ARCHIMEDES OF SYRACUSE:
THE CHEST OF IDEAS

A Historical Novel

I0564002

Monte R. Anderson

1st WORLD PUBLISHING

ARCHIMEDES OF SYRACUSE:
THE CHEST OF IDEAS

Monte R. Anderson

© Monte R. Anderson 2009

Published by 1st World Publishing
P.O. Box 2211 Fairfield, Iowa 52556
tel: 641-209-5000 • fax: 866-440 5234
web: www.1stworldpublishing.com

First Edition

LCCN: 2009927408
SoftCover ISBN: 978-1-4218-9085-2
HardCover ISBN: 978-1-4218-9084-5
eBook ISBN: 978-1-4218-9086-9

This material has been written and published solely for educational purposes. The author and the publisher shall have neither liability nor responsibility to any person or entity with respect to any loss, damage or injury caused or alleged to be caused directly or indirectly by the information contained in this book.

The characters and events described in this text are intended to entertain and teach rather than present an exact factual history of real people or events.

Dedicated to all my childern;

Monte, Brett, Keri, Carrie, Becky and Jen

Central Italy in 1499

CHAPTER ONE

(1499, Central Italy)

In the heat of the summer, a day's ride south of Bologna, Philippe rides his horse in silence across the foot hills of the Appenniniche Mountains, searching for the man who many claim is the best military engineer in Europe, Leonardo di ser Piero da Vinci. The terrain is not easy to navigate because the friable rocks easily erode during the rainy season causing frequent landslides, but it is safer than riding along the old Roman road, Via Emilia. Philippe and his small troop of bodyguards parallel the Via Emilia as much as possible to avoid ambush or chance encounters with enemy scouts who regularly ride on the old road. Philippe has been the commander of the Borgia bodyguards for nearly a decade, a veteran of many campaigns. He rides below the ridge line with his head just above the crest to keep from silhouetting himself against the sky. He knows that he can never appreciate the beauty that surrounds him for he has, what he likes to call, a military mind. As he rides along, he mentally organizes the terrain, and prepares to defend or attack every hill. It is a good mental exercise. No, he can never again look at a landscape, and enjoy the beauty of it. But he knows that it is one of the traits that make him an excellent military commander.

Philippe recalls how Pope Alexander VI appointed his own son, Cesare Borgia, Duke of Valentinois, as the Captain-General of the papacy military forces to replace Cesare's older brother, Juan, Duke of Gandia, who had been assassinated. The Pope then ordered the Papal Army to subdue the city states and dukedoms of Romagna in central

Italy. He wants Romagna to become the nucleus of a papal state. Now Philippe is responsible for protecting the life of the new Captain-General of the Papal Army.

Juan's assassination was not my fault, Philippe says to himself. *Cesare was still a Cardinal, and had insisted that no one, not even bodyguards, carries weapons into mass on Sundays. But the assassins operated by a different set of rules. Juan attended his younger brother's mass that fateful day. How stupid! It is as if Cesare himself was helping the assassins. When Juan was attacked coming out of mass, walking too close to the crowd, there was not much my men and I could do without our weapons. The assassins had mingled in the crowd, and carried daggers under their cloaks. They were on top of Juan before we could stop them. There were a dozen of them but only two would have been enough. In our futile effort to protect Juan, I lost two good men, though we killed eight assassins. None escaped. It was our bare hands against their daggers. I added two new scars to my body in the melee. But no one blamed me for the assassination, and Cesare decided keep me on as commander of his bodyguards. It will not happen again.*

At least as the new Captain-General, Cesare has agreed to let us carry weapons into mass. He is more cautious about his security since the assassination. What a joke he is; a cardinal at twenty two and now, five years later, a Captain-General. Of course, it doesn't hurt to marry the sister of the King of Navarre, and have a father who is elected Pope. He can do nothing without the patronage of his father and family. Look at him. He rides through the countryside as if he were on a picnic. He has much to learn about military tactics. It may be difficult to keep him alive, but if I can, some day he might become Pope, and I could become the Captain-General. Strange things happen in these turbulent times.

As the youngest son, Cesare prepared for the priesthood as customary. However, the sudden murder of his brother, Juan, changed everything. His father, Pope Alexander VI, did not trust anyone outside the family. He needed Cesare to lead the Papal Army. Cesare knows that he is not a good military commander, and has much to learn with little time to learn it. But he has the ability to inspire men, and he prides himself on being a good judge of character. Deciding who can be trusted and who might be a traitor is his strongest talent. In these chaotic times, the key to survival depends on this ability. Cesare uses his talent to further his own ambitions, and the fortunes of the Borgia family. The reason Cesare hired Leonardo lies in his extraordinary insight into individual human character. Cesare knows that Leonardo is a brilliant intellect, and one of the best engineers that he has ever met. And as a quick understudy, Cesare knows he can learn much from a man of Leonardo's genius. Even more important to Cesare, however, is Leonardo's character, his integrity, and trustworthiness. Leonardo is a man of his word, an honest man who speaks his mind. Cesare does not trust those who curry his favor. Of all those who advise and serve him, Cesare needs individuals of the caliber of Leonardo da Vinci most of all.

Cesare had met Leonardo in Milan while studying law. Leonardo was employed as an artist and later as a military engineer by Ludovico Sforza, Duke of Milan. They were introduced in the Duke's palace during one of the elaborate dinners that the Duke was fond of hosting. Cesare was impressed by Leonardo, and the two had many discussions about art, military architecture, and Leonardo's numerous ideas and inventions.

Soon after Cesare was elevated to Captain-General, he learned that Leonardo had fled Milan, returning to Florence when Charles VIII of France drove Sforza out of Italy. He immediately sent for Leonardo, and, after brief negotiations, hired him as his chief military engineer and advisor.

Recruiting Leonardo was an easy task for Cesare. He usually gets what he wants, but, in this case, it was easy. Leonardo fled from Milan after it fell to the French, and was seeking employment. It was in Florence, years ago, that Leonardo was accused of sodomy. Although he was acquitted, he was on the watch list of Florence's Officers of the Night, a fact that Cesare used to discourage other potential employers. Cesare made it clear to Leonardo that, that no one would dare to accuse a member of the staff of the son of the Pope of anything, and that he would be free to live his private life. With no other alternatives, Leonardo signed on.

When Pope Alexander VI ordered Cesare to subdue Bologna, Cesare took Leonardo along. He hoped that Leonardo would devise some easy means to capture the walled city without the loss of many of his troops—troops he would need in the subsequent siege of the walled cities allied with Romagna.

Cesare is traveling with just eight mounted men and Philippe. He is not on maneuvers or on reconnaissance, just looking for Leonardo. Still, Philippe feels uneasy. His eyes dart back and forth looking for any sign of an ambush. The hills are filled with danger; the enemies of the Borgia family are many. Every turn in the road, every grove of trees, every dust cloud in the distance could mean an ambush. Philippe wishes that Cesare would have consented to an additional company of infantry. Philippe deploys the bodyguards as scouts today; two ride point toward the front, two provide security on each flank, and two are rear guards. He has learned the hard way to deploy men in pairs so that one maintains constant visual contact with him, while the other rides in the lead. In an ambush, there is a good chance that one guard can escape or at least fire a warning shot. Philippe trusts these men with his life. All are members of the Borgia family or of families allied to the Borgia. All are veterans, and more than once have thwarted attempted assassinations. Juan's assassination was just plain bad luck.

The bodyguards ride in silence. Philippe controls their movements with hand signals even though by now they pretty much know how he operates. With just a pointed finger or a wave of a hand, he signals them to check out different areas. It is a system developed over the years, and it works well. Suddenly, toward the front, Philippe hears a loud pop. A gesture from the point rider, two fingers pointing toward the eyes, indicates that Leonardo has been found. Philippe motions for Cesare to wait until he can verify the report. He rides over the crest of the next ridge where one of the point riders is waiting, hidden in the shadow of a tree. Together, Philippe and the point man trot over the next hill, and observe a small group of men standing around what appears to be a smoking cannon. With a few more gestures, Philippe posts four of his guards in good vantage points around the surrounding area to provide early warning if needed. Philippe waits for his men to get into position while he watches the small party below. When he is satisfied that it is safe for Cesare to approach, he rides back to his charge. When he is within sight of Cesare and the other guards, he reins up, and signals for them to ride forward. Philippe then leads Cesare to an advantage point where they can observe Leonardo and his assistants.

Leonardo has placed the cannon on a level field in a valley near a small stream. Down range is an outcropping with a large circle painted in red. Little flags mark off set distances from the cannon to the target. Philippe can see no security and no outposts, leaving Leonardo vulnerable to ambush.

The chief Military Engineer with no more common sense than a common soldier, Philippe thinks to himself.

The cannon is unusually small, and not shaped like others with which Philippe is familiar. He predicts that it will take a larger cannon to hit the outcropping. The distance is too great for such a small weapon. Leonardo is directing the loading and firing operations. When the cannon fires, it makes a strange sound. It is not the loud explosion of black gunpowder with the accompanying smoke. It is more of a popping sound. A white cloud appears at first but dissipates quickly. That observation captures Philippe's attention because, in battle, smoke from artillery can get so thick that the gunners must wait valuable minutes before they can fire their weapons again. These tell-tale clouds of smoke give away the location of the artillery, and provide an open invitation for counter-battery fire or a sudden visit by enemy cavalry. Philippe tries to follow the flight of the projectile, which is much longer than a normal cannon ball. He raises an eyebrow when the projectile hits very near the target. Two of the men with Leonardo trot out to recover the projectile.

Cesare trusts Philippe's judgment, and so he waits for him to decide when it is safe to ride out into the open to meet with Leonardo. When Philippe is finally satisfied, he and Cesare ride up to the party of men around the cannon. Leonardo recognizes Cesare at once, and steps forward to greet him.

"Leonardo, I have been looking for you," shouts Cesare, as he reins in his horse.

Leonardo holds Cesare's reins while he dismounts. Stepping back he makes a large sweeping gesture with his hat, bowing very low. Philippe considers it too showy for an exposed position like this one—making it obvious to any uninvited observer that this is an important man.

"You honor me with your presence, your Highness, or should I call you Captain-General?"

"I have hardly gotten use to all my new titles. I am not sure which one will last but to tell you the truth, I still prefer Duke."

Leaning closer to Leonardo's ear, Cesare whispers, "Privately, I wish you would call me friend. I have so few of those." Then straightening up he continues, "But enough of this nonsense with titles, I want to see this new weapon you have been talking about." He looks around at the other men. "For God's sake, Leonardo, where are your guards? I cannot afford to have you captured. Couldn't you at least have your men carry some swords and muskets?"

"I am sorry, Duke. I was not aware of the danger."

Philippe snickers.

"Danger is everywhere, my friend, even in one's palace," says the duke. "Be careful! I will leave two of my bodyguards to escort you back to camp. Now show this cannon to me."

"Yes, sire. You know my pupil, Salai? We were just getting it ready to fire. Would you like to see a demonstration?"

Cesare nods in Salai's direction. He does not care for Leonardo's assistant, and, if the rumors were correct, he is much more than just an assistant. His real name, Cesare recalls, is Gian Giacomo—something, but Leonardo always calls him Salai, meaning the Little Unclean One-the devil. Cesare consented to letting Leonardo keep Salai as part of their agreement. Cesare notices with distain that Salai is wearing a skirt with the hem cropped as short as possible in the manner of the Florentiners. He thinks the short skirt with the tights makes Salai look like a ridiculous dandy. He knows many women who are attracted to Leonardo. After all, he is a strikingly handsome man, but he is not interested in women. Too bad!

"I saw your last firing from the hillside, and I must say that I am very impressed. Is it a cannon?"

"Yes, it is a cannon, but not like any that you are familiar with. It does not use gunpowder."

"Does not use gunpowder? But I saw the projectile fly more than two statia."

"Actually, two and one half statia. It uses steam."

"Steam? How is that possible? Show me."

"Yes, sire. Step closer and I will try to explain."

Monte R. Anderson

"Now remember, I am a simple man so keep your explanation simple."

Philippe raises his eyebrows at that remark. He knows by now that Cesare uses such remarks to disarm people, and as a false show of humility. He is an extremely intelligent man.

Picking up a stick to use as a pointer, Leonardo continues, "Through this chamber I place the projectile in the breech of the barrel. The chamber is secured with a screw mechanism. Around the chamber is a fire box in which we burn wood to heat the inner chamber. When the inner chamber reaches a very high temperature, water is injected from these tanks into the inner chamber."

"Wait! Wait! Are you telling me that the projectile is propelled by hot water?"

"No, sire, by steam."

"By steam?"

"Yes, sire. The water hits the hot inner chamber, and is instantly vaporized into steam. The steam rapidly expands, greatly increasing the pressure inside the chamber. A trigger releases the projectile, and the pressure of the steam propels the projectile a great distance."

"Can steam do that?"

"You have seen for yourself. A small amount of water creates a large volume of steam. By confining the steam in this small chamber, the pressure created is very great. All this happens rapidly, a matter of seconds."

"So the cannon uses only water and wood?"

"Yes, sire."

"But the projectile is not a ball?"

"No, sire", picking up a projectile and handing it to Cesare.

"It looks like a huge arrow."

"I prefer to call it a dart. These fins stabilize the projectile in flight, and give it much more range, not unlike the feathers on an arrow or the wings of a bird. The accuracy and range is greater than any in use today. With this, your artillery can engage the enemy long before the enemy artillery can return fire."

"But Leonardo, unless this dart hits a man directly, it won't kill him. It certainly does not look as if it could destroy a city wall."

"No, sire. This is a prototype just for testing. The final dart will have an explosive head. I will design two types: one for walls and one for troops. And, best of all, the enemy artillery cannot pick these darts up, and fire them back at you like they do with cannon balls."

Now Leonardo has captured the attention of Philippe who dismounts, and steps closer for a better look at the dart.

"Well, it seems to me that this dart will simplify logistics," Philippe interrupts. "We just need to carry these darts and tow these cannons; no gunpowder and no cannon balls. Water and wood are available nearly everywhere."

"Correct! You have immediately grasped one of the many advantages of this weapon."

Cesare ponders Philippe's remark for a minute. He does not like others discovering truths before he does. It makes him feel inferior. He had not even considered the logistical aspect.

"What do you call this weapon?"

"Archimedes' Steam Cannon."

"What does that mean? Wasn't Archimedes Greek?"

"Oh, have you studied Greek, sire?"

"Greek and Latin were part of my training for law and the priesthood."

"I named it after Archimedes. He was a Greek military engineer."

"I am not familiar with his work. Where is he from?"

"Well, he lived fifteen hundred years ago in Syracuse."

"Syracuse? In Sicily?"

"Yes, Syracuse was once a great city."

"Fifteen hundred years ago? I thought that there were no cannons or gunpowder fifteen hundred years ago."

"You are correct, sire. Archimedes was a mathematician and

engineer who studied the properties of water. He proposed a steam cannon but never built one."

"Why not?"

"As you have said, they had no gunpowder or cannons. The science of casting metals was not advanced enough to develop artillery."

"Leonardo, you surprise me. I thought all of your inventions were original ideas."

"By no means, sire. I build upon the ideas and machines developed by those who have gone before. As it is written in scripture, 'We stand on the shoulders of those who came before us.'"

"So, this Archimedes, what else did he design? Any machines we can use now?"

"Archimedes developed the mathematics needed to design war machines, and built many war machines himself. He held off the Romans during the siege of Syracuse using his machines."

"I would like to hear more about this Archimedes. I enjoy history, particularly ancient battles, and I want to hear more about his inventions."

"Sire, time does not permit me to tell you everything today nor is the heat of this midday sun conducive to the study of history. Tomorrow is Sunday, and I know you do not campaign on the Sabbath. And, you have a great chef. Did you bring him with you?"

"Yes, why do you ask?"

"Sire, may I propose that I join you at your headquarters after mass tomorrow. I will tell you all about Archimedes. I presume you have some excellent wines from your collection?"

Patting Leonardo on the shoulder, "Leonardo, you are impertinent, but you have piqued my curiosity. I do admired your wisdom, and I enjoy your company. I also want a full report on this cannon as well."

"Yes, sire."

"Very well! I will leave you to your work. I will have Philippe post two of my bodyguards with you, and they will escort you back to camp when you are ready to return."

"Thank you, sire."

Mounting his horse with the help of Salai, "Until tomorrow then, my friend. Farewell," making the sign of the cross, "God be with you."

Philippe turns and signals to his other guards, starting them back toward camp. With two quick gestures he tells the guards who are staying with Leonardo where to post themselves for the best observation and concealment. He is not happy about splitting up the few guards he has but the camp is not far, and Cesare will ride faster on the way back. Speed is security. Leonardo bows quickly, and turns back toward his cannon.

"What did he whisper to you?" asks Salai.

"He told me to call him 'friend' because he has so few friends."

"That's because his friends usually end up murdered. Their families too."

"I do not intend to call him 'friend.'"

Ω

The Camp Commandant at Cesare's military headquarters set up a large tent for mass. The tent is large enough to cover the altar, the priests, and the few front rows of those in attendance. Benches are available for members of the Borgia family and the staff officers and their families. The rest of the soldiers have to remain outside in the morning sun. It seems that everyone in camp turned out for mass except the perimeter guards. This is to be the final mass before the attack on Bologna—not the time to tempt God. Besides, all the officers made sure that as many men as possible attended this mass. Cesare is not a man to risk angering.

Philippe is more uneasy than usual for mass. Today everyone carries a weapon. It would be so easy for anyone in the crowd to assassinate Cesare as he comes down the center aisle, during mass, or during the recessional. The best Philippe can do is to have all of his men mingle with the crowd, checking unfamiliar faces and anyone who looks out of place. He will be as near as possible to Cesare. Today Philippe wears his dress cape which is hot but it conceals his weapons. He keeps his right hand on his dagger under the cape, sometimes taking it out, and holding it with the blade hidden alongside his forearm or up his sleeve.

It will be impossible to keep this man alive, he thinks half out loud. He realizes that he could be the last person between Cesare and a would-be assassin.

Let's pray there is only one assassin and not more.

As Cesare and members of his family come down the aisle following the acolytes, cross bearer, priests, and a couple of deacons, Cesare sees Leonardo standing near the aisle. He says something to Philippe who approaches Leonardo, and offers to escort him to one of the benches reserved for the Borgia family. Leonardo is hesitant and embarrassed by this public gesture, but it is presented more as a command than a request. Philippe has a way of giving orders that make people want to obey rather than to test him. Leonardo starts toward the front, and pulls on Salai's sleeve to bring him along. Philippe frowns but Leonardo knows he will not object.

Fortunately, mass is uneventful, and when the priest says, "Go in peace to love and serve the Lord," Philippe breaths a sigh of relief. Leonardo and Salai follow along to Cesare's tent. To call it a tent would not do justice to the size or splendor of Cesare's field quarters. It is fitting for a duke and the Captain-General. Leonardo has been there many times but each time he is still impressed. A servant leads Leonardo and Salai to a large room while Cesare and Philippe disappear into one of the other back rooms. Except for the canvas walls and ceiling it could be mistaken for the state room of a grand palace in Naples. It has the finest chairs and couches and a large oak table. The servant leaves Leonardo and Salai there, and returns shortly with two glasses of wine on a tray. He offers the wine to Leonardo and Salai who each take a glass. After stating that the Captain-General will join them shortly, the servant leaves. Leonardo tastes the wine. It tastes like an ordinary table wine. He looks at Salai who is already half way through his glass of wine.

After about thirty minutes, Cesare enters the room wearing just the trousers and shirt of his uniform. He has removed his jacket and boots. He looks relaxed, and is in high spirits.

Coming forward, Leonardo says, "Your highness."

Salai tries to do the same but Cesare stops him short with a raised finger. The servant reappears with two wine glasses and a bottle of wine for Cesare who takes the bottle, and examines it carefully. He hands the bottle back to the servant who opens it with a flourish which Leonardo assumes is for the benefit of Cesare's guests. The servant pours a small amount in one glass. Cesare holds it up and looks intently through it from two or three different angles. He sticks his nose deeply into the glass nearly touching the wine. Leonardo is surprised when Cesare hands the glass of wine to his servant who drinks the glass in one gulp. Cesare stares at the servant's eyes for two or three minutes as the servant stands at attention. When he is satisfied that the wine is not poisoned, a sweep of his hand indicates that the servant should pour him a fresh glass. Cesare takes the glass. As the servant leaves the room, Cesare watches intently.

"One cannot be too careful even in one's own home."

Leonardo and Salai both look down at their glasses and then at each other. Salai shrugs his shoulders, and takes another sip of wine. Leonardo watches for any sign that would tell him something might be wrong with the wine. When nothing happens to Salai, he takes another sip. Cesare sips his wine and frowns.

"This is the wine that I drink for penance. It reminds me of the bitter tasks ahead. However, it is hard to poison because poison dilutes the bitterness. I will have a much better vintage for dinner." Looking at Leonardo, "I had forgotten what a great singing voice you have, Leonardo. You have so many talents. I shudder to think what you could accomplish if you entered politics."

"No, sire. I am too kind hearted for politics." Seeing the frown on Cesare's face, he adds, "It requires a certain ruthlessness, does it not?"

Slightly taken aback by Leonardo's bluntness, "Yes, I suppose you are right. It does require ruthlessness."

"Sire, I have a gift for you." Leonardo reaches toward Salai who produces a small box from one of his large pockets.

"What is it?" asks Cesare as he opens the box.

"It is called a Stomachion."

"That means stomach, doesn't it?"

"Yes, sire. It does mean stomach, and it was invented by Archimedes. I am not sure why he called it that. It is a a child's game. It consists of fourteen flat ivory pieces of various polygonal shapes, and, as you can see, they can be arranged to form a square. The object of the game is to rearrange the pieces to form interesting shapes like people, animals, and objects. Archimedes calculated mathematically that there are over a thousand possible shapes that can be made from the original square."

"Amazing! My children will love this."

"Sire, before I begin, I would like to excuse Salai to tend to our horses, and to do a few errands."

"Of course," Cesare replies, trying not to sound too delighted as Salai bows and leaves. Setting the Stomachion on the table, "Now then, since you brought up Archimedes, let's talk about him, and then you can tell me about your new cannon."

Cesare motions to the couch, and they both sit down.

"Now, tell me, Leo, great artists and military engineers like yourself need a patron. Did Archimedes have a patron?"

Cesare always refers to Leonardo as Leo in private. At first, Leonardo thought it rude, coming from such a younger man. But, Cesare is powerful and influential. Now he is the Captain-General. However, Leonardo has always called him Cesare or duke.

"Yes, sir. He was the advisor to a king who is also an interesting fellow. He was elected King of Syracuse."

Thus, Leonardo begins the story of Archimedes.

SICILIA

CHAPTER TWO

(1499, Cesare's Campaign Headquarters)

Once Cesare is comfortable, Leonardo begins, "First, allow me to summarize for you the history leading up to the time of Archimedes."

"Proceed, by all means," says Cesare, sipping his wine, "This is a day of rest so I have made no appointments today. We should not be disturbed."

Leonardo continues, "Syracuse was originally a colony settled by Greeks from Corinth. The area on the Eastern coast of Sicily is very fertile, and good for growing wheat and other crops. Syracuse traded with Rome, Carthage, and even as far as Alexandria. It prospered, and eventually became the most powerful Greek city in the Mediterranean. Later, the city of Carthage in North Africa grew in power, and succeeded in conquering the western half of Sicily. Meanwhile, the Romans were consolidating and expanding their empire in Italy. They signed a treaty with Carthage that recognized Carthage's control of Sicily if Carthage promised to stay out of Italy.

"Eventually, Syracuse went to war with Carthage over the control of Sicily. At the Battle of Himera, the Carthaginians were defeated by Syracuse and their Greek city allies. As a result, Carthage signed a treaty with Syracuse and the other independent Greek cities that recognized their independence as long as they would not make war against Carthage or ally with the Romans. That left Carthage in control of the western portion of Sicily, and Syracuse in control of the eastern part of

Sicily. The Romans were still consolidating their empire on the peninsula. The stage was set for the events that unfolded during the time of Archimedes.

"Archimedes worked for King Hieron whom the Romans called Hiero. Years before, during an unpopular war with a neighboring city, Hieron and his best friend, Artemidorus, seized command of the army. They then marched home, and took control of the city of Syracuse. Hieron was declared dictator of Syracuse, and Artemidorus was made commander of the army. Hieron married Philistis, the daughter of Leptines, who was head of the most power family in Syracuse at the time. Together, the three plotted to get Hieron elected king."

Salai enters the room followed by two soldiers carrying a cedar chest.

"Ah, good. Just put it down anywhere," says Leonardo.

"What is this chest?" asks Cesare as the soldiers place the chest in a corner.

Salai leaves to continue his chores.

"The ancient Greeks would have called it an 'armaria'. I call it my Idea Box," says Leonardo. "Whenever I have an idea, I make a few notes, and place it in the box to work on when I have time. I asked Salai to bring it over because I keep some information about Archimedes in there."

Cesare walks over to the chest to get a better view. The lid has a relief map of an ancient walled city carved in perspective. The sides have carvings depicting walls, towers, and gates.

"I do not recognize this walled city."

"It is Syracuse, sire. The top shows the layout of the city, and on each side is one of the city gates. See, the city was shaped like slice of pie. It had a wall all the way around it, and was further subdivided by a wall that ran from the Grand Harbor across to the sea on the other side." Pointing to the chest, "There was a small fort here to guard the Grand Harbor and another here to protect the city from a land attack. Until the Romans conquered the city, it had never been captured."

"Please continue," asks Cesare, "You were explaining how Hieron became a king."

Leonardo continues, "Leptines also had a son by the name of Phidias, who was the father of Archimedes. Part of the bargain that Leptines had with Hieron was that Leptines would become Hieron's chief advisor and Phidias would become the Royal Astronomer." After the death of Leptines and Phidias, Archimedes became Hieron's chief advisor. By all accounts, Hieron was a benevolent dictator and king.

Ω

(265 BCE, in Syracuse)

Leptines strides toward the center of the city council chambers, "Fellow members of the Council, I have yet another disturbing report about an attack on one of our merchant ships."

The members settle down to listen. Leptines motions for a man to come forward. A young man with a weathered, pockmarked face steps forward.

"This is Damippus, the merchant whose ship was attacked. Please, tell us your story."

"It is true. I was returning to Syracuse from Alexandria, and while still a great distance from Syracuse we were attacked by these pirates who called themselves the Sons of Mars. I call them the sons of whores."

Damippus spits on the floor as he says this, and wipes the spittle from his cropped beard.

"I was able to escape by jumping overboard in the night as we neared their base at Messana. I made it back here, but I fear my crew is already sold as slaves. My entire cargo of silks, perfumes, glass, and other expensive goods is lost."

Shouts of outrage.

One of the members asks, "Are you certain these pirates were from Messana and not Cilicia?"

"Yes, sir. I will gouge out my eye for you if it will help you believe me."

"That won't be necessary," says a disgusted Leptines. "We must stop these pirates now. We must put a stop to this madness. We must have Hieron lead an expedition to capture Messana. He has been dictator for ten years. It is time for him to demonstrate whether he is a true leader or not."

"Here, Here!" several members shout in agreement.

"All in favor say 'Aye'!" says Leptines.

"Aye! Aye!"

"All opposed?"

Silence. After much discussion, the Council summons Hieron, and tells him to proceed immediately to call out the army, and march on Messana. With the business of the day concluded, all the members leave the chamber to go home. Damippus strolls out with Leptines.

"How did I do, Leptines?"

"You were superb, Barnacle! I almost believed you myself. I will see that you are compensated for your...uh, loss." Both men laugh.

Monte R. Anderson

(265 BCE, in the Roman Senate)

Senator Maxentius stands to address the Senate, "Fellow Senators. An envoy has arrived from Messana seeking help from us. It seems that Hieron, dictator of Syracuse, is planning to attack Messana."

Quinctius stands, "Senator Maxentius, must I remind you that we are currently at peace. Let us enjoy our peace while we can. We have a small navy and no troops on Sicily. We must cross the channel to get there, and we will need a stronger navy to keep the supply lines open. Carthage on the other hand is already on the island. Moving troops to Sicily to help Messana would be considered an act of war by Carthage."

Consul Titus stands, "Senators, it is true we are at peace. We have consolidated our empire on the whole peninsula. We have defeated the Gauls. We have fought hard and prevailed. No army on earth can defeat our army. We do not have to fear these Carthaginians. You all know that the only reason we signed a treaty with them was to buy time for us to subdue the tribes that surround Roma. We did that. Now we must consider how to control the straits between Roma and Sicily. Whoever controls Sicily controls the straits, the sea trade routes, and the very security of Roma itself. We must not let Carthage control Sicily. Our security is at stake."

Quinctius replies, "You know that the city of Messana is no longer governed by Greeks. The city was taken over by the Mamertines, the Sons of Mars. They are all pirates. Let Hieron kill them all. He will save us the trouble. Then we can sign a treaty with Hieron to secure the straits."

"Senator Quinctius, not long ago the Mamertines were our allies," replies Maxentius.

Quinctius rebuts, "So was Hieron! And what of the revolt at Reghium? We fought for ten years, but only with the help of Hieron, was the revolt was crushed."

Maxentius is ready with his reply, "If we do not send troops to help Messana, Carthage will take our inaction as a sign of weakness. Our security is at stake. If we can get a legion to Messana before Hieron can mobilize, we may be able to prevent this war from happening."

After much debate the senate decides to honor its treaty with Carthage, and not send troops to help the Mamertines.

Ω

(265 BCE, in the Carthaginian Senate)

Senator Mago stands, "Senators, the City of Messana in Sicily has requested aid from us to protect them from Hieron of Syracuse who is planning to attack them."

"We have a treaty with Hieron. How can we help his enemies?" asks Senator Bostzer.

"Let's not forget that he aided the Romans in putting down the revolt at Reghium," adds Senator Hanno.

"Yes, it is true that we must not let Roma get control of any part of Sicily. However, we may be able to achieve our goals without going to war. Let's send a message to Roma asking the Romans not to interfere in this matter. Let Hieron attack Messana," says Bostzer.

Senator Bomilcar speaks, "Perhaps there is another way."

"And what may that be?" asks Mago.

"Suppose we do send a fleet to the aid of the Mamertines. But once there, we negotiate a treaty with Hieron to end the war before Hieron can attack," says Bomilcar.

"That may upset the Romans," Mago points out.

"We will remind them of their treaty with us," says Bomilcar.

"And if the Romans decide to send legions to Sicily?" asks Mago.

"Then our navy will not even allow the Romans to bathe their hands in the waters of the straits of Messana."

Mago senses a consensus, "It is settled then. We will send a message to Roma asking them to stay out of this conflict, and to honor their treaty with us. Meanwhile we will send a fleet to Messana. Once there we will negotiate a peace."

Monte R. Anderson

(265 BCE, in Syracuse)

A few days later Hieron calls for a council of war to discuss the upcoming battle with the Mamertines at Messana.

Sitting around a table with Hieron are Patroclus, commander of the fleet: Artemidorus, commander of the army and Hieron's best friend: Phidias the astronomer: Phidias' young son, Archimedes; the commanders of the two legions from Alexandria; and several other commanders from Greek cities on Sicily.

Artemidorus speaks first, "Sir, if we attack Messana from the land side, the Mamertines will just board their ships and escape. Then they will attack some other city, and set up their base again. Somehow we must destroy their ships or block the harbor before we attack."

"Can we capture or destroy their ships at sea before they get to the harbor?" asks Hieron.

Patroclus replies, "Attacking a moving ship at sea is very difficult. The technique is to ram the ship or throw ropes with hooks to lash the ships together, and then board the ship. Ramming a ship under sail is difficult enough, and could result in damage to our own ships. The ropes usually get cut as soon as they are thrown. The enemy ships use their oars to fend off the attacking ship before the ram can strike them. Once a ship is rammed, it is hard to separate them, and both ships could sink. The enemy can also board the ship that has rammed them so a tough fight ensues."

"Can't we throw stones with a catapult or shoot fire arrows?" asked Hieron.

"This too is difficult. Catapults aren't very good at hitting moving targets at sea. Fire arrows are easily put out, and at the same time the enemy ship is firing arrows at us."

Archimedes interjects, "Sir, I have a suggestion."

Turning toward Phidias, "Do you allow your young son to interfere with a Council of War?"

"Sir, Archimedes is old enough to state his opinion. He is very intelligent. I would recommend that we hear what he has to say," replies Phidias.

"Very well then, speak, young Archimedes!" commands Hieron.

"I beg your pardon, sir, for interrupting but I think I may have an idea."

"Well, explain!"

"Sir, the problem is how to secure your ship to an enemy ship, and board the ship with enough forces to overwhelm the enemy."

"That is the general idea," replies Patroclus.

"I think it is possible to use a ramp with a hook or claw on the leading edge. The top row of oars is the longest, and they seem to be about the length of three men. If the ramp were four men long, then the enemy could not reach our ships to fend them away. The ramp could be stowed on deck, and raised as the ship approaches the enemy ship by means of a pulley. Once dropped, the weight of the hook will drive it into the deck, and hold fast to the ship."

"But then the enemy could also storm over or shoot our men with arrows," replies Artemidorus.

"Sir, I think it is a good idea," says Patroclus. "If the ramp is wide enough for three men abreast we could form up to board before the ramp is even down. Once it hooks the enemy ship we can storm across. The first three men would hold their shields in front of their bodies. The second row would hold their shields to the side to protect the flanks. The third row would hold their shields on top to protect against arrows. The formation will, in effect, look like a turtle in its shell. We have used it before. If everyone pushes hard, even if a man in front is killed the momentum will propel him forward. If need be, the dead could be thrown over the side."

"Artemidorus?"

"I think it might work, sir. We should make one, and try it. If it works, we could easily train soldiers on them."

"Phidias?"

"I know nothing of warfare but I think the idea has merit."

"And what of the stars, Phidias?" asks Hieron.

"The stars are favorable. Mars is in a position that favors your victory."

"Very well, then. Archimedes, construct one of these ramps, and show us how it will work. We'll call it the 'Archimedes' Hook.' How soon will it be ready?"

"I can have it ready by tomorrow afternoon."

Ω

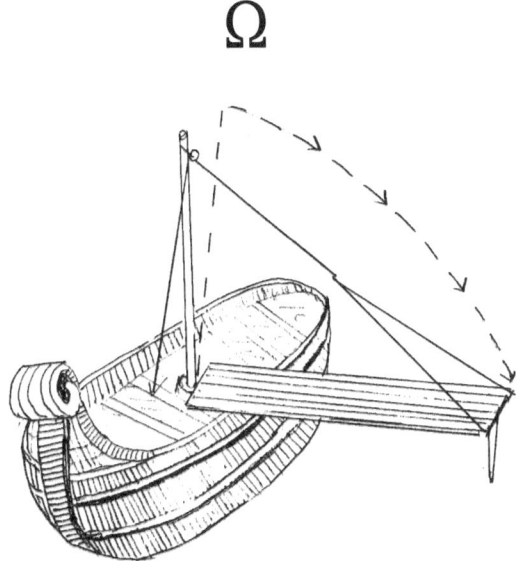

Archimedes and Patroclus work late into the night and the following morning to craft the hooked ramp. Artemidorus provides the crew. In the afternoon, Hieron and the rest of the council of war arrive at the docks on the Grand Harbor. The crew rows out into the harbor where another ship is anchored. It is an older ship about to be torn apart for the lumber, but it will serve the purpose for the demonstration. The crew has been practicing all morning on dry land, and Artemidorus has motivated them until their spirits are running at fever pitch.

As the crew approaches the old ship from the side, the ramp is let loose, and it falls, imbedding itself into the old deck as the marines charge across with their shields in place to protect against arrows. Artemidorus recalls them for another try. This time, as the marines approach the bow of the old ship, Artemidorus and a couple of marines push the ramp rapidly and forcefully down, and they board within seconds in good form. Artemidorus once more recalls them, and recovers the ramp. This time the marines attack from the stern. The marines begin to storm across even before the hook is embedded in the old ship's deck. Their weight adds to the speed and force of impact so that the hook sinks all the way up to the point where it is attached. Each time the marines storm across the ramp, a cheer rises from the small crowd that has gathered on shore to watch these naval maneuvers. When the marines finally returned to the dock there is much cheering.

"Well I think we have a new weapon and tactics to defeat the Mamertines," says Artemidorus as he climbs off the ship onto the dock.

"Excellent! Patroclus, how soon can you equip all of our ships with the Archimedes Hook?" asks Hieron.

"I think we can do it in one week. The construction is very simple."

"Then do it. Artemidorus, how long for you to train the marines in the use of the Archimedes Hook?"

"We'll construct a few on dry land for training, and then use the ships once they have been installed. If I train the commanders, and they in turn train their crews, three weeks."

"Make it two weeks. Patroclus, once the hooks are installed, I want you to start attacking all Mamertine ships wherever you can find them. Destroy as many of their ships as you can. If we destroy enough, they cannot escape from Messana by sea, and will have to fight us on land. The Mamertines have been pirates for so long, they have forgotten how to be soldiers. In two months time I want to march on Messana. That will be enough time for all our allies to send their cohorts to Syracuse. Archimedes, congratulations! You have just built your first war machine."

Hieron turns, and begins to hike toward the palace.

Turning to Archimedes and the others, Artemidorus says, "Gentlemen, drink your wine tonight, make love to your wives, kiss your children, and get a good night's sleep. Tomorrow we begin to prepare for war, and we will not rest until we dine in Messana. Farewell until tomorrow at sunrise."

Everyone goes their separate ways to their homes.

Monte R. Anderson

CHAPTER THREE

(1499, Cesare's Campaign Headquarters)

"Leo! Leo!" calls Cesare, gentling nudging Leonardo's shoulder.

Leonardo opens one eye, and asks, "Oh! Sire, what is it?"

"You fell asleep."

Shaking his head and wiping his eyes, "My apologies, sire. How rude of me. How long was I asleep?"

"About ten minutes. You are tired, I am sure. You have been working hard. I often see a light on in your workshop late into the night. That and the wine. Why don't we stop here, and we can continue tomorrow?"

"No, sire. I want to continue. I don't sleep like normal people. I mean to say, I do sleep but for only short periods of time. Never do I sleep for more than a few minutes. I am fine now."

"Really? You mean you take several short naps during the day?"

"Yes, several. That way I can get much done."

"Amazing! Well, if you are sure you are not tired, please continue. I find this fascinating."

"Where did I leave off?"

"You were explaining how Archimedes invented a hooking device to defeat ships of the Son of Mars from Massena."

Oh, yes, I remember," and Leonardo continues his tale of Archimedes.

Ω

(265 BCE, in Syracuse)

Once inside their workshop, Phidias and Archimedes begin to work on separate projects.

"Abba?"

"Yes, son?"

"You told Hieron that the stars were favorable, but you have never taught me how to predict the future by the stars. I see you gazing at the stars constantly, but you never explain their meanings to me. You have taught me all about astronomy, but I cannot see the future in the stars"

"A person's destiny is not written in the stars. No one can predict the future."

"But isn't that your job—to predict the future?"

"Yes, but confidently between you and me, son, it is all fake."

"Interesting! You can't predict the future in the stars?"

"No! No one can. You are old enough now to know how things work in the palace. I tell Hieron whatever Leptines, your grandfather, tells me to tell him. Leptines is head of our family. He covets power because power means influence, money, wealth, and security. He would do anything to have that power—not for himself necessarily but for the family. When Hieron sought to be dictator, he needed Leptines' influence to get enough votes on the City Council. Leptines was a great politician, much better than Hieron. He agreed to help Hieron, and, in return, Hieron agreed to make Leptines his chief advisor and me, the Royal Astronomer. That way Leptines influences Hieron's decisions. He also agreed to let Hieron marry my sister, Philistis."

"And aunt Philistis went along with this?"

"Well, I told you that Leptines wanted power. Philistis is very much like our father. I think she covets power more than he does. Hieron is very popular with the army, and has the ability to lead the masses. He has all the makings of a future king. It was actually my sister who convinced Leptines that a marriage with Hieron would benefit both families. She seduced Hieron. My sister came up with the plan to put Hieron in power, but made it look as if Leptines and Hieron came up with the plan."

"Does she love him?" asks Archimedes.

"I don't think so but he loves her very much."

"Interesting! Why did you agree to it?"

"For different reasons than Leptines," replies Phidias. "I wanted to be able to provide you a good education, and to provide things for you. As an advisor, I have certain privileges and opportunities."

"Does Hieron always believe you?" asks Archimedes.

"Yes, son, he believes in the stars and in the gods."

"But he is not a fool. He certainly can see the rising and setting of Mars and Venus as well as the location of the constellations."

"Yes, but he does not understand their meaning."

"But you do study the stars, and know their movements?"

"Yes, I have studied them as have many astronomers before me. As a result, we can accurately predict the paths of the stars. I have made charts of my findings, and I have added them to the findings of others."

"Can I see these charts?" asks Archimedes.

"Yes, of course."

Phidias picks up a stack of scrolls from his work bench, and hands them to Archimedes. "Here they are."

Archimedes studies them for a few minutes.

"Interesting! Abba, these charts are very detailed and accurate. I do believe that I can make a mechanical device that would visually show the proper location of each of the planets, the sun, the moon, and the earth. It would save you time."

"Very well, do it," replies Phidias.

"Father, do you believe in the gods?"

"No. There are no gods. I have searched the heavens everywhere, and I see no evidence of any gods."

"Why don't you tell Hieron the truth?"

"Because, son, there is a body of knowledge that is known by only a few scholars. The rest of the world, kings and peasants alike, are not prepared to know such knowledge. They live in fear of the world around them. They fear the night. They fear the weather. They fear the sea. They fear death. They fear everything it seems. So they invent gods, and pray to these gods for protection.

"Men like you and me gaze at the world around us, and try to discover why things are the way they are. Most men think it is because the gods control the world. But I have always taught you this body of knowledge, which is the truth."

"You mean, like there are no gods?" asks Archimedes.

"Yes, and much, much more."

"Like what?"

"Well, for example, the world is round, not flat."

"I thought everyone knew that," replies Archimedes.

"No, son, I taught you that. Very few people believe it."

"What else?"

"Well, the earth is spinning on an axis, the moon revolves around the earth but always has the same side facing the earth, and the earth revolves around the sun," answers Phidias.

"All this I know."

"Yes, but very few people know this."

"What else?" asks Archimedes.

"Oh, there is much, much more. For example, did you know that the tides are caused by the moon?"

"This I did not know. Since you know the rotation and phases of the moon, you can predict the tides."

"Child's play, really," says Phidias.

"Interesting! What else?"

"In good time, my son, all in good time. Much is known, and yet, much more has yet to be discovered. But let me tell you this for now: all of nature is governed by laws; laws that cannot be broken or negotiated. You have only to determine the laws of a subject to master it."

"Interesting! Who else besides us knows these laws?"

"Very few people, but we do correspond with each other. In Alexandria there is a great library with many books and documents. King Ptolemy founded it on the model of Athens and in other Greek cities. It has grown to be the largest library in the world. Along with the library there is a Museum where scholars can go and use the library to do research into the laws of nature. They teach each other. Some day you must go there and study from these great scholars. Those of us who are not living in Alexandria correspond with each other, and share our discoveries."

"How?" asks Archimedes.

"Do you know Damippus, the ship merchant?" asks Phidias.

"If you mean the one they call Barnacle, then, yes, I know of him," answers Archimedes.

"He carries my messages to Alexandria and other cities when he sails. I want you to start working on these laws, and then start corresponding with other scholars in Alexandria."

"What shall I work on?"

"The law of levers," replies Phidias.

"Levers? But levers have been around for a long time."

"True, but the laws that govern them have not been determined."

"What do you mean?" asks Archimedes.

"Well, suppose you wanted to lift a large stone, and you knew its weight. How long of a lever would you need? Where do you place the fulcrum? How many men would it take? What is the ratio of the length of the lever from the fulcrum to the weight being lifted to the length of the lever from the fulcrum to the point where the force is being applied?"

"Interesting! I see what you mean."

"After that, I want you to work on the law of pulleys," says Phidias.

"Why didn't you discover those laws yourself?" asks Archimedes.

"Why, indeed? There is so much yet to be discovered; new laws, great inventions, and universal principles, and so little time. I am old now, and my days on earth are numbered. Anyway, my interests are in the stars. You must find your own interests. I have shown you how to write up your findings in the format laid down by the great teacher, Euclid. See that box over there?" Phidias points to a cedar chest in the corner.

"Yes, and I have always wondered about it."

"Take a look inside."

Archimedes walks over to the chest and tries to open it, but it is locked.

"How do you open it? I see no place for a lock or key."

"Let me show you."

Phidias kneels down in front of the chest. He places his right hand on the right side, placing each finger on a specific brick in the carved wall, and pushes them in slightly. Using his left hand, he places three fingers on specific points in the top carving and slides them to the left. Archimedes hears a click and Phidias opens the chest.

"I built that secret lock to keep prying eyes out."

Archimedes looks into the chest. It is nearly full of scrolls of drawing and notes.

"What is this?" he asks.

"It is my box of ideas yet to be done. Whenever I think of something that I might investigate, I write it down and put it in the idea box."

"But, father, the box is nearly full."

"Yes, well, it is yours now. I do not have enough life left in me to begin even one of those ideas. Perhaps you will work on them."

"Thank you, father. I will begin tomorrow."

Archimedes begins browsing through the various ideas in the chest. After a while he asks, "Father, is Hieron a good man?"

"Yes, I think he is. I have tried to advise him to keep the peace, and to serve the people. He does the best he can."

"How is it possible to stay at peace with Roma and Carthage at war?"

"It is not easy. The fortunes of war change very quickly, and we could be attacked and destroyed tomorrow. Right now the masses are supportive of Hieron but not all of the noble families."

"How so?" asks Archimedes.

"Perhaps half or more of the families of Syracuse think we should end this treaty with Roma, and side with Carthage."

"Interesting! I have not heard that."

"No, of course not. As long as the masses support Hieron, the other families cannot do anything openly. But when the opportunity presents itself, they will act."

"How will they know when there is an opportunity?" asks Archimedes.

"They have spies," answers Phidias.

"Spies?"

"Yes, spies are everywhere so we must be careful."

"Who are these spies?"

"Well, Artemidorus has a network of spies. He has contacts in all the Greek cites in Sicilia, in Roma, and in Carthage itself. My sister, the queen, has bribed servants in every family of Syracuse to supply her with information."

"How does Artemidorus communicate with his spies?" asks Archimedes.

"He also uses Barnacle. Barnacle is an old family friend of Leptines, and a useful person to know. He sails to all these cities to trade, and takes secret messages back and forth. You would do well to make him your friend."

"Interesting! Are there more spies?"

"Yes. Carthage gets information from their supporters inside Syracuse. Roma does the same. Alexandria does too. Alexandria has sent us more soldiers than any other city, usually mercenaries. That way, their commanders are on the war councils where they can learn of our plans. Not much happens in Syracuse that does not get reported to someone, somewhere."

Phidias begins to look at the stars and take notes. Archimedes starts reading the charts and drawing.

After a while, "Abba, what was mother like?"

"I have told you before."

"Yes, but I don't mean what did she look like. I want to know what kind of person she was."

"Well, let me see. She was full of life. She filled our house with laughter. She was devoted to me. She did not care for wealth or influence, but enjoyed the simple things in life."

"And she died giving birth to me?"

"Yes. When we realized that she was dying, the doctor cut her belly, and took you out."

"Did you love her?"

"Very much, but not at first. Our marriage was arranged by Leptines. He wanted to unite our two families. I spoke to her once before the wedding. But we fell in love after we were married. We fell deeply in love with each other."

"It must have been difficult for you when she died."

"Son, I never told you this but if I could have saved her life by killing you I would have killed you myself. Fortunately, that was not a decision I had to make. She was dying, and she knew it. The doctor said he could save either your mother or you, but not both. If the doctor did nothing you both would die. Do you understand?"

"I think so."

"No son, I don't think you do. You have never loved a woman as I loved your mother. Some day you will understand."

"How did you decide what to do?"

"I didn't. She did. She told the doctor to save you. So he did."

Archimedes could see tears beginning to swell up in his father's eyes.

With tears in his own eyes now, "Did she die right away?"

"No. She asked to hold you. She kissed you, and handed you to the midwife. I kissed her. She said to name you Archimedes, that she loved me, and then she died."

His father had never shared these words with Archimedes before. Tears now ran freely down his father's face.

Wiping way tears, Archimedes asks, "Why Archimedes?"

"I don't know. She never got a chance to tell me."

Phidias walks over to the balcony, and begins to gaze at the stars, signaling the end of the discussion. He takes measurements with a device, and records his observations. Archimedes sits at the workbench, reading the charts, and drawing on papyrus.

Suddenly, Phidias sits down on the balcony wall, and cries out, "Ohhh!"

"Abba, what's wrong?" Before Archimedes reaches him, Phidias slumps to the floor.

Turning his father onto his back, "Abba!"

"It's all right, son. I'm dying."

"What is it, father?"

"My heart. I have had a few attacks before but not this bad."

"What should I do?"

"There is nothing to be done, son. Just let me lie here, and watch the stars until I die."

Archimedes kneels beside his father, crying.

"Son, it's all right. I am ready. Just hold my hand."

Archimedes holds his father's hand until his father's breathing stops. He closes his father's eyes which are locked on the stars and cries.

(1499, Cesare's Campaign Headquarters)

"So what happened at Messana?" asks Cesare.

Leonardo explains, "The Carthaginian fleet arrived at Messana first, and sailed into the harbor. The Carthaginian commander was welcomed into the city with all his troops. At the same time, a Carthaginian envoy was negotiating with Hieron to end the war before his attack. Hieron agreed to ally with Carthage against Rome and the Mamertines. The Carthaginian commander, under secret directions from Carthage, planned to turn the city over to Hieron, and to rid Sicily of these pirates. The Mamertines found out, and hurriedly sent another envoy to Rome asking them to expel the Carthaginians. To avoid loosing the fleet, and being trapped in Messana by a Roman fleet, the Carthaginian commander withdrew his fleet from Messana, effectively leaving Messana in the hands of the Mamertines.

"Hieron's campaign to attack and destroy as many Mamertine ships as possible was succeeding, thanks to the innovative invention, the Archimedes Hook. However, the Roman fleet augmented the Mamertine fleet in the harbor at Messana thus preventing an attack by the Syracusan fleet. Rome did not have a strong military presence on Sicily so Hieron decided that he still could defeat the Mamertines in a land battle before the Romans could land enough legions to stop him. Hieron marched his army, supplemented by a large number of paid mercenaries, to Messana to confront the Mamertines. At the same time he came to the conclusion that his non-Greek mercenary forces were increasingly unreliable in battle. The Roman example at Reghium had taught him that mercenaries potentially can turn on their masters. Hieron decided to rid Syracuse of all mercenaries, and to rely only on soldiers from Greek cities.

"Hieron had another reason for wanting personally lead the army. He realized that whenever the city council dispatched the army on an expedition, it invariably resulted in quarrels among the leaders and rebellion among the troops. It was exactly the situation he had used to his own advantage to seize control of Syracuse. He was not about to let that happen again. Leading the army and leading it well would make him very popular within the army. It was the type of support he needed

Monte R. Anderson

badly. Not only was the army needed for the war but many members, particularly the officers, were free Greek men who would vote in any election.

"Hieron drew up his army in battle order near the river Cyamosorus. His Syracusan forces were held in reserve while the mercenaries made the main attack. He told the mercenaries that on a given signal he would attack the flank of the Mamertines with his reserve and crush them. Hieron ordered the mercenaries to begin their attack but withheld his Syracusan reserve when they were badly needed by the mercenaries. The Mamertines cut the mercenaries to pieces and the survivors fled in a rout. At this point, Hieron attacked the flank of the Mamertines, effectively destroying them as a fighting force along with the mercenaries. The Mamertine leaders were captured, ending all further aggression. Those mercenaries that did manage to escape were not allowed back into Syracuse. Hieron did not seize the city of Messana out of fear of a Roman attack. Instead, he retired with his army to Syracuse to await the Romans.

"The Roman Senate sent an army of four legions commanded by two consuls to Sicily. This superior force gained some early victories in the land battles against the Carthaginians. Finally, the consuls prepared to lay siege to Syracuse. Up to that point, Syracuse had not received any support from Carthage, and had not engaged the Romans in battle. The Roman Senate sent an envoy to Hieron with terms for a treaty with Rome.

"Rome offered to guarantee Hieron's kingship of Syracuse, and to recognize him as the leader of all the cities in eastern Sicily if he would ally with Rome; support the war effort with supplies, grains and soldiers; and pay tribute to Rome. In return, the Romans would not attack Syracuse, and all the eastern cities in Sicily would be placed under Roman protection. Hieron agreed to the terms, and signed a treaty with Rome. Hieron offered the Romans the possession of Messana, a substantial part of his other Sicilian territories and a subsidy of one hundred talents annually for fifteen years. Hieron sent Artemidorus with one legion to support the Romans in Sicily. Artemidorus and the Syracusan legion participated in most of the battles in Sicily from that point on.

"Hieron also shared with the Romans the secret weapon called the Archimedes Hook which the Romans then renamed the 'corvas,' which is Latin for Raven. The Roman navy adopted the corvas as a naval tactic to use against the Carthaginian fleet. The corvas was instrumental in many Roman naval victories and ultimately in the defeat of Carthage.

"Syracuse declared Hieron a hero. Leptines forced a vote in the city council calling for free election for king, and Hieron was elected king of Syracuse. He immediately dissmissed the city council. He appointed Leptines as his chief advisor, Artemidorus as commander of the army, and Archimedes as his military engineer. Hieron rewarded his supporters by appointing them to key ministerial positions and ambassadorships. Peace came to Syracuse, and remained for many years."

CHAPTER FOUR

(1499, Cesare's Campaign Headquarters)

"So King Hieron signed a treaty with Rome. Did Syracuse wage war against the Carthaginians?" Cesare asks Leonardo.

"The treaty with Rome ushered in a long period of peace for Syracuse. Hieron did have to support the Romans in their war effort against Carthage, and to send them soldiers, usually a legion. But Rome never demanded that the Syracusan legion leave Sicily. The Romans won the battle for control of Sicily in short order so the legion did not see a lot of action or suffer a lot of causalities. What action the legion did see provided excellent training for the soldiers and officers. Meanwhile, Artemidorus continued to train the army, and to build up the defenses around Syracuse.

"Hieron and Philistis had a son that they named Gelo after a former King of Syracuse and a relative of Hieron. Their second born was a daughter that they named Damarata. Their second daughter was named Heraclia. Leptines passed away leaving his family the most influential in Syracuse. Artemidorus married, and had a son named Adranodoros who married Hieron's daughter, Damarata. Hieron's other daughter, Heraclia, married a nobleman named Zoippos. Hieron's son, Gelo, married the daughter of the famous King Pyrrus."

"Enough of all these marriages, what did Archimedes accomplish during this period of peace?"

"Mostly he worked on mathematics, solving many problems, and sending them to the Museum in Alexandria. Among other things, he discovered the law of buoyancy."

"How did he do that?"

Leonardo continues, "I think it was around the tenth year of the reign of King Hieron."

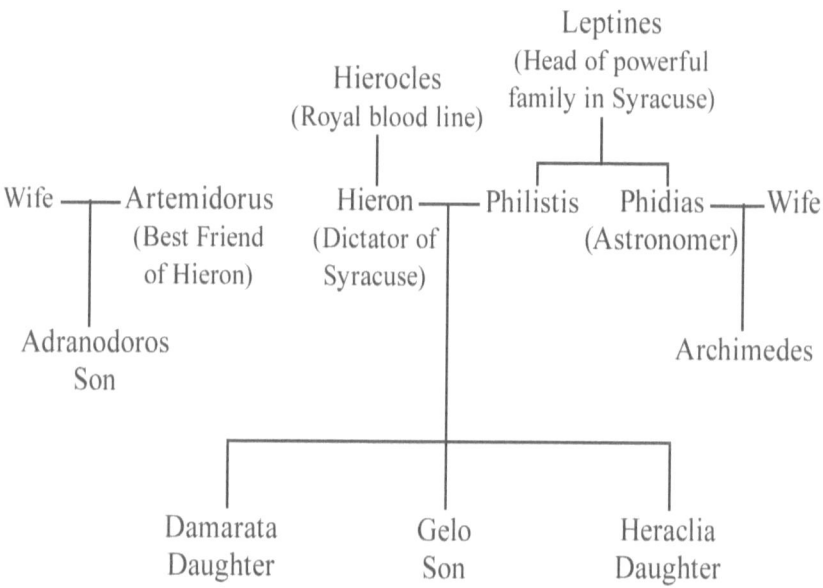

Hieron Family Tree
265 BCE

(255 BCE, in Syracuse)

Archimedes walks into the throne room of the palace.

"You sent for me, sire?"

"Ah, Archimedes. Yes, I have work for you." Sniffing toward Archimedes, "When was the last time you took a bath? Really, Archimedes, this is no way to present yourself to your king. Didn't your father teach you anything about court manners? Even the gods in heaven would be offended."

"Yes, sire. My father was very thorough. However, I seem to get absorbed in my work, and I forget about everything else. Sometimes I even forget to eat."

"Well, I don't care if you don't eat, but I would appreciate it if you took a bath more frequently, and use some ointments or perfumes."

"Yes, sire. Is that the nature of our business today?"

Angry, "Archimedes, don't forget your place! Here is the problem," holding up a beautiful crown of gold.

"To celebrate my victories and being crowned king, I had commissioned to have this gold crown made. It is intended for the temple of Zeus to thank the god for supporting me. However, I have reason to believe that I have been cheated."

"Interesting. Why do you think you have been cheated, sire?"

"Well, I commissioned a certain goldsmith to make this crown, and supplied him the gold. The work is exquisite. But I have been informed by some of his other clients that he frequently removes some gold for himself, and replaces the weight with an equal weight of silver. Can you tell me if any of the gold is missing?"

"Do you know exactly how much gold you gave him?"

"Yes, it was a gold bar like this one," pointing to a bar of gold on the table. "Exactly the same," handing the gold bar to Archimedes.

"Well, sire, if you melt down the crown, the silver will separate from the gold and you will know."

"No, Archimedes. This is a work of art. Look at it! What if we destroy it, and it turns out to be solid gold? No, no, it must not be damaged in anyway. That is the problem. I want you to tell me if this is solid gold without destroying it. Can you do it?"

"I don't know, sire. Let me think on it. Lend me this bar of gold to study, and I will try to figure out a way."

Hieron, dismisses him with a wave of his hand. Archimedes bows and starts to back out of the room.

"Archimedes!"

"Yes, sire?"

"I have another bar exactly like that one, and I expect to get every bit of that gold back."

"Of course, sire. Your word is law."

Archimedes returns to his workshop, and studies the bar of gold for several hours. He weighs it many times, scratches it, heats it, and conducts other experiments on it. Just before supper, Lagus, his personal servant, enters the workshop.

"Sir, you must take a bath tonight before supper. I heard that you offended the king today with your body odor. I must insist."

"Not now, Lagus. I am in the middle of looking for a solution to a problem for the king."

"I knew you would say that so I have figured out a way for you to continue to work while you bathe."

Now showing some interest in the conversation, "Oh? What have you done?"

"I had a square box made, filled it with fine sand, and set the box next to the bath. You can draw your designs and calculations in the sand while I scrub you. Later, if you want, I will copy whatever you design in the sand."

Picking up the gold bar up from his work bench, "This I have to see."

Together, Archimedes and Lagus march down the street to the public baths. They make an odd sight as they go. Lagus carries a basket filled with the soaps, oils, brushes, combs, and towels, that he needs to clean Archimedes and a change of clothes. Archimedes walks with the bar of gold in his hand. Lagus pretends not to notice a stir in the crowd as they pass. He has grown used to the stares and rumors that his master causes every time he goes out in public. Archimedes is earning a reputation as some type of genius but a slightly eccentric person. He does not bathe for months at a time. He wears the same tunic for weeks without washing it. His beard and hair are always unkempt. But today, Lagus is going to bathe Archimedes even if he has to tie him up. At least for a while, he is going to look like the Royal Engineer. Then Lagus will not have to endure the snickers and laughs behind his back from the servants of the other wealthy families in Syracuse.

As Archimedes and Lagus enter the public bath, the master of the bath waddles over.

Snickering, "Ah, Lagus, I see it is that time of year again. I have followed your instructions word for word. Right this way."

He leads them to a smaller bath in a private section normally reserved for wealthy clients. Next to the bath, the bath Master has set up a type of sand box. The box is close enough to the edge of the bath for a man to stand in the bath and draw in the sand.

"Great!" says Lagus.

Archimedes studies the sand box for a moment, "Interesting! I think this will work."

Lagus helps Archimedes get out of his tunic and into the bath. He removes his own clothes, and places his oils, brushes, combs, and perfumes within reach. Taking a sponge, he enters the bath. Archimedes places the gold bar next to the box of sand, and starts making calculations in the sand. Lagus begins to scrub him. Lagus is glad that Archimedes is concentrating on his work, and hardly aware of what Lagus is doing. He shakes his head when he sees weeks of accumulated dirt and grime on Archimedes' elbows and hands. As he takes one arm to wash to scrub the elbow and clean the hands and finger nails, Archimedes allows him to do so, continuing to work with the other hand.

This is working out well, Lagus thinks to himself.

After he finishes Archimedes' body he begins to work on his hair.

The soap for the hair is out of reach so Lagus climbs out to retrieve it. As Lagus leaves the bath, Archimedes notices the change in the water level. As Lagus reenters the bath, Archimedes watches the water level rise.

"Stop!" shouts Archimedes after Lagus enters the water. Lagus freezes, not sure what to do. Archimedes waits for the water surface to settle, and draws a line on the side of the bath at the level of the water.

"Get out!"

Lagus, still confused, obeys. Again, Archimedes waits for the water to calm down, and draws another line with his finger at the new water level. Then Archimedes gets out very slowly, hardly disturbing the water. He goes over to his previous marks, and marks the new water level. Then he reenters the water very slowly, and observes the rise in the water.

"Come back in slowly."

Lagus obeys, imitating Archimedes' slow movements. Archimedes watches the water rise.

"Get me a large bowl! No, no! Bring two large bowls. One must fit inside the other. Hurry!"

Lagus talks to the Bath Master who returns with two wooden bowls. Archimedes takes the smaller of the two bowls, fills it with water, and sets it inside the larger bowl. He reaches for a perfume bottle but Lagus grabs the expensive perfume bottle, and pulls it out of Archimedes' reach. Lagus quickly hands Archimedes a smaller and less expensive bottle of perfume. Archimedes pours the perfume into the bath, and uses the bottle to fill the smaller bowl to its top, eventually finishing by adding one drop at a time with his fingertip. When he is satisfied that the bowl cannot hold another drop, he sponges out any water that spilled into the larger bowl. He takes the bar of gold, places it into the smaller bowl, and watches as the water flows out of the smaller bowl into the larger bowl. He repeats the procedure a second time and then a third. Lagus, realizing that the bath is over, starts to collect his things, and put them into the basket. Finally, Archimedes stares at the bowls for several minutes. Lagus knows this is when his master is working on the solution. Archimedes turns and scribbles something in the sand. He smoothes the sand over, and writes again. He smoothes that over, and writes something else.

Suddenly shouting, "Eureka! That's it! I have found it! I've done it!"

Archimedes bolts out of the bath, heading for the door. Lagus grabs his own tunic, and pulls it on while picking up Archimedes' clean tunic, all the while shouting, "Bath Master! Bath Master!"

The Bath Master comes running, "Quit shouting! Here I am." Lagus is already heading for the door to catch Archimedes.

"Watch that bar of gold. I'll be back for it."

Archimedes runs out of the bath house and into the street causing screams and a few laughs from citizens in the street. Lagus is right on his heels shouting for him to stop. Finally, Lagus is able to get a grip on Archimedes' hair and stops. Archimedes' head jerks back, and he loses his balance, falling backward onto his butt, naked in the street.

"Lagus! What are you doing? Let me go! I have to tell the King. I know how to determine if the crown is solid gold."

Putting Archimedes' tunic over his head, "Master, if you go like this, the King will have you arrested."

"What?"

"You have no clothes on!" answers Lagus.

Looking down, "Oh! Oh! Where are my clothes?"

"Put on your tunic. Besides, the King is probably dining at this hour. Later, when you are properly dressed, you can tell the King."

"Yes. Yes, of course. I still have to test my theory on the crown."

"That's right. We must be presentable for the King. Now let me help you up, and get you home. We will get the gold from the bath on the way."

$$\Omega$$

Two days later, King Hieron looks up from his throne as Archimedes enters the throne room.

"Ah, Archimedes. Have you found a way to determine if my crown is solid gold or not?"

"Yes, sire, I have."

"Well, let's have it."

"Well, sire, gold has a different density from silver. That is why gold is so much heavier than silver. I discovered that if I measured the amount of water displaced by the bar of gold, and compare it to the amount of water displaced by the crown and …"

"Archimedes! You do this to me all the time. Don't bore me with the details. Just tell me if the crown is solid gold or not."

"It is not solid gold. As you suspected, some gold has been replaced with silver."

"I thought so, but I had to be sure. I had the goldsmith arrested after I gave you the crown. I had to be sure, but I did not want him to escape. He has cheated many people over the years, and made himself wealthy in the process. But now he has cheated his king. Thanks to you, it will be the last time he will cheat anyone."

"What will you do?"

"I will confiscate his home and all his gold. Then I will order his thumbs cut off."

"But, sire. If you do that, he will not be able to ply his trade."

"So be it. He can beg in the streets for all I care. It will serve him right, and be an example for others to be honest with me. I will not allow anyone to take advantage of me. You have rendered me a great service once again. Thank you."

"Your word is law," Archimedes bows, and marches out of the room.

Monte R. Anderson

CHAPTER FIVE

(1499, Cesare's Campaign Headquarters)

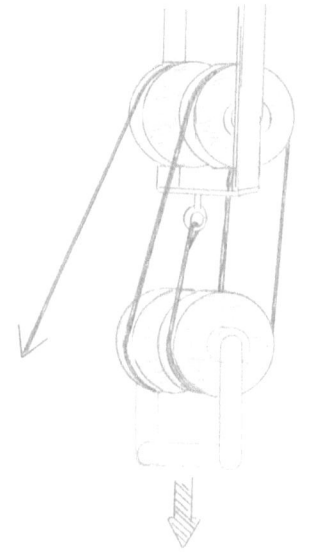

L eonardo retrieves a document out of the chest, and holds it out
to Cesare.

"Here is a document written by the Roman author Plutarch. He
was writing about Marcellus but wrote this note about Archimedes."

Cesare takes the document, and reads aloud, "Archimedes, however,
in writing to King Hiero, whose friend and near relative he was, had

stated that given the force, any given weight might be moved, and even boasted, we are told, relying on the strength of demonstration, that if there were another earth, by going into it he could remove this. Hiero being struck with amazement at this, and entreating him to make good this problem by actual experiment, and show some great weight moved by a small engine, he fixed according upon a ship of burden out of the king's arsenal, which could not be drawn out of the dock without great labour and many men; and, loading her with many passengers and a full freight, sitting himself the while far off, with no great endeavor, but only holding the head of the pulley in his hand, and drawing the cords by degrees, he drew the ship in a straight line, as smoothly and evenly as if she had been in the sea."

Ω

(249 BCE, in Syracuse)

Archimedes enters the throne room and bows.

"Archimedes, there you are," says King Hieron. "I have a task for you. King Ptolemy of Alexandria has been a loyal ally and has supported me in all my efforts. I know that you have been studying floating bodies. I want you to get with Barnacle, and build me the greatest ship ever built."

"Sire, what type of ship?"

"Well, not a war galley. It will be a gift for King Ptolemy for the feast of his father, the first king of Alexandria. It must be a fitting gift. I was thinking of a merchant ship, perhaps, but something big. Make it the fastest and biggest ship ever built. I will name it the Syracusia".

"What do you want built into it?"

"It should be able to out sail any ship afloat. I also want it to be able to defend itself against pirates. You figure out the rest, and don't bore me with the details as you usually do. If it works out, we will see how we can adapt it for other uses. Now go."

"Your word is law." Archimedes bows, and leaves the room.

Ω

For the next six months, Barnacle and Archimedes confer daily. At night Archimedes builds scale models, and tests them in the public bath. Lagus had recommended it as a veiled way to get Archimedes to bathe. While Archimedes is naked, Lagus removes his tunic, and replaces it with a clean one. It becomes a form of daily entertainment for the men of Syracuse to go to the bath about the time that Archimedes is there, and watch him launch his models into the water. Most consider the models mere toys, and Archimedes quite mad. Archimedes makes frequent changes, and launches them again and again.

Down at the shoreline near the docks, the ship is beginning to take shape. The ship has three masts, which is unheard. Archimedes determines that the wind would easily tip over a normal ship with three masts. Therefore, he has additional rudders, called keels, attached to each side. They are very long, and reach deep into the water. This makes the ship very stable, and reduces the amount of roll at sea. He also widens the ship to increase buoyancy, and enable it to carry a large cargo. In addition to the three masts, Barnacle finds that he can add another sail merely by using a triangular sail instead of a square one. The triangular sail is anchored on the top to the forward mast, and the other two corners to each side of the bow. Archimedes adds a boom with a triangular sail to the third mast. The bow sail and the new boom sail are tested on one of Barnacle' other ships and with spectacular results. Archimedes also installs a system of pulleys to help the crew to raise the sails quickly. A unique crane made with beams and pulleys that can load any type of cargo quickly is installed above a cargo hatch. To help bail water during stormy weather, Archimedes builds bilge pumps consisting of large screws inside wooden pipes. One end is anchored in the lower portions of the ship where water normally accumulates, and the other end exits a hole in the side of the ship. Four are installed, two on each side. Each pump is operated by a man walking on the shaft. The pumps are efficient and effective. Barnacle makes sure that only the finest wood and materials are used.

The Syracusia has five banks of rows, if needed, for extra power. It has two towers on each side to ward off pirates. The Syracuse can carry

400 marines in addition to a full cargo and crew. The towers double as platforms for the cargo cranes. There are a dozen rooms amply furnished for the royal family, a bath, and even a small temple.

Finally, the day to launch arrives. It is by far the biggest ship ever built. When the workmen try to pull it into the water, it is too heavy for them. More slaves are added but the ship is still too heavy. When the king sees this, he summons Barnacle and Archimedes to his throne room.

"Archimedes. It is fine looking ship and I do not want to destroy it or damage it while trying to float it. Perhaps we should dig a trench around it with dikes, and flood it until it floats."

"Sire, that would take more time, and the winter is almost here," says Barnacle.

"I was talking to Archimedes!"

"Your highness, that is not necessary," replies Archimedes, coming to Barnacle's defense. "I have figured out a way to launch the ship."

"But how? It is too heavy."

"Sire, there is nothing on earth that cannot be moved. Given another earth, a lever long enough, and enough room, I could move the earth itself by myself."

"Archimedes, you are a pain in the butt sometimes, but I am not letting you get away with that remark. I want you to show me how you can move that ship by yourself."

"It is very simple, sire…"

"Don't tell me. Just do it. I want to have the ship floating in one week, and I want to see you pull it into the water by yourself."

"Yes, sire. Your word is law."

$$\Omega$$

Four days later, Archimedes informs the king that all was ready for the launch. A large crowd has gathered to watch Archimedes make a fool of himself. On the beach, Barnacle and Archimedes have constructed the apparatus to launch the ship. Archimedes determined that one single rope cannot hold the weight of the Syracusia. He attached dozens of ropes to special loop holes along the deck, sides, and masts of the ship. Each rope then passes through a compound pulley. The ropes from each pulley go to another set of compound pulleys. The running ends from these pulleys are wound around a capstan so that only one rope comes off the capstan. The rope then goes to one last set of pulleys. The running end goes to a make shift throne that Archimedes has set down by the shore. The keels are raised.

In front of the Syracusia is a greased ramp shaped much like the bottom of the ship. Every rope and pulley is also greased. It is obvious that if the ship can be positioned on the ramp, it might move to the water under its own weight. Getting it onto the ramp is the challenge. The ship is supported, as it had been during construction, on all sides by large support beams. The support beams are cross braced and anchored so they will not move as the ship travels. Everything is ready. Barnacle approaches Archimedes.

"Everything is in place and working, Archimedes."

"Thank you, Barnacle. I think we can start."

"Before you do, shouldn't I have the crew get off?" pointing to the crew onboard the ship.

"It won't be necessary."

"But it will lighten the load."

"The amount of weight contributed by the crew is small compared to the weight of the ship. I have already included it in my calculations, and I have even allowed for an extra margin."

Spitting, "Damn it, Archimedes! You are as stubborn as a sea lion. What if your calculations are just slightly off? Should we take that chance?"

"Barnacle, I have rechecked my calculations, and they are not off. This will work. Why do you still doubt me? I recall the story about when you when you escaped from the Mamertine pirates. Can this be worse?"

"It never happened."

"What?"

"I was never captured by pirates."

"But I thought…"

"It was all a lie. Your grandfather, Leptines, paid me to tell the City Council that I was captured by pirates. He gave me enough money to buy my own ship. Then he gave me the contract to supply grain to the Romans. That is how I started my business, and made my fortune."

Archimedes notices that Barnacle is looking him straight in the eyes, "Interesting! But what has that have to do with this?"

"Don't you see, Archimedes? I am between Scylla and Charcoal."

"I think you mean Charybdis if you intended the monster."

"You do know the sea monsters, Charybdis and Scylla, who guard the Strait of Messana? If a ship sails to avoid the one, it is attacked by the other."

"I know of them vaguely."

"Well, I owe my business and my livelihood to your family and the king. If I don't do this, the king will seize all my ships and goods. If I attempt it but fail, it will be bad for my business. Everyone will take me for a mollusk, and refuse to do business with me. I will be ship-wrecked."

"And if we succeed, you will have more business than you can handle. That is the risk we must take. You are a businessman and a sailor, you surely understand risk. Beside, you are a barnacle not a mollusk."

Ignoring the last remark, "Yes, I understand risk but I have never taken a risk this great. I prayed to Poseidon this morning. I even prayed to Berenice. If you fail, people will just laugh at you, but I will be ruined." Spitting onto the sand, "Let's get it over with."

"Who is Berenice?"

"I will explain later. Go ahead. My life is in your hands."

Archimedes asks King Hieron to come, and sit on the throne on the beach. Grudgingly, King Hieron marches to the throne, and sits down, shaking sand out of his sandals.

In a voice so low, only Archimedes can hear, "Archimedes, if you embarrass me in front of my subjects, it will not go well for you."

Monte R. Anderson

"Not to worry, sire."

Once the king sits down, Archimedes picks up the rope. A hush comes over the crowd as Archimedes pulls the slack out of the rope. Barnacle darts back and forth from one side of the ship to the other checking support beams, ropes, and pulleys. Archimedes pulls one arm's length of rope, and the capstan begins to rotate, pulling the slack out of the three running ends wrapped around it, but the ship does not budge. Archimedes reaches out his other arm, grips the rope, and pulls. The capstan turns again, pulling the lines between the sets of pulleys taut but the ship stills does not budge. Archimedes pulls again. Finally, the slack in the ropes between the final set of pulley and the ship tighten. The ship still does not stir.

People in the crowd begin to laugh and snicker. Archimedes reaches for another arm's length of rope and pulls. The capstan turns, all the pulleys rotate, the hemp ropes stretch and vibrate rapidly, but the ship does not move. Barnacle scurries faster around the ship, trips, and falls face first in the sand. The crowd roars with laughter. The king shifts in his seat. Barnacle sits up but remains sitting in the sand, spitting sand out of his mouth. At this point he has done all he can do--the rest is up to Archimedes. Archimedes takes up another arm's length of rope as all the ropes tighten, and continue to stretch. He pulls again, and this time the ship starts to stir. It moves slowly at first but as Archimedes continues to pull it picks up speed. The crowd hushes and pushes closer, not sure if the ship had moved or not. Once the crowd realizes that the ship has, in fact, moved, they start to cheer. The king leaps out of his throne in the excitement. Several times he jumps up and down, and claps his hands. He hugs Archimedes, and slaps him on the back several times.

"We have done it! We have done it!"

We? says Barnacle under his breath as he spits into the sand.

"Of course we have, sire," replies Archimedes. "Here," handing the rope to the king, "You try."

The king takes the rope in both hands. Archimedes moves toward the water's edge.

"No, sire. Try it sitting down on the throne, and just use one hand."

The king sits down and takes the rope in one hand. He stares at the rope for a minute. He had expected the tension to be greater but in his hand it feels not much tighter than the reins of a horse. The crowd grows quiet again in anticipation.

"Pull, sire," yells Archimedes.

The king pulls the rope toward him. He is astonished that it takes so little effort. The crowd cheers as the ship resumes its journey toward the water. The king pulls again, and the crowd cheers louder, picking up the chant, "Pull! Pull!" Encouraged by the crowd, the king pulls one arm's length after another, faster and faster. One pulley snaps loose and its ropes go slack but the progress continues. Support beams begin to fall as the ship starts to enter the ramp. Still he pulls, and the crowd cheers. The ship comes up onto the ramp, and begins to slide toward the water under its own weight, but the king keeps pulling the rope. Soon his lap and feet are covered with rope.

The king does not stop until the ship splashes into the water. Crewmembers onboard quickly throw ropes to men on the dock to tie the ship to the moorings. The people of Syracuse have never seen such a feat. The crowd rushes King Hieron and Archimedes, patting them on the back, cheering all the while. Finally, the king raises his arms to silent the crowd. He motions for Archimedes and Barnacle to stand next to him.

"Citizens of Syracuse, today you are witness to the greatness of Syracuse, and the wisdom of Archimedes. This ship shall be called the Syracusia, and it is intended as a great gift to the King of Alexandria. There is none other like it in the world. There is no other city capable of building a ship like this except Syracuse. There is no other engineer in the world as great as Archimedes. From this day forth, we will believe anything that Archimedes says. When he says it can be done, it will be done. His word is law. We will build a great fleet of merchant ships that will sail the world, and trade with other kingdoms. The admiral of this fleet will be none other than Barnacle. This is a great day for Syracuse!"

The crowd cheers, picks up Archimedes and Barnacle, and carries them back to the palace.

Back in the throne room, the king addresses Archimedes, "Archimedes, I must confess I thought you had made an idle boast but you were right, and I was wrong. I did not trust you. Your father, Phidias, was not only my chief advisor, he was a close friend. I admired his intelligence, and trusted his judgment implicitly. I miss him a lot. You, on the other hand, I did not trust until today. You had not proven yourself to be the man your father was. Now, I realize, I was wrong. You are greater than your father. You have earned my trust and my friendship."

"Thank you, my Lord."

"I want you to join me in celebrating the launching of the Syracusia by dining with me in the palace. I am sending you to Alexandria on the Syracusia as soon as it is ready to sail. I want Barnacle to go with you. He will train the new crew from Alexandria. You can visit the Library and the Museum. Stay as long as King Ptolemy desires."

"Your word is law."

"Archimedes," Queen Philistis says, "May I offer you a word of advice?"

"Of course, your Highness. I would welcome any advice from you."

"Well, I think this trip to Alexandria is a great opportunity for you. You are not getting any younger, and I think you should consider taking a wife while you are in Alexandria."

"Yes, your Highness, but why Alexandria and not here in Syracuse?"

"Archimedes, you are my nephew, and I am concerned for your well being. The truth is, I have been seeking a suitable wife for you for a number of years since your father died, and I have had no success. The women in Syracuse know of you and your reputation, and, quiet frankly, they consider you-how shall I say this without offense-somewhat, well, eccentric."

King Hieron begins to chuckle.

"I have even gone to other cities in Sicily but to no avail. Suitable women there have friends and relatives in Syracuse, and they soon find out about you. I am afraid I have not been able to find you a wife anywhere in Sicily."

"I am sorry, your Highness. I did not mean to put you to so much trouble."

"That is not the point. You are family. As near as I can determine, the citizens of Alexandria know of your great work but are not aware of your eccentricities. I think you may have the opportunity to find a wife. I should go with you to help, but I must stay here. You will have to be on your best behavior, and make an impressive appearance."

"What do you mean?"

"Well, for example, don't go running down the streets naked, and don't forget to bathe. Try to meet with people and socialize. Don't work so hard. Enjoy your visit, and make new friends."

"I have many friends in Alexandria already. Many scholars."

"I mean outside of the Museum."

"I will try, your highness."

"And another thing, shave your beard."

"Why must I shave my beard?"

"It will make you look years younger. You are a good looking man, but who can see it? Women are attracted to smooth faces."

"But, your Highness, I will be meeting with scholars from the Museum. Surely..."

Philistis cuts him off, "You will not find a wife in the Museum or Library. You can discuss your mathematics with the scholars after you marry and let your beard grow, but for now, shave off your beard! That is a command!"

Looking at King Hieron, "Sire, please..."

Snickering, "Don't drag me into this, Archimedes. My advice is to do whatever she says. That's what I do. If you don't, you will never hear the end of it, and you probably won't ever get married. Just do it."

"Yes, your highness. Your word is law."

"Archimedes, my friend, I think she may be right," says Hieron, "You are representing Syracuse, and we want you to look your best. I have heard that the women in Alexandria are beautiful. Beside it is a great opportunity for you. King Ptolemy himself has requested your presence. You can study at the great Library, and meet the greatest minds in the world. Then you can return, and share that knowledge with Syracuse."

"I look forward to it."

"Just bring back some useful ideas and not that nonsense about the world being round and spinning around the sun."

Archimedes' mouth drops open, and he stares at the king. He never realized that the king knew anything about the secret body of knowledge.

"Oh, don't look so surprised. King Ptolemy writes to me often, and has told me all about such things."

Astonished, "You know that the world is not flat?"

"Whether I know it or whether I believe it is of no consequence. Of course, I know it!"

"And that the earth orbits the sun?"

"Again, it is useless knowledge."

"Useless, sire? It is of monumental proportions! It underscores all that we know of nature. Surely, you can see…"

"Archimedes, I did not mean to offend you, and I do not want to debate the point. What I mean is that it doesn't make any difference in the manner in which I rule Syracuse. How would it change my life? How will it aid us in battle? Will it add one day to the number of days that the gods have granted me?"

"The gods, sire?"

"Yes, the gods. Zeus favors me because I make sacrifices to him and honor him. He does not seem to care if the world is flat, round or square."

"But, sire…"

Philistis interrupts, "Please, Archimedes, do not get the king all worked up, and then leave him to me to calm down. Have these debates with your peers at the Museum."

"Yes, my dear, you are right," agrees the king. Turning to Archimedes, "You will sail for Alexandria in time for the feast of Ptolemy I."

"And shave off your beard!" interjects Philistis.

"Your word is law."

Monte R. Anderson

CHAPTER SIX

(247 BCE, on the Mediterranean west of Alexandria)

Archimedes strolls out on the deck for his nightly calculations of the stars, picking his path carefully through a mass of bodies. Many of the marines are trying to sleep on deck to catch the sea breeze in the heat of the night. Even in sleep, they hold onto their shields and weapons. The Syracusia does not have its full compliment of rowers, because it is carrying nearly a hundred athletes who will compete in the games at Alexandria. Many of the marines will double as rowers if needed. The athletes too, are on deck trying to sleep.

Archimedes spots Barnacle in the bow gazing eastward, focusing on a small light just on the horizon. Archimedes can see the light but not the land upon which it must rest.

"What is that light?"

Spitting overboard, "That is our guiding light," answers Barnacle. "That is the great lighthouse at Alexandra. It is called the Pharaoh's

Lighthouse. It was built by the first king of Alexandra, King Ptolemy."

"I think you mean Pharos Lighthouse. I have heard of it. How tall is it? Do they keep that fire going day and night? How do they get the light so bright? How far at sea can it be seen?"

Barnacle laughs, "You are asking me? I don't know, but tomorrow you will see it up close."

Together they watch the light in silence until Barnacle asks, "Will you meet King Ptolemy tomorrow?"

"Yes, I think so. This ship is for him, after all."

Scratching his butt, "How I envy you."

"Why?"

"You will probably meet Berenice, Queen of Cyrene. I heard that she is in Alexandria. If you get a chance to meet her, memorize what she looks like so you can describe her to me."

"You mentioned that name, Berenice, once before. I think it was when we were launching the Syracusia. Is she the goddess you prayed to? Who is she?"

Spitting overboard again, "A goddess? Yes, even you must have heard of Queen Berenice, the most beautiful woman in the world. I saw her at a distance once when she was racing. Even at a distance, there is no mistaking her. If she extends her hand to you, hold her hand as long as you can, and do not wash your hand until I get a chance to smell it. I want to smell the perfume that once caressed her bosom."

"I would only touch her hand."

"Yes, but it is the same hand she uses to put her perfume on her bosoms."

"Barnacle, that is disgusting!"

"Maybe so, but I can dream can't I?" grabbing his crotch, and making guttural noises. "You'll probably meet the king's son, Euergeter. He is quite a warrior I understand. He has a chest like Hercules."

"Barnacle, may I ask you a question?"

"Sure, but if it is like your other questions, I probably can't answer it."

"It is a personal question that I am sure you can answer."

"Then ask it."

"Why are you always spitting?"

Reaching into the pocket on his cloak and pulling out something. "Here, try chewing on these."

Barnacle pours a handful of beans into Archimedes' open hand.

Looking at the beans in his hand in the moonlight, "What is this?"

"The natives of the Galla tribe call it kaffa. The beans come from Absentea south of Egypt. My wife in Alexandria trades with the caravans that come to Alexandria for bags of kaffa."

Surprised, "I think you mean Abyssinia. Your wife? I thought your wife lived in Syracuse!"

Looking down at Archimedes' feet, "Did I say wife? I meant to say my partner. You know how I get my words mixed up."

"No Barnacle, you are lying. You clearly said wife. You have a wife in Alexandria and in Syracuse?"

Now looking Archimedes in the eyes, "Well, yes. I need people I can trust to manage my warehouses; one in Alexandria and one in Syracuse. When they are married, women tend to be very loyal and honest. It works for me."

"But you also trade in Carthage. Then you must have a wife in Carthage?"

Somewhat annoyed, "Archimedes, must you know everything? You never gave a damn about my personal life before, and now you are prying into my business."

"I am sorry. I meant no offense. You just took me by surprise. You are a shrewd businessman." Changing the subject to calm Barnacle, "Now tell me about these beans."

"As I said, they are called kaffa. I chew them, and they keep me awake. They have the opposite effect of wine. I swallow the juice, and spit out the beans. Try it!"

"I don't think King Ptolemy would approve of my spitting in his court."

"I would appreciate it if you would keep that knowledge about my wives to yourself. It is strictly business, mind you, but, it would not go well for me if each wife discovered that they are not the only wife."

The next day everyone is topside as the lighthouse comes into view. The lighthouse is the tallest manmade structure Archimedes has ever seen, nearly 300 cubits high. It is built on an island in the center of a large bay. Behind the lighthouse, Archimedes sees a long causeway connecting the island with the mainland, and creating two harbors. The tower has three tiers; a lower tier that is a quadrangular, a second tier that is octagonal, and a third tier that is cylindrical. At the top is a copula under which, Archimedes assumes, a fire is lit at night. Also near the top are two statues; one depicting Zeus the Savior and the other Poseidon, Lord of the Waves. Archimedes hopes that he will get a chance to visit the structure, and to view its plans.

The Syracusia sails past the lighthouse into the large main harbor as Barnacle begins to trim the sails to slow the Syracusia down. The keels are raised and locked along side as the ship glides past reefs on the left and docks on the right. Barnacle steers past a long pier crowded with spectators, and smoothly into the Royal Harbor reserved for the king and his royal visitors.

Pointing toward the city above the harbor, "There it is, the Queen of the Mediterranean," says Barnacle.

The arrival of the Syracusia causes a stir on the docks of Alexandria. Only the Roman and Carthaginian war galleys, called penteres because they have five rows of oars, are bigger, but they are slower in spite of their manpower. Today, the Syracusia also creates a stir because the famous Archimedes is aboard.

Barnacle makes port as early as he can after sunrise. He will need most of the morning to unload the cargo, all gifts for King Ptolemy. Most merchant ships usually avoid the night or hug the shore, but the Syracusia is not an ordinary ship. Barnacle sailed directly across the sea from Syracuse to Alexandria. The Syracusia out maneuvered every Roman and Carthaginian patrol, the fastest crossing Barnacle has ever made.

The harbor is crowded with ships as usual today. Ships from Spain, Africa, and even junks from China line the docks. All are eager to trade for Alexandria's goods. With most of the sails down and using only the bow sail, the drag on the wide hull slows the Syracuse to a crawl as it comes along side the royal dock. Eager hands tie the ship up while a crowd cheers.

Barnacle notices that the usual Nubian guards that meet his ship have been replaced with Greek soldiers--highly unusual. They are keeping a mob of citizens from entering the dock. As soon as the gangplank is down, an officer marches onboard. Barnacle and Archimedes meet the officer on deck.

"Is Archimedes onboard this ship?" asks the officer.

"I am Archimedes."

"I am here to collect all your scrolls and papyri."

"Why? What will you do with them?" asks Archimedes.

"It is our law, sir. We collect all books and documents, and take them to the Library."

"I meant to keep them with me. These are the only copies I have of my work."

"It's okay, Archimedes," a voice bellows from the dock. Archimedes turns to see a younger and rather large man in a long robe carrying a walking stick. The man quickly comes aboard the ship.

"It is I, my friend, Conon of Samos."

Conon seizes Archimedes in a bear hug that takes Archimedes' breathe away.

"Conon! You're Conon?"

"Yes, my distant friend. My friends call me The Bear because I hug so much. At long last we meet. You are pretty much as I expected except I thought you would have a beard."

"Yes, well, Queen Philistis suggested, or rather ordered me to shave. And you! You look much different from what I thought. Barnacle, do you know who this is? This is Conon, the famous mathematician from the Museum. This is the person that I have been writing to for years, and you have carried all my letters to him and his letters back to me."

"We have met," grumbles Barnacle.

Archimedes senses a stiffness between Barnacle and Conon.

"Barnacle, you old sea dog, it is good to see you again, too." Pointing to the Syracusia, "I see that you have moved up in social status."

"Sir, if you please?" interrupted the officer.

Conon explains, "Now listen, by decree of King Ptolemy, King of Alexandria and Egypt, all visitors to the city are required to surrender all books and scrolls to these guards who will take them to be copied by our official scribes. The originals are put into the Library, and the copies will be returned to you. This is how we expand the Library. It is a simple system, but it works. Now tell one of your servants to get all your papyri and models too if you have any."

"I do, but please be careful! You say the copies will be returned to me? Why not the originals?"

"The scribes don't always understand what they copy. Many can't read. Mistakes are made. It is better to have the originals. It was my idea."

"When will I get them back?"

"In a day or two. We have many scribes. But you, my friend, are the guest of King Ptolemy. You will be staying in the palace for now. I will send one of my slaves to pick up all your baggage."

Archimedes instructs one of his servants to gather the documents, and the officer follows the servant below deck.

When they are alone, Archimedes turns to Barnacle, "Were all my personal letters copied?"

"No, sir."

Barnacle opens his wool cloak for Archimedes and Conon to see. Inside the coat are sown several pockets, most containing scrolls and letters.

"Well, I'll be," says Conon laughing along with Archimedes.

"Come on, some more people are waiting to meet you on the dock," says Conon as he starts toward the gangplank. Archimedes follows Conon onto the pier. At the end of the gangplank are three men, on their knees, and bowing with outstretched arms as if worshiping some god.

"Oh great Archimedes. Oh great Archimedes," the three repeated in unison.

Immediately Archimedes and Conon begin to laugh.

"Do you see the type of people I am forced to work with? Honestly, Archimedes, I have tried but no one can teach donkeys. Get up, you asses, before these guards arrest you all for impersonating members of the Museum."

All three stand up grinning.

"Archimedes, allow me to introduce these clowns to you." Pointing to each man in turn, "Here we have Theon, Stobaeus and Eratesthenes. I believe you corresponded with all of them."

"Yes, yes, of course. How great it is to finally meet the three of you," says a delighted Archimedes.

"But first, if you please, Archimedes, give us a tour of this marvelous ship."

As the athletes and soldiers disembark from the Syracusia, Archimedes shows the four scholars all the designs and engineering of the ship: how the pulleys work to lift the heavy sails, the winches he designed to help pull the ropes, and the additional sails. He spares no detail. Barnacle is afraid that after this tour Conon will have the guards haul the ship off to the Library to be copied if it were not for the ship's great size.

After the tour, Conon leads Archimedes and the others through the cheering crowd toward the palace.

"Conon, could I please see the Great Library? I have heard so much about it."

"But of course. I knew you would want to. It is right next to the palace as is the Museum. We will meet King Ptolemy tonight at supper."

"How many books and documents are in the Library?" asks Archimedes.

"Thousands and growing day by day. We have surpassed the Library of Pergamum. We not only collect books from people like you, but we also write them ourselves," answers Theon.

They finally arrive at the main building of the Great Library, the Alexandriana. Conon leads Archimedes inside and down a long hall lined with white marble. Inside, he points toward a larger hall.

"There are ten halls like this one, each dedicated to the ten divisions of knowledge. Each hall has thousands of papyri, scrolls, and models-- all the knowledge of the civilized world under one roof. In these halls, scholars use the materials for general research or study."

Archimedes inhales the air taking in the aroma of the cedar oil used to protect the papyrus scrolls. It permeates everywhere. The aroma reminds Archimedes of his father's cedar chest, the Idea Box.

He looks around at the various halls; medicine, astronomy, geometry, mechanics, and others. Archimedes spots the hall for mathematics, and races into it followed by Conon and the others. The hall is lined with shelves from floor to ceiling. Each shelf bares stacks of scrolls.

"The most important scrolls are wrapped in leather jackets," Stobaeus points out to the awe-struck Archimedes.

Archimedes pulls a scroll from a shelf, and unrolls it.

"Not now, Archimedes," says Conon. "Others are waiting to meet you at the Museum. There will be plenty of time for you to explore the Library later."

He takes the scroll from Archimedes, and puts it back. Archimedes reads the name on the shelf.

"Euclid!" He looks to the left, "Thales of Miletus!" He starts moving down the row, "Pythagoras of Samos! All the great mathematicians of the world!" Moving faster now, "Even Parmenides! Hippias of Elis and Apollonius!" He stops suddenly.

Conon reads the label for him, "and Archimedes of Syracuse!"

Archimedes' mouth drops open as he stares at the stack of scrolls above his own name.

Opening one, "My work on circles!" Then another, "My work on spirals!" And another, "My centers of gravities and floating bodies!"

"Archimedes, we have all the works you sent us except for those you gave us today, and they will be here in a few days," says Conon.

"Oh my!" Looking at another, "My work on the ratio of a cylinder to a sphere."

"Yes!" says an exasperated Conon.

"This is my finest work. For this I will be remembered."

"No, Archimedes, your finest works lay ahead for you. Come, we must go now."

Conon leads Archimedes out of the Hall of Mathematics.

"The smaller and separate lecture halls are for individual or group study or research," says Theon.

Archimedes looks into one of the smaller rooms. The room is built of limestone, and has rows of tiered benches in a semi-circle and a raised center seat for a presenter. Conon takes Archimedes into a large room filled with tables with tens of people at the tables.

"We invited seventy-two Jewish rabbis to work with our scholars to translate the Pentateuch into a Greek version to be placed into the Library."

In another room, Archimedes sees masons working on a stone upon which they are inscribing text in Greek, hieroglyphics, and the Egyptian language called demotic.

"Besides Greek and Roman scrolls, we have oriental texts that were translated into Greek, and placed in the Library, as well as Egyptian, Hebrew, and Persian," brags Eratesthenes.

Conon shows Archimedes laboratories, botanical gardens, and miniature zoos, as well as a theater. A great workshop filled with masons, draftsmen, carpenters, artisans, and scribes is available for any project that needs constructing.

"And this, my good friend, is the Museum," says Conon as he leads Archimedes down a covered marble colonnade to another building, also in white marble. "The Museum is modeled after the Lyceum created by Aristotle. All scholars are housed here, presently about forty. King Ptolemy invites scholars from around the world. Many are Greeks from cities like Athens, and most of them are scientists and philosophers."

Finally, Conon leads Archimedes into a large, circular room full of men seated on marble benches. The room has a dome ceiling, and is surrounded with smaller classrooms. The walls are lined with Lebanese cedar paneling.

"This is called the Great Hall," Conon says.

Everyone stands when Archimedes enters with his escorts. Conon holds Archimedes by his elbow, and starts to make introductions. Many names Archimedes recognizes. He even corresponded with a few of the men. Each in turn welcomes Archimedes. Some even hug him as if they had known him forever. He meets mathematicians, philosophers, astronomers, poets, and other famous scholars. For the first time that he can recall, Archimedes feels that he is among his own peers and friends. He is reminded of his father who knew many of these scholars.

Suddenly, an elderly man with a long white beard makes his way into the room, and the room grows quiet. The man walks with measured steps, using two wooden staffs for support. Obviously in pain, he walks with his head down trying to avoid even the smallest obstacle that might trip him. Half way into the room he looks up to see Conon standing with Archimedes, and walks toward them, the sound of his staffs striking the tile echoing down the halls.

"Archimedes," says Conon, "I would like to introduce you to the famous poet, Callimachus of Cyrene, and now the head of the Museum. Callimachus, this is Archimedes of Syracuse, who has written...."

"Conon, stop your endless patter. I am familiar with Archimedes' works, and I do not need you to explain them to me. I may be old and feeble, but I still have a sharp mind. Now go, and check that everyone is here while I talk to Archimedes."

"Yes, sir," says Conon with a grin as he starts counting the people in attendance.

Bowing slightly, "It is an honor to meet you at last, Callimachus," says Archimedes.

Waving his hand, "Nonsense, Archimedes! You honor the Museum with your presence. I am sorry that I could not be at the docks to meet you when you arrived, but, as you can see, I don't get around very well. As Plato recorded Sophocles as saying, 'I thank old age for delivering me from the tyranny of my appetites.' I am glad you have arrived safely. Please, please, continue to meet all the members. We will talk at length later."

Callimachus shuffles to his chair. After a few more minutes, he stands up with the assistance of a slave, and taps one of his staffs on the marble floor. The sound reverberates off the walls and ceiling. The group falls silent.

"Members of the Museum, please take your seats. We have business to discuss."

All the men begin to sit down on the marble benches that circle the perimeter of the room. Pillows have been placed on each bench. Except for Callimachus, who has a large chair at the head of the circle of benches, there is no special seating arrangement—all scholars are equal. Conon takes Archimedes by the arm, and leads him to the center where one bench sets. Archimedes had heard about this room where scholars have to answer questions and challenges from the others, and to defend or prove their theories. He becomes uneasy because he is not prepared for this. Two Greek guards come in, and speak in whispers to Callimachus who directs them to take their posts, one by each door. Archimedes presumes this is to ensure that the assembly will not be interrupted.

When the guards are in position, Callimachus raps his staff on the floor once again.

"Are all the members of the Museum assembled?" Callimachus barks.

"Yes, we are all present," Conon replies, somewhat formally.

"Conon, you requested this assembly, perhaps you should begin."

"With pleasure, sir."

Conon stands, and begins to meander around the room and around Archimedes causing him to constantly change positions. Conon addresses the other scholars but does not look at Archimedes. Archimedes feels as if Conon has somehow changed from a friend to an inquisitor. He is now on guard.

"Fellow scholars, you are all familiar with the work of Archimedes of Syracuse, and now you have finally met the man who dares to submit his work to this Museum. He was the first to enunciate the laws of the levers, the laws of equilibrium, and the law of bouyancy. You are all familiar with his work on curves, parabolas, and compound pulleys. He was the first among us to figure out how to calculate the center of gravity, and he did so on several various shapes of uniform density. We do not have time today to explore and examine all of his works, but one theory demands our immediate attention."

Turning with a jerk toward Archimedes, "I speak of course about your theory on circles. Now you offered to prove that the ratio of a circle's perimeter to its diamter is the same as the ratio of the its area to the square of the radius."

A mumur races through the crowd, and several men whisper to each other or just nod in silence. Archimedes gets the impression that they are all familiar with this theroy. He realizes now why Conon had called for an assembly. Conon is a politician, apparently, and is putting on quite a show. Callimachus raps his staff for silence.

Talking directly to Ardhimedes, Conon continues, "We have all read your theory, and are particularly disturbed because another mathematcian at the Museum has offerred the same proof but claims to have arrived at his theory nine months prior to you. Furthermore, I attempted to use your ratio, and it just did not work. You had stated that the ratio was three plus one seventh. I have made some calculations myself, and arrived at a different conclusion. Can you explain this?"

Smiling, "Of course, I can. I have been writing to this Museum for many years as my father, Phidias, had before me."

"I knew your father, and considered him a friend," interjects Callimachus. "Please continue."

"I have always put forth my theories in the format laid down by Euclid with theorems, postulates, assumptions, and axioms with all the required proofs based on deduction. Well, on several occasions, after I had sent my theories to the Museum, someone here claimed to have developed the same theory independently but months earlier. So I decided to send three theories with deliberate errors or false assumptions. This theory on circles was one of them."

Everyone turns, and glares at Heraclide of Cyrene who stands up and paces in front of his bench looking away from the group.

Callimachus starts to stand, grimaces, and sits down again. "And, Conon, have you calculated the correct value of this ratio as I have asked, and kept that knowledge in secret?"

"I have, sir," replies Conon.

"And may I have it?" asks Callimachus.

Producing a scroll from inside his cloak, "I wrote it on this papyrus."

Conon strides over to Callimachus and hands him the papyrus.

"So, as I understand, Heraclide of Cyrene claims he discovered this ratio, and Archimedes says he did. The one of you has calculated the number correctly to match what I have in my hand is the true author. Heraclide of Cyrene has already said that the ratio is three plus one seventh, is that correct?

"Yes, sir," Conon speaks for Heraclide.

"Archimedes, what do you say is the correct ratio?"

"By my calculation, it is more accurately three plus ten seventy ones."

Fumbling with the tablet, "Conon has calculated the ratio to be," trying to find the number. "Three plus ten seventy ones."

Murmurs start circulating through the crowd. Several people standup, and shout at Heraclide. Callimachus raps his staff for silence.

Callimachus points his staff at Heraclide, "Therefore, Heraclide is a liar and a thief."

Now everyone except Archimedes begins shouting at Heraclide. Callimachus raps his staff to gain control, and signals the two Greek guards who march to either side of Heraclide, and seize his arms.

Callimachus gets up with some difficulty, walks over to Heraclide, and says, "You have shamed yourself, and disgraced the Museum. Academic freedom does not mean lying and stealing the work of others. You are no longer welcome at the Museum, the Library, or the court of Ptolemy. You are to leave Alexandria at once. You will never again have access to the Library of Alexandria. I will send a letter to all the Greek cities explaining what you have done and that all your work should be considered false. A special courier will escort you to Cyrene with a letter explaining why you have been expelled from Alexandria and the Museum."

Turning to the guards, "See that Heraclide is on the next ship sailing to Cyrene with all of his works."

Glaring at Conon and Archimedes, and shouting as the guards remove him from the assembly, "You have no idea what you have done! You have no idea of the power I have. I will see you both dead. I will appeal my case to Berenice, Queen of Cyrene."

"It is too late for that. There are no appeals to my decisions. I already spoke with Queen Berenice, and she has left your fate up to me. You are expelled. Guards, take him away!"

As the guards remove Heraclide, Callimachus addresses the Assembly, "I am sorry that this happened, but I wanted you all to witness this. We have no room in the Museum or in scholarly work for falsehood. Archimedes, my apology to you for putting you through this, but it was necessary to keep secrecy so we could expose this deception. For that, the Museum thanks you. If you would be so kind as to correct the other two false proofs as soon as you can. We look forward to your lesson on the floating bodies tomorrow night."

Callimachus raps his staff twice, signaling the end of the Assembly. Everyone makes a slight bow toward Callimachus, and remains standing as he exits the room. One by one the scholars file by Conon and Archimedes to congratulate them. Eventually, the room is empty except for Archimedes, Conon, Theon, Stobaeus and Eratesthenes.

"Conon," Theon starts after making sure everyone has left. "I think you enjoyed that too much."

"Well, for too long we have let Heraclide get away with this. But Archimedes deserves all the credit. His simple deception caught Heraclide in a snare like a hare."

"What did Heraclide mean when he was being take out of the room?" asks Archimedes.

"Oh, that was his Parthian shot. He can't do us any harm," says Conon.

"Parthian shot?" asks Archimedes.

"You know. The way the Parthian mounted archers can shoot backwards as they ride away," answers Conon.

"And what did Callimachus mean when he said my presentation?"

asks Archimedes.

"My dear friend," says Eratesthenes, "Now that you are in the Museum, in the flesh so to speak, we want to hear about your theories and works."

"All of them?" asks Archimedes.

"Yes, of course," replies Eratesthenes.

"But that would take months," says Archimedes.

"Of course," says Eratesthenes.

"But I can't stay here for months-a few weeks at most."

"Don't be so quick to leave. Wait until you have seen Alexandria. It is like no other place on earth. For scholars like us, it is heaven. Wait a few months, then decide," says Theon.

Conon interrupts, "Tonight is a banquet, and you are the guest of honor. Let me show you to your quarters so you can freshen up. King Ptolemy is most anxious to meet you. I will come at sunset to show you the way."

Stobaeus put his arm around Archimedes, "After the banquet, this small group of your friends is going to introduce you to one of the delights of Alexandria."

"And what might that be?" asks Archimedes.

"Beer! The best beer in the world," replies Stobaeus.

"Beer is only for peasants!" says Archimedes.

"Nonsense!" says Stobaeus. "We don't brag about it, but the Egyptians make the best beer in the world. Beside, we are not political here. The gods showed the Egyptians how to make beer, and we certainly don't want to anger the gods, now do we? It is a sign from the gods that they want us to be happy."

Everyone laughs except Archimedes.

CHAPTER SEVEN

(1499, Cesare's Campaign Headquarters)

A servant enters the room, and nods toward Cesare with a slight bow.

"Ah, lunch. Keep talking as we partake of a light lunch."

Leonardo follows Cesare into a larger part of the tent where a meal has been spread upon a table. The cook has prepared pigeon crostata; an open tart with a filling made of spit-roasted pigeon and seasoned with prunes and spices. Other cold, pre-cooked items one would hardly expect while on a military campaign are artfully displayed on the table. Biscotti is served with the pigeon crostata, and, of course, a fine Madeira wine. To top off the meal, the cook has made pandoro; a light, delicate, golden bread in the star-shaped style of Verona, lightly dusted with powdered sugar. *A light lunch indeed,* Leonardo thinks to himself.

Cesare says a quick prayer to bless the food, and looking up sees Leonardo frowning, "What is wrong? Ah! I know! I am sorry. I forgot to tell the cook that you do not eat meat. I will have him bring more salad and vegetables."

"Thank you, sire. This reminds me of the feast that was held on the first night of Archimedes' arrival in Alexandria," Leonardo continues from where he left off.

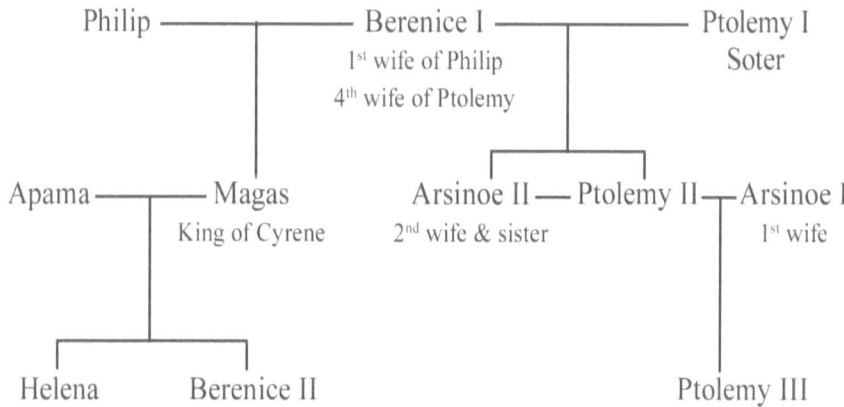

Ptolemy Family Tree

Dinner is served in the Great Hall. Conon leads Archimedes to the table reserved for the royal family of Ptolemy. The table sits on top of a platform from which the royal family can see and be seen. Conon brings Archimedes to king Ptolemy who is seated at the head of the table. The king is wearing a white tunic with a gold-colored silk waist band, and a hood that covers his head. Over the hood he has placed a gold crown. His shoulders are also covered with golden silk. He is carrying a golden flail.

"The king is dressed like an ancient Egyptian Pharaoh to please the masses and the priests," Conon whispers in Archimedes' ear as they approach the throne. The queen sits to Ptolemy's right, and his hound, Peritas sits on a small pillow to his left.

Conon bows and says, "Sire, may I present the famous…."

Interrupting Conon, Ptolemy says, "Conon, I do not think you can do justice to this man. Allow me to make the introductions."

"As you wish, sire." Conon backs away but lingers a few minutes to stare at Berenice before leaving to find his own seat.

"You are Archimedes. I have heard so many stories about you that I thought I would recognize you anywhere, but I thought you had a beard."

Archimedes bows and says, "Yes, sire, I did have a beard but Queen Philistis suggested that I cut it off for my visit."

"Well, I think it makes you look younger. I am King Ptolemy. Welcome to Alexandria. Please, join me at my table tonight. This is my wife, Queen Arsinoe."

Queen Arsinoe remains seated, and does not extend her hand to Archimedes. Archimedes thinks her smile is genuine.

"Welcome, Archimedes," says Arsinoe. "I do hope you will enjoy your stay with us. We are very proud to have you here." Archimedes notices that, like many of the women and men of the court, the queen has rotten teeth, a result of eating rich food.

In spite of her teeth, Archimedes marvels at her beauty.

Pointing with his flail, "And here we have my son, Euergeter who is co-ruler of Alexandria."

Euergeter stands, extending a hand to Archimedes. Archimedes is impressed by his youthful energy and boyish grin. Barnacle was right; he does have a chest like Hercules. Euergeter seems delighted to meet Archimedes.

"This is my niece, Berenice, daughter of the late Magus, former King of Cyrene, and my half brother. Now she is the Queen of Cyrene. Berenice has one of the best chariot teams from Cyrene. She drives them herself."

Berenice does not stand but does extend her hand to Archimedes. He kisses it in the fashion that he has seen men do in the court at Syracuse. Archimedes thinks that Barnacle is right, she is the most beautiful woman he has ever seen. He cannot help but stare.

"Please, sire. It is nothing compared to what Archimedes has achieved," Berenice says with a broad grin.

Archimedes detects false modesty.

"Archimedes, if you would be so kind as to let me have my hand back," say Berenice.

"Oh!" Dropping her hand from his grip, "My apologies, your Highness. I forgot myself for a moment."

He remembers Barnacle's words about holding on as long as possible, and then smelling the perfume later. He had not intended to do it but now it has happened.

"That's quite all right. It happens to me all the time."

King Ptolemy continues around the table, "And here we have my other niece, Princess Helena of Cyrene, Berenice's younger sister,"

Already standing, and extending her hand, "I see that your Highness is in an excellent mood tonight."

Helena nods her head toward Archimedes.

"And why shouldn't I be. It is a night to celebrate; the great Archimedes is here. Helena is a great charioteer in her own right. She will also race this week. As she gains more experience, she might even surpass Berenice."

"Your Highness embarrasses me."

"I don't think that is possible but, none the less, it is true. Archimedes, I am going to give you the most desired seat in the kingdom tonight. Please, sit here between Helena and Berenice. They will take good care of you. Just don't make Euergeter jealous." Winking, "He has his eye on Berenice."

The king motions for Archimedes to sit down. Once everyone in the Great Hall finds his or her proper place, and reclines at table, the king claps his hands twice to begin the banquet.

Moving toward the center so everyone can see him, Ptolemy says, "Tonight we start the celebration of the great achievements of my father who established our dynasty. We are especially honored to have as our guest, Archimedes of Syracuse. Tomorrow morning we will begin the festivities. The first day will be a solemn day of sacrifices. The second day we will have foot races in the gymnasium. After dinner, Archimedes will make his first presentation in front of the Museum. Wrestling and boxing will follow the third day with the pentathlon on the fourth day. On the last day we will hold the chariot races in the morning, and in the afternoon we will see a play by the great playwright, Sophocles. We will end the celebrations with another great feast."

The king pauses and raises his hands to silence the applause.

"You are all invited. Now, please, you are my guests tonight. Enjoy the feast and the entertainment, and be joyous as only Greeks can be."

At a signal from Ptolemy, musicians begin to play, and a troupe of young women begins dancing.

"So you are the great Archimedes?" asks Helena above the din.

Archimedes is pleased to see that she has nice teeth. Helena is wearing a simple green peplos, a type of tunic, trimmed with royal purple at its edges, and fastened at the shoulders with silver pins.

"No, your Highness, I mean, yes, your Highness. That is, I am Archimedes of Syracuse, not the 'great' Archimedes."

"Come, come. You are too modest. We are not as formal as this banquet makes us appear. Call me Helena."

Archimedes had not even thought to speak to her since she was the king's niece.

"You look nervous," says Berenice.

"Yes, your Highness, I am. In Syracuse women do not usually dine with men. One exception, of course, is the queen. But I see several women here."

"We do in this palace," answers Helena. "Many of the royal family and even some of the wealthier families eat together. Do woman make you nervous?"

"Yes, but I do not see any wives eating with the scholars from the Museum."

"Well, rank does have some privileges," replies Helena.

"I heard that," says Berenice, leaning forward so that only Archimedes and Helena can see and hear her. "You speak too loudly.

Pay no attention to her, Archimedes, because that would kill her. My little sister craves attention."

"Hush now, or I will tell Uncle Ptolemy to marry you off to a wart hog of a king, and send you away," snaps Helena.

"As you wish, my dear sister, but when you are through with Archimedes, I would like to ask him a few questions of my own."

"Now then, Archimedes," continues Helena. "I understand you will be explaining your theory on floating bodies tomorrow night. I can't wait to hear about it."

"You plan to attend my presentation?"

"Why, yes, of course. Berenice and I attend most of the presentations at the Museum. Do you not approve of women attending?"

"Yes, I mean no. I mean to say, that in Syracuse women would not attend such a presentation, and I doubt would find it very interesting."

"Oh, my! Then Syracuse is not as advanced as I thought. You will find we do thing differently here in Alexandria. Women here do many things that women in other cities do not. For example, many of us are educated in the arts and sciences, and most of the Greek woman here can read and write. I know women who even write poetry. We enjoy many of the same privileges as free Greek men. We even are allowed to vote on some issues. I think you have a lot to learn about the women of Alexandria."

"So it would seem, and about a great deal about other things too, I imagine," replies Archimedes.

"Your Greek is excellent but you have an accent."

"Yes, I suppose I do. We Greeks in Syracuse have lived there for hundreds of years. While we study Greek writings, our language has adopted some of the local tones. You Greeks here in Alexandria are not far removed from Greece, and have not developed a local dialect yet."

"Are you familiar with our cuisine?" asks Berenice.

"No, not really. I recognize some of the more common dishes but not much else."

"Very well then, tonight we will be your teachers, and you can be our pupil."

"As you wish, your Highnesses."

"Oh, Archimedes, I told you, don't be so formal," says Helena. "Call us Helena and Berenice."

The first course is served. It is an elborate dinner even by Greek standards. Archimedes has never seen so much food, many dishes that he has never seen or eaten. The king is served first, then the rest of the royal family, and then the other guests in the Great Hall. The king feeds scraps of food from the table to his dog, Peritas. From time to time, Archimedes catches a glimance of Berenice and Euergeter holding hands under the table.

Pointing at all the food, Helena asks, "Archimedes, I am sure you recognize eggs, salad, and shellfish, but are you familiar with these?" She points at a silver tray of food.

"No, I don't think so."

"These are snails." She picks up a snail, and tries to place it in his closed mouth. "Come now, don't make a face. You must first try every-thing then you can eat whatever suits you. Now try this."

Archimedes opens his mouth, and lets her drop the snail inside. He was prepared for some unplesant taste but much to his surprise it is tasty.

"Hmmmm. Interesting!"

"That was not as bad as you thought it was going to be, now was it? Now what would you like?" asks Helena.

"I think I will stick to eggs and salad to begin with."

"Archimedes, where is your sense of adventure?" asks Berenice. "You come here to learn and to explore new ideas at the Museum, and here you sit with a closed mind. Tell you what, we will feed you things that we know you will like. You just relax."

The two sisters began picking out items, and feeding Archimedes. Archimedes can barely conceal his delight. Never has anyone fussed over him in this manner. The women keep up a steady stream of chat-ter while Archimedes reclines, and eats whatever they put into his mouth.

Helena is exquisite, obviously much younger than Berenice. She is more tanned than most of the other ladies. She is thin but as muscular as an athelete. Her blond ponytail sways from side to side as she turns her head from the table and back again. Archimedes observes that her eyebrows are painted on, something he has never seen before. Her feet have tan lines from wearing sandles in the sun. Every time her arm comes near his nose he takes in the scent of roses. He decides not to mention any of this to Barnacle. Barnacle would have too many questions and vulgar gestures to be sure.

The second course contains the meat dishes: beef, lamb, pork, chicken, and fish. The fish includes porpoise, mackerel, mullet, oysters, and sole. A variety of wild game such as wild boar, venison, hare, goat, pheasant, duck, goose, partridge, thrush, and turtledove is presented in a pleasing display. Many dishes are new to Archimedes.

"Now what is that?" asks Archimedes, pointing.

"That is crane, and that is flamingo, and that is ostrich-all fowl" answers Berenice.

"Interesting! What type of fowl is ostrich?"

"Ostrich is a large, long necked bird found in the plain of Africa," replies Berenice. "However, we raise them here in Alexandria. Quite tasty, like beef."

"Interesting! And that?" Archimedes points at a tray of strange meat.

"That is zebra, like a horse, but white with black stripes," answers Berenice.

"I think zebras are black with white stripes," jokes Helena.

"Interesting!" says Archimedes, missing the joke. "And that?"

"The natives call it a 'river horse' so we took the name literally, and call it Hippopotamus too, says Berenice. "Helena is more familiar with the native cuisine than I."

"So it is some type of horse?"

"Helena chimes in, "More like an elephant with short legs living in the water. It is hard to describe. You will have to see one for yourself. And this is crocodile, also tasty if cooked right and seasoned with spices; otherwise it is bland."

From time to time, the dog, Peritas goes to Euergeter for a bite of meat. Whenever Archimedes doesn't like the taste of food in his mouth, he waits for Helena and Berenice to turn their heads, and he slips it to the eager Peritas.

Archimedes recognizes many of the vegetables: olives, beans, lentils, chick peas, lettuces, cabbages, and leeks. Helena and Berenice take turns selecting a morsel and placing it in his mouth. Archimedes enjoys every minute. The wine is in abundance and is excellent. Archimedes has never seen such an assortment of breads. Bread is not eaten in Syracuse. Berenice dips a piece of bread in olive oil mixed with spices, and drops it into his mouth. The last course is served: trays of fruits, various cakes, and puddings.

"Here try this. It is called an apricot. I doubt you have ever seen this in Syracuse. Now what else? Oh, I know, almonds. Have you tasted almond nuts before?" asks Helena.

"No, never. Mmmmm. Interesting!" as Helena places an almond in his mouth.

"I will have one of my handmaidens bring up a tray of fruit and nuts to your room. You might be hungry later,"

"I don't think I will be hungry for a week."

Laughing, Helena says, "Good! You have a sense of humor. That is a quality so lacking in most of you scholars."

Helena takes Archimedes' goblet, and holds it up for a wine steward to refill but stops him when the glass is half full. She then reaches for a small bowl containing honey. Using a special stick from the honey bowl, she drops a generous portion of honey into his glass and stirs. "Surely you recognize this," says Helena as she holds the goblet out to Archimedes.

"Of course, an aperitif, is it not?"

"Yes, of course. I guess you must have honey in Syracuse. But try this with our excellent wine."

She makes two more glasses for herself and Berenice but with much less honey. Archimedes thinks this would be what heaven is like if he believed in heaven: plenty of rich food, excellent wines, and the company of beautiful women. The wine is served in glass goblets not like the metal ones to which he is accustomed. He has seen a lot of glass bottles and glass vases tonight, more than in Syracuse. His thoughts are interrupted by Helena's voice.

"I think it is time for the ladies to retire. I see Queen Arsinoe preparing to leave. We must tend to her, and see that she gets to bed. What did you think of our feast tonight?"

"It was…"

"I know, interesting! Until tomorrow then."

Berenice already has the queen by the arm, and is leading her out. Helena extends her hand to Archimedes, and he kisses it. He is surprised to feel caluses on her fingers. As Helena and Berenice escort the queen out of the Great Hall, Archimedes can not resist the urge to smell his hand. Bernacle was right! The sweet smell of perfume lingers on his hand. But is it Berenice's or Helena?

"She is beautiful," says Archimedes as he watches Helena walk away.

"Which one?"

Archimedes turns toward Euergeter, whom he had ignored all during the meal.

"Both, I guess."

"Yes, but tell me, Archimedes, these laws of levers that you discovered, could they be used to build war machines?"

"Of course. Helena is very young isn't she?"

"Old enough to marry if she desires, but right now I don't think she wants to marry anyone. And could you please explain to me your laws of pulleys. I find this all fascinating."

"Can we do this another time, please, King Euergeter. I am very tired, and I see my friends coming to get me."

"Of course. You must be exhausted after your trip. Sleep well. I will talk to you tomorrow."

Conon, Theon, Stobaeus, and Eratesthenes approach the table.

"Aha! I know this gang of troublemakers," says Euergeter. "And I would guess they are up to no good tonight. I will alert the Nubian patrols to be extra alert tonight for a gang of scholars who are terrorizing the city. Good night. I will see all of you tomorrow."

The scholars politely laugh as they bow. Euergeter ambles away to talk to someone else.

Conon speaks first, "How did you enjoy the feast? Judging from the way Helena and Berenice were feeding you, I would guess you enjoyed it very much."

"You are the envy of everyone here tonight," says Theon. "You were seated between the two most beautiful women in the world, and they were feeding you like a couple of female slaves."

"It wasn't like that at all," protests Archimedes.

"What was Euergeter saying to you?" asks Conon. "Was he angry?"

"Why would he be angry?" asks Archimedes.

"Because the woman he loves was fawning over you, an older man who has twice his intellect."

"You guys have over active imaginations. She was not fawning over me, and Euergeter was not mad at me"

"Then what did he say?" asks Conon again.

"He was asking about my theories. You guys are like old ladies who like to gossip. There was really not much to say about it except that I am stuffed, and I definitely had too much wine."

"No time to rest," says Stobaeus. "We have to leave now so we can get to the tavern before the door is locked."

Conon leads the way to a tavern in the Greek Quarter. When the group arrives, the tavern owner greets Conon and the others by name. Apparently, this is a regular meeting place for this group. One of the bar prostitutes sees Conon, waves, and runs toward him. She is wearing face makeup made from white lead and mulberry juice on her cheeks. Archimedes has never seen a prostitute before. He knows Syracuse has them, but he has never frequented any place where they ply their trade.

"Not tonight. I have some business to attend to," Conon tells her.

"Why not? I won't be in the way. I need the money, Conon, honey."

Handing her a coin, "Here! You owe me one. Now go away!"

Pouting, "Okay, but don't forget me."

Laughing, "Not a chance!"

As the prostitute walks away she walks through a puddle of beer on the floor. Archimedes notices that her sandals leave an imprint on the dry portions of the floor. He bends over, and reads, "Follow me. Clever!"

The owner leads the small group to a large room on the second floor. The room is bare except for a long table with chairs. Conon sits in the middle chair. Everyone else sits down around the table while two Egyptian women bring in tankards of beer, baskets of bread, and leave a large bowl of beer on the table. Conon pats one of the women on the butt, and she playfully slaps him. Conon roars with laughter. When the women leave the room, Conon pays the owner, and bolts the door behind the owner.

"We won't be disturbed tonight. We come here to get away from the spies so we can talk in confidence. The walls have mice, and the mice have ears. We are not here to drink beer even though we will."

"I think I have had enough," says Archimedes.

"No matter, we are here to tell you things," says Conon.

"What things?"

"Like whom you can trust, who you need to be wary of, and what is really going on here. I'll start, but first a toast to the Museum," Conon raises his tankard.

All say, "To the Museum," and drink.

All look at Archimedes.

"Well?" asks Conon. "What do you think?"

"About what?"

"About the beer," says Erastesthenes.

"Oh. Yes, it is quite good. Is it barley?"

"Who cares?" replies Stobaeus.

"It is not as tasty as a Samian wine, but it is quite good," adds Conon.

Conon continues, "First of all do not be deceived. We scholars are well cared for by King Ptolemy, but it comes with a price. We are expected to glorify our benefactor with flattery and hints of divine status. For example, Callimachus equated him with Zeus and Apollo in some of his hymns. Manethan, the Egyptian high priest, dedicated his history of Egypt to him, even though Ptolemy himself had requested him to write it in the first place."

"Divine status? Does Ptolemy think that he is a god?" asks Archimedes.

"Yes and no," replies Conon. "The Egyptians make a habit of declaring their kings and pharaohs to be gods. They have already declared Ptolemy's parents as gods. They will probably do the same for Ptolemy and Arsinoe while they are still alive.

Eratesthenes interrupts, "He likes his subjects to say, 'I am obedient to my god and my king' when they are dismissed. We don't have to since we are not his subjects, but be careful. Let him do the talking, and let him finish the conversation. Do not correct him. He hates that."

Stobaeus speaks next, "Then there is the whole issue of politics. Do not be fooled by the friendliness of the court. Ptolemy is deeply involved with politics on a grand scale. He even dabbles in politics back in Greece. He will try to use you. Be careful what you say to him. He can turn on you in a flash. However, he does love the sciences. And Queen Arsinoe is actually his sister."

"His sister?" Archimedes says in shock.

"Yes. She is very powerful. She had left Alexandria, and then returned. Ptolemy was married at the time to someone else who happened to be named Arsinoe also. The second Arsinoe accused the first Arsinoe, of treason, and got her exiled so that she could marry Ptolemy. Everyone calls her 'Philadelphus, Brother Love,' behind her back, but do not let her hear you. She is not to be trusted. She cares nothing for the Museum or Library. Ptolemy's son, Euergetes, is a special case. Publicly, he adores his stepmother, but privately they cannot stand each other. He has not forgiven her for what she did to his mother, the first Arsinoe. But he is loyal to his father. We think Ptolemy made him co-ruler to keep his loyalty. He also supports the Museum and Library. He loves to collect books, and has contributed much to the Library. I am not sure he ever reads them. He is honest, and can be trusted."

"Interesting! What about Berenice and Helena?" asks Archimedes.

Eratesthenes answers, "Berenice is very intelligent, and supports the Museum and Library. She can ask some tough questions. She and Euergeter plan to marry even though they are cousins. Helena is still young, and not involved in palace politics. She has her own interests. She genuinely tries to help the Egyptian peasants. She is supportive of the Museum and Library."

"No, I mean is Helena married?"

Eratesthenes pauses, "No, she is not married." Everyone stops drinking, and stares at Archimedes for a minute.

"I would guess that Helena made an impression on you tonight," says Eratesthenes.

"Get to the point, Beta!" interrupts Conon.

"The point is this; we have a great thing here," Eratesthenes continues, "Here is the world's largest depository of knowledge. If all that knowledge falls into the wrong hands it would be a disaster. We all have plans, if needed, to escape at a moment's notice. We will help you to make arrangements too."

"Interesting!" Turning to Conon, "Why did you call Eratesthenes 'Beta?'"

"Oh, that?" laughs Conon. "It is a joke among our small group. We assign letters to each of the scholars.

Eratesthenes is Beta because he always comes in second. He usually finds the correct solution but is a little slow."

"What letter did you assign Heraclide? Omega?" asks Archimedes.

Everyone is silent for a minute.

Finally, Stobaeus breaks the awkward silence, "Heraclide would have to make much improvement to earn a grade of Omega." Everyone laughs including Archimedes.

"Archimedes, did you ever hear of Heraclide before he came to the Museum?" asks Theon.

"No, I don't believe I did."

"Of course not," says Theon. "No one outside of Cyrene had heard of him. He was hired to be the teacher for Berenice and Helena when they were but children. He was a fair teacher but had never contributed anything to the body of knowledge in any field. When he came to Egypt with Berenice and Helena, King Ptolemy recruited him for the Museum. We think he was placed in the Museum as a spy and for special assignments."

"What type of special assignments?" asks Archimedes.

"We'll explain later," says Conon. "We have suspected him for a long time. When you exposed him as a liar, it gave us an excuse to get rid of a spy without proving his duplicity."

The men talk and drink late into the night, and then go back to the Museum. Conon takes Archimedes to his guest quarters in the palace.

CHAPTER EIGHT

(247 BCE, King Ptolemy's palace, Alexandria)

Archimedes' room is amply furnished with a huge bed, a table, and several chairs. Food is also in abundance. There are trays of fruits, nuts, and sweet breads, not to mention wine. The next day, Archimedes is awakened early by one of Helena's handmaidens, told to eat something, and to join the other scholars in the Great Hall. When Archimedes leaves his room, the handmaiden, a girl no more than fifteen, is sitting in the hallway. She leads him to the Great Hall where most of the royal family is assembled with many of the ministers and priests. Archimedes looks around for Helena or Berenice but does not see either of them.

"Where is your mistress?" he asks the handmaiden.

"She must prepare for the sacrifices at the temple of Isis," she replies.

"Interesting!"

Conon pushes his way through the crowd to join Archimedes.

"Good morning, Conon. I am surprised to see you up so early," says Archimedes, grinning at Conon who is obviously hung over.

"Not so loud! My head hurts. Believe me, if this was not a command performance, I would still be in bed." Turning to the handmaiden, "I think I can take care of Archimedes from here. Go tell your mistress that Conan will see that he gets to where he needs to be."

The young girl genuflects and leaves.

After a few minutes, King Ptolemy arrives. Manethan, the high priest, starts the procession, and is followed by King and Queen Ptolemy and the King's son and co-ruler, Euergeter. The rest of the royal family follows by rank. The order of precedence is carefully orchestrated by one of the assistant priests. Once the royal family and ministers start out of the palace, Archimedes and Conon, along with the other scholars, are given the nod to follow. The procession heads down the main street, named the Canopic, toward the tomb of Alexander, called the Soma.

As the procession passes the Museum, more scholars join the royal procession to the Soma and the tomb of the first Ptolemy. Outside the Soma, the procession stops while the Egyptian priests perform rituals and sacrifices. Afterwards, everyone solemnly files by the tombs of Alexander and the first Ptolemy. Women lay flowers on the tombs.

The precession continues on to the Temple of Apollo. The Egyptian priests refuse to enter the temple so Greek priests take over. Inside there is a wooden statue of Apollo. In front of the statue is a one cubit square hole in the floor containing water from the Nile. The head priest throws an offering of wheat mixed with honey into the hole.

The pageant continues to the Temple of Zeus. Inside the Temple of Zeus is a huge statue of the god. He is portrayed as a regal, bearded man with bare arms and a muscled chest. The face is covered in ivory and gold while the rest of the statue is made of clay and gypsum. In one hand he holds a royal scepter and in the other an eagle. Once again, the Egyptian priests refuse to enter, and the Greek priests take over the rituals. One Greek priest places barley mixed with wheat on the altar.

An ox, which has been prepared for sacrifice, is released. It immediately goes to the altar, and eats the offering. Archimedes wonders if this has been rehearsed a few times. One of the priests, called the ox-slayer, moves from behind the ox, and severs the ox's spine with an axe. The ox dies quickly. The ox-slayer places the axe on the altar, and runs from the Temple. It is an old custom that Archimedes has not seen practiced for years. According to the custom, the ox-slayer goes into exile, probably just a re-enactment now. The ox blood runs down the steps of the altar onto the floor of the temple. Priests catch the ox blood in golden cups, and anoint the two kings and Queen Ptolemy. The head priest turns, and pretends to find the ax on the altar. The ax is quickly put on trial, and presented to the co-rulers for judgment. The kings acquit the ax of the murder of the ox, and the priests are pleased.

The procession ends at the Temple of Isis. There Archimedes sees Helena performing some of the rites of Isis. Archimedes is close enough to see that today she does not paint on her eyebrows. Inside the Temple is a white statue of Isis nursing her son, who is called Harpocrates by the Greeks and Horus by the Egyptians. The statue depicts her with wings partially covering the baby Horus in a protective posture. The altar in front of the statue consists of a large marble top held up by six pillars. Each pillar is shaped like a large cock, the missing part of Isis' lover, Osiris. Scorpions are carved into the sides of the top. Archimedes cringes at the sight of the scorpions.

A long parade of virgins precede single file up to the altar, and each virgin lays various offerings upon it. There is corn, bread, flax, cloth, balsam, and all types of flowers. At the end, Helena pours out water upon the altar. The water is from the Nile, and symbolizes the tears of Isis. The Egyptians believe that the annual floods of the Nile are caused by her lamentation over the death of her lover, Osiris. With that, the sacrifices for the day are over.

Archimedes returns to his quest room, and rests until the nightly feast. Once again, the royal family sits at the head table. Archimedes and Conon take their places among those reserved for members of the Museum. During the meal, Archimedes cannot help but stare at Helena who is flirtatious. Occasionally, she catches Archimedes staring at her, and smiles back at him.

Conon interrupts Archimedes' thoughts by tapping his arm, "You are being summoned."

"What?"

Archimedes looks where Conon is pointing. The king is waving for Archimedes to come over. Archimedes gets up, and strides over to the king.

"Sire?"

"Come join me, my friend. I need some advance knowledge about your presentation tonight so I can appear intelligent to my subjects. Please, sit here by me."

The king's wife, Arsinoe, slides over to make room for Archimedes. When Archimedes is finally settled, he looks up, and sees Helena directly across the table smiling at him.

"Now please, in simple terms, explain your theory to me."

Archimedes begins to talk about his theory starting with what is known, and stating what has to be proven. He clears off a portion of the table in front of the king. Dipping his finger into the honey, he begins to draw circles on the table. Helena notices that nearly everyone at the table is watching and listening. Euergeter stands up, and moves behind his father for a better view. Queen Arsinoe could care less.

At the end, the king laughs, "Archimedes, I have wasted your time. I am afraid that I still do not understand. Perhaps when you speak tonight, it will be clearer to me."

Everyone laughs. Helena sticks the tip of her finger into the honey, and while smiling at Archimedes, licks off the honey. Archimedes feels flushed, and is sure that he blushed. He avoids looking at Helena, and instead, concentrates on straightening up the table. He hopes no one noticed this little scene with Helena. He is relieved when the king stands up, and helps his wife up. Everyone else stands.

"I have some business to take care of before Archimedes' presentation. Please, enjoy your dinner," says King Ptolemy.

He starts to go but stops, and turns back toward Archimedes, "Archimedes, I think it would be good for you to see something of our kingdom outside of the palace and Library."

"I would like to, sire."

"Excellent! You can start next week."

"But, sire, I will need a guide, someone who speaks the native language."

"You are right. Helena will take you."

"Sire? Me?" asks Helena.

"Yes, of course. Who better than you?"

Bowing, "I am obedient to my god and king."

After the king leaves the room, Helena turns to Archimedes.

"So, I guess I will be your guide next week. Until tonight then."

She offers her hand to Archimedes who kisses it. She follows the queen out of the room. Once again, he cannot resist smelling her perfume on his hand.

Conon, scampers to Archimedes' side. "Archimedes, did you hear about poor Heraclide?"

"Poor Heraclide? No! What happened?"

"Well, it appears that he drowned at sea," replies Conon.

"What? How?"

"Apparently, he climbed into a lead box, sealed it from the inside, carried it over to the railing, and threw it overboard with himself inside."

"Conon, that is a terrible joke. It makes no sense. How could he do that?"

"Don't be naïve, Archimedes. He was murdered."

"How horrible! Who would do that? Wasn't Heraclide tutor to Queen Berenice? Do you think she could have ordered his death?" Archimedes could not believe that the beautiful woman who had hand-feed him could be capable of killing her own teacher, but he had to ask.

"No," replies Conon. "I would not believe it. She could have arrested him before we exposed him. She knew what we were planning. No, it has to be someone else."

"Then who?" asks Archimedes.

"Who indeed? King Ptolemy probably had him killed to avoid any embarrassment."

"Are you serious?"

"We told you that he is not a man to be trifled with. Had I known this would happen I never would have exposed Heraclide. I feel terrible. "

"How could you know? There has to be more to this. No one would kill a man for stealing my theories."

"You may be right. It seems like a lot of trouble for such a small crime. Someone did not want him to show up in Cyrene. While he was here at the Museum, he was no danger. He must have had a secret too important to be revealed," says Conon.

"How did you find out?"

"The ship was not out of the harbor more than an hour. You remember the woman at the tavern who asked me for money?"

"Yes, you gave her a coin, I recall."

"Yes, that is the one. She does business with some of the crews of the ships. She told me."

"What kind of business?" asks Archimedes.

"Now what type of business do you think?"

$$\Omega$$

The room where Archimedes is to make his presentation is larger than the Assembly Chamber, and is modeled after the style of an amphitheater. The marble benches have no cushions, and are tiered very steeply in concentric semi-circles. At the bottom of the amphitheater is a circular area with a square box in the center filled with very fine, damp sand. Two long poles with narrow points lay along side a short bench which is near the top of the circular area. The room is brightly lit with numerous oil lamps.

Archimedes strolls in with Conon who is explaining the layout and the format for the presentation. When Archimedes explains his theory and assumptions, he can demonstrate in the sand with the long poles so all can see. A slave kneels next to the sand box ready to smooth over the sand when Archimedes tells him.

"Interesting! Where did you get the idea for the box of sand?" asks Archimedes.

"From you, of course."

"What?"

"Don't you recall writing me how your slave—what was his name?— had a box of sand installed next to your bath?"

"He was a servant, not a slave, and his name was Lagus. He died a few years ago. An excellent servant and friend."

"Well, anyway, it seemed like a good idea. I added the long poles and the slave to smooth the sand. We wet the sand. It works well."

"Interesting!"

A slave marches down each hallway of the Museum and Library announcing that the presentation is about to begin. In years past, many scholars would be so engrossed in their research that many times they missed the lectures or arrived late. This custom was started to put an end to that. Members of the Museum and the royal family are invited to attend all presentations but attendance is not mandatory. Sometimes, more than one presentation is made at the same time but not tonight. People wander in, and the room begins to fill. Everyone wants to see and hear the famous Archimedes.

When the room is full, people line up in the hallways. Conon acts as usher, ensuring that all the royal family are seated down front, and all the members of the Museum get a seat somewhere in the room. Scribes, who are recording every word, sit on the floor with the tools of their trade: papyri, brushes, and pots of pigment. Finally, when there is no more room, Conon nods toward Archimedes, and he begins.

"Good evening your Highnesses, members of the royal family, members of the Museum, and guests. Tonight I will explain some of my work on floating bodies. I will consider the first three propositions of the nine that I have proven. The remainder I will demonstrate at my next lecture. I will start with my second proposition since it the easiest to understand, and does not require proving the first proposition, and that is this: the surface of any fluid at rest is the surface of a sphere whose center is the same as that of the earth."

Thus, Archimedes begins his demonstration, drawing figures in the sand. After half an hour he notices that all the scholars are leaning forward, watching intently, their chins on their hands. The royal family, on the other hand, is sitting up straight or leaning backward slightly which gives them a look of being aloof and feigning interest. That is, all except the king, his nieces, Helena and Berenice, and, of course, Euergeter. The queen is not in attendance.

Ω

The second morning activities open in the gymnasium with foot races, jumping, and javelin throwing. Conon explains the various events, and points out the favorite athletes. Archimedes is amazed by Conon's knowledge of athletics. As a youth, Archimedes never competed in any athletic events. His interests were confined to studying.

Archimedes is disappointed to see that there are no women, particularly Helena, among the spectators. For all of Alexandria's liberal ideas, some traditions still hold. The athletes compete naked. There are three foot races; the shortest race is one stade, the second is two stades, and the final race is seven stades.

In the jumping event, the jumpers stand at the start line with weights called halteres in their hands. They start their jump by swinging their arms and weights forward, and at the end of their jump, throw the weights backwards. The event causes a debate among the scholars as to whether or not the halteres improve the athletes' performance.

Archimedes notes that the discus is made of bronze instead of stone. Conon says that is because in the last games, the discuss broke, and nearly caused a riot. The javelin is thrown by use of a leather loop attached in the middle. The scholars have an endless debate on the proper angles to use for maximum distance. King Ptolemy presents wreaths to the winners in each event. Merchants are selling food everywhere. Flute players entertain the athletes on the field.

At lunch time, Conon and Archimedes go down to the harbor, and eat aboard the Syracusia. Barnacle has prepared a light meal of breads, fruits, nuts, and beer. Archimedes is beginning to acquire a taste for

Egyptian beer. The crew of the Syracusia spent the morning scrubbing the ship from top to bottom to make it ready for tomorrow's presentation.

Helping Barnacle serve is a young, beautiful Greek woman.

"Why Barnacle, you old sea dog," shouts Conon. "You have brought your wife."

Conon and Archimedes stand up, and Conon takes the giggling woman's hand and kisses it. Her teeth are stained by kaffa beans just like Barnacle's teeth.

"Sit down Conon, you old fool," the woman says. "Don't be an ass in front of Barnacle. You know how angry he can get."

Barnacle glares at Conon who just grins. Archimedes thinks that her remark is odd. In all the years that Archimedes has known Barnacle, he has never once seen him angry.

Finally, Barnacle says to the woman, "My dear, you must meet my old friend, Archimedes."

Extending her hand to Archimedes, "But of course, my husband speaks highly of you."

Taking her hand, "At last we meet," says Archimedes.

This time Barnacle gives Archimedes a look that seems to say that is enough of that. The woman continues to help her husband serve the food without another word. She and Barnacle take their lunch to another deck, and leave Conon and Archimedes alone.

After the two are out of sight, Archimedes says, "I see that Barnacle has taught his wife about the kaffa beans he chews on."

"Oh, that? You have it backwards. It was his wife who taught Barnacle about the beans."

"Have you tried them?"

"Yes, and they kept me awake all night. I did not care for them. But old Barnacle likes them. He has the energy of a man half his age. He needs them with a beautiful wife like that. He does well. Did you know that he cannot read or write?"

"Interesting!" replies Archimedes to avoid a lie.

"That old sea dog! I'll bet he has a wife in Syracuse too."

Archimedes does not answer, and tries to change the subject.

"What is all this fuss about Alexander and the first Ptolemy about?" asks Archimedes.

Conon's eyes widen as he slaps the table. "I knew it! He does have a wife in Syracuse. Why that sly dog!"

"I didn't say that he did," protests Archimedes.

"You did not have to. I could read in your face. But, nonetheless, it is no concern of mine. You want to know about the ceremonies today? Well, it is really a simple matter of politics. When Alexander died in Babylon, he had no heirs. His generals set up a Council of State to rule the empire, and appointed a regent to govern. The generals then divided up the empire among themselves. The first Ptolemy, who took the name of Soter, ended up with Egypt where Alexander built the city that bares his name. Alexander had intended to make Alexandria the capital of his vast empire, and to rule from here. Soter managed to bring Alexander's body back here. That gave him both political and religious advantage. Soter could claim that he was the legitimate heir to the empire. Many wars were fought over that issue."

"What was the religious advantage?" asks Archimedes.

"Well, that too is pretty simple. When Alexander liberated Egypt from the Persians he was declared Pharaoh of Egypt. Soter also claimed that title, and adopted many of the Egyptian customs, one of which is to declare the Pharaohs living gods. Soter was declared a god. King Ptolemy wishes to continue that tradition so he must honor his father as if he were a god. The Egyptians believe strongly in an after life so this is very important to them. If King Ptolemy did not honor his father, it would undermine his own authority with the Egyptians."

"Does he actually believe that he is a living god?" asks Archimedes.

"No, of course not. But he knows that the Egyptians do, and that is the important point."

"So the rest of us must go along with this farce to impress the Egyptians? This is not religion, it is politics."

"Precisely. Welcome to the world of politics. Doesn't King Hieron believe in the gods?"

"Yes, he does, but he doesn't force his religion upon his subjects."

"And have you told him that you do not believe there are gods?"

"Of course not. I am not a fool."

"Then, even the great Archimedes plays politics."

Conon laughs loudly as he washes down some bread with a bowl of beer.

After lunch, Conon spends the rest of the day showing Archimedes the Library and Museum. The Library is actually a shrine to the nine muses, and each muse has a statue near the appropriate hall. Archimedes is attracted to the Egyptian sections where several priests are compiling the history of Egypt under the leadership of Manethan, the Egyptian high priest. As the other scholars return, Archimedes is pressed into answering their questions, and talks late into the evening.

$$\Omega$$

The next morning, it is back to the gymnasium for the boxing and wrestling competition. Archimedes quickly loses interest, and walks down to the harbor to prepare for his presentation of gifts to King Ptolemy. After lunch, King Ptolemy leads the procession onto the dock along side the Syracusia. Barnacle has erected a platform on the dock, and the King walks up the steps to greet Archimedes and Barnacle. Archimedes makes a little speech about the ship being the biggest in the world and a special gift from King Hieron of Syracusia.

"Archimedes, please convey to King Hieron that Alexandria accepts this gift, and thanks him and the great city of Syracuse. To honor this friendship between our two great cities, this ship's name shall remain Syracusia so that all who see her will know from whence it came."

King Ptolemy walks from the dock onto the Syracusia. Archimedes and Barnacle give King Ptolemy and King Euergeter a private tour of the Syracusia. They are very impressed. At the end of the tour, the King starts to head to the gangplank.

"Sire!"

"Yes, Archimedes?"

"This ship is not just a great gift to behold. It must be experienced to be appreciated. Please allow Barnacle to demonstrate its full capabilities at sea."

"But Archimedes, you do not have a full crew."

"This ship needs only a small crew."

"Very well, how many passengers can we bring along," pointing to the crowd on the dock.

"We can bring all of them."

"All of them? But there must be over three hundred people."

"The Syracusia can handle more than five hundred, sire."

"Very well!" King Ptolemy waves for everyone to come onboard.

The crowd rushes onboard, and each person finds space wherever they can. Barnacle takes the helm, and orders one sail to be hoisted. The crew operates a capstan to raise the anchor and the pulleys to raise the sail. Soon the Syracusia is sailing out of the harbor toward the open sea.

"Archimedes, could you demonstrate the Syracusia's capabilities inside the Grand Harbor?"

"No, sire. The ship is so fast that at full sail, it would cross the harbor in minutes."

"Oh, my!" says Queen Arsinoe.

The wind is blowing gently out of the west. Barnacle barks out commands to a well-trained crew, eager to demonstrate their skills. He orders all sails hoisted. Soon the Syracusia is gaining speed. Barnacle turns the wheel, an innovation that controls the tiller through a system of pulleys, so that the ship is heading east, running with the wind. He then orders the keels raised. Crew members crank wenches that pull the hinged keels along the sides of the ship. As the ship gains speed, Barnacle orders the bow and the stern sails hoisted. The crew eases out the sails to catch as much wind as possible. They push the boom on the stern sail perpendicular to the ship.

Barnacle sees that the wind is blocked from the bow sail by the main sails. He orders the sail pulled to the side opposite the main. The Syracuse begins to approach top speed. Without the keels fully extended, the ship is not as stable, and begins to rock. The speed is impressive.

Queen Arsinoe becomes frightened, and clutches to Ptolemy's arm. Berenice and Helena, who are used to high-speed chariot races, dash toward the bow for the full effect of the speed.

After thirty minutes, Archimedes tells Barnacle to return to Alexandria. Barnacle barks out more orders. Some of the sails are trimmed to slow the ship down. He orders the keels lowered, and the ship begins smoother sailing. Then Barnacle starts to turn the ship into the wind by turning the wheel, slowly at first, then more rapidly. The crew takes in the bow sail. Barnacle straightens the course as the sails are filled, and sets a northwest course.

"Archimedes, Barnacle is not heading straight back to the harbor," King Ptolemy points out.

"No, sire. We can't just head straight into the wind. Instead, we have to zigzag. By sailing back and forth as close to the wind as possible, we will make the quickest progress against the wind.

As the ship starts back, Barnacle watches the sails, and trims them to keep them full of wind. After tacking a couple of times, the Syracusia sails past the lighthouse and into the Grand Harbor. Barnacle approaches the dock slowly from the downwind side. A cheer goes up from all the passengers as the crew throws lines to tie up the Syracusia to the dock.

After the crowd has dispersed, Helena and Berenice request a private tour of the Syracusia as well. Euergeter and Barnacle have a lengthy discussion on how best to train an Alexandrian crew and the construction of a war galley modeled on the Syracusia.

Ω

The fourth day is the final competition in the gymnasium. The events include the finalists for the pentathlon. There are two new events; pankration, which is a martial art consisting of wrestling and boxing combined, and a team race in full hoplite armor. Each city team in the hoplite races is made up of a single cohort of men. Each man wears a helmet with cheek protectors, a small shield, a long spear, and boots. The race is one stade long. The winning cohort is the first to have all of its men cross the finish line. The Alexandrian cohort includes

King Euergeter. The other teams judiciously let the king's team win but not by much. King Euergeter chastises them for letting him win. Late in the afternoon, King Ptolemy declares the winner of the pentathlon, Victor Ludorium. Following tradition, the winner, a young man from Athens, reads a short and amusing poem he has written for the spectators.

At supper, Archimedes is disappointed to see that Helena and her sister, Berenice, are absent. Conon says that they are probably preparing for tomorrow's races.

CHAPTER NINE

(247 BCE, in Alexandria)

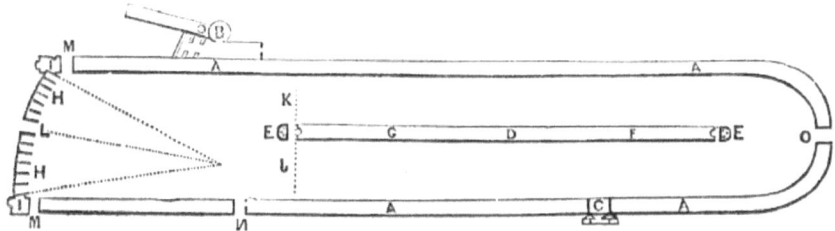

The next day, after breakfast, Archimedes and Conon follow the crowd to the Hippodrome for the chariot races.

"How many races today?" asks Archimedes.

"I believe there are only four," Says Conon. "There are thirty-six teams, but only twelve race at a time. After the first three races, the top four from each race will race in the fourth and final race after lunch."

Archimedes and Conon sit in the section reserved for members of the Museum. It is centered on the racing track and half way up the tiered seats of the Hippodrome. Cushions are provided. Their seats are behind the king, the royal family, and members of the court. The track is wide with two straight-aways and a semi-circle at both ends. In the middle is a low wall or a spine that divides the two straight-aways. On top of the spine are lap counters in the shape of dolphins.

Archimedes looks for Helena but doesn't see her. The members of the Museum begin talking among themselves, usually discussing their work but also some of the earlier sporting events. Conon buys some wine to share with Archimedes. They talk as they watch slaves preparing the track; leveling the ground, filling in holes, and sprinkling water on the track to settle the dust. The Hippodrome quickly fills with spectators.

"Did you know Barnacle's wife before?" asks Archimedes.

"Of course, we were lovers. Didn't that old sea dog tell you?"

"No he did not, but it explains why he is uncomfortable around you."

"Is he? He shouldn't be."

"Interesting! Why didn't you marry her?"

"Archimedes, I am already married. My wife and children live in Samos. I didn't want to marry her. I was just having fun. Barnacle came along, and offered her a partnership in his business. They made a deal, were married, and that was that."

A roar goes up from the crowd at the sound of a trumpet, signaling the beginning of the opening procession. King Ptolemy leads the pageantry dressed as a pharaoh. He is wearing the same white tunic he had worn the first time Archimedes met him. Today he carries a small crooked scepter instead of the flail. The scepter is gold plated and reinforced with blue copper bands. At first, Archimedes is impressed by how straight and steady King Ptolemy looks in his chariot. Then he realizes that the king has tied himself into the center of the chariot with ropes. He is riding in a decorated war chariot driven by a bodyguard, followed by musicians and dancers. Behind them are chariots carrying statues of gods who will watch the races. There are statues of Zeus, Isis, Poseidon, and others. There is even a statue of Ptolemy's father. Archimedes wonders what the gods do when two competing charioteers pray to the same deity for victory. The statues are followed by all the officials for the race: the umpires, assistants, and medical staff.

The crowd cheers as everyone climbs to their designated seats, and the statues are placed on pedestals in the center spine. The chariot teams follow next. Leading the chariots is Berenice. She is wearing a silver helmet which designates her as last year's winner. She is also wearing a tunic covered by a leather cuirass and trousers re-enforced with leather and greases. The reins of the four horses are wrapped around her waist. She moves and twists her hips as well as using her hands to steer the horses.

Archimedes is surprised to see Helena following Berenice. She is dressed the same as Berenice except without the helmet.

"Are both Berenice and Helena racing today?" he asks.

"Usually they do not race each other," says Conon. "They are both in the Royal Stable from Cyrene and, therefore, on the same team. I presume that Helena needs more experience, and that is why she is racing. It is unusual to have two teams from the same stable."

Helena's chariot is one of four in the line abreast behind Berenice. The rest of the competitors follow four abreast. In addition to Alexandria and Cyrene, there are chariots teams from Numbia, Samos, Antioch, Crete, and Sparta. There is even one from Syracuse. The crowd cheers their favorite team.

The chariots for the first race enter their assigned stalls, which had been chosen by lot before the race. Each stall has a hinged bar placed across the stall to keep the horses inside. Berenice enters the first stall reserved for the defending champion. Another trumpet sounds, and the crowd becomes quiet. All eyes are on King Ptolemy as he raises his arm. In his hand is a white cloth. Ptolemy holds it at arm's length for a minute, and then lets it fall. Immediately, an assistant on top of the stalls pulls a lever that opens all the stalls at the same time. The race is on!

All the chariots dash forward at once into the straight-away, each in their marked lane. After a short distance, the markings stop, and the chariots begin to change lanes, fighting for the inside lane occupied by Berenice. Here the first accidents happen. One chariot is overturned, and the chariot breaks away from the horses. The driver cannot get out of his reins, and is dragged half way around the track. Another chariot losses a wheel. A collision happens seconds later with one chariot losing a wheel, but the other charioteer maintains control, and stays in the race. With each collision or near collision, the crowd cheers, and Conon holds his head.

"Are you ill?" asks Archimedes.

"Could you ask the crowd to keep the noise down? I had too much beer last night."

"I don't think I can."

"Then, please, kill me to take me out of my misery."

"Have some more wine. I understand that it will take the sting out of your pain."

"I don't think so, but I will try it," drinking more wine.

Berenice has the coveted inside lane, and takes an early lead. Now she must fight to keep her position. She moves her horses as close as possible to the spine for the turn. As she enters the first turn, she shifts her weight to lean the chariot into the turn. This maneuver makes the chariot easier to turn left but is very dangerous. The chariots are made lighter by removing the floor. The drivers must balance on the center yoke, and leaning to either side is tricky. She gives the outside horse his head by twisting her hips to the left. This also pulls in the reins on the left side horses. She calls the right outside horse by name, and strikes him with her whip to start the first turn. The left hub of the chariot misses the spine by a hand's width.

Slaves run out onto the track to remove the injured drivers, and young boys run out to clear the debris. The boys removing the debris are too slow, and are nearly struck by other chariots. One leaps up on the spine and out of harm's way. The others cannot make it that far so they fall flat on the track, and lie parallel to the spine, trying to make their bodies as small a target as possible. They are lucky this time. No one runs over them.

Berenice is able to keep the lead position by blocking her challengers. Just before each turn she moves in closer to the spine. On the straight-away she steers the chariot farther out to keep the drivers behind her from cutting inside while lengthening the distance they must drive to pass her on the outside. These tactics enable her to easily win the first race.

Helena is in the second race but is in a stall several lanes over from the inside track. She will have to fight to gain the inside track. She manages to reach the inside track four chariots behind the lead chariot from

Samos. Her chariot swings wide around the first turn--too wide. Helena realizes her mistake, and tries to regain the inside position but two chariots cut in ahead of her before she can move over. She curses herself for taking the turn too fast to hold the position, and vows not to make that mistake again.

Conon is feeling better, and begins to take some interest in the race. Archimedes fears the worse for Helena. She is still in the race but some six chariots behind the leader. His heart races along with the horses, and he sways left or right with every move Helena makes. More than once he yells to warn her of near collisions. Everyone is shouting or cheering so no one pays any attention to Archimedes.

The chariots approach the second turn. Helena slows the chariot slightly, and is able to hold the turn. Her left hub misses the spine by three finger's width. Before she is out of the turn she spurs the horses on to accelerate. This gives her the extra speed to cut inside the chariot in front of her. The driver had taken this turn too fast and swung wide. Ahead of her, another chariot loses a wheel, and is out of the race. One of the dolphin counters is pulled down to signal one complete lap. Helena is in fifth place.

Archimedes' heart jumps whenever he sees Helena nearly colliding with another chariot. Helena spends the next two laps trying to get inside the chariot to her front. However, the driver is an experienced driver from Pythia, and holds onto the inside track. On the next straight-away, Helena pulls away from the inside, and moves to the outside of the Pythian chariot. Going into the next turn, she drives her horse to keep abreast of the Pythian chariot. It is a tactic that Berenice taught her. By staying abreast in the turn she is actually racing faster, and pulls ahead in the straight-away. Now she moves back inside. This same tactic works on the next chariot too. Most seasoned drivers will pass only on the straight-away because they consider passing on a turn to be too dangerous. They are right. Helena knows she is among the top four chariots, and concentrates on holding her position. She successfully blocks any attempts to pass her, and finishes the race in third place. She and Berenice will both be in the final race. Archimedes is relieved to see that Helena has survived the first race.

Helena and Berenice take their places with the royal family to watch the third race but do not socialize. They discuss tactics. Berenice will have a good chance to win the final race, but anything can happen. She coaches Helena on how to achieve a position where she can block some of the other drivers, and help ensure victory for the Royal Stables. They are the only two teams from the same stable, and by working together, they will have an advantage over the other teams.

"What is the matter with you?" a finally sober Conon asks Archimedes. "You are sweating as if you were in the race yourself."

"I guess I got caught up in the action."

The fourth and final race starts with Berenice in the first stall. Helena is in stall number eight. She knows she must fight hard to even place in this race. Bernice takes an early lead, and slowly but steadily increases it. Helena tries to gain the inside position but ends up in a cluster of chariots. It is very rough going trying to move inside while trying to avoid collisions. Several times her chariot bumps hubs with other chariots. Each bump jerks the chariot. If she loses her balance and is thrown to one side or the other, the reins around her waist will pull in the reins on the opposite side, turning the horses in that direction. This will cause a collision. Suddenly, she is trapped between two chariots--hub to hub. Each driver tries to move forward but cannot gain ground. They continue to battle for position for two laps. One of the drivers tries to hit Helena with his whip, but Helena sees it coming and ducks. She twists her hips to jerk the horses into the offending driver. The impact causes him to fall to his left, jerking his horse to the left, into the path of another chariot. The collision causes one chariot to overturn, and the driver of the other chariot to lose his footing, and to fall off his chariot.

Helena now has a clear shot for the inside track, and gets there before the chariot to her right can make it. She is not sure what place she is in, and the next chariot is at least half a lap ahead of her. As she makes the next turn, she sees a lot of debris on the track. There must have been a major collision. The larger pieces have been removed by the young crews. Helena does not see Bernice's chariot, and that is a good sign. However, there is still much debris on the track, and Helena slows down to maneuver around it. Striking something on the track might injure a horse or throw a wheel.

Suddenly, Helena hears hoof beats behind her. She turns to see Berenice racing down on her. Berenice has lapped the competition, and is now behind Helena. Helena tries to move to the outside to let Berenice pass on the inside but Berenice is already moving to the outside. Berenice quickly jerks the horses back to the left to avoid a collision with Helena. The two chariots enter the turn neck and neck with Berenice in the inside. Helena did not move over far enough, and Berenice is dangerously close to the spine. Berenice's inside horse strikes the spine with his left shoulder. Her chariot jerks violently to the right into Helena's chariot. The inside horse stumbles and falls, breaking the yoke of the chariot. Berenice's chariot, boxed tightly in between the spine and Helena's chariot, does not turn over. The pinched chariot abruptly slows down as three of the horses continue to gallop ahead, pulling Berenice out of her chariot. The yoke of her chariot digs into the track, and flips end over end behind Helena. It is the type of accident that in the past has killed drivers who remained in the chariot. Berenice is dragged by her reins which cause the horses to eventually stop. The crowd is on their feet; some concerned for Berenice, some angry that two chariots from the Royal Stable have collided, and others hoping that with Bernice out of the race, their team can win.

For several seconds, Berenice does not move. Finally, she gets up. The crowd realizes that she is not injured, and cheers wildly. Helena turns her chariot around, and drives up to Berenice who has stopped to pick up her whip. Helena dismounts, and the two meet face-to-face on the track. Archimedes fears they will be run over.

"I believe Berenice is going to strike Helena with her whip," says Conon. "Helena not only caused the accident and made Berenice lose the race, but now has taken herself out of the race. Berenice must be furious."

The crowd watches as the two women face each other for a few tense seconds. Suddenly, Berenice embraces Helena. As Berenice climbs onto Helena's chariot, the crowd yells their approval. Berenice re-enters the race, and leaves Helena standing on the track. By now the other chariots have caught up, and are charging right for Helena. When she turns to face them, they are nearly upon her. It is her greatest fear. Berenice frequently told Helena that she takes too long to make decisions. Races are won or loss on hundreds of split second decisions.

Berenice always seemed to make the right move quickly while Helena always waited too long. The results were many near misses and lost opportunities. It could also mean the differce between life and death, or at least serious injury. This is one of those moments that called for a split second decision and it had to the right one.

Her first impulse is to move into a gap between two chariots but the four chariots are hub to hub. Her next thought is to lay flat like the young boys who clear the track, and take a chance on getting trampled. Finally, Helena runs for the outside, leaping head first to get out of the horses' path. The outside chariot misses her by the width of one hand. Helena picks herself up, and dusts off her tunic and trousers. She has cheated death once again.

Most of the crowd does not notice the near miss as they watch Berenice battling to win. However, Archimedes is terrified. He holds his breath, and finally closes his eyes, not able to bear watching Helena be trampled. When he opens his eyes again, he is relieved to see Helena dusting herself off.

Berenice passes chariot after chariot, and in the final stretch, wins the race by one chariot length. She starts on her victory lap, and stops to pick up Helena. Both women acknowledge the cheers of the crowd. Berenice stops her chariot in front of King Ptolemy's throne and dismounts. When Helena stays in the chariot, Berenice turns and holds out her hand for Helena to join her. Hand in hand, they approach King Ptolemy. They kneel on a cushion before the King. King Ptolemy holds up a palm branch and laurel wreath, and awards them to Berenice. The crowd pours out of their seats, and mobs Berenice. It is the most amazing race Alexandria has ever seen.

A play by Sophocles follows later that afternoon. Archimedes and Conon take their seats in the section reserved for members of the Museum directly behind the royal family. Archimedes is pleased to see that Helena appears to be all right after her ordeal at the races. Berenice appears to be in pain, and moves about rather stiffly. Conon suggests that she might have broken a rib when she was dragged by the horses.

The play by Sophocles is *The Women of Trachis*. Archimedes has seen the play many times, but these actors are professionals, and quite good. The female parts are actually played by women not men, something Archimedes has never seen. The actress who plays the part of Deianeira, Hercules' wife, is beautiful, and reminds him of Helena. The way she portraits a woman driven by jealous fears makes Archimedes wonder if Helena has ever been jealous. He spends more time watching Helena than watching the play. As everyone is leaving, Helena's handmaiden, the young girl that escorted Archimedes on the day of sacrifices, approaches him.

"Excuse me sir, but my Lady wants to know if she can begin to show you Egypt starting tomorrow?"

"Why, yes. Tell her I would be delighted."

"Very well. I will come for you after breakfast."

The young girl genuflects and leaves.

"It looks like you will have fun tomorrow," says Conon.

That night, Archimedes dreams of Helena for the first time.

CHAPTER TEN

(1499, Cesare's Campaign Headquarters)

Cesare folds his napkin, and stands up.

"Let's go back into the other room so my staff can start setting up for supper."

Leonardo follows Cesare back into the living room of the tent. A servant enters behind them before they can sit.

Still standing, Cesare looks at the servant and then toward Leonardo. "Oh, yes, I promised you some wine. What would you like?"

"Sire, you promised me some fine wine. I already tried the table wines. But you are a better judge of fine wines than I. I will defer to your judgment."

"Very well. If you would like a Rosa, I would recommend Aglicanico. It is a varietal grown in Basilicata. The name is Greek, so it seems appropriate for our discussion. It is spicy and rustic. On the other hand, if you prefer a white wine, I would recommend Nuragus. It is an ancient varietal from southern Sardegna. It is light and tart."

"I am familiar with both wines. Excellent choices! I would like the Nuragus. It is more like an aperitif, and best suited for after lunch."

Cesare instructs the servant to bring the wine. He sits down, and motions for Leonardo to sit.

"So Archimedes was smitten by Helena, but the feeling was not mutual. Ah, unrequited love! Did she ever fall in love with Archimedes?" asks Cesare.

"Well, they were the most unlikely couple to begin with. Their relationship certainly got off to a rocky start. Archimedes was the smartest man in the world, nearly twice her age, and although from a noble family, not royalty. Helena was young, beautiful, a princess, and niece to the King of Alexandria."

Leonardo continues the story of Archimedes and Helena.

Ω

(247 BCE in Alexandria)

The next morning, Helena's young handmaiden arrives just after breakfast to fetch Archimedes. She leads him into the palace courtyard where Helena is waiting in a two-horse chariot with a Greek bodyguard. The chariot is much different from the other Greek or Roman chariots Archimedes has seen. It is lighter, probably due to the limited sources of wood, and also very handsomely decorated. The axle is lined with copper plate, and greased to cut down noise. The spokes are thinner, and nicely shaped. There are six spokes instead of the usual four—a war chariot. There is more room to stand than in a racing chariot which has hardly any floor. In a racing chariot, charioteers must balance themselves on the yoke, but a war chariot has room for a driver and an archer or a javelin thrower.

Two Nubian guards stand on either side of the chariot carrying spears but no armor, helmet or shield. In fact, the guards wear only a loin cloth, and are barefooted.

She intends for them to run along side, Archimedes thinks to himself.

"Come up here, Archimedes," beckons Helena.

Archimedes climbs onto the crowded chariot, next to the guard and behind Helena.

"Hold on now," Helena commands.

The way Helena is standing forces Archimedes to put one arm on either side of her to reach the front edge of the chariot. Helena smiles as he does so. The chariot lurches forward as Helena cracks her whip, and her body sways backward, striking Archimedes. He nearly looses his footing. The two Nubian spearmen travel along either side effortlessly. Archimedes marvels how well the Nubians run along side the chariot, but do not appear even to breathe hard.

Helena is totally in command. The horses obey even the slightest pull on the reins. Today she does not wrap the reins around her waist, using just her hands to control the two horses. She is wearing her hair up, in the style of a peasant. She wears a peasant tunic and a beautiful necklace with a large ornament hanging from the center. Her usual assortment of rings is absent today. Archimedes smells her perfume on the breeze and in her hair when it brushes against his face. When she leans forward to loosen the reins, her buttocks thrust backwards against his groin so close he can feel the tautness in her buttocks. Helena does this on purpose, of course, and is pleased with the response.

Helena takes Archimedes through Bruchium, the Greek Quarter: through the Jewish Quarter, which is almost as large as the Greek: into Rhakotis, the original village around which Alexandria was built: and finally into the new Egyptian Quarter. The streets are crowded with two wheeled wagons, and people who move over when they recognize the royal seal on the chariot. The Nubian guards have no problem keeping up in these crowded streets. Helena drives past peasant houses built out of mud bricks with straw. Some have stones added to strengthen them. Some of the brick walls are covered with plaster. Archimedes sees Egyptian men wearing short hair while the women seem to prefer a smooth, close coiffure with a natural wave and long curls. Young boys have their heads shaven, except for a long lock of hair on the side of the head while the young girls wear their hair in plaits or a ponytail. Slaves and servants tie their hair in a loop at the back of the head.

Helena drives the chariot out the west gate of the city and past olive groves where Egyptians are pressing olives for their oil. Archimedes asks Helena if they can stop so he can see this process much closer. Helena and Archimedes dismount, and stroll over to the olive grove, and Helena speaks to the Egyptian overseer. Helena tells him to continue making olive oil so Archimedes can observe. First, a wooden tub is filled with ripe olives. The tub has slats in the bottom and sides for the oil to drip down into a vat. A round board fits into the top of the tub, and heavy rocks are placed on top of it. The weight of the rocks squeezes the oil out of the olives. The overseer says something to a slave who darts off, and soon returns with three glasses and a bottle of olive oil. The overseer takes the bottle, and pours a sampling of the olive oil into each glass for Helena and Archimedes to taste.

Turning to Archimedes, Helena says, "This is one of the king's olive groves. This man is in charge of making olive oil for the palace."

"Interesting! I can show him a better way to press the olives. I think it will increase the yield, and improve the quality of the oil."

Helena translates, and the overseer motions for Archimedes to demonstrate. Archimedes picks up a stick, and draws in the dirt. The overseer nods in agreement. Archimedes tells Helena to ask the overseer to find a very long pole. As she does, the overseer suddenly starts barking orders, and slaves dash off in different directions. They return shortly with all the parts that Archimedes needs. Soon Archimedes is hard at work with the help of the overseer. They fasten one end of a long pole to a tree to use as a pivot point and fulcrum. The tub is placed next to the tree and under the pole. Another short beam from the long pole is fastened to the top of the round board. A basket to hold rocks is tied at the far end of the long pole. Archimedes has tied his tunic around his waist leaving his arms and chest exposed. His muscles flex and glisten with sweat. Helena is impressed. She has never seen a scholar do manual labor like Archimedes.

Finally, they are done, and the tub is filled with olives. The overseer has two of his men start loading the basket with rocks. After a few rocks the lever crushes the olives farther down than the overseer has ever seen. A few more rocks are added, and the olives are crushed so fine that the overseer cannot get his finger under the board. He takes his glass, and catches the olive oil dripping into the vat. He drinks, tastes it for a minute, letting the flavor swirl around his tongue. He smiles. Helena and Archimedes take their glasses, taste, and agree that it is excellent.

As the overseer speaks to Helena, she translates, "He says I bring him good luck whenever I visit. He also says you must be a wizard to do such magic."

"It was mathematics not magic."

"Nonetheless, you made their work easier. Do you have a name for this press?"

"You could call it a mechanical olive press."

"I will see to it that all the olive overseers learn how to make this 'Archimedes' Olive Press. Thank you, Archimedes."

She kisses his cheek. The overseer starts toward Archimedes. Archimedes isn't sure if the overseer will kiss him or hug him, but he decides not to wait around to find out. He strides quickly toward the chariot.

After a few minutes of driving, Helena stops near a stream for lunch. The bodyguard sets out a basket of fruit and a jug of wine. They sit down to eat in the shade of a palm tree near the shoreline. After watching Archimedes eat for several minutes, Helena speaks, "Archimedes, you are amazing."

"What do you mean?"

"What you did for the overseer, improving upon the olive press. That was amazing!"

"How so?"

"Archimedes, the old style olive presses has been used for decades, maybe centuries. All your scholarly brethren have seen that type of olive press in their own kingdoms and cities, and yet not one could improve upon it. You spend just a few minutes watching, and instantly you figured out a better system. You are amazing!"

"In defense of my scholarly brethren, I should point out that I have worked for a number of years with the laws of levers. I could clearly see the solution."

"Yes, but that is not the point. You wanted to help, and you did not hesitate to jump right in to make the olive press better. I am utterly amazed. I will do something nice for you."

"That is not necessary."

"Archimedes, after we eat, I want to show you something," says Helena. After lunch they continue riding along side the river. Just ahead, Archimedes sees a crowd of people. Two priests dressed in white and with shaved heads are taking people one by one, and ceremonially dunking them into the river. Helena stops the chariot as a servant of one of the priests comes over to greet her.

"Welcome, my Lady," gesturing toward the river.

"What are the priests doing?" asks Archimedes.

"Baptizing new converts."

"Converts to what?"

"To the goddess, Isis. The first Ptolemy adapted this current form of the religion based on an older Egyptian religion. He built a temple to Isis in the Egyptian quarter. The religion is based on a trinity of gods which consists of Isis, Harpocrates, her son, and Serapis. When a person converts to this religion, the priests baptize them in the Holy River Nile or, at least, with water from the Nile."

"What is the purpose of the baptism? Is it an initiation rite?"

"The ceremony removes a person's sins. This is a necessary step for salvation. We believe in an afterlife where we will be judged for our sins."

"You said 'we.'"

"Yes. I am a believer. Isis is a fertility goddess. She is the mother of all, and the cleanser of sins. She understands women. She is our mother, sister, and friend. It was Isis that ordained that women should be loved by men, and bear children. She has suffered through childbirth, and knows our pain. She invented the marriage contract."

"Interesting! And you believe this?"

"Yes, I am a priestess of Isis."

"Is that why you shave your eyebrows?"

"You are very observant! Yes, and that is not all. I shave all my body hair except on top of my head at least every three days."

"Why?"

"To cleanse my body for the Rites of Isis."

"Interesting!"

Archimedes and Helena dismount, and walk over to the bank of the river to watch the ceremony. At its conclusion, one of the priests says something to the new converts, and as he does, all the converts turn to look at Helena who acknowledges them. Many of the Egyptian children and women gather around Helena who begins to address them. As she talks to the children and women she touches them on the head. Archimedes realizes that she is blessing them, and in return the converts all want to touch her. Many kneel down, and kiss her feet.

Archimedes has never seen a woman treated with such adoration, not even the Queen of Syracuse. The lessons from his father, and the admonishment about no gods haunt him.

"I find it amazing that you know the native language, and you seem so comfortable among them."

"Archimedes, I am going to reveal to you something about myself because I trust you, but do not judge my family by what I tell you."

"If you wish."

"I am not like the other Greeks in Alexandria. Alexander came here, and conquered these people. They were ruled by the Persians. Most of the Persian nobility that did not die in battle fled. When Alexander died, all the conquered lands were divided up, and Ptolemy was given Egypt. The Ptolemys now own all these lands. In effect, we Greeks are the masters, and the Egyptians are our slaves. We can be very cruel taskmasters. The peasants lead miserable lives working in the fields or mines for their Greek masters. We Greeks treat each other with great respect, and we say we honor equality and freedom, but we do not extend that freedom to the Egyptians. Look at them! It is a hard life, and the only escape is through death. I tell you that these people welcome death as a relief from their drudgery. That is why the afterlife has always been a part of their culture and belief. They want to believe that the afterlife will be better than this one."

"You don't approve of the Greeks as masters?"

"No, I do not! The Greeks in Alexandria live off the labor of these poor Egyptians, and yet do not attempt to help them. Most Greeks don't even bother to learn the Egyptian language. Euergeter and Ptolemy do seem to care about them, and want to improve their lives, and I agree with them, but we are a minority. I think that if we don't do something, the Egyptians may revolt someday. Certainly, they will not defend us against any invaders that might be a liberator for them."

"Interesting! How are you trying to help improve their lives?"

"Well, the religion and the worship of Isis is one way. But, I fear that the Egyptians feel we are just corrupting their old gods. We are not getting many converts."

"Do you have proof of this afterlife?"

"No, Archimedes, this is not a mathematical problem. You either believe or you do not."

"But you must have some proof."

"The proof is all around you. Look how beautiful the world is." Pointing toward the Nile, "Look at that river of life. It floods every year so the Egyptians can have fertile soil for their crops."

"Does the river flood because the people live here or do the people live here because the river floods? I believe in logic and reason. The truth is found through deduction not through blind faith."

Angry now, "Blind faith is it? I see more blind faith than logic in the members of the Museum. You scholars treat the Library with the same reverence as a temple. You hold onto a secret knowledge passed down to you by Aristotle. You select a high priest called the head librarian. You have your own rites and rituals you call formula and theories."

"Helena, I am sorry. I did not mean to offend."

"No, I am sorry. I guess I get a little defensive of my faith. So many members of the Museum act so superior with their knowledge of things but won't lift a finger to help. They dribble out their secrets of the universe in meager droplets that only create thirst without quenching it. At least some of us are trying to help these people."

Archimedes had never been talked to like this by a woman.

"I apologize on behalf of the Museum."

"No, Archimedes. You are not responsible for their actions. But, I sense that you are different. You don't seem like the others. Maybe, because you are new here. I hope they do not corrupt you, make you indifferent to the suffering of the masses."

"What else are you doing for the Egyptians?"

"We have shown them how to reclaim land for cultivation through irrigation, and we have introduced crops such as cotton and better wine-producing grapes. I will show you."

"I have been admiring your necklace," says Archimedes. Pointing to her necklace, "What is that ornament hanging from it?"

"It is called a 'scarab'. It is like a beetle, and sacred to the Egyptians."

"Interesting! It is very beautiful."

"Thank you. Do women in Syracuse wear jewelry?"

"Not as much as the women in Alexandria. I don't think the women in Syracuse are as beautiful as those in Alexandria."

Laughing, "Archimedes! I think that is a compliment for the Alexandrian women but not for the woman of Syracuse. You should be careful not to always to speak your mind. It will get you into trouble."

Helena takes Archimedes to large fields outside the city. She drives on top of canals built to direct the Nile flood waters to more distant fields. Archimedes sees reservoirs built to contain some of the water for use during the dry season. He observes farmers using long poles balanced on horizontal wooden beams with counter weights on one end and buckets on the other. The beams are used to raise water from wells or ditches for irrigation. Archimedes is fascinated by this primitive use of the beam, fulcrum, and scale. Helen stops at a well where the natives have constructed a large wheel that is turned by wrapping a rope around the shaft several turns, and having a pack animal pull it. As the wheel turns, buckets scoop up water, and dump it at a higher level. Archimedes thinks there must be a better way.

Helena takes Archimedes next to a building in the Egyptian quarter of Alexandria where Ptolemy has established a school for the children of Egyptians.

Helena explains, "Most of the students are middle class, children of nobility, or children of priests. The children learn reading, writing, and mathematics. But the students are taught Greek culture not Egyptian."

"Why not Egyptian culture?"

"Ptolemy considers Egyptians to be uncivilized."

"You teach girls?" observes Archimedes.

"Yes, until they reach puberty."

After the school, Helena takes Archimedes to the harbor where the royal barge is waiting for them. As the barge travels up the Nile river, Helena points out various sights and landmarks, and explains whatever she knows about them. Archimedes thinks that her knowledge is extensive for someone so young. Helena explains much more about Egyptian culture and traditions. At one point, Archimedes stands very close to her so that he can look along her out-stretched arm at something. Suddenly, Helena steps back.

"Do you like my perfume?"

"What?"

"Do you like my perfume?"

"Why, Yes. I have been admiring it all day."

"It is called 'Susinum.' It is made from lilies, myrrh, and cinnamon with a base of balanos oil. It is very hard to make but smells wonderful when I wear it. Don't you agree?"

"Yes, it smells wonderful."

"Well, you don't smell wonderful."

"What do you mean?"

"Archimedes, anyone that comes near you knows that you have not been to the bath since you arrived. Your hair smells like salt water. Your clothes smell like sweat. And your body...well, I am too refined to describe it. I will show you how we bathe here in Alexandria before we dine tonight."

"Then, perhaps we should start back. It is getting late."

"We are not going to eat in Alexandria tonight."

"Where are we going?"

"You like to discover things. Well, this is a surprise."

Soon on the bank of the Nile, Archimedes sees a pier next to a large palace. Steps lead from the water into the structure which is covered with pink marble. As the barge approaches, people began to gather on the dock.

"What is this place?" asks Archimedes.

"My home. My father, Magas, built it many years ago before he was King of Cyrene. Berenice and I stay here sometimes when we visit Alexandria."

"What happened to your father?"

"My father was Ptolemy's half brother. Ptolemy had sent him to subdue the region of Cyrene. He did subdue Cyrene but later declared himself king. He was visiting Alexandria when he died on a hunting trip. I was only ten at the time. My mother died a few years later while I was still young. I come here sometimes to get away from the royal court. We will dine here tonight, and then return to Alexandria after dark. The Nile is beautiful at night."

"Interesting! So your sister became Queen of Cyrene after your father's death?"

"No, my father's successor was Demetrius the Fair. He and Berenice were engaged to be married. Berenice suspected he was having an affair. One night, she caught him in bed with another woman. Berenice had intended to kill the woman with a dagger, but the woman turned out to be our own mother. So, she killed Demetrius instead, and banished my mother. My mother died in exile."

"Then you and Berenice fled to Alexandria?"

Laughing, "No, we did not flee. Berenice was crowned Queen of Cyrene, but she knew that she had to make accommodations with Ptolemy, so we came here. It was intended as a diplomatic mission, but she met Euergeter, and we have been here ever since. Perhaps too long."

As the barge docks, servants come out to greet Helena. As Helena walks up the white steps and into the palace she points to a male servant, "This servant will show you to the bath. I will meet you there. We dine in one hour."

When Archimedes enters the bath, the servant pours him a generous glass of wine, and then removes his clothes to be cleaned. Archimedes steps into the hot bath water. Obviously, this is no ordinary bath like those in Syracuse. The water has some type of spice or fragrance that makes his skin tingle. The wine, the hot bath, the spices are too much to absorb. For the first time since his arrival, Archimedes truly begins to relax. He thinks of Syracuse, and how different it is from Alexandria. How different these Alexandrians are from any people he has ever met, different even from other Greeks. They are not colonists like the Syracusans but conquerors that arrived from Macedonia with Alexander, the city's namesake. Archimedes admires how advanced Alexandria is. He thinks about his meetings with Ptolemy, and how friendly he seems towards all the members of the Museum. Yet, he recalls what Conon told him about the death of Heraclide.

And Helena! He has never met any woman like her. She is attractive and yet intelligent. She converses with scholars and does not sit in the background like other Greek women. He cannot recall any other woman that spoke directly to him other than Queen Philistis, his aunt. These Alexandrian women are so independent and proud. Most are educated, and can read and write Greek. Helena even speaks damotic, the Egyptian language.

Archimedes is lost in these thoughts when he hears the sound of bare feet on the tiled floor. He turns to see Helena leading a procession of four handmaidens. Helena and the handmaidens are all dressed the same, naked except for a white linen wrapped around the waist. Their hair is tied up high on their heads, and each carries a small tray of oils and spices. Their skin appears to be oiled, and the lights from the oil lamps reflect off the curves and angles of their bodies. Archimedes tries not to stare at their breasts, especially Helena's, but he cannot resist. Women are not allowed into the baths with men in Syracuse. The only woman's breasts he has ever seen before were on statues, but they were made of cold marble. These breasts are live, warm flesh and blood, bouncing with each step as they come closer.

Archimedes frantically looks around for a robe or something to cover himself, but there are none. The servants have seen to that. He considers getting out of the bath, and hiding behind a pillar, but it is too late. Helena and her handmaidens reach the bath, and place their trays near the edge, remove their linen wraps, and walk into the hot water naked. Archimedes retreats to the farthermost corner of the bath, trying to use the water to hide his nakedness. Each of the women is much more beautiful than the marble statues in Syracuse. Their legs and buttocks glistened in the lamp light. Archimedes sees something covering the groins of the handmaidens which he thinks is a small, linen loin cloth, placed strategically, no doubt for modesty. But these women, especially Helena, are anything but modest. Archimedes is used to women who avert their eyes and look down. These Alexandrian women dare to look directly at him, smiling, and making him feel very uncomfortable.

Now he fully understands what Helena was trying to explain to him earlier about shaving her body hair at least every three days. She is clean shaven—no loin cloth. Suddenly, he realized that the handmaidens are not wearing loin cloths either. It is body hair. Archimedes had assumed that all women were hairless except on their heads like the statues he had seen. These women have hair in their groins and under their arms. This is a new discovery! Interesting!

Led by Helena, each of the women picks up a small bottle from their tray, and advances through the water toward Archimedes. Helena is first to reach him, and Archimedes starts to protest.

Helena places the tips of her fingers on his lips, "Don't talk. Archimedes, you are in Alexandria now. We do things differently here. You should honor our customs, and enjoy yourself. Just touch only what we tell you and behave yourself, and I will reward you later. Now just relax. You will like this. We will take good care of you." Placing a sprig of mint in his mouth, "Here chew on this for awhile, it will freshen your breath."

She takes his wrists, and gently pulls them off his groin where he had placed them to cover himself. She places his hands on her shoulders, and grabbing him by the elbows slowly leads him to the center of the bath. A handmaiden hands her a bottle, and she begins to pour something from the bottle onto Archimedes' shoulders and arms. Archimedes can detect thyme and sage but cannot identify the other spices. He decides to cooperate. Her voice is so compelling, and her breasts so pleasant to look at as they float in the water.

For several minutes he has forgotten the handmaidens. One is stationed near the trays on the side of the bath, and is handing various bottles to the others, taking bottles from them, and placing them on the trays. Archimedes recognizes the teenage handmaiden who was his guide on the Day of Sacrifices. He blushes when their eyes meet, and she giggles and smiles. Handmaidens are positioned on each side of him and another one behind. Archimedes decides that the first liquid is some type of soap. The women wash him from head to toe, gentling nudging him to shift this way or that without saying a word. Now and then Archimedes can feel a nipple or a breast brush his skin which is already sensitive from the spices.

Helena looks into his eyes, smiles, and gently shifts his hands from her shoulders where they had been to her breasts. She holds onto his wrists, and with a slight pressure pulls his hands against her breasts. Archimedes is startled, but does not resist. Although he can feel her hard nipples in the palms of his hands, he resists the urge to caress them. He does not want to offend her by resisting or seeming to enjoy the moment too much. He was not sure what he was expected to do when suddenly he realized that the three handmaidens are washing his groin and ass. He wants to stop them and clean himself but he does not want to pull his hands away from Helena's breasts, so he allows them to finish their work.

From the beginning Archimedes had tried to avoid getting aroused thinking it might be considered rude. But now, with his hands on Helena's breasts and all this activity in his groin area, he can no longer restrain himself. One of the woman giggles at this but does not stop. She grabs his erect organ and washes it. This causes Archimedes to swallow the sprig of mint. The woman washing his cock says something in Egyptian, and all the women giggle, even Helena.

After a couple of minutes, the women are finished. Helena takes him by one hand, and leads him out of the bath. The women use warm towels to dry his skin, and then wrap a warm towel around him. They lead him to a low table, and remove his towel. His erection returns. The women have him lie face down on another long towel with a pillow for his head. Another oil is poured on him, and Archimedes recognizes ben oil. The women begin to massage his body: the back and then the front. The ben oil softens his rough skin. When the women are done, they scrape off the ben oil using small wooded knives that are curved to conform to the body. After drying him, the women pour on sweet almond oil with a hint of anise and orris root, and rub it into his skin. That is followed by a mixture of spices that leaves him smelling like eucalyptus with a refreshingly cool feeling on his skin.

At this point Helena helps him into a white tunic that the male servant brought into the room. The tunic is made of a fine Egyptian cotton.

"A gift from me to you. You are an important man in Alexandria, and you must look important."

Then she has him sit on the edge of the table. One of the hand-maidens comes with a small tray of items.

"I said I would reward you if you behaved yourself, and you did. Now close your eyes."

When he closes his eyes, she takes a blindfold from the tray, and ties it around his head, covering his eyes.

Whispering so near his ear that he can feel her warm breath, "Don't look and don't touch. Open your mouth."

He does.

"Not so wide!"

Archimedes obeys. He feels her hands on his jaw pulling his face slightly forward, and then he feels a nipple in his mouth—and something else. Something sweet! Honey! Delicious, sweet honey. Archimedes sucks the honey off her nipple. His erection returns. After a minute, the nipple pulls from his mouth, and it is over. Archimedes sits, not knowing what to do next. He can hear the patter of bare feet on the tile floor as the women leave the bath.

After several minutes Archimedes again hears the sound of bare feet on tile but it sounds different this time—heaver, stronger—a man's feet.

"I will show you to dinner."

The announcement in a man's voice startles Archimedes, and he removes his blindfold, embarrassed. He sees that Helena and the other women are gone. The same male servant who had led him to the bath is now in front of him with his sandals. The servant puts the sandals on Archimedes feet, and laces them up. Archimedes has always put on his own sandals but somehow, here in Alexandria, it seems like the right thing to do. The servant leads a more relaxed and cleaner Archimedes to dinner. As he walks, Archimedes realizes that for all his education and wisdom he has not spoken a word the entire bath.

Helena and Archimedes dine on a much simpler meal than he had had in the royal palace. Helena sits up next to him while he reclines, and they talk about everything and anything. Helena picks up his head, and places it in her lap. She takes various pieces of a food and feeds Archimedes. After he eats it, she tells him what it is. He then frowns, smiles, or just nods his head and raises his eyebrows. Archimedes is delighted. He is full of questions about Egypt, Alexandria, and the royal court. Helena seems to know everything.

After dinner, Archimedes and Helena board the royal barge for the return journey. The river seems to come to life with all sorts of creatures such as crocodiles, waterfowl, and other animals coming down to the river to feed. Helena and Archimedes sit on cushions as Archimedes points out all the different stars and constellations to Helena. Her perfume fills the night air. As the barge floats down the river past villages, the villagers rush to the shore to wave, hoping to catch a glimpse of some nobility onboard. Helena has sweet treats to throw out to the children. The city of Alexandria finally comes into view with all the lights and fires reflecting off the water. Towering above the city is the Lighthouse of Pyros. Archimedes hates to see the day come to an end.

As the barge docks in Alexandria, Helena says, "My servant will fetch you after breakfast, and we will continue your tour. Good night, Archimedes. Sleep well."

She touches his arm, climbs into her chariot that had been made ready, and drives off into the night. The teenage handmaiden escorts Archimedes to the Museum where Conon is waiting for him. Conon leads him to a room in the Museum that is prepared especially for him. All his things from the Syracusia, including his father's cedar chest, have been relocated into the room as well as copies of all his works that the guards had taken when he arrived. Archimedes soon falls asleep, and dreams again of Helena.

The next morning Archimedes goes to breakfast at the Museum. King Ptolemy is there, and approaches to discuss one of Archimedes' theories.

Stopping in the middle of a sentence, and looking Archimedes directly in the eyes, "I see that Helena has introduced you to her version of the royal bath."

Archimedes is dumb struck. He cannot believe that Helena has told the king or, perhaps, one of her handmaidens is a spy.

The King sees the puzzlement on his face. "It's your fragrance! The eucalyptus gave you away. She tends to favor it. She likes her men to smell like eucalyptus."

"Her men?"

"Yes! Did you think you were the first?"

"Your Highness, I assure you that…"

"Come, come, Archimedes, please do not say anything or you will sound like a fool. You are not her first, and you won't be her last. I am sure that right now your mind is on Helena, and not mathematics so we will talk of mathematics some other time. Please, enjoy your stay with us."

Ptolemy acknowledges Archimedes' bow with a slight head nod, turns, and walks away.

CHAPTER ELEVEN

(247 BCE, King Ptolemy's Palace, Alexandria)

Ptolemy's aide finds Helena at breakfast, and brings her to King Ptolemy on the Grand Balcony viewing the panorama that is the city of Alexandria. The sun has risen, and it is getting warmer, but a slight ocean breeze makes it bearable. The King is accompanied by his favorite hunting hound, Peritas, a direct descendant of Alexander's hound.

When he hears Helena's footsteps, "It is beautiful, isn't it?"

"Yes, sire."

"I swear by whatever Gods that may be that I love this city more than all the greatest of Greek cities, more than Athens itself. I will do anything I can to make this the greatest city in the world." Pausing, "I see that you have your claws into Archimedes already. He smells like a temple whore."

Feigning surprise, "Uncle Ptolemy, whatever do you mean?"

"Don't be coy with me about this. I am very angry with you. And stop calling me uncle. This is official business, so call me your highness."

Genuflecting, "Yes, your Royal Highness."

"Helena, stop mocking me or I swear by Isis that I will feed you to the crocodiles."

"Your Highness, now I can see that you are upset. Tell me what I have done to displease you, and what I must do to please you."

Sternly, "I want you to leave Archimedes alone."

"But what did I do? I gave the man a bath. He smelled like a goat. I couldn't stand to be near him. You should thank me not scold me."

"I know very well the kind of bath you gave him. You do this all the time. You like to make men fall in love with you, but you never return their love. You want them to worship you, and to shower you with gifts, and then you break their hearts. To you, it is all just a game. Then they leave Alexandria, and never return."

"But Archimedes has not showered me with gifts," protests Helena.

Shouting now, "That's because he is different!" Calming down, "This man is a true scholar and not a prince. He is not royalty. He does not value worldly possessions. He values research and intelligence—the search for knowledge. This time you have chosen to seduce the wrong man. He is not like normal mortals like you and me. I have never met a man with such wisdom. I feel like a block of wood when I am around him. He is probably the smartest man in the world."

Ptolemy stands staring at the city, rocking back and forth on the balls of his feet as he gathers his next thought.

"Mere mortal men know nothing higher than themselves, but the gods have given some men certain talents, men like me, so that we instantly recognize genius in others. Archimedes is a genius. I tell you, Helena, he does not live in this world."

"What do you mean?"

"His body is here but his mind is in a world of mathematics where he is constantly trying to solve problems. Occasionally, he returns to his body, and appears normal but only for a short time. He sees things differently. To him, the world is made up of formulae and equations not shapes and substances. You and I look at the sunset, and marvel how beautiful it is. Archimedes looks at that same sunset, and wonders how far away the sun is and how to calculate its size and weight. You look at a soldier, and you see him holding a spear. Archimedes sees a man holding a lever. I warn you, this time it is you who will get hurt."

"How can he hurt me?"

"Helena, Archimedes can't love you. He already has a mistress, a mistress who demands his full attention. He is in love and will always be in love with mathematics. You would always come second. He will break your heart, and not even know it. For him, happiness is finding a problem and solving it."

"Then I will become a problem for him to solve. Besides, I think he does love me."

"No, Helena, listen to me. Right now he lusts for you, but he cannot love you. Do you even understand the difference? You are the one who will get hurt this time if you continue this little game."

Louder now, "I am a free woman, and I can love whomever I want."

Raising his voice even louder, "Helena, remember your place! Do not take liberties with me! I am the King, and I will confine you to the temple if you drive Archimedes away. Love whomever you want, but you will marry whom I tell you."

Helena decides that this is not the time, nor the place, to argue against arranged marriages. She tries to change the subject.

"But why? Why should Archimedes be so important to you? You never spoke to me this way before."

"Because I want Archimedes to become the head of the Museum to replace Callimachus."

"But what of Callimachus?"

"He is old, and not in good health. He has told me that he wants to return home. He will leave as soon as there is a suitable replacement. Archimedes is the best choice to replace him. He is respected by all the other scholars, and his reputation is worldwide."

"I thought that the Museum was totally independent, and elected its own headmaster? You're hiding something. You are not telling me everything. Tell me what you know."

"Oh, Helena, you are a clever girl, but you have no idea what's going on in the world. It saddens my heart even to think about it. You live your life of pleasure and wealth as if life will go on this way forever. Well, it won't. Alexandria could cease to exist, our kingdom destroyed, and all of us sold as slaves sooner than you think. It could all end in tragedy. You have no idea."

"What do you mean?"

"It is complicated."

"Tell me!"

"Only if you promise to keep this information strictly between us. I tell you this so you will understand how important it is for Archimedes to stay in Alexandria." Pausing to gather his thoughts, "You know that Roma and Carthage are at war. Both want to build an empire around the great sea."

"Yes, of course, I know that."

"Well, so far we have not been drawn into that war. We have managed to stay neutral. We have no treaty with either side. However, Carthage has a great navy, and they dominate the sea passages. We need the sea open for trade. We are a major supplier of food and grain for Carthage so they would like that to continue. We also get gold from the mines in Kush to buy goods from Carthage. Carthage needs that gold to keep its navy supplied. Right now both cities are very busy fighting with each other, but some day that war will end. It does not matter who wins; either one could attack Alexandria. We could not hold out for very long. We do not have the resources to defeat them."

"Why would anyone attack us?"

"To secure the food and the gold mines. We would then be a buffer between their empire and Syria. Roma and Carthage are not Greek cities. When Alexander conquered Egypt, Carthage and Roma were merely warring tribes. There is no feeling of kinship toward us."

"We might defeat them."

"No, girl. We have no navy to speak of. Our ships are merchant ships not war ships. Our city walls have been neglected and need repair. Our army is weak. We have relied on Nubian mercenaries to fight our battles."

"What can you do?"

"I'm not sure. Many things are possible. We might be able to sign a treaty with whoever wins this war. Meanwhile, we should start to rebuild the city walls, build up our army and navy, and eventually get rid of the Nubians. If we can present a formidable defense, we would be in a better position to negotiate. Then there is the whole issue of Macedonia and King Antigonus. The Athenians long for freedom from Macedonia as does Sparta and King Areus. They have formed a league they call the Achaean League. Secretly, I have been supporting them with money."

"What does this have to do with Archimedes?"

"A lot! As you said, the Library and Museum have always been independent from any city. Carthage and Roma both see the value of the Library. However, the Museum would be an even greater resource for either one to make war. Great war machines could be designed to defeat any wall. Fortifications could be designed that no machine could defeat. Terrible war galleys could be built to patrol the sea. I think whoever owns the Museum could rule the world for centuries. When it was founded, it was intended to be used for only peace. Until now, the scholars have confined their interests to scholarly pursuits and not politics."

"What do you mean, until now?"

"I need the knowledge of the Museum to rebuild Alexandria, and make it the greatest city once more. Archimedes is famous in Roma and Carthage as well. He is from Syracuse which has a treaty with Roma. There is a chance that if he were head of the Museum, Roma might not disturb the work of the Museum."

"But what if Carthage wins?"

"If it looks as though Carthage might win, we could try to sign a treaty with them to guarantee grain and gold supplies so that that when the war ends, they can focus their attention on Spain and not Egypt."

"And if Carthage doesn't sign an agreement?"

"We must prepare for whatever may come. That is why I asked Archimedes to come to Alexandria."

"What? You asked him? I thought the Museum invited him here."

"Well, yes and no. Callimachus has been trying to get Archimedes here for years. I try not to get involved in the affairs of the Museum. But Archimedes would not come so long as he was employed by King Hieron. So a few months ago, Callimachus approached me to use my influence with King Hieron, which I did. I explained to King Hieron that it might be advantageous to cultivate friends among the Carthaginian allies, just in case."

"But the war could go on for years. It might never end or it could end with a peace treaty."

"The longer the war goes on, the more time we have to prepare. That is the other reason I invited Archimedes here. He is not like the other members of the Museum. The others just research, and work on theories and formulae. They do not know how to translate what they do into something useful that people can use: they cannot make the theoretical practical."

"And Archimedes can?"

"Oh, my dear, you have no idea what this man has done. You have heard of his theories, but have you not seen his machines? You saw the ship called Syracusia."

"Yes!"

"It is the fastest ship sailing the seas. King Hieron is planning to build a fleet of them just for trading. It is faster than any war galley. Archimedes designed and built it. "

"I did not realize."

"Now that it has been presented to me as a gift, we can copy it to make the largest war ships the world has ever seen. I think it could hold five banks of oars with forty oars to a bank."

"Is that huge?"

"Yes, and not only that, but Archimedes has designed and built unbelievable war machines and fortifications to defend Syracuse. He has redesigned, and rebuilt the city walls. He discovered the law of levers, and made good use of them. And what he did with.... Now what did Conon tell me they were called? Pulleys! That's right, they are called compound pulleys. Archimedes figured out how to combine several pulleys in a group to lift enormous weight."

"How do you know these things?"

"The officers I send to Syracuse have told me. And did you know that he gave the Romans a weapon that helped them to defeat the Carthaginians years ago? The Romans called it the 'corvas'. It was a

Monte R. Anderson

hook that the Romans used on ships. It helped the second rate Roman navy defeat the superior Carthigian navy and the world's best navy at the time."

"So he has done these things. What do they have to do with Alexandria?"

"Unless we do something to help the Egyptians, I fear a revolt soon. Archimedes is a practical man. He can find ways to help the poor. I need him to win the support of the Egyptians. He could also rebuild our navy, and repair our walls."

"But if he becomes the head of the Museum, what makes you think he will do this for you?"

"I have a plan. Archimedes is a very practical man. Maybe he will help us on his own without the help of the Museum. With time, I am sure I can persuade him. Right now I do not need you to break his heart, and chase him back to Syracuse." After a long pause, "Do you understand what I have told you?"

Helena nods her head in agreement.

Louder, "Well, say something! Why don't you say something?"

Genuflecting, "Sire, until now I never knew you to be so intelligent, and strategically aware of the world. I am naive. I am in awe. I should be worshipping you and not Isis. I am your humble servant. Command me!"

"Lately, I have been thinking that it is about time you married."

Jumping up quickly, "If I have a choice, I would rather be fed to the crocodiles."

Smiling, "How can I stay angry with you? I promised my brother that I would take care of you. But this matter is very important. Please!"

"Alright, Uncle, because you said 'please', I will obey," kissing his cheek.

"Thank you," says Ptolemy. "Now let's return to breakfast and remember, not a word about this to Archimedes."

CHAPTER TWELVE

(247 BCE, the Museum of Alexandria)

L ater that afternoon, Archimedes and Conon are sitting in one of the lecture halls discussing one of Archimedes' theories when Barnacle enters the room.

"There you two are. I have been searching the Museum for you."

"Ah, Barnacle, what is it?" asks Archimedes.

"I come to say goodbye. I leave for Syracuse tomorrow. I wanted to see if you had any messages for King Hieron."

"When do you sail?" asks Conon.

"I will sail with the high tide about mid morning. I must get the athletes back, and see to my business. Euergeter has given me a full crew to train. They will bring the Syracusia back to Alexandria."

"I will write a note for King Hieron, and have it delivered to the Syracusia before you sail," promises Archimedes.

"Will you tell Queen Philistis that you met Helena?" asks Barnacle with a wink.

"No! And don't you say anything!"

"I am sure King Hieron and Queen Philistis will be excited enough when they hear that Berenice and Euergetes are betrothed," Barnacle says casually.

"I have something," says Conon as he reaches inside his tunic, and pulls out a sealed scroll. "Can you see that this is given to the King of Athens."

Looking at the inscription on the scroll, "But Conon, this says it is for the King of Samos, your own master."

Jumping up and pointing at Barnacle, "I thought so! You can read!"

Fear comes over Barnacle' face as he looks down at Conon's sandals, "No! No! Just a few names and letters and the names of cities. That is all. I cannot read."

"You are lying, Barnacle. You have always said that you could not read," yells Conon.

Archimedes tries to calm Conon, "I knew he could read. What is the problem with his being able to read?"

"I will tell you," Conon replies, a little more calm. "That comment about Berenice and Euergetes being betrothed. How did he know that? Has anyone made such an announcement?"

"No, I don't think so," replies Archimedes.

"I think it is common knowledge," interjects Barnacle.

"No, it is not because no such announcement has been made. You tripped up when you said it. The only way you would know that is if you read it in a letter from King Ptolemy to King Hieron. You are a spy. You read all those letters while everyone believes that you cannot read Greek."

"But I knew he could read," interjects Archimedes.

"Yes, it is true. I can read," confesses Barnacle. To Archimedes, "I did not know that you knew. How did you know?"

"My father told me years ago. He told me that you were a spy, but that I should make friends with you."

"Ah! Well, that makes sense now. Leptines taught me. He set me up in business, and in return I spied for him. It could only work if people thought I could not read the messages and scrolls they sent with me."

"Well, it must stop now!" yells Conon, his temper starting to rise once more.

"No! It cannot stop! You don't understand. My life would be in danger if people found out I can read."

"Who do you work for?" asks Conon.

"King Hieron, of course, but people do not know that. Everyone thinks I am independent, but my loyalty has always been to Syracuse and King Hieron."

Puzzled, Archimedes says, "I have been the chief advisor to King Hieron for years, and never once has he said you were working for him as a spy. Something does not make sense. Barnacle, you must explain yourself."

"Well, it is a little complicated. When your grandfather, Leptines, set me up in business, and taught me to read, he encouraged everyone to use me to deliver messages. He told everyone that I could not read so secret codes were not necessary. That put me in a position to read all the letters. I reported whatever I read to Leptines."

"Not to King Hieron?" asks Conon.

"No! Only to Leptines. Leptines was father-in-law to the king, and wanted to know what the king was saying to other monarchs. The king never knew that I could read."

"And after Leptines died?" asks Archimedes.

"Well, I couldn't tell the king that I had been reading his letters all along, now could I? I would report to the king that I had heard such and such from other merchants and shipmasters."

"Then you read my letters?" asks Archimedes.

"I did at first, but you scholars write only of mathematics or science and in terms I hardly know. Boring stuff really. I stopped reading your mail years ago."

"I think King Ptolemy and King Hieron would like to know what you have been up to," says Conon.

"No! You must not tell anyone. They would kill me if they knew I could read."

"Barnacle, you are a spy, the scum of the earth. I never trusted you," says Conon.

"Please, Conon, you must not tell anyone," pleads Archimedes.

"Oh, he won't tell anyone," replies Barnacle as his old confidence begins to return. "He knows that I know too much."

"What could you possibly know about me?"

"Well, for starter, your wife in Samos meets my ship when I dock there. I could tell her of some of your affairs here in Alexandria."

"Yes, that would be bad, but I have survived many affairs before."

"Perhaps, I should take my wife to meet your wife in Samos. I am sure they have many things to discuss."

"Wait a minute, Barnacle. What has your wife told you?"

Looking Conon directly in the eyes, Barnacle relies, "What do you think? She has told me everything she had seen and heard about you when she was your mistress. Many disturbing things. Some of those things your king might even want to know."

"Ah, now we are at an impasse. While I don't mind my wife finding out some things, there are others that I would not care to share with my king," replies Conon.

Still looking directly into Conon's eyes, Barnacle asks, "Then we have an understanding?"

Somewhat shaken by this turn of events, Conon replies, "Yes, I hope we have an understanding. You don't tell anyone about my past, and I won't tell anyone that you read their mail."

"Agreed! Then I sail with the tide." Turning to Archimedes, "Until we meet again, my friend. If you need me, my wife will know how to find me."

Barnacle leaves a stunned Conon to face Archimedes.

"What was all that about?" asks Archimedes.

"There are some things that are best kept secret. I cannot tell you, not now, not ever.

Monte R. Anderson

CHAPTER THIRTEEN

(247 BCE, the Museum of Alexandria)

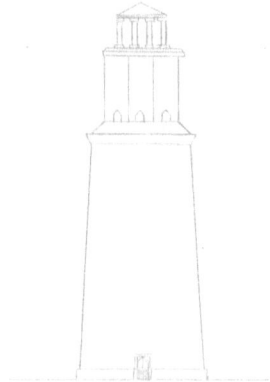

After breakfast the next day, one of Helena's servants arrives to take Archimedes to the dock to board the royal barge. Helena is already onboard.

"Helena, I must ask you about the bath."

"Yes? Did you enjoy it? You smell much nicer now, and are more pleasant to be around."

"I am sorry. I did not mean to offend you or the king. It has been a long trip, and I am excited to be here. My father talked often about Alexandria."

"I am surprised that he never mentioned the Alexandrian women."

"I would have been surprised if he had. He never showed any interest in other women after my mother died. Helena, I have never met anyone like you. You are amazing. And that thing you did with the honey."

"That was not me!"

Stunned, "But... I thought it was you."

"You were blindfolded. After I put on your blindfold, I had one of my handmaidens put honey on one of her nipples, and put it in your mouth. It is just a silly game we play on visitors."

"A game?"

"Yes. It makes their visit more memorable, and creates a certain air of mystery and excitement. Don't you agree?"

"Helena, I am sure it was you. I could smell your perfume."

"Don't be ridiculous! I make all my handmaidens wear the same perfume. I can't have men paying more attention to my handmaidens than to me, now can I?"

"I don't believe you."

"Look, I know you men. You don't even look at a woman's face. You just look at her breasts and body. You spent an hour with me and my handmaidens naked in the bath, and I will wager that if we covered our faces, you could not tell one person from another."

"What do you mean?"

"You like to conduct experiments, well, I am proposing an experiment. If you can pick me out from my handmaidens, I will let you into my bed."

"What?"

"We will go to the bath again tonight, but before you come in I will cover all the handmaidens' faces as well as my own. If you can pick me out from all my handmaidens, I will send them away, and you and I will go to my bed. How is that for an experiment?"

"I just have to pick you out of all the women?"

"Yes. It is a simple test to see if you actually paid attention to me or not."

"Helena, I didn't mean to imply…"

"Yes or no? But if you fail, we will never speak of last night again, and we will not have another bath together. If you refuse, I will tell my uncle to deport you back to Syracuse on the next ship."

"But, Helena!"

"Yes or no?"

"Yes, I guess, but this does not seem fair."

$$\Omega$$

This time the royal barge sails out into the harbor, and makes the short trip to the Pharos Lighthouse. Their arrival interrupts the discussion on the experiment.

Archimedes is delighted to be able to explore the lighthouse up close. Helena explains that the original idea for the structure was from Alexander. They disembark and walk toward the lighthouse. The approach to the lighthouse is a long ramp with beautiful vaulted arcades. At the base Helena points out an inscription that bears the name of the architect, Sostratos of Cnidus. Inside the base are several service rooms and a stable for the pack animals that bring firewood up to the third tier to feed the fire that is the light source. After climbing up some stairs Archimedes and Helena come to an observation platform at the top of the first level where merchants are selling food. Helena leads the way up to the second level where several statues stand depicting different gods. Helena and Archimedes continue to climb to the top of the eight-sided tower where a small balcony provides an impressive panoramic view of the harbor, sea, and city.

Archimedes, however, is not interested in the view. He begins to examine the light source which provided the light he had seen at sea. The fire pit is open and at the very pinnacle of the structure. Archimedes spends the rest of the morning examining the lighthouse. He and Helena have lunch onboard the royal barge as it makes its way up the Nile back to Helena's palace.

When the barge arrives at Helena's palace, Helena says, "Wait onboard until a servant comes for you."

Finally, Helena's servant arrives, and leads Archimedes to the bath.

At the door the servant says, "You are to wait until you are called, then go inside."

Shortly Archimedes hears his name, and steps into the bath. Near the bath he sees ten women with their faces covered with a very fine cloth. Archimedes thinks that the women can see out through the cloth, but he cannot see their faces or eyes. Their breasts are not covered. From the waist down each wears a skirt and is barefooted.

The servant explains, "You must choose Helena. You cannot touch. The women will not speak. You have only one chance."

The servant leaves Archimedes to his test.

Archimedes is silent for a moment trying to figure how to make the correct decision. It is a challenge. The women all look identical. Their breasts and nipples are all the same shape and size. All are fair-skinned without any blemish of any kind, or any scars, freckles or birthmarks. All the women are remarkably similar in height and build.

Apparently, they have played this game before. If they all look a like, then the difference has to be in what they do.

He tries to look at their hands thinking that Helena's hands will show the calluses from the chariot reins but the women have their hands hidden in pockets of their skirts.

That Helena is clever. She thought of that, no doubt. But I am on the correct path. I must proceed from what is known to be true to the truth that needs to be found. At first, all the women appear alike. This I know to be true. I will assume that the others stay in the palace for the most part.

He remembers the feel of Helena's buttocks in the chariot, the firmness of it. He tries to examine their legs and buttocks, but their skirts hide them. Then he remembers her perfume. When he smells each woman, he remembers that Helena said that they all wear the same perfume. He tries to recall the activities of the past two days.

What did we do today that would leave a mark? Of course! We were in the sun a great deal. She wore sandals.

He looks down at the feet for the tell tale signs of sandal straps marks left by exposure to the sun. That narrows it down to three or four women. Then he remembers her necklace. *"What was on the necklace? Yes! A scarab!"*

He looks at each woman's chest for a faint outline of a scarab sunburned into her skin. There was only one. It must be Helena. Impulse overcomes Archimedes, and he kisses the side of her neck. All of the other woman gasp. It is Helena! Never before has anyone ever guessed correctly. She is startled by the kiss, and tries to push Archimedes away, but he pulls off the cloth from her face, and she stiffens. Archimedes kisses her again on the mouth. The handmaidens begin to giggle, and remove their head cloths. Helena does not know what to do, and struggles with what to say. Finally, she looks at Archimedes, and takes one step back to regain her composure. She is used to winning this game of teasing men. She is used to being in control, and dictating her desires. This never happened before. She looks at her handmaidens who are as surprised as she is. She is losing control.

Shouting, "Leave us! Leave now!"

The women immediately leave the bath. When she is sure the handmaidens all have left she turns to Archimedes.

"I will keep my word."

"Helena, that is not necessary. You were playing a game, and sex with me doesn't mean a thing to you. It would certainly mean a lot to me, but I don't want to go to bed with you by winning a wager or by playing a stupid game. This may be the way you do things in Alexandria, but this is not my custom. You are the most remarkable woman I have ever known, but this is not right. I will bed the woman I love, and who loves me and not anyone else. What you say to the king is up to you. Let me know if you still want to be my guide."

Archimedes turns and walks out of the room leaving Helena standing alone, and for the first time in her life, speechless.

She watches him leave. No man has ever turned her down. She has always picked the man she wanted, and decided the time and place for sex, but love had never entered into it. She did not intend to have sex with Archimedes. She never thought he could pick her out of the group of woman. But when he kissed her, something came over her—lust, desire, and maybe love. She is not sure. When she decided to keep her promise, and to go to bed with Archimedes, he would not have her. She has never been rejected. She is disappointed. She suddenly realizes that she really does desire sex with Archimedes, not want but desire. Angry at being rejected, she thinks for a moment about revenge. *I can tell the king to send him back to Syracuse. Wait a minute! It was the king that insisted she be the one to show Archimedes around. He knew this would happen! Wasn't it he who said that Archimedes would break her heart? No, she cannot tell him. Besides, he wants Archimedes to stay, and probably would not send him away no matter what. Now what?* She does not accept defeat that easily.

Helena undresses and enters the bath. She takes her time bathing. After a while she dresses, and rings a small bell. Quickly, her handmaidens return.

"Your Highness! Is Archimedes gone?"

"Yes, he just left"

"And how did it go? Did you two go to bed?"

"Yes, and it was wonderful. I had forgotten how sweet it is to have sex with a virgin. He did anything I asked, anything."

"Anything?"

"Yes, the best sex I have ever had. Do not tell anyone. Tomorrow I am going with Archimedes to Cairo for four or five days. We leave around noon, so have all my things ready. I will leave you ladies here. Just Archimedes and me and our bodyguards."

"How romantic."

"Remember, don't tell a soul about tonight."

Helena saunters out of the room, certain some of her handmaidens are spying for the king. He will know first thing in the morning. Helena is going to teach her uncle a few things about manipulation. She dresses for dinner but when she arrives, Archimedes is not there. A servant informs her that he had asked that his dinner be brought to him onboard the barge. She asks that her dinner brought to the barge as well. She instructs a servant girl to adjust the pin on her peplos so that it hangs lower, revealing more cleavage. The servant places a wool himation around her shoulder to ward off the chill of the evening. Helena tries to adjust it so it does not cover much of her breasts. After several attempts to make it hang just right, she takes it off, and hands it back to the servant.

"I think it will be better if I don't wear this tonight."

She joins Archimedes onboard the barge as they set sail back to Alexandria. At first Helena and Archimedes eat in silence.

Finally, Helena says, "Archimedes, don't be like this. I like you. I am sorry that you did not approve of my little game tonight. You are the first man who ever picked me out. I was surprised. I realize now that you are not like other men."

"How many men have played with you in this game?"

"Now see, I have made you jealous, and that is not what I wanted to do. The truth is that those men meant nothing to me. It was the excitement. It was all a tease. No one, until you, passed the test, and so none ever got into my bed. That is the truth."

"I am not jealous, just curious." More silence as they continue to eat.

Finally, Archimedes breaks the silence, "So you are a virgin?"

After chocking on a bite of food, "Archimedes, I have acted like a whore so that men would be attracted to me but the truth is, I am a virgin," she lied. "My uncle, the king, would marry me off to someone I never met, and probably could never love. This way, perhaps, I can find someone that I love, and who loves me. Someone who is not interested in making me his queen but who is actually attracted to me, to my body, to my intelligence, to my personality. Do you understand?"

"I think so, but still, it is a mean thing to do."

"Oh, come now. I think you enjoyed the bath I gave you yesterday. Now it is your turn to be truthful. Tell me."

Blushing, "Yes, I enjoyed it. Now tell me what the spices were so I can get them in Syracuse."

"There, that is better. Now let us start over, and just be friends. I don't think you can get all those spices in Syracuse. I will supply you with what you need. Now you help me learn the constellations."

"Surely you must know the constellations after attending so many lectures at the Museum."

"No I don't. I never really paid any attention. Usually I go to those lectures only if the queen goes." She lied again.

Helena and Archimedes lie down on the cushions and pillows so that Archimedes can point out the stars.

"Do you see that band of stars that runs across the sky?"

Helena puts her head on his shoulder so she can see where he is pointing.

"Yes. I see."

"That is called 'The Road of the Gods.' It is made up of many, many stars, and is not really a road at all."

"Oh."

"Can you see Orion, the Hunter?"

"Where?" Helena places her hand on his chest, and presses her cheek against his shoulder.

"There! The bright star is his left shoulder. See his belt and those three faint stars that make up his sword?"

"How beautiful! Don't you agree?"

"Beautiful? No. They are just stars. They are not like a work of art, created to please. They are there to tease men like me into discovering their secrets. There is no beauty in them."

"Oh Archimedes, how can you say that? Can't you see the beauty? Doesn't it cause something to stir within you?"

"No, I cannot say that I feel anything."

"Now, Archimedes, you felt something in the bath. You had passion. We all saw it. You were aroused."

"If you mean urgings, yes I had them. It embarrassed me. I have always tried to keep my urging under control."

"Urging is such a crude word. I like passion better. But why try to deny them? They are a gift from the gods, especially Isis."

"These urging or passions get in the way of logic. They confuse the mind. These passions are the root of anger, fear, and hate."

"No wonder you do not see the beauty in the stars. You showed passion again tonight; first in the bath when you chose me, and after when you were angry with me."

"Yes, I lost control. I am sorry."

"Would you say that I am beautiful?"

"Yes, very much so."

"Do you think that you will always think of me every time you take a bath from now on? Will you remember how my breasts felt? The smell of the perfumes? The softness of my skin?"

"Yes, I am sure of it."

"And will that memory stir your passion?"

"Yes, I am sure it will."

"Then that is a start. Please continue."

"Over there is Leo the Lion."

Now Helena has her cheek on Archimedes' cheek. "I'm cold."

Archimedes puts his arm around her shoulders. As he reaches for a blanket to pull over them, Helena kisses him. Archimedes freezes.

"Archimedes, since you taught me about the stars, let me teach you something."

"I am afraid to ask what."

Laughing, "That's better. You do have a sense of humor. You are a terrible kisser. Let me teach you how to kiss."

"I would like that."

"All right, then." Taking something out of a basket nearby, "First, eat this." She hands him an apple studded with cloves.

"What does this have to do with kissing?"

"The apple will clean your teeth, and the cloves will freshen your breath."

"But don't we just use our lips?"

"Archimedes, I am the teacher tonight. Now you must trust me about this."

Archimedes eats the apple and cloves.

"Now I will teach you to see the beauty in the stars. After tonight, whenever you see the stars, you will remember this night, and you will remember me. You will remember how beautiful I was, and how bright and beautiful the stars were."

The rest of the trip back to Alexandria, Helena teaches Archimedes how to kiss, first in the Greek fashion and then the Egyptian fashion. With Helena as the teacher and Archimedes as the student, they hug and kiss for hours. When the barge arrives in Alexandria, Archimedes is disappointed that the trip was so short. He agrees to go with Helena to visit Cairo for four or five days. As he walks back to his room, he looks up one more time at the beautiful stars and see Helena in them.

Ω

The next morning Archimedes comes to the Museum dining hall for a breakfast of fruit. He notices that several of the servants are talking behind his back, and pointing at him.

Conon ambles over. "Congratulations, old friend. I understand that Helena has shown you some wonderful sights, if you know what I mean," adding a wink.

"No, I do not know what you mean."

"Come, come, old man. Don't be shy. The rumor is all over the palace and Museum that you bedded Helena."

Angry now, "Well, it isn't true." Archimedes throws down the fruit he is holding, and storms back to his room.

Around noon Helena's servant comes to get Archimedes.

"Tell your mistress that I changed my mind, and I am not going with her. Not now, not ever."

The servant goes away, and returns later with a message from Helena.

"My mistress says that you must go with her. The king commands it."

"Tell her that he is not my king. I will do as I please. Now go!"

The servant leaves. About half an hour later, Helena comes to Archimedes' room.

"Archimedes, what is the meaning of this? We must leave if we are to make Cairo on time."

"I am not going. You lied about me. You told everyone that I bedded you."

"Most men would have been pleased."

"Well not me. You have tried to pull me into your fantasy world of palace games and tricks, and now you have spread a rumor about me. I will not be a party to these lies and deceit.

Besides, I don't have time for sightseeing. I have to return to Syracuse. I left a lot of work unfinished."

"You can't go back now. The king had hoped you would become the head of the Museum."

"Someone else can do it. Conon can do it. The Museum got along just fine without me before I got here, and they can do it again after I leave."

"Archimedes, I have offended you again, and I am sorry. Please stay."

"No. I will not stay here and be part of your games any longer. Now get out."

Helena leaves and starts hurriedly back toward the palace. This did not go well. This is not what she had intended. Now Archimedes will leave, and the king will be furious. She goes straight to the Great Hall where the king is eating breakfast with the queen. The king is feeding scraps of meat to Peritas. By the time Helena arrives she is in tears. She kneels down beside the king's chair, and places her head on his thigh.

"Well, my niece, I thought you might be coming to me this morning."

"You have heard?"

"I think all of Alexandria has heard by now. Isn't that what you wanted?"

"No! You're not angry?"

"Of course, I am, but you were true to your nature, and now you have chased Archimedes, one of the finest minds in the world, back home to Syracuse where he will be of no use to me. I have not yet decided on a suitable punishment for disobeying me."

"What shall I do?"

Dismissing his servants with a wave of his hand, "Did I tell you to stop playing your games with Archimedes, that he was different?"

"Yes, sire, you did."

"And did I tell you that he would break your heart?"

"He didn't break my heart!"

"Then why are you crying? Why are you here?"

Pausing, "Why am I crying? I don't love him. He's in love with me."

"Then why are you crying?"

"I don't know."

"Stupid child," interrupts Queen Arsinoe. Standing up, "With all your fooling around, and playing games with Archimedes, you fell in love with him." Looking at her husband and Helena, "The two of you are a fine pair! Partners in crime! You," pointing at Ptolemy, "are worse than her because you should be above such things. Helena is just a child but you, with all your politics and meddling, are just as guilty of driving Archimedes away. Did either of you even consider his feelings? Do either of you care about Archimedes? Do you care about what he wants? I don't think you do. You make me ashamed of you. You both disgust me. I used to be so proud of you two but now I am just disgusted. Husband, I think it is time for you to leave, and let us women talk."

"You cannot talk to me this way! I am the king! You are my queen! You don't command me!"

"I didn't command the king. I am your wife. I commanded my husband and my brother. Helena and I will take care of this mess without your help. Now leave us."

Getting up, "It is a fine situation when a king cannot command his own queen, but I will obey my wife and my sister." Kissing his wife on the forehead, "You are right as always, my dear." He winks at Helena, and starts to leave followed by Peritas.

To his back, "I will deal with you later, husband. We are not finished with this matter. Don't think you can get away with just a kiss."

Monte R. Anderson

Waving his hand but not turning around, "Yes, my beloved." By now Helena is sobbing, kneeling on the floor.

"When is the last time I held you in my arms?"

"It has been a long time, Auntie."

Extending her arms, "Come here."

Helena and Arsinoe embrace. Arsinoe strokes her hair, kisses her head, and together they sit down.

"You are like a daughter to me. For too long I let you behave badly. You have made a bad reputation for yourself. I should have stepped in sooner, and now you have gotten hurt. It is time for you to grow up."

"Oh, Auntie, what can I do?"

"You have tried to trap Archimedes in your web like you have other men, and you have tangled up yourself. He is not like other men. When did you realize that you are in love with him?"

"Just now. Just today when he said he is going back to Syracuse. I thought he loved me. I thought I had more time. Now, because of me, he will leave Alexandria, and never come back."

"Does he know that you love him?"

"No. He thinks I was just using him, toying with him."

"And he is right."

"I don't know what to do. He wants to go home to Syracuse, and I think he means it. I need Ptolemy to stop him so I can talk to him. Maybe I should tell him that I love him."

"It's too late for that now. You have hurt him. Men have such frail egos. You may have lost him. If you tell him how you feel now, he will only think you are playing with his feelings again. However, there is still hope for you, but no one can help you. It is really up to you."

"What do you mean?"

"If Archimedes really loves you he will look for the opportunity to stay. If he stays then it proves that he loves you."

"How can I make him stay?"

"Stop talking like that. You cannot make him stay. It is up to him.

He is the one to decide whether to stay or go, not you. Get that through your thick skull."

"All right."

"Stop being selfish, and start thinking of Archimedes' feelings. Find out what he wants. Archimedes is an honorable man. Honorable men are the easiest to handle because they require only honesty and trust. He trusted you. But you violated his trust, and spread lies about him. It will be difficult for you to earn his trust again. He wants to leave so you won't hurt him again. You must appeal to his good nature."

"What do you mean by 'good nature'?"

"Listen to me. I have heard great things about this man. He is kind, and wants to use his knowledge to help people. He did that many times in Syracuse. If you ask him to stay to help the Greek citizens of Alexandria he probably will not stay, but if you ask him to help the Egyptian peasants, I think he will do it, not for Alexandria but for Egypt."

"That is all I have to do?"

"No, that is not all you have to do. You also have to beg for his forgiveness, something you are not very good at. Beg, don't ask. Be serious this time, from the heart. If he does stay it will give you more time to let him see your good qualities. Love needs time to grow. If you don't beg, he is gone"

"I can beg."

"I mean it, Helena. If you don't do this right, he will be sailing on the next high tide. Now don't wait. Go to him. Go now! I have to talk to my husband. He is not as dumb as he wants people to believe, but not as smart as he thinks he is. His heart is in the right place. What he does, he does for Alexandria and Egypt."

"Thank you, Auntie. Can I ask you a personal question before I go?"

"Yes, of course, my dear."

"Do you love him?"

"Who, Archimedes?"

"No. I mean the king. Do you love him?"

"Of course. He is my brother."

"No, I mean do you love as your husband? Really love him?"

"Of course not! It's not the same as you and Archimedes. Our marriage is political, pure politics. He is much younger than I, and he is my brother. I love him like a brother, but it's not the way you love Archimedes."

"Does he love you?"

"Perhaps. Who knows? I wish sometimes that he had a concubine."

"Why did you marry him?"

"Silly girl. I had a choice. I married the King of Samothrace—what a horrible place. It is not at all like Alexandria. I got bored, and came home. Then I decided that I did not want to remain the Royal Sister but I wanted to be the Queen. So when his first wife committed treason, and was exiled to Coptos, I married him."

"Any regrets?"

"Yes, my dear. No man has ever really loved me for myself. I would rather be a peasant girl, and know without a doubt that a man truly loves me than to be a Ptolemy and never know true love."

"You would like to be a peasant?"

"No, of course not. I am trying to make a point here. I made my choice years ago. Now you have a choice to make, too. The king will use you. He hopes to marry you off to some other king to seal a treaty or some other political ambition. He doesn't really care about you. You can be a queen, and live in luxury or you can be the wife of Archimedes, and know that he loves you everyday. It is up to you. Now choose!"

"Thank you, Auntie. You may be a great queen, but you are a better aunt."

A few minutes later Helena is outside Archimedes' door. "Archimedes."

"Go away. I don't want to talk to you ever again."

Marching into his room, kneeling in front of him, and taking his hand in both of hers, "I don't blame you for being mad at me. Everything I did to you was wrong. I realize that now. You trusted me, and I let you down. I have hurt you badly. I beg you to forgive me. If you won't forgive me, I will understand, but please stay for the sake of the people. Don't leave because of what I did."

"I told you, the Museum will get along just fine without me."

Tears begin to flow down Helena's cheeks, "I am not talking about those people. I mean the Egyptian people. I saw you yesterday at the olive grove with the olive press. You want to help. You can help. You are different from the other scholars in the Museum. I am not worthy of your forgiveness, but don't leave and punish the Egyptians for I did. Yes, I played games with you. Yes, I tried to seduce you. But above all of that I wanted to ask you to help ease the burdens of the Egyptians. Please say you will stay for their sake. Please!"

"How can I help them?"

Wiping away tears, "The other night when we were gazing at the stars I was sure that Isis had sent you to me. I realize now that she did not send you to me at all. She sent you to Egypt to help the Egyptian people. You are very clever. I will show you how the peasants live, the problems they have, and the hardships they must endure. When you see all of that you will think of something. I know you will."

"I suppose I can. But I can't stay long. I have work to do in Syracuse. I will stay for the sake of the Egyptian people, but no more games from you."

"Thank you. Thank you. I promise, no more childish games."

"Just honesty between us. No more lies."

"Yes. No more lies from now on. Just the truth."

"Then it is settled. We leave after lunch."

Monte R. Anderson

CHAPTER FOURTEEN

(247 BCE, in Alexandria)

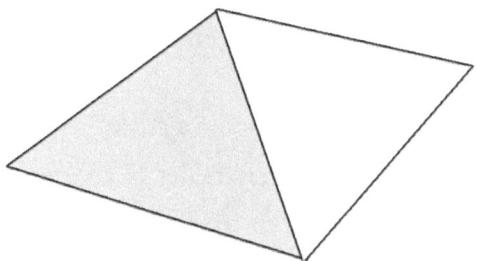

Helena is already onboard the royal barge when Archimedes arrives. Once Archimedes boards, the barge sails for Cairo. Helena and Archimedes sit on cushions and talk for hours. In the evening, the barge stops at a vineyard where Helena and Archimedes build a fire, and dine on waterfowl, bread, dates, nuts, and fruit. After dinner the barge continues on to Cairo. Archimedes lies down on the cushions with his arm around Helena, and continues to explain all the constellations to her. Toward midnight, he notices that she has fallen asleep. With the smell of her hair in his nostrils, he finally falls asleep, and dreams of her. When he awakes in the morning, he finds the barge docked and Helena in her cabin. The skipper has prepared a breakfast of fruit and nuts. When Helena comes out for breakfast, she is dressed in white from head to toe, with just her face showing. After breakfast Helena gives Archimedes a large white robe.

"You will need to put this robe on. It will be hot but it will protect you from the sun, and conserve your body moisture."

Archimedes goes into his cabin to change. When he returns, Helena is standing next to a caravan of camels with her Greek bodyguards and a cohort of Nubians, courtesy of the governor of Cairo. They are dressed all in white. Archimedes stares at the camels.

"Are you familiar with camels?" asks Helena.

"Well, yes and no. I have read about them, but I have never seen one up close."

"Very well. For long trips in the desert, camels are the best means of transportation. The natives call them 'ships of the desert'. It is a little tricky to get on and off and to ride them, but by the time we get back, you will be an expert."

Helena taps one of the camels on the knees with a stick, and the camel kneels down.

"Here, get on," handing Archimedes a stick.

After a couple of attempts Archimedes is able to climb onto the camel. Helena tells him how to hold the reins and how to sit. On a signal from Helena, everyone mounts their camel, and two of the Nubian riders start out to scout the route ahead. Helena and Archimedes are followed by Helena's bodyguards and then the rest of the cohort of Nubians with camels loaded with tents, food, and water. The small caravan winds its way through the city, and finally reaches the west gate. In the distance Archimedes sees pyramids, not clearly at first because of the shimmering heat waves, but soon as distinct points on the horizon. As they get closer to the pyramids, they appear as three triangular red points floating on the horizon.

Finally Archimedes sees the Great Guardian to the pyramids.

"What is that?" he says, pointing at the Great Guardian.

Helena smiles, "The priests call it a Sphinx. It has the body of a lion and the head of a man."

When they are close enough, Archimedes begins to estimate the size of the pyramids and the Sphinx. His mind races as he tries to determine height, weight, angles, and all sorts of mathematical relationships.

When they finally reach the pyramids, Archimedes is totally lost in his thoughts. The caravan stops, and Archimedes nearly falls in his haste to dismount. As he regains his footing, he scampers off toward the pyramids. Helena watches in amazement as Archimedes darts back and forth, sometimes counting paces and sometimes holding his arms in different angles. He is lost to her in his mathematical world, and she does not like it one bit.

After a couple of hours, Archimedes approaches Helena where she is seeing to the camels' watering.

"Where is the base line?"

"What are you talking about?"

"The base line! Where is it?"

"I don't understand."

"In order to build anything of this size, the engineers must have a baseline, a starting point. It must be level, and it must be straight. All measurements are made from this line."

"I don't know. I have never seen anything like that here."

Archimedes turns and hastens back to the pyramids to begin closely examining the ground near the base. After a few minutes he finds what appears to be an ancient trench now filled with sand that runs completely around each pyramid. He scoops out several hands full of sand.

"Eureka!"

Helena rushes over to him. "What is it?"

"I think I have found it. See! The soil here is a different shade than the surrounding soil. I think the builders of these pyramids dug a small ditch around the pyramid in a square shape. This is how they started. It was easy to make sure the ditch was square and straight using stakes at either end with a cord stretched between them. But they had to have it level, and the ground here is not level. Look here!" pointing to a mark on the side of the trench that he had uncovered. "I think they filled the ditch with water which will find its own level. Once the water was smooth and not disturbed, they drained it, and then drew a line at the water mark. Now they had a straight and level line around the structure. Any measurements could be taken from any side of the pyramid."

Mimicking Archimedes, "Interesting! What does all that mean?"

Oblivious to her teasing, "It means that the four sides would all be straight. A small error in any angle or line in the beginning would cause a large error as the structure progressed. That could cause a failure in the structure."

Archimedes turns, and begins to explore the sides of the pyramids. Helena and the Greek guards watch him in wonder while they make camp. The Nubians post lookouts, and set up a separate camp nearby. Soon a campfire is blazing, and the cook begins to prepare dinner. Helena soon tires of watching Archimedes darting about taking measurements. She sits down with the Greek guards to discuss plans for the next day. The shadow of the largest pyramid begins to reach the camp site as the sun sets behind it. Suddenly, they see movement on the edge of the shadow. Helena and the guards turn toward the pyramids to see Archimedes climbing up the side of the pyramid. Loose stones and dirt break away, and tumble down the side.

"He is like a child with a new toy," says one of the guards.

The commander of the Nubian guards trots over to Helena and her bodyguards. He bows, and points off to the east. Helena and her bodyguards jump up when they see the gathering clouds of a dust storm moving swiftly toward them.

"Dust storm!" yells one of the guards as he hurries off to tie down the tents.

"Archimedes!" yells Helena. But he is too far away to hear her. Grabbing the other guard, "Quickly, go get him."

The guard sprints, yelling to get Archimedes' attention, but he is too absorbed in studying the pyramid to heed the call or see the storm. In a few minutes, the storm strikes with all its ferocity. The sand stings Archimedes' face, and gets into his mouth and eyes. He covers his face and tries to turn back, but it is impossible to keep his eyes open more than a few seconds. He cannot see more than an arm's length to his front. He lets go of the block he is climbing, becomes disoriented, and steps off the block, sliding down the side of the pyramid. Suddenly, he is in mid air. He lands on his feet, falls forward to his hands, and strikes his knees on the hard stone. He lies face down very still, and tries to cover every opening he can with his clothes.

"Archimedes!" It is the Greek guard.

"Over here!"

The guard pulls Archimedes half upright, and drags him toward an opening in the side of the pyramid big enough for one person.

"We'll stay here until the storm passes. It is too dangerous to try to climb down now."

The guard places Archimedes into the opening, and helps him cover his face and hands. Then the guard covers his own face with his hands, and presses up against Archimedes to protect him with his body. The storm rages for over an hour, and just as suddenly as it hit, it moves on. A layer of sand covers everything. The guard helps Archimedes out of the cavity, and together they begin to climb down the side of the pyramid. They arrive in camp just after sunset. Archimedes dusts off his robes, and enters Helena's tent.

"Archimedes!" She falls into his arms, "I thought I had lost you."

"I am all right, thanks to your guard."

He starts to kiss her, but she pulls away.

"What's wrong?"

Laughing, "If you could see yourself." Holding his face in her hands, "You have sand in your hair, in your eyebrows, all over your face except for a small area around your lips. Here, look!" She hands him a mirror. "Let me clean you off." Archimedes looks at himself in the hand mirror, and begins to laugh. Then he becomes fascinated by the mirror. Helena takes it away. Using a cloth and a bowl of water she brushes off as much sand as she can, and then washes his face. She washes dried blood from his hands and knees. As she finishes one area, she kisses it, and starts on another. Archimedes sees tears in her eyes. When she is finished with the exposed parts of his body she stops, and looks him over.

"Well, I washed the areas I could see. Now take off your robe so I can clean the rest of you. I will pour you some wine. Dinner was ruined by the sand but I did manage to save some fruit and salad."

"It will do, thank you."

As Archimedes removes his robe, a scorpion falls to the carpet.

Archimedes yells, and leaps onto Helena's bed. Helena is stunned for a moment.

Archimedes waves his arms, shouting, "Kill it! Kill it!"

The sight of this famous mathematician afraid of an insect is too much for Helena. She starts laughing uncontrollably, and falls to ground holding her sides. Two bodyguards dash into the tent. They see Helena on the ground holding her sides, and breathless, unable to speak. They turn and see Archimedes standing on Helena's bed. Not sure what has happened, they draw their swords, and turn to face Archimedes.

"No! No!" yells Helena, finally able to get air into her lungs. Pointing at the scorpion, "There!"

One of the guards walks over and steps on the scorpion. The guards look at Helena, and realize that she has not been stung. They see Archimedes on the bed shaking with fear, and they begin to laugh as they leave.

"Spiders! I hate them."

"Actually, that is much worse than a spider. It must have crawled into your clothes during the dust storm.

"Well, it's not funny."

Laughing all over again, "Yes, it is."

Finally, Archimedes calms down, and he too begins to laugh. After Helena cleans the rest of Archimedes, they sit down, and eat the small dinner of vegetables and lettuce served with a dressing of oil and vinegar. Along with the salad are figs, dates, pomegranates, melon and bread with honey. As they eat, Archimedes begins to explain his theories on how the pyramids were built. After a couple of hours, he goes back to his tent. The bodyguards have cleaned out most of the sand, and prepared a bed for him. He did not realize until now how exhausted he is. In all of his excitement in seeing the pyramids, he raced about and climbed for hours. Now every muscle is starting to ache. He climbs into bed, and quickly falls asleep.

After an hour, Helena enters his tent. A flash of moon light awakens Archimedes as she opens the tent flap. He recognizes her perfume immediately.

"Helena! What is it? What do you want?"

"I am cold."

"Do you want my blanket?"

"No, Archimedes. I want you."

"Well, Helena, I don't think…"

"Now stop, and listen to me. Whenever I get cold at the palace or on one of these trips, some of my handmaidens come to bed with me. Their bodies keep me warm. It is the only way I can sleep when I am cold. I did not bring my handmaidens this time. I want to get into bed with you so that you can keep me warm with your body."

"But, Helena, I don't think…"

"Oh, quit complaining. I am not going to attack you. You don't have do anything. I'll just sleep close to you, and if it makes you feel better, we can put a blanket between us. I am freezing."

Tired, he relents, and holds open the covers for Helena.

Helena drops her robe, and stands silhouetted in the moon light from the tent opening. She is naked. Trying not to stare, Archimedes fusses with the covers and pillows. She climbs into his bed, and snuggles with her back close to his stomach. He can smell her hair and her perfume.

"Even in the dark, I can tell that you are blushing."

"Don't tease, Helena, I have never done this sort of thing before. Yes, I am a little embarrassed."

"Put your arm around me." Archimedes puts his arm around her.

"Today when I saw you disappear into that storm, I thought I had lost you. I was so afraid. Don't ever scare me like that again. Now go to sleep."

In spite of their exhaustion, neither can sleep. After a while, Helena takes Archimedes' hand, and places in on her breast. Archimedes feels her hard nipple. He feels emotions stir within him that have been dormant for years. Helena turns around to face him, and wrapping her arms around his neck she begins to kiss him. Their legs intertwine. At first Helena plans to fake her passion. She believes that with all the men she has bedded, Archimedes could not give her pleasure. But her plan is soon forgotten as she begins to fully enjoy what is happening.

Archimedes has no idea how to please a woman. He is as gentle as possible, and becomes aware for the first time how rough his hands are, and how soft Helena's skin is. He tires to be careful not to hurt her but his gentleness only fans her passion. The combination of rough and smooth, of pain and pleasure excites her. She has had rough lovers before but they only hurt her. This is different and much, much better.

Finally, Helena can resist no longer and pulls Archimedes on top of her. Once they become one, she wraps her legs around his and locks her heels behind his knees. Then, for the first time in his life, Archimedes becomes as one with a woman. Suddenly, Archimedes screams as sharp pains shoot up the back of his legs. He tries to roll off of her but she has him locked up so tightly that he can barely move. His struggles only excite her more. He tries to straighten his legs to relieve the pain but cannot. He screams again and Helena reluctantly untangles her legs. Archimedes hops out of bed, and hobbles around the tent rubbing the backs of his legs.

"Archimedes, what is wrong?"

"My legs! Cramps in both legs! Oh, that hurts."

"Come here, and I will massage them."

Archimedes climbs back into to bed, and Helena massages the back of his legs until the cramps go away. The massage arouses them and they resume their love making. The cramps come back quickly and they repeat the massage. It happens again and again. While this interrupts their love making, it has the added affect of prolonging it. This scene is repeated several times during the night until, finally, they consummate their relationship, and fall asleep totally fatigued but satisfied.

The next day Helena and Archimedes lie in bed, and laugh about their first attempt at love making. They had to stop several times to massage the cramps out of Archimedes' legs, and remove the sand that had gotten into the wrong places. In spite of everything, they both agree it was wonderful. Just talking about it gets Archimedes aroused, and so they try one more time. When they are done, Helena gets out of bed, and puts on her robe.

Handing Archimedes his robe, "Come with me. We can talk."

They walk over to Helena's tent. The cook and the guards are up, but pretend not to notice the two lovers. The Nubian guards, on the other hand, giggle and laugh.

"Do you think we were too loud last night?" asks Archimedes.

"What do you mean 'we'? Every time you got a cramp in your leg, you howled."

"Well, it hurt. Besides, you were not exactly the princess of decorum."

Laughing, "Never mind them. They are just jealous."

Once inside Helena's tent, Archimedes watches as she gets ready. First, she washes herself with soap and water from a bowl. She then rubs on a lotion to moisturize her skin, followed with perfume. Finally, she puts on a girdle and her tunic. She sits down on a camel saddle, and taking out a metal hand mirror, begins to comb her hair. She pours some water into a wide, shallow dish, and sets it aside. Archimedes is again fascinated by the mirror, examining it closely. It does not show a true reflection but one which is distorted.

"Is this a good mirror?" he asks.

"Good mirrors are hard to find. That is why I use this dish."

Archimedes leans over to look at his reflection in the water filled dish.

"Archi," she decides to call him Archi. "If you could invent a good mirror, every woman in Alexandria would gladly bed you to get it."

Startled, "I, I, I don't think I could handle that."

Laughing, "I was just teasing. Besides, I am not willing to share you with anyone."

Archimedes studies Helena's hand mirror for several minutes before handing it back to her. Once they are both dressed, they join the bodyguards for breakfast. The bodyguards have placed all the camel saddles around a small fire to ward off the chill as they break camp. Nearby, the Nubians are eager to move out, and are singing and dancing while they wait for the slower Greeks.

"What are they singing about?" asks Helena.

"I have never heard that one before," answers one of the guards. "I will go, and ask them what it means."

The guard returns after a few minutes, laughing to himself.

"Well?" asks Helena.

"It seems that they are singing about you two. It is an old folk song."

"What do you mean about us?" asks Archi.

"It is a folk song about two young lovers who mate for the first time, and all the pleasures they discover in each other. Apparently they heard you two last night."

"They don't know what they heard," says Helena.

"They have also bestowed a title on Archimedes."

"What title?" asks Archi.

"They now refer to you as the Lion of Alexandria".

"What does it mean, the Lion of Alexandria?" asks Helena.

"They intend to honor Archimedes by the title. It has nothing to do with the strength or courage of a lion. As the Nubian commander explained to me, the lion is known for sexual prowess. It seems that lions can mate frequently and for hours, many times with more than one lioness."

"That is disrespectful!" says Helena, starting to get annoyed at the conversation.

The other guards begin to giggle.

"What do you mean? Did they think that my yelling was something sexual? I had leg cramps," protests Archi.

"Apparently so. Any way, that title is much better than the one we came up with."

"I am afraid to ask. What title did you dogs come up with?" asks Helena.

"We decided Archimedes' title should be, The Scorpion King."

At this remark, two of the guards fall off their camel saddles laughing.

Now Helena is angry. She stands up and throws a piece of fruit at one of the laughing guards. Pointing a finger at the guard who is talking, "If any one of you could bed a woman as well as Archi, your sons would be kings."

Helena stands up and, straddling Archi, sits on his lap, wraps her arms around him, and kisses him. Then she storms off to her tent. Before entering, she turns, and makes a gesture that she has seen young Egyptian girls do when they are mad at a man.

The bodyguards are stunned. They have seen a lot in their roles as bodyguards to Helena, but never have they seen such a public display of affection. They all stop laughing, and stare at Archi. Archi considers going to his tent but it comes down with a thud as the Nubians begin to pack it.

Finally, Archi says, "I hope you don't get into trouble over this."

"No, we won't," says the commander. "Helena knows we are only teasing. We would not dare to act so bold if we thought for a moment that she would punish us. We know all the royal family, and I can tell you that Helena is the best of the family. Berenice may be more beautiful but no one else is half as nice as Helena. Of all the women in Alexandria, you have chosen the best."

"I did not choose her, she chose me, I think."

"Should we address you as Archi now, or Archimedes."

"Perhaps, until Helena cools off, you had better be more formal."

After breakfast, the caravan starts out toward the east. On the far side of Cairo, they crest a large hill.

"Stop! Stop!" yells Archimedes.

The caravan stops, and Archimedes jumps down, scanning the horizon in every direction.

"Eureka!" he shouts.

"What? What have you found?" asks Helena.

"Yes, yes. It can be done."

"Archi, what can be done?"

"I believe it is possible to build a canal that would link the Nile

River with the sea to the south."

"It has been considered before but the two seas are at different levels, I am told. If the seas were connected, one would empty into the other, would they not? At any rate, the engineers never built it because it was impossible."

"Nonsense! All that is necessary is a series of locks. Locks would raise or lower the ships to the proper level while keeping the waters back."

Helena watches in amazement as Archimedes' mind fades out of her presence and into that mathematical world of possibilities inside his head. He uses his camel stick to begin drawing in the sand.

"Archi!" No response.

"Archi, look at me!" Still no response.

"Archi, I am not going to compete with an imaginary canal for your attention."

Archi continues drawing, oblivious to Helena.

"Archi, I warn you! Do not ignore me when I am here with you."

Archi sights along his outstretched arm into the distance. Helena turns, and climbs up a nearby sand dune. After several minutes, one of the bodyguards comes over, and stands on Archi's sand drawings.

"Out of the way! Don't disturb me!"

"Archimedes, you need to attend to Princess Helena right now."

"Why? Has something happened to her?"

"Well, yes. See for yourself," pointing toward a sand dune. Archi sees Helena at the top of a dune with her arms out stretched, facing the sun, naked.

"What is she doing? Is it a religious ritual? How long has she been like that?"

"I think she is trying to get your attention."

"What? Why?"

"I am sure she is not doing this for our benefit," pointing toward the Nubian guards who are watching Helena.

Monte R. Anderson

"Please, make them stop. I will go and get Helena."

The guard smiles mischievously, "Do you need help?"

"I think I can manage. Now, please, go and have the guards look away."

"Yes, sir."

Archi rushes to Helena, and helps her dress.

"What are you doing?"

"Archi, I will not allow you to ignore me. If you do, I will take off my clothes no matter where we are."

"Helena, you are absolutely crazy!"

"Me? What man in his right mind ignores a beautiful woman? You are the crazy one here!"

"I must get back to my drawing before it blows away." Helena starts to remove her clothes again.

"Wait! Wait! I promise not to ignore you. Now, please, get dressed."

"I mean it, Archi. I am more important that some stupid canal. Pay attention to me when I am around you or I will find ways to get your attention."

"Helena, you are right. I am sorry for ignoring you. It won't happen again."

"Archi, you are a bad liar. Of course it will happen again, but I hope that in time you will grow to love me more than these projects of yours. It would be easier to compete with another woman than to fight these problems you work on in your mind. At least, another woman is flesh and blood, and I could gouge out her eyes or pull out her hair. But how do I fight an image in your head? This is the only way I know how."

"Are you really jealous of my work?"

"Yes! I did not know it myself until the storm the other night when I thought I had lost you. I am jealous of anyone or anything that might take you away from me."

"Interesting!"

"I should hope so."

Helena puts her arms around Archi, and kisses him. The Nubians, who ignored the orders of the bodyguard to avert their eyes, cheer, and once again begin singing of new love.

The next day, after Helena has dressed, Archi borrows her hand mirror. While the caravan travels across the desert, he experiments with it, reflecting the sun in various directions. As they crest a large sand dune, Archi stops.

"Why do you stop, Archi?" asks Helena.

"I want to conduct an experiment. I want to use this mirror as a signal, but I need know how far away it can be seen. See that hill in the distance?"

"Yes."

"I want you to send one bodyguard to that hill and another to the larger hill beyond."

"Archi, this is not a good spot to stop. We are very exposed, and there is no water here. The farthest hill will take over an hour to reach."

"I know, but nothing else can send a signal that far. If this works, it would be possible to send signals over great distances very rapidly."

"If you insist."

Helena tells everyone to set up camp, and sends out two bodyguards. She tells them to return if they see Archi' signal. After two hours, Archi uses the mirror to reflect sunlight toward the hills. Within an hour, an excited guard returns with the news. He saw the signal. Two hours later, the other guard returns with the same report. They saw it quite clearly. For the next hour, Archi rants about using mirrors in a string of signal towers, for signaling in battle, and for command and control of military units. With the help of the bodyguards, he brainstorms every possible use of mirrors. When it is over, he has won the respect of the guards.

After a couple of more days of touring the ancient sights of Egypt, observing the natives and their culture, and taking pleasure in each other at night, Archi and Helena return to Alexandria. Helena tries to bribe the Greek guards for their silence. She does not want to have another rumor started that might offend Archi. They refuse saying that they would not do anything to disrespect Archi, and destroy the trust they have built up over the last week.

Before Archi and Helena depart, the commander of the Nubian guards gives Archi a small, wooden figurine. He shows it to Helena who starts giggling.

"What is it?"

"It is a small figure of one of the Nubian gods."

"Which god?"

"The fertility god." Laughing, "It seems that the Nubians have high hopes for you."

"I am glad that they found this so entertaining."

"Archi, they are honoring you. They do not give gifts easily."

Ω

When Archi gets back to the Museum, he locates Conon.

"Conon, I need your help."

"Advice on the affairs of the heart, I presume."

Archi is stunned for a minute on how Conon always seems to know everything before he can tell him.

"Conon, be serious. I have some projects to help the Egyptians. Help me find a map of the Nile."

Conon tells a scribe what to look for, and the scribe returns with his arms loaded with maps. Conon searches through them, selects one, and rolls it out on the floor.

Archi studies it for a while and says, "Just as I thought. It can be done."

"What can be done?"

"A canal! We can build a canal to connect the Nile with the Red Sea. See here," pointing to the map. "We can build it from the Pelusiac branch of the Nile."

"It has been attempted before and failed."

"That's because there were no locks in it. It must have locks." Archi explains how the locks would work. "Tell the king that we have a recommendation for a canal, and that I can show his engineers how to build it. I have another idea to help in irrigation."

"What is it?"

"It is a simple type of pump. I used it on the Syracusia. It is easy to build. It is a screw inside a hollow pipe. One end is put into a lower body of water, and the screw is then turned. Each time the screw turns, the bottom end scoops up water. The water will slide up in the pipe until it finally pours out from the top in a continuous stream."

"How big is it?"

"That's the great part. It is small enough for a man to carry to any field."

"Won't it leak?"

"It does not need to be perfectly water tight as long as the speed of turning is enough to deliver a volume of water greater that the volume that has leaked. However, we could seal it with pitch."

"How does a person hold this screw?"

"I will design a frame work that is light enough to be carried, and that will hold the device and allow it to turn."

"Great! Let me get the carpenters, and you can get started."

Monte R. Anderson

CHAPTER FIFTEEN

(1499, Cesare;s Campaign Headquarters)

Cesare interrupts, "Leonardo, excuse me, but your story about the canal reminded me of a question I have been meaning to ask you."

"Yes, sir, what is it?"

"Is it possible to change the course of a river with such a canal?"

"Well, that depends on several factors. I would have to know the terrain, the river's depth, and the river's width. Which river do you have in mind?"

"Are you familiar with the river that runs through the city of Pisa, the Arno?"

"Yes, sire, I am."

"Well, for centuries, Pisa has prospered because of its strategic location near the mouth of that river. The Arno gives the city of Pisa access to the Tyrrhenian Sea and thus makes it a sea port. Their profits have funded their navies and armies over the years. Now they have taken advantage of the current political unrest to break away from Florence, a papal ally, and to form the Second Pisa Republic. They have encouraged other cities to join, and, in many ways, have been a bad influence. The Pope wants me to break up the Republic, bring Pisa back into line, and to make an example of them. However, storming the city walls could be costly and a blockade without a strong fleet, impossible. It occurred to me that we might be able to reduce their profits for years to come if we could build a canal to permanently divert the river so they would not have access to the sea. They would no longer be a sea port."

"Well, sir, if you have the financial backing, I am sure it can be done."

"Excellent! Or, should I say, Eureka? Start working on the design of the canal after you finish the steam canon."

Ω

(247 BCE, the Museum in Alexandria)

One day while Helena and Archi are talking outside the museum workshop she asks, "Archi, what did you do about making me a better mirror?"

"Let me show you."

Archi leads Helena into the workshop. On his worktable are several types of hand mirrors.

"Each of these mirrors is made of a different metal, hammered thin, and made to conform to different shapes. Some of the round or rectangular shapes are flat. Others are made concave or convex by inserting the thin metal into a bowl or by covering the outside of the bowl. The metal is one single sheet. After it is hammered thin, it is bent to conform to the shape of the bowl using mallets made of leather. The metal is then polished with different compounds and tools. I am experimenting with different sized bowls. As for hand mirrors, silver seems to work best."

He hands Helena a silver hand mirror. She looks at her reflection, and begins to adjust her hair. The metal smiths begin to chuckle.

"Actually, this shows the greatest potential," handing Helena a mirror made of glass with a thin silver backing covered with black paint.

Looking at her reflection, "It is better than I had expected. Archi, this is good." Looking at herself for a minute or two, "Do I really look this bad?"

A silversmith working nearby drops his hammer, and several other workmen snicker. They know that there is not a good answer to that question. They stop to wait for Archi's response.

"No, Helena, you are beautiful. I got the idea from your dish of water that you use. Let me show you how I am experimenting with the mirrors."

Good strategy, *change the subject,* the metal smiths think. Archi picks up a concave shaped mirror inside a shallow bowl, and goes over to an open window where the sun is shining through. He uses the concave mirror to focus the suns' rays onto a small pile of hay. After a few seconds, the straw begins to smolder.

"I believe that once we perfect the surface of this mirror, I will be able to start fires!"

"But Archi, there are simpler ways to start a fire, especially at night."

"True, but I am thinking of something much bigger."

Pointing toward another section of the workshop, "This larger mirror is what I am really working on."

Helena sees a large concave mirror the height of a man. On all sides of the large mirror are smaller mirrors on hinges. The entire structure is on wheels. Archi, with some help, rolls the mirror out onto a balcony and into the sunlight. In the yard is a large pile of hay about one half a bow shot away. Turning a small crank, he moves the mirror toward the sun. Looking down upon a small sundial, he turns two other cranks until there is no shadow on the sundial. Now he turns another handle which causes the mirror to reflect the sun light onto the pile of hay. Once he is satisfied with the alignment of the mirror, he begins to adjust the smaller side mirrors which intensify the sunlight. The pile of hay begins to smolder, and bursts into flames.

"Archi! How did you do that? How is it possible?"

"I just used the mirror to concentrate the sun's heat."

"How will you use it?"

"I am not sure yet. It needs more work. I need to extend the range, and increase the power. Certainly, mirrors can be used for signaling. If I can perfect it, it could be used to burn ships at sea, either from another ship or from the city walls beyond the range of arrows or catapults."

"That is amazing! How soon will it be ready?"

"I am not sure. There are many problems to be worked out."

As Helena walks back through the work shop, she picks up the mirror with the black paint on the back, and takes it with her.

Ω

A few weeks later, Archi loads the large mirror onto the royal barge for a journey to the Pathos Lighthouse. Helena watches from the bow. Once the mirror is off loaded, it is attached to a crane and pulley device that lifts it to the top of the lighthouse. After some maneuvering, the mirror is in place. Helena uses a smaller hand mirror to signal Conon on one of the ships in the harbor. In a few minutes, Conon sails out, past the lighthouse, out of the harbor, and toward the open sea. On another signal from Helena, both Conon and Archi turn over a large hourglass timer filled with sand, and graduated in fifteen minute increments. Thirty minutes later, Archi uses the large mirror to signal Conon's ship on the horizon--three short flashes. Conon, out at sea, sees the signal, and takes notes. Then, using a hand mirror, he signals back with six short flashes.

Fifteen minutes after sending the first signal to Conon, Archi turns the large mirror toward the land, and sends two flashes toward the palace. There, on the Great Balcony, are Eratesthenes, Euergeter, and Berenice. They reply with four short flashes on a small hand mirror. The first test signals go well. Thirty minutes later, Conon's ship is just a tiny speck on the horizon. When Archi sends his signals, Conon replies once again with six short flashes. Archi, Helena, and the others cheer when they see flashes come from the tiny speck. Archi measures the azimuth to Conon's ship. At the palace, Eratesthenes also measures the azimuth. Within a few minutes, the ship disappears from sight. Thirty minutes later, Archi sends another signal. This time there is no reply. He tries it again but still there is no reply.

Archi and Helena break for a small meal that they share with the others. There is almost a festive mood. The experiment went well. Soon, they are joined by Eratesthenes, Euergeter, and Berenice from the palace. Archi explains what has happened so far. Using Eratesthenes' measurements and his own, Archi determines the distance to Conon's ship by triangulation. Days earlier, he and Eratesthenes had determined the distance between the lighthouse and the palace. Using these measurements, Archi determines that the distance from the Lighthouse to Conon's ship is very great. The light can be reflected a long way off.

Euergeter is excited about the prospects of using mirrors for command and control of the army. He talks with Archi and Eratesthenes about setting up signal towers for early warning, about using hand held mirrors to control military units, and using mirrors at sea for ship-to-ship communications. From that moment, Euergeter has the highest admiration for Archi, Conon, and Eratesthenes.

As the sun sets, Archi re-sets the timer as the last of the sand runs out. Workers start the lighthouse fire. Archi makes adjustments to the mirror. One hour after sunset, Archi uses the mirror to send out three signals using the fire as a light source. He continues to do this every thirty minutes.

After a couple of hours, the lights from lamps tied on top of the mast of Conon's ship comes into view. In another hour, the ship docks at the lighthouse. Conon leaps down the gangplank, yelling. He grabs Archi in a bear hug, then kisses Helena. He starts toward Euergeter and Eratesthenes who both stick up their hands to stop him. He turns toward Berenice but thinks he had better not try to kiss the Queen.

Conon shouts, "Success! Success! Archi, it worked!" By the light of a lamp, they compare notes.

"The distance is very great." says Archi.

"Then there is no doubt about using mirrors on the lighthouse?" asks Helena.

"No doubt! If I set up two mirrors, they can serve as a beacon to ships at sea as well as to travelers on land. I can design a system to make them rotate."

Euergetes adds, "I will order the construction of smaller towers all the way to Cairo and beyond. We can use them for early warning of an invasion."

Euergetes invites the group for a late dinner in the palace. Everyone is in a festive mood except Archi. His mind is already working on the design for a mechanical system to rotate the mirrors on top of the light-house.

Ω

Monte R. Anderson

CHAPTER SIXTEEN

(1499, Cesare's Campaign Headquarters)

Philippe enters the room, and whispers into Cesare's ear. Standing up, Cesare says, "Excuse me for a few minutes, I must confer with Philippe about tomorrow's campaign."

After sitting alone a few minutes, Leonardo walks over to a cage on the table containing a small songbird. He had guessed it to be a warbler but is not sure which species. Examining the gray on the back and pale underneath, he thinks that it might be a reed warbler, but it does not have the characteristic flattened head. The way it mimics other warblers but with punctuated squeaks and whistles convinces Leonardo that it is a marsh warbler. He opens the cage door, reaches in, and gently seizes the bird. He walks over to the entrance of the tent, kisses the bird on the head, and releases it.

Leonardo, quite satisfied with himself for freeing the warbler, returns to his seat. A few minutes later, Cesare returns.

"Leonardo!"

No response.

"Leonardo!'

"What? Oh, sire, I must have dozed off."

"Perhaps we should continue this later. You look tired."

"No, sire, this is the way I sleep—a few winks here and there. I never sleep for a long period of time. I am fine."

Convinced that his little ruse has worked, Leonardo continues where he left off, hoping that Cesare does not notice that the warbler is missing.

Ω

(247 BCE, in Alexandria)

Ever since Archi started his relationship with Helena, he felt guilty about knowing certain things about her father's death that she did not know. The friendship between Archi, Helena, Berenice, Euergeter, Eratesthenes, and Conon has grown into a firm bond. Archi feels that the time is right to tell the sisters the truth about their father's death. He is hesitant to include Euergetes, but is willing to leave that up to Berenice. He is not sure how Euergetes will react when told about his father.

One evening, Helena and Berenice accompany Archi, Conon, and Eratesthenes to their favorite tavern. Callimachus arrived earlier by sedan chair, and is waiting in the upper room. Soon everyone is seated around the table.

Conon begins, "Helena, Berenice, there is no way I can soften this. We think that King Ptolemy killed your father."

"No!" shouts Berenice. "It is a lie! I don't believe it! My father died hunting. It was an accident. He fell from his horse, and drowned in a stream."

"No, he was drowned to make it look like an accident," replies Conon. "He had come to Alexandria to reconcile with your uncle, his half brother. They went hunting lions. During the hunt, Ptolemy had your father drowned. All of your father's staff was promised high positions in Cyrene to keep quiet. They returned to Cyrene with his body, and announced that he had died while hunting. Ptolemy selected Demetrius to succeed your father even though, by rights, the throne should have gone to your mother. Demetrius was a trusted agent of your father's. I think you know what happened after that."

"How could you know this? It must be a lie," says Helena.

Archi takes her hand, and puts his arm around her.

Eratesthenes answers, "I am from Cyrene and so is Callimachus. When you two came here, you brought your teacher, Heraclide. He was on that hunting trip. After your father's death, he was invited by King Ptolemy to join the Museum even though he had contributed nothing to the body of knowledge. His membership in the Museum was his reward for his participation in the murder plot. We think Ptolemy was also using him to spy on the Museum. When he arrived, Callimachus and I brought Heraclide here to drink with fellow countrymen, and to talk. We all had too much beer but Heraclide had much more. While in a drunken stupor, he let the truth slip out."

Tears start to form in Helena's eyes, "But why?"

"That's the simple part," Eratesthenes answers. "Ptolemy never forgave his Magus for setting up a separate kingdom to the west of Egypt. He had broken away from the family. To secure his borders, Ptolemy would like to reunite Cyrene with Egypt."

"What do you know about the first Queen Arsinoe?" asks Callimachus.

Helena wipes her tears away, "Well, the queen told me that she was exiled to Coptos in Southern Egypt. The queen had something to do with it."

"There is some truth to that. She is the second Arsinoe to marry King Ptolemy. When she returned to Alexandria, she wanted to be Queen of Alexandria and Egypt but there were two problems; Ptolemy already was married, and he was her brother. So she came to the Museum, and asked one our scholars to research if there was any history of Egyptian kings marrying their sisters. It turns out that there was."

"Who was the scholar that did this?" asks Berenice.

"It was Heraclide, of course, and because he knew too much, he was murdered by Ptolemy."

"Murdered?" both sisters blurt out.

"I thought he drowned at sea," said Bernice.

"He had help, you could say. We have information from a reliable source that he was locked in a lead box, and thrown over board," says Conon, without revealing the source.

"Arsinoe knew that Ptolemy feared an Egyptian revolt, and would do nearly anything to please the Egyptian priests. She figured she could convince him to marry her based on the historical precedence if she could get rid of the first Queen Arsinoe."

"How did she get rid of her?" asks Berenice.

"Ptolemy did that. He had grown tired of her anyway. She was pressuring him to conclude a treaty with Athens, her homeland. The treaty favored Athens but not Alexandria. The king intercepted a messenger going from Alexandria to Athens carrying a note from Queen Arsinoe. It was, of course, a forgery, written by the second Arsinoe herself. The king had his own wife tortured until she confessed, and then exiled her. But she was innocent."

"That's terrible!" interjects Helena.

"You have taken a great risk in telling us this," says Berenice.

"Yes, we realize that. Our very lives are at stake. What we tell you, we say in confidence because our friend, Archi, asked us to. We tell you this as friends, and to warn you. It may help you decide what course of action to take in the near future," says Callimachus, referring to Berenice's pending marriage to Euergetes. "Your lives are at stake too. Whatever you decide to do, you will have our support."

With that, Bernice stands up, and leaves the tavern, followed by Helena and Archi.

Once outside the tavern, Helena stops and asks Berenice, "Now what should we do?"

"I don't know. I have to think about it. For right now, let's not tell anyone, especially Euergetes. I think he wants to marry me but I am not sure how he will react if he hears this."

"Do you think he would not marry you if he knows?" asks Archi.

"No, I think he might kill his father."

Ω

After much thought, Archi decides to ask King Ptolemy permission to marry Helena. A few days later, he goes to the throne room of the palace.

"King Ptolemy, I wish to marry Helena."

King Ptolemy looks at Archi for a minute and replies, "Absolutely not! Nothing personal, Archimedes, but it is out of the question. What could you possibly offer her? I know that you are related to King Hieron by marriage but not by blood. Helena should marry a king. She is a Ptolemy and of royal blood. What are you? A court advisor! Your employment could be terminated on a whim. And what about a palace? You don't even own a palace. And look at the difference in your ages. You ask too much. Besides, what would I get out of this?"

"I have given that some thought. We would stay here, and I could become your chief engineer."

Pausing for a minute, "It is a tempting offer, I agree, but Helena is more valuable to me as settlement of a treaty or to seal a bargain with an allied kingdom. The answer is still no. Now go away, and don't bother me again about Helena."

Later, when Archi tells Helena, she is furious. She immediately tells her sister, Berenice, and together they go to the King's bedroom at a time they know he is getting ready for bed, and will be alone.

As the women enter Ptolemy's bedchamber he stands up to greet them, "Helena, I was expecting you. Berenice, I was not expecting you. Have you come to support Helena in her petition?"

"You might say that," Berenice answers curtly.

Ptolemy's dog, Peritas walks over to Berenice to be petted. Berenice removes a leather pouch from her waist band, and pulls out a large piece of meat for Peritas. She tosses into the hallway. As Peritas leaves the room, Helena closes the large wooden doors, and bolts them.

"I guess this is serious," says the king.

Berenice walks over to the bed, and searches it for a dagger or weapon. She finds none. Arsinoe had mentioned once in passing that King Ptolemy always kept concealed weapons nearby for his own protection. Now Ptolemy fears for his life, and dashes toward a large curtain. Helena is quicker, and trips him so that he sprawls on the floor. She pulls back the curtain to reveal a sword hidden behind it. As the king starts to stand, Berenice runs over, knocks him down, and sits on him with her own dagger at his throat.

"We are going to talk, and you are going to tell the truth for once. If you cry out for the guards, I will kill you. I have killed one king before, a second should be easy," says Berenice.

"All right, but get off me, and let me up. This floor is cold."

"No. I don't trust you any more," pushing the dagger closer to his throat.

"All right! All right! What do you want to know?" asks the king.

"I know that you killed our father. I want to hear you say it."

"I didn't kill him."

"You liar!" yells Helena as Berenice raises the dagger to stab him.

Grabbing her forearm, "Let me finish! I didn't personally kill him. I ordered it done. He was killed by his own staff, not by any of my people."

Bernice pulls her arm free, and places the point of the dagger over his jugular notch. Killing him now would be easy and quick. He is weaker than her, and too old to stop her.

Pleading, "Are you going to kill me now?"

"I haven't decided. I have more questions. Tell me how you killed him?"

"We went on a hunting trip. I had bribed his staff so that they were all in my employment. When we crossed a stream, I had them seize him, and drown him. I wanted it to look like an accident."

"Why didn't you just arrest him, and then kill him?" asks Helena.

"Cyrene has been a problem for years. If I openly did anything, there might have been a revolt."

"But why did you kill our father?" asks Berenice.

"It was politics. I wanted to put Cyrene back under my control. Your father had broken with the family when he declared himself King of Cyrene. He was a traitor."

Helena shouts, "He was our father!"

"Helena, keep your voice down! The guards!" says Berenice.

"Was Demetrius your agent too?" asks Berenice.

"Yes, of course. You caused me a lot of trouble when you killed him."

"He deserved to die," replies Berenice.

From behind the bolted doors a guard asks, "Are you All right, sire?"

Berenice pushes the point of the dagger into Ptolemy's throat enough to draw blood.

Whispering, "I can kill you before the guards can save you."

"Yes," answers the king, "I am all right. It was just a dream. Go back to your post."

"I am obedient to my god and my king," replies the guard.

After waiting a minute to be sure that the guard is not outside the door, Helena asks, "Why didn't you kill Berenice and me when you killed my father?"

"You were both so very young. I thought we might work something out, an arrangement. I do love you. I know that sounds strange but I do. I have no ill will against you two. What your father did had nothing to do with you two. Your father's death was political."

"If you say that one more time, I swear, I will kill you," growls Berenice. "Now I know who the traitors are in my kingdom. Every member of the staff that was on that hunting trip, and told me that he had drowned is a traitor. I will have them arrested and executed."

"No! You must not do that," says Ptolemy. "If you do, they will all confess that I paid them off, and ordered my own half brother killed."

"That is the truth!" interjects Helena.

"I know! I know! But if the truth comes out, Cyrene may revolt. I cannot have that. It is not in your best interest either. We are on the verge of war. I must secure my borders in case we are attacked by Roma or Carthage. Cyrene must be part of Egypt."

"And another thing," asks Helena, "Did you and Queen Arsinoe have the first Arsinoe tortured, and then exiled?"

"That was pure...," Looking into Berenice's eyes, "Yes. It was my sister's idea but it suited my plans."

"You killed your brother, and tortured and exiled your own wife?"

"She was not innocent! She was melding and conspiring against me but I couldn't prove it. So I made up a crime and had her confess to it. But I didn't kill her. I loved her."

"I know! It was politics! But you did kill Heraclide," says Helena.

"He was an embarrassment to me and to the Museum."

"That is not why you had him killed, is it? The Museum had already exiled him. You killed him to keep him quiet," Helena replies.

"Oh! You know about that?"

"Yes, I know. What about all the other things you did; the religion and the Egyptian schools? All of it?"

"What can I say?"

"Politics! The Museum and the Library?"

"My father started those. I only continued them. They will be my crowning achievement."

"It is all about you, isn't it?"

"Berenice, kill me now or let me up. My back is killing me."

"What about Archi?" asks Helena.

"What about Archi?" asks Ptolemy.

"My whole life has been a pack of lies. Archi is the only good thing to happen, and you forbid him to marry me?"

"Helena, be reasonable."

"What would happen if we told everyone, all the Greek cities, and the people of Cyrene about what you have done?"

"They would probably recall their ambassadors and scholars from the Museum. Cyrene would cause trouble. A war may start."

"It would not be difficult to burn down the Library too," says Helena.

"You wouldn't? Would you? You would! Helena! Berenice! Not the Library! I have done many bad things in my life but the Library is a good thing. Please, do not destroy it. Tell me what you want me to do. I will do anything."

Helena answers, "Here is what you are going to do. You are going to let me marry Archi. After the wedding, you will make him the Royal Engineer."

"Is that all? If I do this, you won't tell? You won't burn down the Library?"

"From now on you do not have any authority over Archi or me. We are free," says Helena.

"And if I do?"

Your dirty secrets will remain hidden as long as there is no more 'politics'. Understand?"

"Agreed! Now let me up, please."

"Wait a minute!" says Berenice, "This was too easy. You are still hiding something. You want Helena to marry Archi, don't you?"

"Yes! Yes! Now let me up!"

"Helena, why doesn't Archi wear a beard?"

"His queen told him he would attract a wife if he cut his beard off."

"Exactly! He came here looking for a wife. I think he had help. I think the Queen of Syracuse wrote a letter to Queen Arsinoe asking for help. Arsinoe told her husband."

Helena, suddenly enlightened, "That is why Ptolemy sat Archi beside me at the banquet!"

"Yes, and it was Ptolemy who suggested you be Archi's guide in Egypt. He was hoping you would offer to bathe him. He was hoping you two would fall in love."

"But that cannot be. He told me to stay away from Archi."

"You naïve woman. He knows how you are. The best way to get you to do something is to tell you not to do it. He knows you too well. He manipulated you. He is good at using people to get what he wants. He has had years of practice."

"Then why did he oppose the marriage when Archi asked?" asked Helena.

"He did not want it appear too easy. He was hoping for concessions from you and Archi. He did not want you to return to Syracuse after you married."

"Oh, no! You are right! What shall I do?"

"Well, it seems clear to me that you cannot marry Archi now."

Silence from Helena.

Berenice looks at her, "What?"

"I love Archi. He loves me. I want to marry him."

"And let this asshole get the best engineer in the world to work for him?"

"We don't care about that."

"Of all the men you bathed, and hopped into bed with, why did you fall for this one? He is not a king. He is not like Euergetes."

"No, he is not like Euergetes. He is not like anyone else."

"Damn you!"

"I am sorry. We just want to get married. That is why you and I came here, isn't?"

"Yes, I suppose so. Wait a minute!" Looking down at Ptolemy, "What about Euergetes and me? Was that just politics too?"

Ptolemy looks sheepishly into Berenice's eyes.

"I knew it! It is politics!" shouts Berenice. "You have been throwing the two of us together ever since I got here. You wanted us to fall in love. You are hoping that we would marry. That would reunite Cyrene with Egypt, wouldn't it? You old fool! I should kill you now."

"But I thought you loved Euergetes?" asks Helena.

"That is a problem. We did fall in love and now we want to marry. I am so angry that it was all a plot." Pushing the dagger into Ptolemy's throat a little deeper, "Does Euergetes know about this?"

"No, he knows nothing about it," says Ptolemy. Arsinoe said that if I just put you two together it would happen. You are both so beautiful."

"If I find out that he knew about all along, I will kill you both like I did Demetrius. Do you know how I kill him?"

"Yes, you found him in bed with your mother, and stabbed him with a dagger, just like this one."

"Oh, I didn't just stab him. I cut off his balls and cock. My mother screamed the whole time. Then I threw them at her as a memento of their undying love, which died anyway. That is what I will do to you and Euergetes."

"Please don't! I am old but Euergetes is still young. He will father many children. He is an honest man, and fair to look at. The way I see it, you are giving up Queen of Cyrene to be the Queen of Egypt and Cyrene. Your children will inherit a much larger kingdom. Beside, you do love each other, don't you? It would be a marriage of love, not politics. And you Helena, you love Archi, don't you? He will become a wise and powerful minister. Is that so bad?"

"It is only bad because it pleases you," replies Helena.

"He is right." says Berenice. "But, I would like to cut off one of his balls just for good measure."

"Let him up. We got the truth we were looking for and more than we wanted," says Helena.

Berenice lets Ptolemy up. He has trouble getting up so Helena helps him stand up.

Flexing his back, "Berenice, you will be a great addition to this family. We need you to put some backbone into the blood line. I fear they are getting soft. You will stiffen their spines."

"If not, I will create a lot of eunuchs, and the bloodline will die out."

"So after all this, you get what you always wanted," says Helena.

"So do you! It is fair for all," replies Ptolemy.

"I think we have still more to settle," says Benenice. "First, there will be a double wedding for Helena and myself and you will pay for everything. It is going to be really big."

"Of course."

"Second, after the weddings, you will abdicate your throne and make Euergetes the sole King of Egypt. You will do it in such a way that Euergetes will never know I had a hand in it. Once Helena and Archi marry, you will make Archi the Royal Engineer."

"You drive a hard bargain, but all right. You must promise not tell anyone about this, not even Euergetes."

"You also must keep your promises. If you don't, Helena will go to Syracuse, and I will return to Cyrene. We will make trouble for you. I should think that the King of Syracuse will declare war with you or, at least, stop trading with Alexandria. Before we go, we will burn down the Library, and castrate your sons."

Grimacing, "I said all right. I vow to do as I have promised."

Berenice throws her dagger at his bed, and it sticks into the pillow up to the hilt. "See that you do."

With that, Berenice and Helena unbolt the door, and walk out of the bedroom.

As they leave the palace, Helena asks Berenice, "Did you really cut off Demetrius' balls and cock?"

"No, I stabbed him in the heart. I only said that to scare Ptolemy. Kings are so protective of their genitalia."

"Oh, I see. And that remark you made about me hopping into bed with other men."

"Yes?"

"Well, Archi doesn't know that. He thinks I am a virgin, or at least, that I was until I met him."

Laughing, "What? You did go to bed with him, right?"

"No, not right away. Later."

"Well, surely, when he entered you, he knew you were not a virgin?"

"How could he? He was a virgin too. I mean, he had never had sex with anyone but me, and I would appreciate it if you never brought it up again."

Laughing harder, "All right little sister. And if you can be a virgin, then so can I."

"I'm serious. This is not funny."

"Helena, I will try but I am not sure I can keep a straight face when I see the two of you together."

"Well, try! And when did you learn to throw a dagger?"

"That, sister, was pure luck. Impressive, wasn't it? So how goes it with you and Archi? Do you really want to marry him?"

"Yes, I do but I worry about it," replies Helena.

"What do you mean?"

"He is a hard man to understand. When his mind starts working on a problem he can become so absorbed in solving it that he becomes oblivious to the world around him, even me. It is as if he is in a trance."

"Helena, men aren't that hard to understand. Once you go to bed with them you control them. You two did go to bed together, right?" asks Berenice.

"Is that how it was with you and Demetrius?"

"All right, so it does not work all the time. I was much younger then, and Demetrius desired an older flesh pot."

"I never understood why you killed him. I know he cheated on you but if you truly loved him, how could you kill him?"

"I guess I did not really love him. Suppose you found out that Archi had a wife back in Syracuse, what would you do?"

"I couldn't kill Archi!"

"You don't know what you are capable of doing in passion."

Somewhat puzzled, Helena asks, "If you did not love Demetrius, then why were you engaged to him?"

"Helena, if I tell you, you will be angry with me."

"It was politics wasn't it? I don't believe it! You really are a Ptolemy. You are as bad as the king."

"All right, I admit it. I am capable of some politics myself. Our father chose Demetrius as next in line to the throne. It should have been our mother and then me but father thought a strong king was needed. The only way I could rule was by marrying Demetrius. Beside, he was called Demetrius the Fair for a reason. He was really good looking, and quite good in bed. Maybe I did not love him, but when I found out he was cheating on me, I was really angry. I guess it was easier to kill him because I did not love him. Finding him in bed with our mother helped too."

"How did you find out he was cheating?" asks Helena.

"Someone told me."

"Our mother should have been queen," says Helena. "I think she realized that with Demetrius as king, and if you married him, then she would be powerless and cast aside. I think she was playing her own game of politics. She was hoping to marry Demetrius. She is no different that Queen Arsinoe. But surely, whoever told you that Demetrius was cheating on you, must have known that he was bedding our mother, and that you would catch them together. Who told you?"

Helena's words startle Berenice and she blurts, "It was Heraclide, our teacher!"

"Heraclide! Heraclide probably told Ptolemy that Demetrius was bedding our mother and Ptolemy told him to tell you. Ptolemy was counting on you doing something drastic. If you did not kill Demetrius, Ptolemy could invade Cyrene under the pretext of protecting you, the rightful heir to the throne. Killing Demetrius was a bonus."

The realization hit Berenice, "That asshole! That is why Heraclide had to die. He was in the plot to kill our father, and to dethrone Demetrius. We should have figured this out sooner. I guess all men are liars and cheats."

"Not Archi!" Helena blurts out. "He is different. He is honest, and detests palace politics. He prefers scholarly pursuits. He would never lie to me or cheat on me."

"But you lied to him," Berenice points out.

"I know but that just shows you how much better a person he is than you or I. That is one of the reasons I love him."

"Well, I still say that you can control him with sex."

"Archi is not like that. No one can control him. He loves mathematics. Sex is not as important to him as mathematics. Sometimes, when he is with me, he goes into a trance, thinking about problems, and paying no attention to me. When he is in that trance, the only way I can get his attention is to take my clothes off."

"So I have heard. But if that works, what is the problem?"

"I can't keep taking my clothes off just to get his attention. It will not work forever. It is taking longer and longer to pull him out of his trances."

"Helena, I tell you that with sex you can make him worship you."

"No, I think you are wrong. There must be another way. The tricks that work on most men will not work on Archi. I have been getting advice from you and the queen but none of you really know Archi. You can't help me. I must find a way. I cannot marry someone who loves something else more than me."

Well, then, you must find someone who knows Archi well enough to advise you."

Ω

A few days later, Helena approaches Conon as he is reading a scroll in the Library.

Startled, "Your Highness! I apologize. I did not hear you come in."

"That is precisely what I have come to talk to you about."

"What does your Highness mean?"

"Conon, you are Archi's closest friend. I need your help."

"What is it?"

"First, you must promise not to repeat anything I tell you to Archi."

"Yes, of course. I won't repeat anything to Archi. You can trust me."

"Donkey dung! You cannot be trusted. You gossip like an old lady, and you know it. And when you drink, every secret you know is told. You are worst than my handmaidens. I mean it, Conon! If you repeat one word to Archi, I will come after you. He is so sensitive about his reputation. Now swear to it!"

"All right! All right! I swear that I will not repeat a word of what you tell me."

"I don't trust you but I have no choice. This is the problem; sometimes, Archi slips away in his mind. He loses touch with reality as he tries to solve problems in his head."

"Yes! I know exactly what you mean. I have seen him do that. When he is like that, you cannot talk to him. He forgets to eat or bathe."

"Yes, well, I think I solved the bathing problem but I tell you, sometimes when he does that, I can stand naked before him, and he does not take notice."

"Are you sure? I don't believe it. Try it with me, and let's see what happens."

"Conon, I am serious! I love him, but I won't be a concubine to a mathematical wife."

"Oh, love is it?"

"Yes, you old fool. Now tell me what to do."

"All right! All right!" After a long pause, "Well, I think you are taking the wrong approach with Archi."

"What do you mean?"

"I mean, if you can't beat him, join him."

"Huh?"

"Look! Archi is the way he is. He can't help it. Mathematics is for him like air is to normal people. He can't live without it. Do not try to compete for his attention. Join him."

"But how?"

"Take an interest in his work. Ask him to explain it. Ask questions. Let him try out his ideas on you. Be his partner. Ask him to solve other problems. Give him ideas. Soon he will include you in his mathematical world."

"Do you really think so?"

"I know so. You will be his touchstone with reality. Helena, it is a very fine line between genius and insanity. Without you, he may disappear into that mathematical world one day, and never come back. Take care of him. Be his beacon, his lighthouse back to this world. He needs you. I think in his own way, he is very much in love with you."

"Conon, you are right. Archi is lucky to have a friend like you. I will do it! Now, remember, not one word to Archi."

Helena hugs Conon, and rushes out to find Archi. She finds him in the Geology Hall pouring over maps.

"Archi."

No response.

Helena looks over his shoulder at the map on the table. It is an old map depicting the canal that was proposed years earlier, started, and then abandoned.

"Archi, I know where the old canal is located. It does not follow the map exactly."

Turning to Helena, "Oh, hello, Helena. You have seen this old canal?"

Finally getting his attention, "Yes. Bring your maps, and I can show it to you. You can make corrections to the map." Pointing to notes on the map's margin, "Are these your notes?"

"Yes, I am making calculations to build the canal."

"Archi, your notes are hard to read. Why don't you use a scribe like the other scholars do?"

"The scribes make mistakes. They do not understand mathematical symbols. It is better if I do it myself."

"What does this note say?" picking out one of his scribbles.

Archi studies his own handwriting for a minute, "I am not sure. I can't read it."

"Your handwriting is very bad, and your Greek is worst. Let me write your notes for you. You can tell me what to write, and I will write it down neatly."

"Very, well. Let's try it."

Archi gathers up the maps, and together they ride out of the city in Helena's chariot. They spend the greater part of the day surveying the old canal, and updating the old maps. Archi dictates to Helena, and she writes everything down in a clear, strong hand. Helena is delighted. They are working together in his world.

$$\Omega$$

Within weeks Euergetes asks to marry Berenice, and Archi asks to marry Helena. A wedding date is set. Six months later, Helena and Berenice approach the altar in the temple of Isis. They kneel down, and pray for a few minutes. Then they stand, and turn to face their hand-maidens. One of the handmaidens is holding a small pillow with a pair of scissors on it. Helena takes the scissors, and cuts off a lock of Berenice's hair. Berenice in turn, cuts off a lock of Helena's hair. Normally, this ceremony is conducted by the mother but under the cir-cumstance, the sisters do it. With the aid of their handmaidens, the women undress, and take off the girdles they have worn since puberty. They place the locks of hair and the girdles on the altar as a dedication to Isis. Helena and Berenice, together with their retinue, move to another part of the temple where the ritual baths are located. These baths are used only for baptisms and for young virgins about to marry. The waters are carried from the Nile by slaves. They bath to induce fer-tility.

After the bath, Helena and Berenice are dressed by their handmaid-ens for the wedding. The wedding banquet is at the palace. As is the custom, veils hide the young women's faces. The banquet is a splendid display of King Ptolemy's wealth. He has made good on his promise to pay for everything. Flowers are everywhere, along with music, dancing, and plenty of food. Both couples wear crowns of garlands. After dinner, King Ptolemy takes Helena and Berenice from the royal family table to a special table where Archi and Euergetes sit. Taking the women, one in each hand, he leads them to their grooms. Each groom takes his bride's hand from King Ptolemy, lifts the veil, and kisses her. The music and dancing resumes for a couple more hours.

Late into the evening, the king leads both couples and a procession of wedding guests outside the palace. Helena and Berenice climb up into their chariots which have been decorated with flowers. At first Archi takes the reins from the groomsman but realizes he does not know how to drive a chariot. He hands them over to a smiling Helena. Euergetes never attempts to take the reins, deferring to the better driv-er, his new wife, Berenice. The royal family and wedding guests follow the chariots on foot, bearing gifts. In the procession, Queen Arsinoe and her ladies-in-waiting carry torches to light the way to the dock where the royal barge waits to take the couples to their palace on the Nile. The flames of the torches, the sound of the music, and the danc-ing are intended to frighten away evil spirits. All along the dock is a Greek cohort honor guard. As the happy couples approach the dock,

Ptolemy barks out a command, and the honor guards extend their spears overhead to form an arch.

"Welcome into the Ptolemy family, brother Archi," says Euergetes as he hugs the protesting Archi.

As the couples climb aboard the royal barge, the wedding quests shower them with fruit and nuts symbolizing fertility and prosperity. The Royal Family and wedding guests proceed up the gangplank, and deposit their gifts on the barge. The gifts include vases and baskets filled with greenery, pots, furniture, jewelry, combs, and perfumes. After the Royal Family, the members of the Museum follow with their gifts. The gifts include all sorts of handmade mechanical devices, books of poetry, maps and other assorted academic gifts. Finally, everyone is back on the dock, and the royal barge sets sail up the Nile.

CHAPTER SEVENTEEN

(1499, Cesare's Campaign Headquarters)

A servant enters, interrupting Leonardo, and announces that supper is ready. Cesare stands, and motions for Leonardo to join him in the next room. The meal is a common meal but still rich considering Cesare is fighting a war in the field. Leonardo admires the skill of the cook who must labor under these conditions to satisfy a Duke, especially the Captain-General of the Papal Army.

Arranged on a table more elaborate than lunch are ravioli stuffed with capon breast, cheese, and herbs lightly cooked in a saffron broth. There is also duck and various side dishes—plenty of vegetable dishes for Leonardo. The baker made pannetone—sweet egg bread flavored with raisins and citron. Leonardo is disappointed to see the same Madeira wine that was served at lunch. It must be one of Cesare's favorites. Once they start to eat, Leonardo continues his story about Archi.

Ω

(247 BCE, in Alexandria)

As the Royal Engineer, Archimedes designs new defenses for Alexandria. An early warning system of signal towers using fires and mirrors is constructed along Egypt's borders. Signal ships extend the network to the horizon at sea. No army or fleet approaches Alexandria undetected. It has the added advantage of alerting local merchants that cargo ships and caravans are approaching. The fleet, with many ships modeled after the Syracusia, is greatly expanded. Work is begun on the new canal. The next three years are happy ones for Helena and Archi. Helena is constantly at Archi's side taking notes, and working on his drawing and plans.

As members of the royal family, Helena and Archi have an open invitation to dinner in the palace. One night during dinner, Euergeter arrives with a Roman officer, and begins to make introductions.

"Berenice, may I present the ambassador from Roma, Consul Marcus Claudius Marcellus. Berenice is my wife, Queen of Egypt and Cyrene."

Berenice turns and extends her hand to the good looking young man before her. He is clean shaven with short hair but in spite of the causal atmosphere, he is wearing the dress uniform of a Roman officer, complete with helmet and sword. Behind him stands another Roman officer who turns out to be Marcus' translator. As the interpreter translates Euergetes' introduction, Marcus chuckles. As he takes Berenice's hand, he turns toward Euergeter, and in poor Greek says, "You honor me, King Euergeter. I am just an ambassador. I am much too young to be considered for consul. However, I would have known your wife from the stories I have been told by visitors to Alexandria. Even in Roma her beauty is legendary."

Marcus waits for his interpreter to finish before kissing Berenice's hand.

"And you, sir, are also a liar, but I will take that remark as a compliment," replies Berenice. She watches for a reaction as the interpreter translates her words. Marcus smiles and nods his head.

"And this is Archimedes of Syracuse, my Royal Engineer."

Upon hearing the name, Marcus does not wait for the translation.

"Yes, I have heard of your work. Syracuse is a good ally of Roma's. How is King Hieron?"

Through the interpreter, Archi replies, "I have not been home in some time but I understand he is well. His wife, Queen Philistis pasted away recently."

"I was not aware of that. Anyway, I have several letters from scholars in Roma for you. When word got out that I was coming to Alexandria, I was swamped by scholars asking me to give you messages. You are popular in Roma."

Euergeter continues the introductions as the interpreter translates, "And this is Princess Helena of Cyrene, Berenice's sister and Archimedes' wife."

"Of course, I should have guessed. Beauty runs in the family."

"My, my, my, you are full of flattery tonight," says Helena.

"It comes with the responsibilities of an ambassador, I am afraid."

"How did you manage to be appointed ambassador at such a young age?" asks Helena.

"He is a hero in the war against Carthage," interjects Euergeter as he leads Marcus to another table.

The next day, Archi and Helena are reclining at dinner in the palace with Berenice and Euergeter when a Greek guard interrupts them.

"Sire, you had better come at once to your father's bedchamber. We fear something is wrong. He asked to be awaken for dinner but we cannot wake him."

Euergeter jumps up, kicks off his sandals, and sprints barefooted down the hall to the king's bedchamber. Archi, Helena, and Berenice follow as quickly as they can. At the king's bedroom door, Euergeter rushes by several guards who are milling about looking inside. Two of Ptolemy's aides are at his side trying to wake him with loud voices and gentle shakes. Euergeter takes his father's wrist, and feels fruitlessly for a pulse. Archi feels the old king's forehead, and bends down to listen for a breath. Ptolemy's body is cool and lifeless. Euergeter drops the wrist, and straightened up.

"King Ptolemy is dead. His body is cold so he must have died over an hour ago."

Turning to the captain of the guards, "Has anyone been in here in the last few hours?"

"No, sire. The king came in alone. No one else has entered or left all afternoon."

"Go find the court physician." Then to one of the aides, "Go find Queen Arsinoe."

Helena volunteers, "I will go too."

Euergeter motions for everyone except Archi to leave the bedroom, and closes the doors, leaving them alone with the body.

"Archi, I fear that my father was murdered by someone. He was in good health. Look around and see what he was drinking or eating."

Picking up a piece of meat from the table, "I think he was eating this."

"I doubt that it was poisoned."

"Why not?"

Euergeter points to King Ptolemy's dog, Peritas, lying on a pillow in the corner of the room. "My father used his dog as a taster. He always gave the dog the first bite of food. If that meat was poisoned, the dog would be dead too."

"Interesting!" Archi points to a wine cup, "There!"

Euergeter picks it up, and smells the contents, "We need to test this wine."

They both look at the dog. Archi, hands the meat to Euergeter who takes it, dips it in the wine, and tosses it on the pillow near Peritas. Peritas sniffs it, and eats it in one gulp. After a few minutes, Peritas closes his eyes. His breath becomes very shallow, and finally stops. Euergeter tries to wake the dog, but Peritas is dead.

"I suspect it is hemlock."

"Interesting! Greek?" asks Archi.

"Not necessarily. The Egyptians use hemlock too," replies Euergeter.

"It would have to be someone close to the king, someone he would trust," Archi points out.

"Don't say a word about this yet. Let's see how things unfold."

As Archi and Euergetes stand watching Peritas, the king's personal physician enters the bedchamber followed by the captain of the guard and one of the aides. The physician feels Ptolemy's neck for a pulse, then opens one eyelid, and looks into the eye.

Turning toward Euergeter, "Sire, King Ptolemy is dead."

"How? Why?" asks Euergeter.

"It appears that he died peacefully in his sleep of old age. He would have been sixty three this year."

Archi raises one eyebrow, and glances toward Euergeter who is pretending to believe the doctor.

The other aide rushes into the room, "Come quickly! The Queen is dead."

Euergeter turns toward one of the guards, "Stay here with my father. Don't let anyone touch the body. The rest of you come with me."

Euergeter races down the hall following the aide with the guards trying to keep up. The physician and the others follow close behind. The aide leads everyone to a courtyard below the grand balcony. Helena is kneeling beside Arsinoe's body which is in a pool of blood.

With tears steaming down her checks, Helena says, "We found her here, like this."

The physician kneels down, and begins to examine the body. Standing up, the royal physician announces, "The Queen is dead. She must have fallen or jumped off the balcony. Her skull is fractured. I think she jumped off the balcony in her grief. She probably found Ptolemy in his bed, dead, and she killed herself."

At that pronouncement Euergeter strikes the physician in the face so hard that the physician falls to ground. Euergeter jumps on top of him trying to choke him. The commander of the guard pulls Euergeter off the physician.

Euergeter commands, "Seize him!"

It is an unnecessary command since the commander already has the physician by the throat. Two guards grab hold of his arms. Euergeter points down with one finger, and the guards force the helpless doctor to his knees. Euergeter takes the commander's sword, and places the tip down on the physician's shoulder just behind the collar bone.

"Euergeter! He should have a trial," shouts Archi.

"This is a trial. I am the judge and executioner," replies an angry Euergeter.

"Do you know this type of wound?" Euergeter asks the physician.

With trembling lips the physician answers. "Yes."

"A stab wound here is always fatal. The blood gushes out, and cannot be stopped. Death is quick."

"I know, but why me?"

"Berenice, Helen, what do you say about the queen's death?"

Berenice laughs, "She never had a great love for her brother. Not like that. She would rather rule as the widow Queen of Alexandria. When I saw the King dead, she was the first person I suspected. She never would have killed herself."

"She told me so herself," adds Helena. "She only loved him as a brother. Never as a husband."

"We know that my father was poisoned, and now we know that you did it," says Euergeter. "You are going to die. If you confess, and tell me who put you up to this, you will die quickly. If you do not tell me what I want to know, you will die a slow and painful death."

Euergeter pushes down on the sward until blood starts to flow a little.

"Yes! Yes! I did it." yells the doctor.

"Who put you up to this?"

"Laodice!"

At the sound of the name, Euergeter grabs the hilt with two hands, and thrusts the sword downward into the physician's chest. Blood squires up and onto Euergeter's tunic. Helena turns into Archi's chest to hide her eyes while Berenice watches. The physician lets out groan, and slumps to the ground, dead.

"King Ptolemy was wrong," whispers Berenice to Helena behind her hand. "Euergeter does have enough backbone."

Servants pick up the queen's body, and take it to Ptolemy's bedroom. Euergeter and Archi follow the servants while Helena and Berenice walk back to the throne room.

"Why were you crying over Arsinoe's body?" asks Berenice. "Those two were not innocent people. The evil they did has come back to kill them."

"She was good to me. But I will shed no tears over King Ptolemy."

A few minutes later the four are in the throne room.

"How did you know?" Berenice asks Euergeter.

"Archi and I took wine from a cup in the king's bedroom. We dipped a piece of meat in it, and feed it to Peritas. In just a few minutes, Peritas was dead.

"That confirms that the king was poisoned, and the queen killed," says Archi.

"What?" yells Berenice.

"You killed Peritas!" screams Helena. "He was a good dog, Why did you have to kill him?"

"We had to be sure," replies Euergeter.

"Don't you think there has been enough killing for one day?" yells Berenice as she rushes out of the room followed by Helena.

After a moment of silence, a remorseful Archi says, "I guess we did not have to kill poor Peritas."

"No Archi, we had to be sure, and there was no time to test the wine on another animal. Besides, the Egyptians would entomb the dog with King Ptolemy anyway. The women are more upset about the death of the dog than they are about the death of my father and step mother. That is odd, don't you think?"

"Who is Laodice?" ask Archi.

"Ah, yes," says Euergeter as he sits down on his throne. "Laodice was once Queen of Antioch. As you may know, Ptolemy gave my older sister, Berenice Syra, to Antiochus in marriage as part a peace treaty. At the time, Antiochus was married to Laodice. In the terms of the treaty, Antiochus was forced to repudiate her. He settled by giving her a vast territory and a large sum of money. However, she was very angry about it."

"Interesting! She must still be angry."

A frantic Conon rushes into the room.

"I just heard that King Ptolemy is dead and the queen too."

Conan stops when he sees the blood all over Euergeter' tunic. "Are you wounded?" he asks.

"It's not my blood. It's true! The king was poisoned, and the queen thrown off the grand balcony. The physician did it," says Euergeter. "It is his blood you see. I avenged my father's death."

"Shall I disband the Museum? I can tell everyone to leave tonight. We can meet in Athens."

"I think that the Library and Museum will be all right. No harm will come to the scholars. There is no immediate danger," replies Euergeter.

The next day, Archi decides to talk to Euergeter to determine what happened, and what he can do to help. He finds King Euergeter in the throne room with ambassador Marcus.

Looking up as Archi enters, Euergeter says, "Oh good, you are here. I was going to send for you."

"Sire, have you learned any more about your father's murder?"

"Archi, sit down. This will come as a shock. Marcus was sent here to warn us. However, the assassins acted too soon. Either that or Marcus' arrival prompted them to act swiftly. For some time we have been at peace with Antiochus of Syria. Now, Marcus has informed me that Antiochus died a few weeks ago."

"It's true," adds Marcus through his interpreter. "And what's more, we suspect he was also poisoned."

"We think that Laodice had Antiochus and my father poisoned in revenge for being thrown out of Syria. If what Marcus tells me is true, then my sister's life is in danger. She has a son who should become king but he is still very young. The whole situation is very tenuous. I have sent an envoy to find out what is going on. Meanwhile, we must make the army and fleet ready. If my sister or my nephew are harmed or killed, I will march on Antioch."

"Interesting! What must be done first?"

"I will have a council of war as soon as I hear from the envoy. Marcus has offered me a treaty with Roma if we must make war against Antioch. I will leave my wife as head of state in my absence."

"Yes, sire."

"Meanwhile, we are all in grave danger. If Laodice was brave enough to kill my father in his own bedchamber at the risk of war between Syria and Alexandria, then she must be prepared for war. There was great planning in this double murder. I think she would not hesitate to kill me, my wife, or Helena."

"Helena? Why Helena?"

"If I am killed, Berenice becomes the sole ruler of Egypt and Cyrene. If she is killed, Helena would become queen because I do not have heirs yet. We need to separate Berenice and her sister. Archi, I think you should take Helena to Syracuse. The death of my father makes it clear that even in this palace, no one is safe. Syracuse has been at peace for a long now. It is safer there. If anything happens to Bernice and me, Helena will be queen."

"But what of my work here?"

"I think that it is developed far enough that my engineers can complete the rest. You need to go home with your wife, and start a family of your own."

"Yes, it has been a while since I was home. I think you are right. I will make the arrangements."

Helena and Archi begin planning to return to Syracuse. While reclining at dinner, Helena asks, "Archi, I have many slaves and servants. How many shall I bring with me to Syracuse?"

"Syracuse has not been at war for a long time. There are very few slaves there, just servants who are free men and women. I have never owned a slave, and I don't care to. I do not like the idea of owning another human being."

"What shall I do with all my slaves?"

"Set them free. Bring just the servants you will need but free all your slaves."

"Archi, you are right. I will do it."

Helena consults with the slave master, and the next day all the slaves and servants are gathered to hear what Helena and Archi have to say. Many have heard rumors about going to Syracuse. The slave master raps his walking staff for silence. It is the same staff that he has used in the past to discipline disobedient slaves.

Once everyone is silent, Helena says, "I know all of you must wonder what is going on since the death of King Ptolemy and Queen Arsinoe. It appears that war is imminent. If there is a war, Archi and I will go to live in Syracuse where we will be safe. We cannot take all of you. Therefore, I am setting you all free."

The pronouncement impacts the slaves like a storm. Many slaves fall to their knees, and beg not to be set free. Others demand to know what they have done that was so wrong that they are to be turned out into the streets in this manner. Some stare in disbelief. A few of the women begin to pull their hair shouting, "What will become of us?"

The slave master raps his staff several times to silence the pandemonium. After everyone is silent Archi says to Helena, "This is hardly the reaction I thought we would have."

"They are like frightened children, thinking we are throwing them into the streets," replies Helena. Then to the slaves, "We are not turning you out into the streets. Those of you who want to return to your homes may do so. We will give you some money, and arrange for your safe passage. Those who want to stay here will be paid a fair wage for your labor as servants. Some of you we will ask to go with us to Syracuse. We won't force anyone to go. I will find work in the palace for those who stay behind. No one will be forced out of the palace."

Helena's words are met with laughing, crying, and dancing. The former slaves rush up to kiss Helena's feet or say thank you. Many volunteer to go to Syracuse. Over the next few days, Helena draws up a list of the servants she will need in Syracuse.

Ω

Two weeks later, Conon finds Archi in the Mathematics Hall.

"Archi, you have a visitor."

Archi turns to see a grinning Barnacle standing beside Conon. He runs over to Barnacle, and hugs him, a practice he has learned from Conon.

"It is good to see you, my old friend."

A somewhat shocked Barnacle replies, "You are a pleasant sight for these old eyes yourself."

Monte R. Anderson

"So what is new in Syracuse and with you? It has been a long time."

"Well, I am now building ships like the Syracusia. When I heard that old King Ptolemy had died, I thought you might want to return home. I came to pick you up."

"Interesting! Yes, King Euergeter has asked me to take Helena to Syracuse to protect her. Alexandria may soon go to war with Syria."

Barnacle continues, "King Hieron is most eager for your return. He wants you as his Royal Engineer and Chief Advisor again. He made his son, Gelo, co-ruler. You have been away for nearly three years. How about you and Helena, any children yet?"

"No, not yet. I am sure that when we do, you will hear about before I do."

All three men laugh.

"Well, I must tend to my business, and see my wife," says Barnacle. "I will return tonight to update you on all the news back home. We can finalize the plans for your trip back to Syracuse."

Barnacle turns and walks down the hall.

Ω

A few days later the envoy returns from Syria, and Euergeter calls a council of war. The news is not good. Euergetes' sister and nephew have both been murdered – killed outright. The council decides to march on Antioch as soon as the army and fleet are ready. Euergeter tells Archi to leave for Syracuse with Helena as soon as possible. Helena decides to ask only a dozen servants, some Greek, some Egyptian, to go with her to Syracuse. All those she asks agree to go.

Berenice and Helena walk into the temple of Isis. At the altar, Berenice takes a pair of scissors, cuts off a lock of her hair, and places it on the altar. She and Helena pray for the safe return of Euergeter from the war.

A few days later, a servant informs Berenice that the lock of hair has been stolen. Berenice rushes to the temple to see for herself, and finds the lock of hair gone. She is furious. It is impossible to find the thief because there are no clues.

Later that night, Helena finds Conon in the Museum.

"Conon, you must do something!"

A startled Conon asks, "About what?"

"About the missing lock of Berenice's hair."

"Yes, I have heard about it. I fear there is nothing to be done. Every man in the city would give anything for a lock of her hair. It would bring the owner good luck. There are too many suspects."

"I don't care about that. Berenice is so angry that she might do something rash. Euergeter considers it a bad omen, and is so depressed he hardly comes out of the palace for fear of his life. He is afraid to avenge the murder of his father and sister. If you don't do something, the war with Syria will be lost before it has begun."

"Oh my! But why me? What have I got to do with any of this?"

"I don't know but I know you can think of something. You know that Euergeter admires the sciences and all the scholars. He trusts you. He will believe almost anything you say, if it believable. Think of something! Use your influence with Euergeter to end this crisis. Do something!"

"All right. Let me think on it"

Later the next day, Conon meets with Callimachus to concoct a plan.

Ω

A few days later, Conon and Callimachus rush into the throne room where Euergeter and Berenice are holding court.

"We have found it! We have found it!" shouts Conon.

"Found what?" asks Euergeter.

"The lock of Berenice's hair," says Callimachus.

"This better not be a joke."

"No! No! Of course not," answers Conon. "The lock of hair is not missing. It was taken by the gods, probably Isis or Aphrodite. Every night I gaze at the stars, and look at the constellations. Last night I discovered a new constellation. It is the lock of hair. It is in the stars. I immediately told Callimachus so that he could witness what I found. I can show you the new constellation tonight, if you like."

"I was so excited," interjects Callimachus, "that I sat right now, and wrote a poem. I call it The Lock of Berenice."

Callimachus slowly reads the poem for all the court. As he reads, Berenice begins to cry while Eueregetes nods his approval.

"What does this mean, Conon?" Euergeter asks.

"It is a good omen, sire. It means that you will return safely from this war. No one can harm you as long as the constellation is among the stars."

At that news, Berenice jumps out of her chair, runs to Conon, and hugs him. It is the first time Berenice has hugged Conon, and he treasures the moment. Euergeter is right behind her, and also hugs Conon and Callimachus. Conon and Callimachus leave the throne room quite pleased with themselves.

The next day Euergeter leads a vast army toward Antioch as a ship carrying Archi and Helena sails free of the harbor for Syracuse.

CHAPTER EIGHTEEN

(1499, Cesare's Campaign Headquarters)

"So, did Euergeter use Archimedes' machines to seize Antioch?" asks Cesare.

"Not really. Archimedes' machines were built for defense, and usually were too large to move around. He often needed elephants to make them work. Euergeter did use signal mirrors for command and control. Antioch was sacked and occupied for a time. Euergeter campaigned in Babylonia for the next five years until he had to returned to Alexandria to put down dissidents who were causing trouble."

"So, Conon and Callimachus were right after all when they said that Euergeter would not be harmed in battle when they claimed to discover Berenice's hair in the stars."

"It certainly seemed to be true."

"What about his navy with the large ships?"

"Well, it turns out that the great size of the ships was a disadvantage in the shallow waters near the shore and coastal areas where most of the sea battles took place. Euergeter fought a great naval battle off Andros and lost."

Cesare protests, "But Leonardo, I am interested in the machines that Archimedes invented, not all the details of his life. I would also like to know how he defended Syracuse against the Roman army and navy. There might be something there we can use."

"Yes, sire. Archimedes formulated all the tactics that Syracuse eventually used against the Romans. Shortly after Archimedes returned to Syracuse, Rome won a decisive naval battle against Carthage near the Aegadian Islands off the western coast of Sicily which ended the war. The Roman terms were severe. Carthage had to evacuate Sicily, and surrender it to Rome with all adjacent islands. Rome demanded an immense indemnity paid over ten years. Carthage also agreed not to make war in the future against King Hieron or his allies. Hieron's territory was expanded, and Syracuse's independence as a free city was guaranteed. Messana and a few other cities were likewise made free cities allied with Rome. The rest of Sicily came under Roman jurisdiction administered by a governor sent annually from Rome.

"The years after Archimedes and Helena returned to Syracuse were relatively peaceful years. Let me summarize that period, and bring us up to the point that caused Syracuse to switch their allegiance from Rome to Carthage.

"Archimedes and Helena were welcomed back to Syracuse, and initially set up house in the palace. Immediately, the women of the royal family tried to involve Helena in various intrigues in palace politics. But after her experiences in Alexandria, Helena would have nothing to do with politics. Out of frustration, she asked Archimedes to build them a home away from the palace.

"The profound influence Helena had on Archimedes prompted him to invent many useful devices to help the people of Syracuse. Seeing that women of Syracuse were not as educated as those in Alexandria, Helena started a school for girls where she taught reading, writing, poetry, dance, and many other subjects. She would not allow the children of the nobility to attend. For many years Archimedes worked on the walls and defenses of the city. In addition to being the chief advisor and engineer, Archimedes was the teacher of all the children of the royal family.

"In time, Helena gave birth to a daughter she named Arsinoe in memory of the first Arsinoe of Alexandria who had been tortured, and died in exile. Both Helena and Archimedes became very popular with the people of Syracuse, peasants and nobility alike. Eventually, Archimedes became the king's closest friend and confidant. King Hieron's son and co-ruler, Gelo, had a son named Hieronymos."

"Did Archimedes and Helena ever return to Alexandria?" asks Cesare.

"No. But, of course, Archimedes continued to write to Conon and the other scholars. Berenice continued to race chariots. The year after Helena left Alexandria, Berenice won the Nemean Games, six year later, the Isthmia Games. The war with Syria lasted five years, as I have said. Euergeter and Berenice had a son. Euergeter reined for 24 years and died. His son was crowned King of Alexandria. Berenice was poisoned by her son the very next year."

Ω

(216 BCE, Syracuse, Sicily)

Archimedes walks to the gymnasium to observe the training of soldiers. The soldiers practicing with wooden foils against posts planted in the ground so that they stick out about the height of a man. They strike the post with the foil and shield; first from the front at the head and neck, then the sides, and finally at the hamstrings and legs from the rear. The shields are made of wicker and hardwood so that they weigh twice the weight of a real shield. Other soldiers practice throwing the pilum, a type of spear, at wicker shields attached to the posts. Archimedes sees Hippokrates, a grandson of King Hieron, sparring with his brother, Epikyoles. They are using the wooden foils but have real shields. The brothers are called Hippo and Epi. Archi has been their teacher since their childhood.

After several rounds, Hippo takes a break to refreshen, and to drink some water.

Seeing Archi watching, Hippo asks, "Teacher, what do you think of my swordsmanship?"

"Probably less than you do."

Laughing, "Do you find fault with my techniques?"

"Certainly!"

"What do you think I am doing wrong?"

"You don't use your head."

"Use my head? I use my head. Whenever I am close enough I strike my opponent with my helmet."

"That is not what I mean. I mean to say, you use your muscles, and do not try to out smart your opponent. You try to overpower your opponent. If your opponent is more powerful, you will lose."

"In all of Syracuse only five soldiers can beat me, and they are the best in Sicily."

"Is that so? Even I could beat you."

"You, Teacher? I think not. You are not trained, and are surely too old."

"I do believe the Teacher has challenged you to a duel," laughs Epikyoles.

"Lend me a shield, and come here at this same time tomorrow. I will duel with you."

"Very well, Teacher, I accept your challenge," says Hippo.

Hippo lets Archi choose from several shields. Archi examines each shield until he finds one that suits his purpose.

"Take my wooden sword, Teacher. You will need it to practice."

"No, the shield is enough. I won't need the sword."

"Oh, the gods preserve us! Archimedes intends to defeat you with only a shield," exclaims Epi.

Archi picks up the shield, and heads toward home.

After Archi is out of hearing, Hippo asks, "What do you suppose he is up to?".

"I don't know," answers Epi. "He is not a proud man, but he does not make idle boasts either. I guess we will see tomorrow."

That night Archi instructs one of the servants to polish the shield.

Later at supper, Helena asks, "Is it true? You are going to fight Hippokrates?"

"Yes, it is true. It is only a practice duel. I want to teach him a lesson."

"Are you crazy? He is the grandson of the king. If you should strike him, the king could have you arrested. He is also a young man, and you are not. You could easily be hurt or even killed. And what if you should win? You would embarrass him in front of his peers. You will make an enemy of him. There is no way you can win in this situation. Why did you challenge him?"

"What are you two talking about?" asks Arsinoe from across the table.

"Your father has challenged the king's grandson, Hippokrates, to a practice duel."

"Really? When?"

"Midday tomorrow at the gymnasium," replies Archi.

"Abba, I did not know that you knew how to sword fight."

"He doesn't!" interjects Helena. "That is the whole point. He is finally crazy. We will all be arrested, and thrown in prison."

"I don't think so," says Archi.

"Hippokrates is so good looking. I am going to watch. Are you coming too, mother?"

"Of course I am coming. Someone has to talk some sense into these two idiots."

"Hippokrates is called Hippo by all the girls. Do you know why?"

Helena sits up, and stares at her daughter, "Hippo? That means horse. Is it because he is as tall as a horse or as stong as one? Does he smell like a horse?"

"No mother, it refers to a different part of his anatomy." Somewhat shocked, Helena asks, "How would you know?"

"Oh come mother, it is not big secret. Some of my girl friends have brothers that go to the gymnasium. All of us girls know which of the boys have big..."

"Stop!" yells Helena. "Archi, do you hear your daughter?"

"What?" asks Archi, his thoughts interrupted. "I was not paying attention. What did she say?"

"She said," yells Helena to her husband, rather annoyed. "She is attracted to Hippo because of the size of his brains."

"Really? Interesting!"

"Men!" yells Helena as she storms out of the room.

Archi turns to Arsinoe, "What was that all about?"

"I don't really know father."

Arsinoe knew from early childhood that when her father is working on a problem, he does not hear anything said around him.

"Well, I don't know either, but Hippo is very smart. I taught him, you know."

The next day, Archi goes to the gymnasium, followed by his wife and daughter. Hippo is already there with Epi and several other young men. Hippo sees Helena and Arsinoe waiting outside the gymnasium.

"Who is that, Teacher?" asks Hippo.

"I think you know my wife, Helena. The younger one is my daughter, Arsinoe."

"Archi, I think everyone has their clothes on today. Why don't you ask them to come inside?"

"It will only cause problems."

"Nonsense!" says Hippo, signaling to the women to come into the gymnasium.

The gymnasium master immediate starts to stop them but a gesture from Hippo stops him in his tracks. The women come in, and sit down. Both men put on their armor with the aid of some of the athletes present, and Epi gives Archi a wooden sword. Both agree that Epi should serve as referee. When they are ready, he reviews the rules with both men.

The mid-afternoon sun is beating down on the small group as the match begins. Everyone in the gymnasium gathers to watch. Archi looks toward the sun, and then takes a position so that he faces the sun. Hippo takes up a position opposite Archi. At a signal from Epi, the two men begin to circle each other. Hippo darts back and forth looking for an opening. Archi holds his shield up high, and by moving it about, eventually is able to reflect a bright spot of sunlight onto Hippo's face. Blinded and frustrated, Hippo lunges forward with his sword over his head to strike Archi. But Archi dodges to the outside of his swing, and with a back hand swing strikes Hippo in the back of his leg.

Epi immediately stops the match, and looks at Hippo's leg. The spectators in the seats stand up for a better view, debating whether the blow is good or not. Some of the men make wagers on the final outcome with Hippo highly favored to win. Helena closes her eyes, and refuses to watch. Arsinoe can't take her eyes off Hippo. The strike has left a red line on the back of Hippo's leg just above the knee where the leg is not protected. Epi declares Archi the winner of the first match with what would have been a crippling wound.

"All right old man, I was prepared to be merciful but you have left me no choice," growls Hippo.

"You talk too much," says Archi taking up the same position, and projecting a spot of sunlight on Hippo's chest.

As soon as Epi gives the signal, Hippo attacks. Archi shifts the sunlight into his eyes, and this time shifts to his right. Hippo swings blindly hoping to strike Archi. That maneuver puts Archi behind him, and he swings hard, striking Hippo in the back just below his armor. The blow knocks the wind out of Hippo, and he falls to his knees trying to draw in air. Helena and Arsinoe bolt out of their seats, and race toward the combatants, Helena to Archi and Arsinoe to Hippo. Archi drops his shield and sword, and starts toward Hippo but before he can reach him, Arsinoe confronts him.

"You have killed him!" she yells at her father.

She shoves her father so hard that he steps backward, and falls over his shield. Immediately, Helena grabs Arsinoe, and the two women start to fight. The spectators cheer the women on.

Finally getting air into his lungs, Hippo cries out,

"Ahhhhh! I am not killed!"

He turns to see the two women fighting and Archi on the ground.

"Stop!"

"I do think you were killed, brother," says a grinning Epi. Tuning to the stunned crowd, and pointing to Archi, "Archimedes has won the match. Best two out of three."

The crowd cheers. The women stop, and Helena lets go of Arsinoe to help Archi. Arsinoe hurries over to Hippo to see if he is wounded. Hippo extends his arm to pull Archi to his feet.

"Archimedes, you have proven once again that you are the teacher, and that I am but your humble student."

Turning toward mother and daughter, "If I had an army of women such as you two, all the legions of Roma and Carthage would shake with fear. I think you two have caused enough damage for one day. Now leave so that Archi and I can discuss tactics."

Arsinoe hugs Hippo, "Thank the gods you are not hurt."

She sprints out of the gymnasium with her mother in pursuit leaving a very embarrassed Hippo standing in a circle of his peers.

"Usually, it is the victor who gets the maiden's kiss," laughs Epi.

"What were they fighting about?" asks Hippo.

"I told you there would be trouble," answers Archi. "I think Arsinoe likes you, and was afraid that I had killed you."

Laughing, "In a real fight, you would have. Now show me this new technique"

Archi shows Hippo and the others the highly polished shield, and how it could be modified to be even more reflective.

Ω

Over the next week, in Archi' workshop, Archi and Hippo try different shapes on the shield. Arsinoe delights in preparing meals for them much to Helena's disapproval. Finally, a modified rectangular shape that looks like a flat pyramid cut in half in the center of the shield is selected. This shape can capture the sun's rays from nearly any position, and project strong light into an enemy's eyes. Hippo spends another week with Epi perfecting the fighting techniques needed to make it work.

At the end of two weeks, Hippo arranges a demonstration for his father, Adranodoros, commander of army. He fights opponents who have bested him in the past, and defeats them all. He continues to fight several more men, and wins every match. In the end, Adranodoros is convinced, and orders all shields altered to the new shape, and for training to begin at once on its use.

CHAPTER NINTEEN

(1499, Cesare's Campaign Headquarters)

"Why did Syracuse switch from supporting Rome to supporting Carthage? That was a strategic error on their part," says Cesare.

After accepting another glass of wine, Leonardo responds, "Well, there were many parties in Syracuse that did not like the treaty with Rome including some members of the king's own family. But without something happening to change the king's mind, everyone was powerless to act. The change involved Adranodoros, who was the son of King Hieron best friend, Artemidorus. He was commander of the army and son-in-law to King Hieron.

"Sire, if you will recall your history, Carthage sent Hannibal to attack Rome by crossing the Alps. In his first campaign he broke Roman resistance north of the Apennines River. Then he destroyed the Roman army at Lake Trasimene in Etruria. The road to Rome was now open to him. Rome requested two legions from Syracuse; the first time Rome had asked Syracuse to send soldiers anywhere off the Island of Sicily. King Hieron appointed Adranodoros to lead the two legions. Adranodoros took his two sons, Hippo & Epi as legion commanders. King Hieron also appointed Zoippos, another son-in-law, as ambassador to Rome. You could say that the die was cast at Cannae."

"Wait, I know the history of that famous battle," says Cesare, interrupting Leonardo's story. "The Roman army prepared for battle in the Apulian plain, near Cannae. The Romans were commanded by two

Consuls, Varro and Paullus who had been elected on a platform of taking the war to Hannibal. They alternated command of the army every day, a foolish thing to do. Hannibal's army consisted of his own Carthaginians supported by Gauls, Gallic, Iberian Celts, and Numidian cavalry; a total strength around 40,000 men, I believe. The Romans numbered between 70,000 to 80,000 men. Varro was eager to fight Hannibal while Paullus was reluctant to force a battle on terrain chosen by Hannibal. However, since he expected Varro to support him the next day, Paullus supported Varro on the day of battle.

"As the two armies met, the Roman right flank first engaged the Numidian cavalry commanded by Hasdrubal, Hannibal's brother. The more experience Numidian horsemen quickly over powered the Roman citizen legionaries who were more enthusiastic than skilled. Instead of forming ranks in the face of superior force, the Romans panicked, and started to flee. Unfortunately, their backs were to the river, and Hasdrubal forced them into it. Many drowned or scattered, leaving Husdrubal in control of the right flank. Seizing the opportunity, Hasdrubal pushed his attacking cavalry into the rear of the Romans."

"Yes, my Lord, the Roman plan of attack called for a frontal assault led by the two legions from Syracuse. Consul Varro, who was commanding that day, planned to sacrifice the more experienced Syracusan troops to exhaust Hannibal's soldiers before attacking with the main Roman army which was less experienced than the Syracusans. The Syracusans began to severely punish the Celts to their front, pushing them back, and causing many casualties. They used their shields to blind the Celts with tactics developed by Archimedes. However, the Celts fell back in good order without breaking. It was a feint by Hannibal to lure the Romans into a trap, and destroy them.

"Unknowingly, Adranodoros pushed his soldiers on, hoping to force a rout. Hannibal had deployed his veteran Carthaginian heavy infantry on the flanks of the Celts. Even as the Celts were being pushed back, the heavy infantry held their ground. As the Syracusan legions pushed deeper into the Carthaginian front, they were being surrounded by Hannibal's heavy infantry on their flanks and Hasdrubal's cavalry to their rear. The more the Romans pushed in the center the more encircled they became. By the time Varro sensed the trap, it was too late. Just as his center was near the brink of disaster, Hannibal gave the signal for his heavy infantry to attack both flanks, and for Hasdrubal to attack from the rear. As his forces pushed the Romans into a compacted square, Hannibal unleashed his archers and slingers, who had been held in reserve. The results were disastrous for the Romans.

"Consul Varro, who was located near the rear of the army, gathered a few bodyguards, and fled the battlefield through Husdrubal's cavalry who were so busy cutting down every Roman soldier they came to that they let him escape. Zoippos, who was with Varro at the time, escaped with him to Rome. Consul Paullus saw Varro flee the field, and tried to assume command of the army that remained. In the slaughter that followed he was slain by an arrow. So many Roman soldiers were now fleeing that the Carthaginians started cutting their hamstrings to cripple them so they could continue to chase the others, and return later to kill the crippled.

"Adranodoros and his sons were captured, and taken to Hannibal who extracted from them a vow never to fight against Carthage, and in return, he released all the prisoners from Sicily. Adranodoros received a severe leg wound, and was sent back to Syracuse a day ahead of the other Syracusan survivors."

Ω

(216 BCE, Syracuse, Sicily)

Feeling disgraced and depressed, Adranodoros arrives in Syracuse. He goes directly to see the king. In the throne room, sit the king and Archi. Upon seeing Adranodoros, King Hieron rushes to greet his son-in-law.

"Adranodoros, I am so glad to see you! Zoippos came back a few days ago, and said that you had been killed."

"I nearly was. I was captured by Hannibal."

"And your sons?"

"They were captured as well while trying to protect me."

"And all our soldiers? Killed or captured?"

"Mostly killed. They died while fighting bravely. Only about a cohort survived. Hannibal released them, and they should be here in a day or two."

"Released them? Why?"

"He made me take an oath never to fight him again as long as I live. The men too. He said he would kill everyone if we did not swear."

"I understand. You had no choice. A few days ago I thought we lost everyone, and now I discover that some survived."

"But so many died because of me."

"Adranodoros, we have been spared so many times. Fate caught up with us finally. It was ordained by the gods."

"Sire, the battle was decided before it began. Hannibal chose the terrain to defend. He outmaneuvered the Romans on the battlefield. It was a trap, an ingenious tactic of double envelopment. Only Hannibal could think of it, and only the Carthaginian soldiers could execute it. It was brilliant."

"You are wounded I see," says Archi, pointing at Adranodoros' leg.

"I am healing now, thanks to Hannibal's personal physician. I may limp for the rest of my life."

"Adranodoros, the people are filled with grief," says Hieron. "Everyone in Syracuse has lost a family member, many husbands and sons. We have never lost so many men in one battle. Our Sicilian allies are demanding that I arrest you and the other officers. I have never seen this much anger. I fear for your safety. The families still loyal to Carthage want me to renounce my treaty with Roma, and sign a treaty with Carthage. We are on the verge of civil war."

"Sire, you coddle your people. We are at war, and disobedience should be punished."

"Adranodoros, the citizens are still free men," reminds Archi.

Turning toward Archi, "The Carthaginians are unbeatable with Hannibal leading their soldiers. He treated me well. I think the Carthaginians are more civilized than the Romans. Maybe we should sign a treaty with them. But if we wait until they burn Roma, they will dictate terms to us. Sign a treaty now while we still some influence."

"We'll talk politics later. Now tell me of the battle," orders King Hieron.

Adranodoros tells the king everything that had happened including the things his sons had seen after the battle. He tells of the bravery of the soldiers, and how at first they were pushing the Celts back. He explains how the Romans had used them to preserve their own soldiers. He explained how Hannibal had baited the Romans, feigned retreat, and then sprung the trap, boxing in the Romans and their allies. As he tells King Hieron how the river Aufidius ran red with blood, and how bodies were piled five or six deep in places, Hieron begins to weep. He has known battle and death, but never as bad as this. Hieron can hardly bare the news. Tears run down his face at the report of so many brave Syracusans dying. He stands up at one point, and begins to pull out tufts of his hair and to beat his chest. Seeing that the king has heard enough, Adranodoros tells him of the kindnesses shown by Hannibal to himself, his sons, and the prisoners. He talks of watching Hannibal give full military honors to the Roman Consul Paullus who was killed in the battle.

When Adranodoros is finished, King Hieron stands, and weeps openly for several minutes. He drinks a full goblet of wine, wipes his face, and tries to regain his composure. After a few more minutes, he sits down by Adranodoros.

"I am crying like an old woman. I am not the warrior I once was. I am glad that the queen is not alive to hear this.

"You weep for your people, sire," says Archi. "There is no shame in that."

Turning at last to Adranodoros, "Son, the tactics that the Romans used were the same that your father and I used at Cyamosorus when we were fighting the Mamertines. We let the Mamertines destroy the mercenaries. Now, after all these years, the gods have punish me for my treachery," beating his chest.

"No, my Lord. It is all my fault. I should have seen the trap. I should have sensed the treachery of the Romans. I am ashamed of my actions. When I realized that the battle was lost I only tried to save myself and my sons. I should have died on the field with my men. My body should have been carried off on my shield. I have dishonored my family and you. I have dishonored Syracuse."

"Adranodoros, your father was my best friend, even before I was king. We grew up together. We fought side by side against the Carthaginians and the Romans. He was very popular with the people as was I. The election for dictator could have gone either way. He could have been elected dictator. Then he would have been king, and when he died, he would have made you king."

"It was neither his destiny, nor mine," replies Adranodoros. "He told me while I was still young, that he did not want to be dictator or king. He said kings are different from soldiers. Kings are politicians, and are not to be trusted. In turn, they can trust no one. Whoever speaks to a king has some ulterior motive--they want something. Soldiers, on the other hand, deal with truth, loyalty, and trust. They must in order to survive."

"That is true. It was not his destiny, nor yours. But if things had been different, you might have been sitting here hearing this news. If your father were alive and king today, what would he tell you to do?"

"I know what I have to do," replies Adranodoros, placing his hand on the hilt of his sword. "I spared myself this long only so you could hear the truth from someone you could trust."

With tears in his eyes, Hieron says, "Adranodoros, your sword."

Adranodoros takes out his sword, and hands it to the king. By now tears are again flowing down the king's cheeks.

"No, my Lord!" cries Archi.

"This is the hardest decision I have ever made. I wish there was another way."

"May I see my wife first?" asks Adranodoros.

"Adranodoros, she grieved once for you when she thought you had died. Why make her grieve again? She may not want to see you under these conditions. I could give her a message."

"Please tell her that I have always loved her. Tell her that her sons fought bravely, and are not dishonered. They only thought to save me. They are innocent."

"What should we do with your body?" asks Hieron.

"Burn my body, and throw my ashes into the sea so that the stain of my cowardice does not stain the soil or any part of Syracuse."

"It will be done as you have asked. Goodbye, my son."

King Hieron kisses the sword, and hands it hilt first to Adranodoros. Adranodoros walks over to the window to gaze upon Syracuse one last time. He places the point of the sword under his armor so that when he falls on the hilt, the point will pierce his heart. Just as he prepared to fall on his sword, his wife, Damarata, rushes into the throne room, and up to him.

"You are alive! Thank the gods!" shouts Damarata.

"Damarata, let him go. He must fulfill his last duty," King Hieron tells his daughter.

"What do you mean? What last duty?" Damarata asks.

"The King has asked your husband to kill himself," says Archi.

"No! But why? What has he done? Why must he do this?" she asks.

"The people demand it!" shouts Hieron.

"The people demand it? When did you ever care what the people demanded? When Liptines was alive, you told the people what was best for them but now you bend to their will," says Archi.

Shouting at Archi, "He fled the field of battle!"

Archi shouts back, "He was wounded! He had to be carried off the battlefield! You think he was a coward? When was he a coward? When in battle did he ever hesitate to fight? When did he ever not do your bidding. His only thoughts have always been to serve you and his soldiers. "

"That was in the past," says Hieron.

"Was he a coward at Cannae when the Romans sacrificed the Syracusans?" asks Archi. "Was he a coward when he fought until wounded severely in the leg? Was he a coward when he tried to save as many of the prisoners as he could? Was he a coward when he saved his sons, your grandsons? Was he a coward for taking an oath to save the soldiers who had fought bravely but were captured?"

"Hippo and Epi are alive?" asks Damarata in disbelief.

"They are on the way home. They are fine," answers Adranodoros.

"When your grandsons arrive, will you have them kill themselves too?" Archi asks. "And what about the other survivors?"

"Archi, please. It has to be this way," says Hieron.

"No, it doesn't! You are the king. Stop this now!" shouts Damarata. "Don't kill my family! Your family!"

"Damarata, don't!" pleads Adranodoros.

Damarata reaches into Adranodoros' belt seizing his dagger, and tries to stab the king. Adranodoros is quicker, and grabs her round the neck with his forearm.

"Let me go!" she screams.

"Would you kill your king?" asks Adranodoros.

"Yes!"

"Would you kill your father?" asks Hieron.

Damarata collapses to the floor in tears, "No!"

The guards rush in only to be stopped by a hand signal from the king.

"You are both right. It is my decision, not the people's. I am the king. The decision is mine to make. I don't want you to kill yourself, Adranodoros. I need you. The people need you."

"Sire?"

"You heard me. Too many have died already. I need you to command the defenses of the city. Put your sword away."

"Your word is law, Sire."

Damarata and Adranodoros embrace. "Come, husband. I'll take you home."

Adranodoros leans on her and limps as they leave together. The king turns toward Archi. "Thank you, my friend, for saving me from myself. I almost killed my son-in-law. Thank the gods you were here."

"I only asked you to see all the facts before you made a decision. You always make the right decision."

Hieron embraces Archi.

Once Adranodoros bathes and eats, he repeats the entire story for his wife, Damarata.

Damarata says, "I have never liked those Romans. Now they have gone too far. We should never have sided with them. Hannibal will defeat them, and we will be treated as slaves. I have heard rumors that King Phillip of Macedonia will soon join with the Carthaginians."

"Yes, I think you are right."

"Husband, I agree with you. We should side with Carthage. The Romans have never treated Syracuse as an equal."

"Yes, I know, but the king will want to honor his treaty with Roma."

"Perhaps we can change his mind. He ended the treaty with Carthage years ago. He can betray the Romans now."

"How can we make him do this?"

"You should be king or, at least, dictator. The king is old, and is getting feeble."

"Feeble?"

"Yes. You don't see it because you are away fighting battles so much. I see it because I am here every day. His hands tremble, and he spills his wine often. His walk is unsteady now. He must move more slowly to keep from falling. Watch him when he stands. He is stooped over. He has a hard time remembering names and details. I don't think he will live much longer."

"I did not realize. But if he dies, Gelo will be king, and I think he will side with Roma."

"And who would be king when Gelo dies?"

"His son, Hieronymos."

"But who would be king if Gelo died before Hieron dies?

"Then the crown should pass to the next oldest living child." Adranodoros suddenly realizes where his wife is leading him. "That is you!"

"Yes, my dear. Me! I would be queen. I should be queen. With you at my side, we would rule Syracuse and one day the whole of Sicily."

"Do you realize what you are saying?"

"I know exactly what I am saying. Do you understand what I am saying?"

"Are you suggesting that we kill Gelo?"

"If Hieron dies while Gelo is still co-ruler, then Gelo might live for a long time, and the throne will eventually pass to his son. Carthage will defeat Roma and destroy Syracuse before we can do anything. Don't be naive, dear husband, Gelo must die first. My father is already dying and can't live much longer. Then I will be made queen. We must act now to save Syracuse!"

"That would be treason!"

"It was treason when my father and Leptines plotted to put themselves in power, and cheated your father out of the kingship. If your father had wanted to be dictator and not the army commander, he would have been elected king, and now you would be king."

"Damarata, if we do not have the support of the other members of the family, the other noble families of Syracuse would not allow it."

"No one will know. It must look like he died of natural causes."

"Still, we will need support."

"I have been working on this. We can count on support from Harmonia and Themistos and even young Hieronymos as long as he does not know we plan to kill his father, Gelo. Zoippos and Heraclia support Roma. Zoippos was won over ever since he went to Roma. He and Heraclia will seek to be king and queen themselves. They only care about theirselves and not the city. Somehow we must neutralize them."

"We know Hieron and Gelo favor Roma."

Ω

The next day Hippo, Epi, and the other survivors from the battle of Cannae return home.

After talking to Hippo and Epi, King Hieron calls a council of war the next day to decide what course of action to take. In the throne room King Hieron and Gelo sit and listen to the arguments. Zoippos speaks first.

"As you may know, I was at the Battle of Cannae. As our ambassador to Roma, I was at Varro's headquarters when he decided to withdraw, and regroup to protect Roma."

"You mean he fled the battle with his tail between his legs," interrupts Adranodoros.

"It was as I have said," replies Zoippos, glaring at Adranodoros. "While I was in Roma, I took measure of the Romans and their army. Do not be fooled. Roma lost an army at Cannae, yet are raising another. They do not know defeat. They will not give up until Carthage is destroyed. The other tribes and kingdoms that are allied with Roma have not changed their allegiance because they know that Roma will win in the end. Hannibal prevails alone against Roma. He is not getting any support from Carthage, and must live off the land. He is not strong enough to invade Roma itself so he must do battle in the country side. We have always honored our treaties, and I recommend that we continue to do so."

Adranodoros speaks, "I was also at Cannae. We lost many good men that day because the Romans sacrificed our soldiers in order to preserve their own fighting strength. We mean nothing to them. They will only use us. On the other hand, my sons and I were able to observe the Carthaginian general, Hannibal, up close. He is young. He is a brilliant general. He will defeat the Romans eventually. He is also more deserving of our respect. He had his personal physician tend to our wounds, and allowed all the prisoners to go home. The Carthaginians are more civilized than the Romans. The Romans would have crucified everyone. They are barbaric. Carthage will prevail. We would be wise to denounce our treaty with Roma, and sign a treaty with Carthage. I believe King Philip of Macedonia will soon join Carthage against Roma. More cities will follow his lead. We should not wait."

King Hieron speaks, "What the Romans did is exactly what I have done in the past, and I would have done if I were the Roman commander on the battlefield that day."

A murmer runs through the throne room from those present who lost sons in the battle.

The King continues, "We did not expect any special treatment. We have no illusions about warfare. We cannot fault them for the way they deployed our troops."

King Gelo then speaks, "Hannibal is a smart general. He knows that these acts of mercy towards you and our soldiers will help him win support against Roma. The kindness Hannibal showed you and your sons was done to persuade you to convince us to quit our treaty with Roma, and ally with Carthage. If King Philip of Macedonia enters the war, then King Ptolemy of Alexandria will ally with Roma. The fact is; Hannibal is isolated in Italy. Eventually, he will run out of supplies, money, and men."

King Hieron speaks again, "We have decided that we will continue to support Roma, and fulfill our obligations. Thank you for your advice. Adranodoros, we wish to talk to you and Hippo after the war Council. Dismissed!"

Everyone bows, and leaves the throne room. Adranodoros approaches the throne.

"While we have heard your recommendations, and not ruled in your favor we are still concerned about our treaty with Roma," says Gelo. "Our treaty does not state anywhere that we must send troops outside of Sicily nor does it say we cannot. We think we can make a strong argument that the language implies that sending troops to fight in Italy is not covered by our treaty, and therefore we will not send more troops. Roma needs our support so I do not think they will object. At the same time, we need to rebuild our army to cover our losses. We fear an attack against the city so we need to redouble our efforts to defend the city.

"We have jointly decided that you will remain as commander of the army," continues King Hieron. "Hippo, you will work with Archi, and rebuild our defenses,".

"Thank you, your Highnesses. Your word is law," Hippo says while bowing.

Hieron continues, "Now with this business concluded, I understand that you intend to marry Archi's daughter, Arsinoe?"

"Yes, sire."

"Well do so quickly but do it privately. The city is full of grief and anger. Many people lost sons and brothers at Cannae. They resent me, my family, and your family. I think this wedding may cause a riot. You have my blessing."

"Your word is law, sire."

Hippo and Arsinoe are married in a private ceremony at the palace. The guards turn away an angry mob at the palace gates.

CHAPTER TWENTY

(216 BCE, Syracuse, Sicily)

A couple of months later, Damarata goes to the throne room to talk to King Gelo.

Genuflecting very low, "King Gelo, may I approach the throne?"

Somewhat surprised by her gesture, Gelo says, "Come, sister, why so formal? You know you are always welcomed here."

"Thank you, brother, but after what I have been through these last few months, I am not sure that I am still welcomed into your presence."

"Nonsense! We are family. Besides, you have done nothing wrong."

"Thank you. You are always so kind to me and my sons."

"Yes. Now, what can I do for you? You have only to ask."

"You and King Hieron have been so kind to me, and restored honor to my husband. I want to thank you. If it would not offend you, we have a fine wine cellar." Holding out a bottle of wine, "I know this wine is one of your favorites. Please accept it as a small token of our appreciation from my husband and me."

"Of course it does not offend me. Good wine has no master. I will share this with father tonight."

"That won't be necessary. I will give him a bottle when I have an opportunity. Save this one for yourself after dinner."

"All right, I will do that. Thank you."

Backing out of the room, Damarata says, "Once again, you honor me by accepting this small gift."

The next morning, Gelo is found dead in his bed apparently having died in his sleep. Hieron takes the death of his son very hard. Normally it would have been a grand funeral but since Syracuse is still mourning the loss of so many of its sons, the funeral is somewhat subdued.

The day after the funeral, Hieron summons Archi to the throne room.

"You sent for me, your Highness?"

"Archi, my good friend. Thank you for coming." Gesturing for Archi to sit beside him, "I still cannot believe that Gelo is dead. Children are supposed to out live their parents. Now he is gone. I can't believe this is happening. I have lost favor with the gods."

"Yes, sire. It is a shock to all of us. He was a good king."

"Yes, we prepared him well, you and I. Now what must we do?"

"Sire, you have many good years left."

"No, Archi, you know that is not true. I am ninety-one years old. I grow feebler every day. Look at this." King Hieron holds out his trembling hands.

"Yes, sire, I have seen the tremors."

"I have had it for the last few years but it is getting worse lately, harder to control. I try to hide it. My memory is not so good either. I don't feel well. I don't think I will live much longer. I have seen many years, most of them in peace."

"Yes, sire. You have had a long and prosperous reign. You will be long remembered. We have had fifty years of peace."

"But if I die now, who will be king?"

"I think you know. Had Gelo died after you, his son, Hieronymos would have assumed the throne. Since you and Gelo shared the throne, the kingship reverts back to you, and when you die, your eldest daughter will become queen."

"What is your opinion of Damarata's abilities to rule Syracuse? Be honest with me as you always have been. I need your advice now more than I ever had in the past. The fate of Syracuse depends on who will rule after me."

"Sire, I have taught all your children since they were old enough to walk. I think I know their minds as well as their hearts. We had always assumed Gelo would be king after you so his training was the best. Your two daughters are more involved in palace politics and petty intrigues. They both lack the skills needed to rule Syracuse."

"I agree with your assessment. My daughters would require many advisors to guide them, but I fear they will not listen. Damarata and her husband favor a treaty with Carthage. If she becomes queen, that would end the peace, and drag Syracuse into a war with Roma. Heraclia, on the other hand, favors the treaty with Roma but I don't trust her husband, Zoippos. He is ruthless and self-centered. I fear that he would plunder the treasury. My daughters do not care about the people of Syracuse. They look down their noses at the citizens. What of Nereis, Gelo's wife? She is of royal blood."

"Yes, sire, but she is not part of your family. If she marries, the kingship would pass out of your family entirely. Furthermore, she is not from Syracuse. I don't think the nobility would find her acceptable. Since you were co-ruling with Gelo, she is no longer a queen."

"Should we have open elections?"

"I don't think there is a clear majority. Elections could start a civil war."

"I am afraid so. We are on the verge of civil war now. That leaves my grandson, Hieronymos."

"Yes, sire. He is very young but very bright. He has the look of a king. With good advisors, he will learn to be a good king."

"I think you are right. Thanks for being honest with me. I will die in peace knowing there are advisors like you who will guide the future of Syracuse. I will appoint Hieronymos to succeed me. I will appoint suitable advisors for him."

"Sire, if I might be so bold as to suggest that you crown him as co-ruler before you die. It will prevent problems that might arise if you die before Hieronymos is made king. You can guide him for the remainder of your years. If you live a while longer, he will be older and more mature."

"Again, you are correct. I will do so as soon as we select the advisors. There is much to learn in many different areas. He will need more than one guardian. Each guardian would have an area of expertise. But there must be a head guardian to resolve differences. But who?"

"I suspect that your Highness already has Adranodoros in mind."

"Archi, you are so wise. I did have him in mind but I wasn't sure that was the right decision until now. He is strong, and Hieronymos will need a strong hand. Help me to pick the others."

"Sire, I don't think you should appoint Adranodoros as the head guardian. His is very much in favor of a treaty with Carthage. I fear what he might do. You might consider making Nereis the head guardian. She has no loyalty to anyone except Hieronymos."

"I have to appoint Adranodoros. His father was my best friend. Without his father's help, I would not be king. I almost had Adranodoros kill himself. I owe him this much. He will do what is right for Syracuse, despite his personal feelings. I will have him take an oath to abide by our treaties."

"Very well, sire. I hope you are right. As for the others, Zoippos is experienced in politics with Roma. He is a little hot headed; but if he is ambassador to Roma and living in Roma, he will not cause much trouble here. I could be responsible for the sciences and construction of the city's defenses. Hippo could be the advisor for military affairs and Epi for relations with the other cities on Sicily."

"Good! Good! Excellent! Let's finish this list right now."

King Hieron and Archi sit and talk for hours, and finalize the list of fifteen guardians.

The next day, King Hieron gathers together all the royal family and members of the court to make the pronouncement.

"I have decreed this day that my grandson, Hieronymos shall be co-ruler with me, filling the vacancy left by the death of Gelo. Tomorrow, I will crown him co-ruler and King of Syracuse."

"Father, No!" cries Damarata. "I am the rightful heir to the throne!

I am your daughter! Hieronymos is just a child! Don't do this!"

"Silence! It has already been decided. Hieronymos is young and will live long, and be a good king. Had I died before the death of his father, he would have been king by now. It is better this way. He has much to learn so I am appointing guardians to guide him until such time as he can make the right decisions in ruling Syracuse. As head guardian, I appoint my faithful army commander, Adranodoros."

"No father! This is not right," shouts Heraclia this time. "Adranodoros and Damarata will hand Syracuse over to Carthage."

"This is a gross miscarriage of justice!" shouts Zoippos. Looking at Adranodoros, "You have not heard the last of this. We will not be party to this treason."

Heraclia grabs Zoippos by the arm, and they storm out together. Hieron continues in spite of Heraclia's departure.

"Adranodoros will lead the other guardians in recommending the right course for Hieronymos. After Archi reads the names of the other guardians, you will take an oath of office and allegiance to Hieronymos."

"What of Heraclia and Zoippos, your highness?" asks Archi.

"Keep them on the list. I hope they will change their minds. I will talk to them."

As Archi completes the reading of the names of all the guardians, King Hieron administers the oath. The next day, in a simple ceremony, King Hieron crowns fifteen year old Hieronymos, co-ruler of Syracuse.

Late that night, Helena awakes in bed alone. She gets up, slips into a robe, and strolls out onto the balcony where Archi is taking measurements of the stars.

"Archi, how long have you been out here?"

"What? Oh, Helena. Did I wake you?"

"No, not really. I am having trouble sleeping too."

"I am nearly done. Go back to bed."

Helena picks up his tablet, and examines it.

"You are not nearly done, and your writing is worst than ever."

Showing him the tablet and pointing, "What is this number?"

Archi looks at the number, "I don't know. I can't read my own hand writing."

"Of course not. You read the numbers to me, and I will write them down."

Continuing his measurements, "How did you know I was out here?"

"Archi, most women would be worried if they woke up in bed alone. But I always know where you are. If it is daylight, you are either in your shop or advising the king. If it is night, you are here on the balcony, gazing at the stars."

"Interesting!"

"I am proud that you have always been faithful to me, and never looked at another woman. Not many wives can say that. But you love your mathematics and sciences more than you love me. But it is all right, I was warned. I accept it. I enjoy helping you. We are a great team, and have accomplished much."

"Seven three and seven tenths."

Helena writes the number on the tablet.

"Just once, I wish you would look at me like you do the stars."

"Forty one and one tenth."

"Can't you calculate something about me?"

"Like what?"

"Something like the size and mass of my breasts."

Without looking at her, "I did that already."

"Archi, you are joking. When?"

"Back in Alexandria."

In disbelief, "Did you really?"

"Yes, of course. I needed some way to compare you with all the other women in Alexandria that were after me."

"Archi, you are teasing me. I know for a fact that you never looked at another woman after you met me."

Monte R. Anderson

"Don't be so sure. After I perfected the hand mirror, a lot of women made me offers."

"Archi, you are lying!" Putting her arms around Archi's neck, "Did you really measure my breasts?"

"Yes, of course. I had to be sure I was getting the best breasts in Alexandria."

"And just how big were they?"

"A hand and one half."

Poking him in the ribs, "That is not a proper measurement. Measure them again." Helena opens her robe to expose her bare breast. Archi cups her breasts in his hands.

"Oh no!"

"What is it?"

"I made a mistake. They are not one and a half hands, they are only one hand. Our whole marriage has been based on faulty measurements."

Poking him in the ribs again, "Now stop teasing me."

They continue their work for a few minutes.

Helena interrupts, "Archi, I have to tell you something. It is a secret that I have kept from you, and I regret it because you have been such a great husband."

"What is troubling you?" asks Archi.

"Well, this is awkward. Do you remember when we fell in love, and I told you I was a virgin?"

"Of course, I remember."

"Well, I wasn't. I mean, I was not a virgin. I lied to you, and now I feel terrible."

"I know," replies Archi.

Surprised, "You know! How long have you known?"

"I have always known," says Archi.

"All these years and you never said anything! It was Conon, wasn't it. He told you."

"No, not Conon. He always had the highest respect for you. I found out from several people. Even the king made a couple of remarks. I am not stupid you know."

Somewhat hurt, she asks, "Why didn't you say something?"

"I thought you lied because you wanted me to love you. After a while, it wasn't important any more."

"Well, you are a better person than I," says Helena.

Archi and Helena continue to work together.

Finally he asks, "Why are you having trouble sleeping?"

"I was thinking about the death of Gelo. Does the death of Gelo trouble you?"

"Yes, of course. He was still young and a good king. I worry what will happen when Hieron dies."

"No, I don't mean that. I meant the manner of his death."

"What do you mean?"

"Well, remember when King Ptolemy died in Alexandria while we were still there?"

"Yes, of course."

"Remember how at first it appeared he had died in his sleep, and Arsinoe killed herself in despair?"

"Yes, and we discovered that they had both been killed by his enemies."

"Well, I was never convinced it was his enemies, but the point is that I think that Gelo was poisoned."

"Interesting! It is possible, but who would do it?"

"I think that someone who opposes the treaty with Roma."

"That would include most of Hieron's family and half of the nobility in Syracuse."

"And don't forget that my sister, Berenice was also poisoned within a year after Euergetes died. I am certain it was her own son who murdered her. Power corrupts even families. Someone in the palace probably killed Gelo."

"I cannot accuse a member of Hieron's family without proof. We are not sure he was poisoned. It was different with King Ptolemy. We had the evidence."

"I know, but I have a funny feeling about this. I want you to tell King Hieron about my suspicions."

"All right, I will discuss it with King Hieron tomorrow."

"Thank you, Archi. I feel better already." Poking him in the groin, "Now if you have forgotten how to use this organ, I am giving a lecture in the bed room right now."

"You go ahead, I will be there in a few minutes."

Grabbing Archi by his beard, "No Archi! You are lying again. When you come out here, you lose all track of time. You are coming with me right now."

Helena leads a protesting Archi by the beard toward the bedroom. Archi put up token resistance while grinning in anticipation. They have played this game many times.

The next day, Archi talks with King Hieron in the throne room.

"Sire, I want to talk to you about the death of King Gelo."

"Yes, Archi?"

"Sire, Helena and I were living in Alexandria when King Ptolemy died. He was poisoned, and his wife was also killed. Helena sees many similarities between his death and the death of your son. We think Gelo may have been poisoned."

"What? Do you have proof of this? Who did this?"

"No, sire. We do not have proof, but we suspect that his murder was committed by someone who is against this treaty with Roma."

"Half of Syracuse is against this treaty."

"I know, sire. Until we have proof, you should be on guard. Whoever killed Gelo may try to kill you. I recommend you use body-guards, and employ a food and wine taster."

"It has been many years since I felt the need to have bodyguards. But, you always provide wise counsel.

"Did you know that King Ptolemy had a pet dog that he used as a taster? It was less conspicuous."

"A dog? Yes, I suppose I could do that. I will do it immediately."

"Another thing, sire, it would be wise not to tell anyone what you suspect. It might tip off the murderers."

"Agreed!"

Archi bows, and leaves the throne room just as Adranodoros enters.

"Adranodoros, I am glad you are here. I want you to arrange for bodyguards for me."

"Yes, sire. I will make the arrangements but we have not done things like this before."

"Yes we have, but it was long ago, before your time."

"I saw Archimedes leaving. Did he say something to upset you?"

"Yes, he advised it, and I think it is a good idea. And another thing, I would like to get a dog."

"Yes, sire. Your word is law."

Later that night as Adranodoros and Damarata are dining alone in the palace.

"I think that Archimedes suspects that someone poisoned Gelo."

"Does he suspect us?"

"No, I don't think so, but he advised the King to post bodyguards. I am to make the arrangements."

"Good! That is perfect. Make sure you select bodyguards that are loyal to us, and that we can control. It might prove useful later on."

"What about Archimedes?"

"That meddling fool will pay for his interference. I will take care of him."

Ω

One week later, Archi and Hippo are installing a new war machine near the Epipolai gate to the city. It requires using two elephants to lift a huge stone. Once the huge stone is lifted, the workmen tie the supporting ropes to an anchor in the city wall. As the stone is suspended the elephants are disconnected to move a large timber structure into place beneath the stone. As the workmen are starting to harness the elephants, Helena and Arsinoe arrive with a lunch of wine, bread, and cheese for Archi and Hippo. Archi tells the workmen to untie the elephants, and to break for lunch.

Archi and Hippo join the women in the shadow of the suspended stone for lunch.

As the four sit upon a blanket the women have spread upon the ground, Arsinoe says, "What a nice day. I love this weather."

"Yes, so do I. In Cyrene, on a day like today, I would race my sister to the sea, and we would look for sea shells," says Helena.

"Really? I can't imagine you running," teases Arsinoe.

"Well, I was very fast when I was your age, and could beat all the boys."

"Mama, you are making that up. I don't believe you."

"I bet I could beat you even now."

"Mama, stop. You are too old and fat to beat me."

"Why you little wrench!"

Helena reaches for Arsinoe but she dodges her mother's reach, and races off. Helena starts after her. The men just continue eating and laughing. After a few minutes, Helena returns all out of breath.

"I think she may be right. I am too old to catch her."

"Well, I can catch her," says Hippo as he stands up and runs after Arsinoe.

Helena sits down, knocking over a basket of apples that roll down the slope.

"I'll get them. You sit and eat," says Archi as he gets up and starts after the apples.

As he moves from under the stone, one of the ropes holding the stone races through a pulley attached to a crane. The stone begins to swing as all the weight shifts to the other pulley that tears loose from the crane. The stone crashes down and lands on one end. For a moment, it stands on end teetering.

"Run, Helena!" shouts Hippo.

But Helena is frozen to the spot, staring at the teetering stone. She has not had to make a split second decision since she stopped racing chariots. Which way to run? Which way will the stone fall? She was never good at this. She hesitates. The stone stops teetering, and starts to fall toward her. In less than a second, the huge stone crushes her to the ground.

"Helena!" Archi shouts, and hurries to the stone.

Hippo is already running toward the elephants. Finding a rock to use as fulcrum, Archi grabs a nearby beam, and tries to leverage up the stone. Several men rush to help, but the stone is heavy, and the beam breaks. Hippo and two elephant handlers quickly connect a fresh rope around the stone and to the elephants. Within seconds the stone is lifted off, but it too late.

When the stone is removed, it is obvious that Helena is dying. The masons, who have seen such accidents before, silently wonder why she was not killed instantly by one of her own broken bones. Every major bone, both legs, and both arms are broken; some bones protrude out of her skin. Her ribs are broken and caved in making it very painful to breath. Her neck appears to be broken, and her back is most certainly broken. She is covered in blood which gushes from several wounds with each pump of her still beating heart. Amazingly, she is still alive. Archi touches her but she screams, not a loud scream but a painful one. Archi backs off in despair. Arsinoe kneels down by her mother. Helena's eyes are closed, and her breath is shallow and raspy. Bloody foam gushes out of her mouth and nose. She moans with each breath.

"Mother, can you hear me?"

"Hmmmmm"

"We can't help you. You've broken many bones."

"Ohhhh, I know," whispers Helena with much effort.

"You are dying."

"Ohhh, I know. I'm so sorry."

Archi kneels beside his daughter, "I'm sorry. I should never have taken you away from Alexandria."

"No," pausing as blood drips out of her mouth. "I am not sorry for that." Spitting blood, "My time with you were the best years of my life. I will always love you."

"Do you want me to return your body to Alexandria?"

Opening her eyes, and attempting a slight smile, "No! I belong here with you." Pausing to gather some strength, "This is my home now. Bury me near the sea. I so love the sea." Coughing up blood, "Arsinoe?"

"I am here, mother."

"I love you. Take care of your father. He is getting old now."

"Of course, mother."

Caughing up more blood, "I hurt. Make the pain stop, Archi. I want to go now."

Taking out his dagger, Hippo offers it heel first to Archi.

Looking up at Hippo, "No! No! I can't do it."

Arsinoe stands up, and places her hand on Hippo's shoulder, "Hippo, you will have to do it. Please! Quickly!"

A mason steps forward, and offers Hippo his wooden mallet. Taking the mallet, and kneeling down, Hippo says to Arsinoe, "Cover her eyes, and say goodbye."

Placing the dagger over her heart, he raises the mallet. Sobbing, Arsinoe shields Helena's eye from the dagger.

"Goodbye, mother. I love you."

With one blow of the mallet, Hippo drives the dagger to the hilt through Helena's heart. Helena's head rises slightly and falls. Her breath is still. She is no longer in pain. The blood stops pumping out of her body. Hippo reaches over, and closes her still open eyes. Archi collapses in sobs as Arsinoe holds him.

After a few minutes of crying, Arsinoe kisses her mother, and turns to Hippo, "Thank you."

Hippo replies, "I am so sorry." Then to Archi, "Let me take you and your daughter home. I will have the workmen pick up Helena's body, and bring it to your palace. She will get a royal burial."

Archi is sobbing, and cannot speak so Arsinoe nods her head.

Hippo speaks to a couple of the overseers. One of the masons brings the running end of the rope to him. It had been cut. Someone killed Helena, and tried to kill Archi. Hippo takes the rope to show his father later. Helping Archi to his feet, Arsinoe and Hippo make their way through the crowd that has gathered. As the procession snakes though the city, people begin to hear what has happened. Peasants follow the procession to Archi's palace. Soon, hundreds of peasants are flowing toward the house. A large crowd gathers outside to keep a vigil throughout the night.

After dark, Archi makes his way to the home altar dedicated to Isis. He kneels down at the altar for a few minutes in silence. It was the first time he has ever approached any altar. He does so tonight in Helena's honor. Finding Helena's priestly robes, he places them on the altar. Finally, he blows out the sacred lamp that Helena had instructed the servants to burn day and night. He weeps all the way to their bedroom.

The next day, the Egyptian servants ask permission to prepare Helena's body for burial in the traditional Egyptian custom, a rare honor for a non-Egyptian. First her eyes and mouth are shut to secure the release of the psyche. Her body is washed and anointed. All her body hair is removed except on top of her head. Eyebrows are painted on. She is dressed in her priestly robes. Her hair is cut and combed in the Egyptian style, and her body is adorned with flowers, and covered. Her body is placed on public view for two days.

Nearly all the city's citizens file by, dressed in black, to pay their last respects to the woman who had done so much for them, and who was loved by all. Many bring offerings of fruit and oil made by Archi' olive presses. Standing guard over Helena's body are the women servant, raising their hands to heaven, tearing out their hair, and singing prayers and ritualized laments.

Before dawn of the third day, the servants carry the body to Helena's chariot, and lead the horses to the Archimedes family tomb. Barely able to stand, Archi rides in Helena's chariot beside her body. In proper order, King Hieron and the other male members of the court follow in their chariots while the female members follow on foot. The route is illuminated by servants carrying torches. They sing songs and dance as the procession moves along. Behind the royal family are hundreds of peasants following on foot. Helena's body is placed in the tomb near the bones of Archi' mother and father. Once she is laid to rest, the horses are killed, and both the chariot and horses are placed in the tomb, and the tomb sealed.

After the burial, the singing and dancing ceases and the men and women leave the funeral separately. There is to be a banquet in Helena's honor, so the women must leave first to help prepare the meal. Archi is already planning a more fitting tomb over looking the sea.

At the banquet, Hippo speaks privately to his father and Archi about how Helena was killed. Her death was no accident as the cut rope clearly shows. He explains how Arsinoe, Archi, Helena, and he were together eating lunch. Had he not chased after Arsinoe, and Archi moved to pick up apples, all four would have been killed. It appears that Archi was the intended victim so the assassin waited until Archi was alone with Helena. It is not clear why anyone would want to kill Archi.

Later, that evening, Adranodoros speaks to his wife about Helena's death, and how Archi narrowly escaped. He is furious that Hippo might have easily been killed in the attempt on Archi.

Ω

Within a few weeks, Hieron dies while reclining at dinner. After the funeral, Adranodoros immediately calls for a meeting of the guardians, but without King Hieronymos and Archi. He knows that Archi will argue in favor of the treaty with Roma, and that he is very influential with the guardians. Adranodoros also fears that somehow he may tip off Archi that it is he who was behind the plot to kill him to silence suspicions that Gelo was poisoned. He cannot look Archi in the eye, and avoids contact with him as much as possible.

The old arguments for and against a treaty with Roma are discussed. However, this time Adranodoros speaks from a position of considerable more power, and the other guardians recognize it. Zoippos and Heraclia attend the meeting, and voice their opposition. Damarata backs her husband. In effect, the royal family is evenly divided on the issue and neutralized. Zoippos and Heraclia again storm out of the meeting leaving Adranodoros in control. Out of fear, the other advisors don't speak up. In the end, a majority of the guardians vote for breaking with Rome, and signing a new treaty with Carthage.

The next day, based on Adranodoros' recommendation, and without consulting Archi, King Hieronymos approves the decision. In no time, mobs supporting the pro-Carthage party, led by Damarata begin to attack supporters of the pro-Rome party led by Zoippos and Heraclia. The pro-Rome party decides to send Zoippos to warn Appius, the Roman Praetor of Sicily. Fearing a major revolt, Appius convinces Zoippos to sail with him to appeal to the Roman Senate. Heraclia and her daughters stay behind to lead the pro-Roman party. Damarata and Adranodoros begin to plot the assassination of the young King Hieronymos. Now firmly in command, Adranodoros sends Hippo and Epi as envoys to Carthage to negotiate the terms of a new treaty.

Ω

King Hieron had been a popular king but he never had the support of all the noble families of Syracuse. The city was on the verge of civil war when Hieronymos became king. On his very first public appearance he demonstrates that he is not the same man as his grandfather or father. Hieron and his son, Gelo, had always dressed humbly without any distinguishing marks of royalty such as crowns, jewelry, and royal garments. Hieronymos immediately begins wearing royal purple, a diadem, and much jewelry. He travels everywhere with armed attendants--something King Hieron never felt the need to do. Hieronymos keeps his distance from the people, and does not mingle with the crowds as his father and grandfather had done before him. He begins driving from the palace in a royal chariot with four white horses. In the palace he shows contempt for all but family members, and refuses to listen to advice even from his former guardians. All this strange behavior does little to subdue the rivalries inside the city.

(1499, Cesare's Campaign Headquarters)

Cesare stands up, stretches his legs, and lights some candles.

"So that is how Syracuse ended up allied with Carthage, a fatal mistake. Wasn't Rome preoccupied with Hannibal in Italy at this time? How did the war in Sicily start?"

"Good questions," replies Leonardo. "It would have seemed logical for Rome to defeat Hannibal in Italy prior to moving across Sicily, and eventually to attack Carthage itself. And it probably would have happened that way if it were not for two people; Marcus Claudius Marcellus and Zoippos. Rome had placed Marcus in command of its southern army, and he fought Hannibal to a terribly bloody draw. For the first time, Rome began to believe that Hannibal was beatable. The Roman Senate began to call Marcus, 'The Sword', and to plan for the defeat of Hannibal."

CHAPTER TWENTY ONE

(1499, Cesare's Campaign Headquarters)

"Leonardo, I think your story is now beginning to sound like one of our modern day intrigues. Do you know my good friend, Niccolo Machiavelli?"

"Yes, I know of him."

"And what is your opinion of him?"

"To be honest, I hardly know him."

"You are just being polite. Truth is, he has few friends but he considers himself a friend of mine. He and I have had many discussions about politics and power. In fact, he is writing a book. He plans to call it *The Prince*. I think it is a veiled attempt to write about my own life and exploits, but he denies it. The book is a practical guide on strategy and politics. Now Niccolo would say that all wars are about seizing power and politics. Now tell me, if you please, whether it was politics and intrigue that sealed the fate of Syracuse or was it the might of the Roman army?"

"You are very astute, my Lord. The might of Rome could never have defeated Archimedes and Syracuse if it had not been for politics and intrigue."

"Aha! I thought as much. Please go on. This has to be the best part."

$$\Omega$$

(215 BCE in Rome, Italy)

After the short trip from Messina, Appius and Zoippos arrive in Rome. The Senate is in session, so Appius leads the way straight to the Curia, the Senate House in the Forum Romanun. Although Zoippos had seen the Curia before, he had forgotten how small the structure is for such a powerful body of men. As the two enter the senate chamber, all heads turn toward the familiar face of Appius, a former quaester and now praeter of Roman Sicily, and Zoippos, the former ambassador from Syracuse. Cornelius, head of the senate, motions for the current debate to stop, and for everyone to sit down. He then nods toward Appius. After telling Zoippos to stay where he is, Appius walks toward the center of the chamber.

"Permission to address the senate?" Appius asks, more for dramatic effect than for protocol.

Cornelius nods again. Appius, frowning at the condescending attitude of Cornelius, begins,

"Senators, please hear me. I have come from Sicily with an urgent matter to report to you, and I have with me Zoippos of Syracuse, son-in-law of King Hieron."

"We are waiting," says Cornelius, impatiently.

"It appears that while our attention has been focused on Hannibal in Italy, hostilities are about to resume on Sicily after many years of peace. I have spies in the Carthaginian senate that tell me that since Carthage is having problems supplying Hannibal's army in Italy, they have decided to make another grab for Sicily. They think that if they can conquer all of Sicily they might be better able to support Hannibal. Carthage is sending an army consisting of 25,000 infantry, supported by cavalry and elephants to Sicily."

Holding up a hand to silence the rumbling of the senators, Cornelius turns toward a man in the back row of the senate, "Marcus, you are our best military strategist, what do you have to say about this new threat?"

Everyone turns toward Marcus Marcellus, the only general to gain any success against Hannibal. Marcus slowly stands, and gathers his robe, the scars on his face turn bright red.

"It is a good strategy for Carthage to adopt. Whoever controls Sicily, controls the sea and the back door to Roma itself. Hannibal does not have the strength for a direct assault on Roma but he is still a force to be reckoned with. There are many cities that secretly support Carthage and others, like Capua and Terento, may turn against us when it becomes convenient to do so. In time, we will defeat Hannibal but we cannot do it quickly. Unlike Hannibal's veterans, our new army is made up of untrained citizens full of spirit but unsteady in battle. We must discipline and train them. That takes time. If Carthage can seize Sicily, and if a few cities on the mainland shift their support to Carthage, they might be able to bring several fresh legions to the very gates of Roma."

Uneasiness comes upon the senators who shift in their seats, and begin to whisper among themselves.

Finally, a senator stands and asks Marcus, "What do you recommend?"

"I think we can contain Hannibal's army in the field. I could lead an army to destroy the Carthaginian army on Sicily, and end that threat once and for all. Then I could recruit some legions from Sicily and return with more than enough force to destroy Hannibal. He has no hope of reinforcements. We will defeat him."

"How much time?" someone shouts.

"Six months maybe, but less than a year," says Marcus.

"But Marcus," asks one of the Senators. "Instead of battling Carthaginian armies on the island of Sicily, would it not make more sense to attack Hannibal's supply line that runs all the way through Spain?"

The senators murmur again.

"Yes, you make a good point. But Spain is far away, and Sicily is nearer. If Hannibal does decide to attack our city, while I am in the field, I can quickly return from Sicily. However, once an army is sent to Spain, it could not return for months."

More murmuring.

"How soon could you be ready?" asks Cornelius.

"Two weeks. The army is ready. We can gather supplies in Sicily from our allies."

Cornelius senses a consensus, and calls for a vote. The vote is unanimous to send an army to Sicily.

"So be it!" announces Cornelius as senators rush to congratulate Marcus. Remembering that Appius is still standing in the center of the chamber, Cornelius asks, "Praeter Appius, is that satisfactory?"

"Yes, but there is another matter related to this that the senate should now consider."

"What is it now? We have much to discuss in support of Marcus. Make your case quickly."

"It is the matter of restoring the throne of Syracuse to the rightful heir," interjects Zoippos, stepping forward.

The senators return to their seats, and quiet down.

"Zoippos, we have not seen you since the defeat at Cannae. Are you here to ask for your legions back?"

Laughter.

"That was a sad day for Syracuse as well, senators. Syracuse lost many sons at Cannae too"

"Of course! Since you have imposed yourself upon us, go ahead and speak." Cornelius settles back into his seat with a flourish.

Zoippos bows slightly, and moves toward the center as Appius backs away. "Thank you. I am Zoippos, son-in-law of King Hieron of Syracuse and former ambassador to Roma. My wife is Heraclia, daughter of Hieron and rightful heir to the throne of Syracuse. You may have known that Hieron and Gelo were co-rulers until Gelo died unexpectedly. You may not know that King Hieron also died recently. They were murdered by Carthaginian supporters, people who want Syracuse to switch its loyalty from Roma to Carthage."

The senators stare at Zoippos, not certain they heard him correctly.

Now that he has everyone's attention, Zoippos continues, "By all rights, the throne should have passed to Hieron's heir, his daughter, Heraclia. However, he had decreed that the kingship should pass to Gelo's son, Hieronymos, a mere child of fifteen."

"Zoippos", replies Cornelius as he stands and gestures to the senators, "King Hieron had every right to proclaim his grandson as king. What concern is this to Roma?"

Zoippos shouts, "Everything!" Regaining his composure, "King Hieron was an ally of Roma for many years, and always honored his treaties with you. But before he died, he appointed guardians to guide young Hieronymos. The head guardian is his son-in-law, a man by the name of Adranodoros. Adranodoros has a great influence over young Hieronymos, and bends the young man to his own will."

More murmurs. Cornelius raises his hand for silence.

"Wasn't he the commander of the Sicilian army at Cannae? We thought he died in battle."

"Better for you if he had. Hannibal captured him and his two sons. Adranodoros was badly wounded, but lived. He made a vow to Hannibal not to fight against Carthage. I believe that he and his sons made a pact with Hannibal in return for their release. Furthermore, I have proof that it was Adranodoros who poisoned King Gelo."

"So Adranodoros is alive after all?"

"Yes, and he has persuaded the other guardians to renounce the treaty with Roma, and to negotiate a new treaty with Carthage. Many Sicilian cities that have been loyal to Roma but look to Syracuse for leadership have also begun to negotiate with Carthage. If you do not act soon, Carthage will conquer the whole island without a battle."

"You just heard us decide to send Marcellus to Sicily. What more must we do?"

"I can be of great assistance. I have friends in high places in all the cities that were loyal to King Hieron. If you will let me go with Marcellus, I am sure I can persuade many of these cities to remain loyal to Roma. At the very least I can use my agents as spies, and gather good intelligence for Marcus."

"And, I suppose, you want us to restore the throne of Syracuse to your wife?"

With a slight bow, "You will find her a loyal ally but that is only the least of my request."

Sitting down with a sigh, Cornelius says, "Let's hear the rest."

"I want to be appointed governor of Sicily."

"Why you little snake," says Appius as he takes a step toward a defiant Zoippos.

Now the senate is in an uproar. Several senators are shouting at Zoippos. Cornelius stands to assert authority over the body of angry men. Once the senate is quiet again, he says, "Appius, I do believe Zoippos wants your job."

Marcus interjects, "Sicily is much too important to have an outsider appointed governor. For years, it has been divided between a Roman Sicily, now governed by Appius, and that part of Sicily ruled by Syracuse. Beside, Messina must now return to Roman control. It is too important."

Zoippos answers, "Yes, Sicily is too big for one governor. Give me the portion that Syracuse now rules. It will continue as it has since the last war with Carthage."

Turning to Marcus, Cornelius asks, "What say you?"

"It seems reasonable to me."

Turning to Appius, "Appius?"

"I say that he must deliver Syracuse to us and most of its former client cities or he gets nothing."

Seeing no dissent, Cornelius announces, "So be it. It costs us nothing, and it is within our power. As you said, you might be useful to us. Go as advisor to Marcus Marcellus."

As Appius and Zoippos leave together, Appius says in a whisper, "I should kill you for not telling me your true plans."

"You would not have brought me here otherwise."

"You lied when you said that your wife was the rightful heir to King Hieron. Doesn't she have an older sister?"

Zoippos is taken back by Appius' remark. Apparently, Appius knows more about Syracuse than he admits. "A small lie. Her sister, Damarata is married to Adranodoros. They lead the faction that wants a treaty with Carthage. You would not want her crowned Queen, now would you?"

"True, but I don't like being used. Besides, you fail to grasp the reality of the situation that you yourself have created."

"What do you mean?"

"Do you really think that Roma will appoint you, a non-Roman, governor of half of the largest province in the Republic, the very bread basket of Roma? You are naive. It will not happen that way."

"But they just voted to…"

"Never mind what they voted. This is war. It is expedient to grant you small favors. After the war, there will be a different mind set. They will want to ensure the peace. A Syracusan governor of Sicily will not work."

"Perhaps, but at least my wife will be Queen of Syracuse."

"Stupid! Wrong again! Do you think for one minute that the senate is going to let the heirs of a king who turned against Roma rule Syracuse?"

Zoippos stops walking, and stares at Appius.

Appius moves his face very close to Zoippos' face. Lowering his voice, "Here is what will happen. If you do as I tell you, you might be king of Syracuse. But, you must make sure that there are no surviving heirs to the throne. If you can do this, the senate may reward you with the kingship of Syracuse."

"What do you mean?

"Zoippos, even you cannot be that stupid. I mean kill them. Kill them all. Kill every person that has any blood line to King Hieron."

"That would mean my wife, too?"

"Finally, you figured it out. Yes, everyone. If you don't, you will end up with nothing or even crucified for your troubles. Understand?"

"It is very clear. I will see to it."

Ω

(215 BCE, in Eastern Sicily)

Marcellus lands in Sicily, captures a few cities, and then marches on the city of Leontini in Eastern Sicily. Adranodoros counters by sending Hippo and Epi with one legion each to attack Marcellus' supply line back toward Rome. Hieronymos, fancying himself a military commander, proceeds with a larger army into the city of Leontini to help defend it.

Zoippos, aware of Hieronymos' plans, has his agents in Leontini occupy a house overlooking a narrow street the king would have to use to go to the forum. Several armed assassins are placed in the ground level of the house. The day after the king arrives in the city, as he passes by the house on the way to the forum, the assassins push a cart through the doorway, cutting off the king's bodyguards. Several of the assassins rush out, and stab Heironymos several times before his bodyguards can climb over the cart. When the bodyguards and other attendants, see the king lying dead in the street, they flee.

Ω

(214 BCE, Leontini, in Eastern Sicily)

With the death of the young king the Syracusan army become ineffective, and the defense of the city quickly falls apart in disarray. Marcus' superior numbers easily push aside the Sicilian forces under Hippo and Epi, and capture the city of Leontini. Badly outnumbered and in an effort to maintain their strength, Hippo and Epi withdraw with a large number of soldiers to Syracuse. The next day Marcus calls for a council of war in the throne room of the former King of Leontini.

Marcus opens the council of war with a question, "How shall we garrison Leontini?"

Appius answers, "Sir, we have many prisoners. If we have to guard the prisoners, and defend the city against a Carthaginian attack, it will take half a legion. We already have garrisons in the other cities we have captured. If we do the same in every city we capture, we will soon have no soldiers left to fight Hannibal."

Marcus replies, "Messana is the key city on our supply lines with Roma, and must be well guarded. Other than that, we can't spare half a legion for garrison duties. Either we kill the entire population or we destroy the city totally, and sell the inhabitants as slaves."

"That won't be necessary, sir," interrupts Zoippos. "A large number of Leontini's citizens are supporters of Roma. The rest can be kept in line. Turn the prisoners over to me, and I will punish the Carthaginian supporters. In a few days we can take over the defenses of the city from your garrison. In two weeks we will field a legion to join your army."

Smiling, "I like your plan, Zoippos. Any objections? None? Very well, so be it."

"As you command," says Appius.

As the others leave, Appius stays behind to speak to Marcus.

"Sir, I have a little private matter I wish to bring to your attention." He motions to a man in the back of the room. Appius had hardly noticed him, and mistook him for a servant. The man walks across the throne room with his sandals flopping and slapping the floor with each step. Appius recognized the gait immediately as belonging to one of the Lost Brethren. The Lost Brethren, as they are called by the Roman soldiers, are the soldiers who fled the battlefield at Cannae. Hannibal's cavalry was so busy chasing the Romans that they took to cutting the hamstrings of their captives so they could return latter, and round them up. Some, apparently this one, managed to escape in spite of their cut hamstrings. All the survivors, wounded or not, were rounded up as they returned to Roma, branded as traitors, and exiled to Sicily.

The veteran stops in front of Marcus, stands as straight as possible, and salutes.

"You were at Cannae," Marcus says as a statement, not a question.

"Yes, sir."

"And you ran in the face of the enemy, and left Roma defenseless against Hannibal. It was pure luck that Hannibal did not continue his attack all the way to Roma."

"There is no glory in being slaughtered like pigs. We were betrayed by our own generals who were too cocksure of victory to sense the trap."

Marcus sits back in his chair, and looks the soldier over for a minute, "You did not come here to debate tactics with me. What do you want?"

"Sir, what I want, and many others like me, is to have my honor back. You can give it to me."

"Even if I could, I could not go against the senate, and besides, I ...."

"Appius, touches Marcus' shoulder, and indicates with a nod that Marcus should hear what the soldier had to say. As Marcus pauses in mid sentence, the soldier takes the cue.

"Sir, I was a Centurion. I do not defend my actions at Cannae, but, I think we were punished enough without banishment. But here I am. I just want a chance to prove myself, to prove that I am a good soldier and a good Roman."

"And how would you do that? Your are handicapped, no good for fighting."

"Sir, there are many of us here, perhaps a legion or more. Some are crippled like me but many others were not wounded, and can still fight. They are good soldiers. Those who can fight are willing to form cohorts, and join your legions. If they prove themselves in battle, perhaps you will let them return home."

"I cannot promise that. It is up to the senate."

"I know sir, but you could testify to the senate about our bravery."

"I can do that much. What is your name?"

"Lucius, sir."

Very well then, Lucius, tell your veterans to report to Appius as soon as possible. But there will be no pay, just booty."

"We won't disappoint you. Give us the toughest assignments. We will prove worthy of your trust."

"Oh, I intend to. Fight well, and I will talk to the senate." Marcus stands to signal an end to the discussion but Lucius does not move.

"There is another thing, sir."

"You try my patience. Yes, what is it?"

"Well, there are many, like myself, who cannot march but who can still carry a sword. I think we can garrison some of these captured cities, help guard prisoners, and act as sentries. There are many duties we can perform."

"I think you are right. Very well then, have anyone who wants to join my army report to Appius."

"Thank you, sir. You will not regret it."

The centurion salutes, and limps out of the room.

Turning to Appius, "How did you find him?"

"He is my brother."

"Really? When he reports for duty, bring him to me. I want him to be my personal bodyguard. I think he would die before he would ever run again."

"As you command. Lucius could never run under any circumstances."

Ω

Zoippos calls his own council of war with his Roman sympathizers in Leontini. Once everyone is present and seated, Zoippos starts by saying, "Marcus has agreed to turn over the prisoners to us as well as the defenses of the city."

"What of the king?" asks one of the sympathizers.

"I will send him in a cage to the Roman Senate."

"And what of the queen?" asks another.

"We will kill her and all the royal family."

"What?"

Angrily, "What did you expect? What would they do to us if we had failed? No! All of them must die. In a few weeks we will hold an election to elect a new king, one who will support us. We have until then to get rid of all who oppose us."

"What do you mean?"

"I mean when we get custody of the prisoners, we will release any who are supporters of Roma. They will have to take an oath of loyalty. Then I want the rest beaten and beheaded. That includes all the royal family and anyone who supported Carthage and opposed us. It would mean our deaths if any escape. We will make an example out of Leontini."

"But will Marcus allow this?"

Pounding the table with his fist, "I am the new governor of Eastern Sicily, not Marcus. I am Roma! Now do it quickly!"

Zoippos stands to signal an end to the meeting. Everyone else stands, says farewell, and departs. Zoippos beckons to a young man standing near the door. He approaches as Zoippos motions for him to sit. His name is Dinomenes, once one of King Hieron's bodyguards but now an agent for Zoippos.

"Dinomenes, I have work for you to do in Syracuse."

"Yes, sir. You have only to command me."

"What we do in Leontini, we must also do in Syracuse."

"What do you mean?"

"I mean that I want you to begin killing all the royal family in Syracuse. There must not be any heirs to the throne left alive when Marcus captures the city. Do you understand?"

"You want me to kill all of King Hieron's family."

"Yes. Take command of the Pro-Roman party, and use them to help you but act quickly," Handing over a letter to Dinomenes, "This is a letter of introduction to my wife. She will tell the current leaders of the Pro-Roman party to follow your orders. Start with Adranodoros."

"The women too?"

"Of course, stupid."

"But what of your wife?"

"Her too."

"You want to kill your wife? She is a strong supporter of Roma. Why kill her?"

Shouting, "Don't question me! Just do what I tell you." Calming himself, "And stay in Syracuse until I arrive. I may need your to help to capture the city. Now go!"

"Yes, sir."

$$\Omega$$

Monte R. Anderson

(215 BCE, Syracuse, Sicily)

Dinomenes arrives in Syracuse, and immediately begins to plot the murders of the royal family. He comes up with a simple plan to kill Adranodoros. It only takes a few hours to put the plan into operation. No one in Syracuse is aware that Dinomenes is working for Zoippos. He is still considered one of the king's bodyguards. He uses his former position to gain access to the palace, and is ushered into the throne room where Adranodoros and Themistos are sitting at a table looking over a diagram of the city defenses. They look up as Dinomene enters.

"I have a message from the King of Selinus in western Sicily."

Adranodoros stands up, and motions for Dinomenes to come closer.

"I was told to tell only you, sir," Dinomenes says, glancing at Themistos.

It's alright," replies Adranodoros, "You know that Themistos is an uncle to the king. You may speak in front of him."

Dinomenes leans forward as if to whisper which causes Adranodoros to also lean forward. Suddenly, with one hand, Dinomenes, grabs Adranodoros by the back of the neck, and with the other hand plunges a dagger into his heart, killing him instantly. Themistos steps back to draw his sword but it barely clears the scabbard when an arrow pierces his chest. That arrow is quickly followed by another from two archers standing in the doorway. Themistos slumps to the floor.

Turning to the two archers, Dinomenes asks, "The guards?"

"Both dead," replies one of the killers.

"Very good. We can do no more tonight." Dinomenes heads for the door. "Let's go."

Ω

Following the murders of Adranodoros and Themistos, a civil war begins between the pro-Roman party and the pro-Carthaginian party over control of Syracuse. The pro-Carthaginian party is barely able to keep control of the palace for the time being. The next day, news of nearly 2000 people beaten and beheaded in Leontini reaches Syracuse. As word of this brutal reprisal spreads throughout Syracuse and to her allies, it only strengthens their resolve. Another rumor, started by Zoippos himself, says that it was Marcus who ordered the mass killings. Dinomenes uses the rumors to convince the pro-Roman party that they must seize control of Syracuse, and turn the city over to Marcus or suffer the same fate. He also convinces them that it was the royal wives who had influenced the men to decide to go to war. That night, Dinomene leads an angry mob to seize the palace.

Archi is informed about the pending attack on the palace. After telling Arsinoe to hide in his house, he rushes ahead of the mob to warn the royal family. He finds the women, Damarata, Harmonia, Heraclia and her two daughters, huddled in the throne room.

"Quickly, you must flee the palace. It is not safe here anymore," Archi shouts to the women.

"Where are the guards," demands Damarata.

"They have already fled. Come, we must go now."

It is too late. The mob breaks into the throne room with Dinomenes at the front.

"Well, well, well. What have we here?" asks Dinomenes.

Archi steps in front of Dinomenes to confront him. "There are only women and children here. Leave them be."

"Out of the way, Archimedes. We have no quarrel with you. It is these women we want, this den of vipers."

"Dinomenes, you know me, and you know my husband, Zoippos," says Heraclia. "You know that we support Roma." Pointing at Damarata, "She is the one you want. She is the one who betrayed Syracuse. She is the one who killed my brother, Gelo. Take her!"

Dinomenes motions for the mob to seize all of the women, including Heraclia.

"You are all guilty of poisoning the minds of your men, leading them to violate the treaty with the Romans. Your meddling has plunged us into a war that we never wanted and cannot possibly win. For this act of treason, you all must die. Take them out!"

As the mob move toward the door, Archi tries to push them back. Dinomenes strikes him in the face, knocking him to the floor, unconscious.

The mob drags the kicking women down to the harbor defenses to one of Archi's catapults. They bind their hands and feet, and tie a stone into their skirts. They start to gag their screams but Dinomenes pulls off the gags.

"No! No gag. I want to hear their screams."

"Give me a sword, and I will show you how to die, you coward!" shouts Damarata.

Dinomenes walks over to her, "Still trying to play the queen?"

Give me a sword, you pig, and I will show you who is master here."

"Very well, my lady," answers Dinomenes. He draws his sword, and runs it through Damarata's stomach. "Here is your sword."

"What about the children, Dinomenes?" someone asks. "Do we have to kill them?"

"Of course! Little vipers grow up to be big vipers someday. Kill them first so their mother can watch."

The youngest sister is taken to the catapult, and set into the basket. Dinomenes walks over to the trigger.

"Goodbye, my dear," he says as he trips the trigger, and the girl is hurled over the wall of the city into the bay, screaming until she hits the water. Finally, fully realizing their fate, all the women start to cry except for Damarata, who curses the mob with her dying breath. One by one, each woman is catapulted over the walls into the harbor, with the half-dead Damarata being the last.

The next day, too late to save the women. Hippo and Epi march into the city, and with their soldiers easily gain total control of Syracuse, re-establishing order. Hippo assumes total power as dictator.

CHAPTER TWENTY TWO

(213 BCE, off the Eastern Coast of Sicily)

On his flag ship with the fleet, Marcus convenes another council of war. Appius, praeter of Roman Sicily and commander of the land army, is present as well as all the legion commanders. An uneasy Lucius stands behind Marcus' chair with his hand on the hilt of his sword, keeping a watchful eye on everyone. Not all the commanders are Romans, and this makes him uncomfortable. Standing next to a sand table constructed in the bow is Zoippos.

After Marcus opens the meeting, Appius is the first to update the situation for all present. Pointing to a map tacked to the mast, "Sir, we have taken Messana, Tyndarius, Naxos, Catania, and Leontini. Carthage still controls many of the western cities of Sicily. The independent cities not subject to Syracuse or Carthage have declared their support for Roma. Carthage has not put up much of a fight, and cannot support Syracuse."

"Very good, Pro-Praetor," says a grinning Marcus.

"What did you say?" asks a stunned Appius.

"You heard me!" Marcus pulls open a scroll from his tunic, "The senate has authorized me to promote you to Pro-Praetor effective immediately. Congratulations, Appius Claudius."

All the commanders cheer, and congratulate Appius. Marcus motions everyone to gather around the sand table near Zoippos. The table is waist high, and about as large as a regular table. On it is a great deal of sand covering the table top which is painted blue. Using wooden blocks and sticks, Zoippos has constructed a crude model of Syracuse, clearing away the sand so that the blue painted area represents the harbor. He draws his sword, and as he does, Lucius' grip on his own sword tightens, and his eyes narrow on Zoippos' face. He moves closer to Marcus so at the first sign of an attack he can protect him. At a nod from Marcus, Zoippos begins to use his sword to point out the various features on the sand table.

"The small fortress on Otrigia Island guards the Grand Harbor. A wall encircles the whole of the city. The height of the wall varies with the terrain, and will be difficult to breech. There are level stretches of flat ground where it may be possible to assault the wall. However, Archimedes has placed various types of military machines all along the wall, especially in the more accessible areas. The western approach is guarded by a fort named Olympia. The eastern approach is protected by cliffs and rough terrain. This southern part of the city is called Achradina, the wall of which extends almost to the water's edge. It is surrounded by water on three sides and a wall on north side that stretching from the sea on the east and the harbor on the west. The city has a second interior wall that connects with this wall and devides the city proper into thirds. The western part of the city is called Neapolis, and the east part, Tycha. The city is well defended. They have enough food and water stockpiles to last several months or maybe even a year. I would recommend a siege and not a direct assault."

"A siege will take too long, and tie up too many troops," says Appius.

"What is the morale of the army?" asks Marcus, ignoring Appius' comment for the moment.

"The morale and determination of the army is good. The rumors that your troops beheaded 2000 Roman supporters in Leontine seem to have stiffened their resolve."

Pounding the sand table, causing several of the wooden walls to fall, Marcus shouts at Zoippos, "It was you who beheaded the 2000."

"It doesn't matter, you are the overall commander. The people blame you," snaps Zoippos.

Lucius takes one step toward Zoippos, his sword half out of the sheath, and only stops when Marcus places his hand on his chest.

"Why you little snake," says Marcus. "I should feed you to the sharks. Unfortunately, the Roman Senate was impressed by your show of brutality, and the sight of the King of Leontini in a cage. I will see to it that it never happens again. Now what of the Syracusan commanders?"

"The king appointed Adranodoros as the commander, but he was assassinated by one of my agents. The new dictator is Adranodoros' son, Hippokrates. Hippokrates has appointed his brother, Epikyoles, as commander of the army."

"And the morale of the people?" asks Appius.

"That is not good. My agents in the city managed to engage the pro-Carthaginian party in a civil war. Unfortunately, Hippokrates has put down the unrest and reestablished order. Only the fear of your invasion has caused everyone to quiet down and cooperate. However, under the proper circumstances, open revolt could happen."

"Can we count on any help from your supporters?" asks a legion commander.

"Many of my men have been arrested but we can still make limited attacks as needed. We will do what we can, but Hippokrates has eliminated all those who support an alliance with Roma from any important position, and has arrested many of my family and supporters. We will seek opportunities to assassinate Hippokrates and Epikyotes and all the other commanders."

"Thank you, Zoippos. You are a loyal friend of Roma, and will be amply rewarded in time," says Marius sarcastically. "Now if you will excuse us we will plan our attack."

"It would be better if I stayed. If I know your plans, I can better support them."

"I think not. So far you have proven yourself to be a murderer who kills defenseless prisoners and nothing more.

Seize power in Syracuse, and I will welcome you to the war council."

"As you wish," Zoippos leaves to board a small boat that takes him to one of the other Roman galleys.

As soon as Zoippos has departed, Marcus begins, "Gentleman, our main attack will be from the land side of Syracuse. It will be easier to support such an attack. Appius?"

"Yes, sir?"

"You will march immediately with four legions to attack Syracuse. We attack in three days." Marcus glances at Lucius, "Put the Lost Brethren legion in the front lines. They can redeem their lost honor or die trying."

An approving nod from Lucius lets Marcus know that this is the right decision.

Marcus continues, "I will sail with the fleet to lead the diversionary attack from the sea. I will start the attack sometime mid morning, and attempt to draw many of the defenders to the sea side of the fort. Time your arrival for the afternoon. I do not want the Syracusans to know you are in position until they are committed against my attack. On my signal, you will start the main attack."

Appius asks, "If the main effort is from the land side, isn't that where you should be?"

"No, I am sure there are spies among our ranks. If they see me with the seaward attack, they will conclude that it is our main effort. Besides, I know you Appius. You are as able as any commander to plan this attack. I think the seaward attack may be the most difficult part of the plan. I should be there."

"If the seaward walls go almost to the water, it will be difficult to get a footing on the land in order to breech the walls. How do you propose to do that?" asks Appius.

"Remember that the sea attack is a diversion. The main attack is from the land. However, I have the engineers working on building three huge Sambuca, each aboard six ships lashed together. They will be able to attack once we get a foothold. Of course, we also have several catapults."

"How do we treat the people of Syracuse after we take the city?" asks one of the Sicilian commanders.

"Syracuse is a grand and beautiful city. It was our loyal ally for nearly fifty years. Many families in Syracuse still support us. Our supporters have killed the king and many others. We will occupy the city, and preserve it. Seize all the royal palaces, money, and goods, but leave everything else alone. Zoippos will provide us with a list of loyal supporters and guides to point out their homes. I want guards sent to protect these people and property from looting."

"But, sir, the men have not been paid because we expected a large booty. Syracuse has had every opportunity to surrender or negotiate, and has not done so. Unless the supporters can deliver the city to us before the battle, they must be punished. It is the Roman way."

Pounding a fist down on the sand table sending sand flying up into the air, "Don't lecture me about the Roman way. I am well aware of our customs. But I also know that more battles are to be fought in Sicily. If I show mercy in Syracuse, perhaps the other cities will surrender. The Carthaginian faction in Syracuse has been the head of this snake. Once we cut the head off, the resistance will die. Then we will have even more legions with which to fight the Carthaginians. My orders stand! Now go, and make ready."

"As you have commanded."

Ω

Two days later, Marcus sets sail with his armada of sixty galleys, each with five rows of oars. To ease his span of control he divides his fleet into three legions of roughly twenty galleys each. In the leading legion, he places most of the marines who are to assault the walls of Syracuse. In the second, he places most of the archers and slingers. In the third legion he locates his siege machines and catapults.

As the fleet approaches the Grand Harbor of Syracuse, Marcus can just make out the silhouette of the fortress guarding the harbor. The city is black; there are no fires or lights of any kind—not even signal fires.

"This is a good sign," Marcus says to Lucius. "We may still have the element of surprise."

"Sir?" interrupts another officer.

Marcus turns from the ship's railing to face Brutus Fabius, his second in command. He had been with Marcus since the war started but lacks the experience of the more seasoned veteran. Marcus does not particularly like him because on two occasions Brutus caused the death of several soldiers. He knows that as the commander he is responsible for everything his command does or fails to do, and Brutus' failures reflect poorly on his leadership. That is the price of command and glory. However, Brutus is well connected to an influential Roman family and is the son of the very popular General Fabius. It is best to treat Brutus with respect even though Marcus doesn't care for him personally. Beside, Brutus is well educated in Greek—both written and spoken. Marcus has spent his whole life in battle, and has not had time to master any language or science. He can barely read at all. He needs Brutus to read and write all his orders and letters.

"Yes?"

"Sir, we should anchor here for the night."

"Are we out of range of their weapons?"

"Yes, Sir. We should be safe here. We can lash the ships together in groups of four for security, and post sentinels in every group."

"Fine! And tomorrow?"

"At sunrise we can consult the priests, and read the omens. If the weather holds, and the omens are good, we can attack with the tide about mid morning. The sun will be toward our backs and in the defenders' eyes."

"Do you believe in the gods, Brutus?"

"No, sir. If any gods exist, they don't seem much interested in our affairs."

"I think you are right about the gods. If the gods decree when each man should die, when a ship sinks at sea, why do all the men aboard die the same day?"

"But that is not the point, is it? Many of our soldiers do believe in the gods and omens. And so does the senate. Tomorrow at sunrise we will bring the chickens on deck and feed them. If the chickens eat, it is a good omen."

"Brutus, I plan to attack tomorrow no matter what the chickens do."

"I know that, sir. That is why I ordered the chickens not to be fed today."

Smiling at the cleverness of his second in command, "Careful, Brutus, you may anger the Gods." Both men laugh. Marcus' cook approaches, and hands Brutus a dish of boiled eggs.

"Speaking of chickens, I had the cook gather these eggs, and prepared them for tonight's dinner."

The standard bearer and the bugler, called a Cornicen, who are trying to sleep nearby, begin to snicker. They have campaigned with Marcus before, and know what is going to happen next. Even Lucius, who is usually straight faced, begins to grin.

"Did you cook enough for everyone on board this ship?"

"No, sir. There are just enough for you and me."

"Then you can eat them all yourself. I eat whatever the men eat."

Disappointed, Brutus walks over to the two snickering soldiers, and drops the bowl of eggs at their feet. The men eagerly stuff themselves with the eggs. When he walks back to Marcus, Marcus hands him a scroll.

"This came from the senate two days ago. You had better read it."

Brutus takes the scroll, and immediately sees that the senate seal is unbroken. That can only mean that Marcus has not read the scroll yet. Brutus unrolls the scroll, and moves around to catch the moon light so he can read it. He reads it to himself, and looks at Lucius and then back at Marcus.

"Sir, it is the Senate's reply to your appeal to have the Lost Brethren reinstated after the war. They have rejected your appeal once again."

"I am not surprised. I have enemies there. My enemies want to have a different commander to battle Hannibal."

"Who do they favor?"

"Cornelius Scipio! Do you know him?"

"Yes, he is a brave commander."

"I am a brave commander, but generals are not chosen for their bravery. They are chosen by politics. I now believe that I was trapped into this useless campaign in Sicily in order to get me away from the Senate. How stupid of me."

Turning to Lucius, and placing a hand on his shoulder, "I am sorry my friend. I won't give up."

"I know, sir," replies Lucius. "But I think we should not tell the Brethren about this latest appeal. It is better that they still believe that there is hope."

"As you wish. And don't you give up. I will make another appeal in a few months. A victory tomorrow could make all the difference."

Out of the corner of his eye, Marcus sees lights behind the fortress wall. Brutus, is already looking toward the strange lights. The three men walk over to the railing.

"What are they up to?"

"Sir, it looks like as if they are lighting camp fires, perhaps," replies Lucius.

"Why? Something is going on. They know we are here!"

"It doesn't matter. We are out of range," Brutus points out.

"Look!" cries Lucius, pointing toward the fortress wall.

From behind the fortress wall comes a glow of fires being lit, small at first but growing with each passing second. It appears as a solid band of light along the top of the wall but obviously behind the wall. Suddenly, there is the sound of "Thump, thump, thump" in rapid sequence. Marcus has heard the noise before, and immediate recognizes the sound of catapults launching. The band of light rises, clears the wall, and turns into a band of fire. The three men watch the band of fire come closer, and as it does, it separates into individual balls of fire heading toward the Roman fleet.

"They're attacking us!" yells Marcus.

"I think they will fall short, sir," says Brutus. The three men stand at the rail, and stare in silence for a few seconds as the fire balls grow bigger.

"Curse the Gods, they are going to hit us!"

"No, sir!"

"Brutus, I say you are wrong!"

"No, sir! We are out of range."

The first of the fire balls begin to fall among the ships. Many pass harmlessly overhead but some explode among the sails and riggings of the ships. Some fall into the water between and around the fleet. Two or three hit Marcus' flagship.

"What in Hades are they throwing at us? Fire bolts?"

The crew scrambles around trying to put out the fires with sand from buckets placed around the deck. Other ships cut loose their burning sails to keep their ships from catching fire. After a few frantic minutes, Brutus reports, "Sir, I think we have the fire under control."

Marcus points into the water, "Look, the fire balls continue to burn in the water. Go get one and bring it to me."

Brutus gives orders for the crew to use their oars to retrieve one of the floating fire balls.

Suddenly grasping the full impact of what just happened, Marcus says to Brutus, "The fire balls weren't intended to damage us. They used them for light so they can see us. They have our range now." Shouting, "Centurion, turn this ship around immediately. We have to get farther out to sea. Get the men on the oars. Now! Cornicen, sound the signal for withdrawal. Do it now!"

The Cornicen grabs his bugle, and begins to play as loudly as he can. Horns on ships in each legion begin to echo Marcus' command to withdraw. The ships come alive with activity and shouting. Men scramble to get into place at their assigned oars. Oars pop out of the sides of the ships, and enter the water. In Marcus' flagship, under the direction of the ship's Centurion, one side of the ship's oarsmen row forward while the other side rows backward, spinning the ship in place. The ship begins to turn in place in a manner of minutes but it seem like an eternity to Marcus.

"Row! Row! Your lives depend on it."

The ship, now pointed seaward, slowly begins to make headway toward the open sea. The other ships follow Marcus' example.

"Thump, thump, thump."

Marcus turns to look back toward the fortress. No fire balls this time. In the black of the sky he cannot see what, if anything, is being thrown at them.

"Well, Brutus, now we will see if they have our range or not."

Suddenly, Marcus hears a crash as loud as a thunder clap coming from the ship closest to his flagship. The light from the remaining floating fire balls let him make out a huge stone striking mid ship. The stone appears to be as long as the ship is wide. It snaps the ship in two like so many kindling sticks, and the ship goes straight to the bottom. Only a few men on deck survive while most drown at their oars, screaming in the night. Another large stone hits the water behind Marcus' ship right where it had been only a few minutes ago. The stone creates a giant wave that rocks the ship, and sends a couple of men overboard. The wave splashes cross the deck, and knocks Marcus and Brutus to the deck. Large stones continued to fall for a few minutes more. Marcus estimates each stone to be between eight to ten talents in weight.

Marcus turns to see one of the Sambuca war machines being struck two or three time by stones. The Sambucas were built to allow men to climb to the top of the city walls protected from arrows. From the top to half way down the apparatus is torn away, and falls into the sea. It is dislodged from its anchors, but the lashings hold, and the rest of the machine does not go overboard. The ships themselves are saved from sinking because they are lashed together. Men jump from the sinking ships onto the other ships that have been spared. Survivors floating in the water are not so lucky. They cry out for their comrades to turn back and save them. Those who can swim try to follow the ships but the ships move too fast. The ships' centurions are fearful of turning back under the range of the catapults. Soon, the cries are too faint to hear. Then they fall silent.

As the fleet begins to make headway out to sea, the shower of stones subsides, and no more ships are lost. When Marcus feels that the ships are finally out of range, and no longer in danger, he orders the fleet to stop for the night.

To his aide, "Find out what damages we suffered, and report back to me."

Brutus walks over to Marcus, "Sir, here is the fire ball we recovered. It is a gourd."

"You mean a vegetable?"

"Yes, sir. It has been hollowed out, and filled with some type of oil. A wick was inserted into the top, and a weight added to the bottom. I think it was intended to float in the water as some type of marker. Of course, if it hit a ship, it certainly could start a fire. I imagine, some broke on impact with the water and sank, but a number did burn for while."

"You idiot! Not markers! The fire balls provided the light for the engineers to see us so they could adjust their range."

"Yes, sir"

"Have you ever seen a catapult throw a stone that large?"

"No, sir. The largest stone we can throw is around five talents."

"And at what range and with what accuracy?"

"About half the distance that we were engaged tonight. We are lucky if we hit anything moving. Catapults are best when used against fixed fortresses with troops massed inside. We seldom see the target."

"Tell that to the Syracusans who found our range quickly, and fired accurately. It was not luck."

The aide returns and salutes, "Excuse me, sir. I have the damage report"

Marcus turned to the aide, "Yes?"

"Sir, we lost three ships and have five damaged. One of the Sambuca machines was badly damaged. The damaged ships have managed to rejoin the fleet, and are making repairs."

"How many men killed, wounded, or lost?"

"Nearly all the crews of the three ships that were sunk. Several others on the damaged ships were also killed or wounded, but I do not know how many."

"Thank you. That is all for tonight. In the morning get a full accounting.

"As you have commanded, sir."

"Three ships lost with their crews, and we did not even get a chance to attack. Yet we have been forced to retreat. It is a bad start for the campaign."

The next morning Marcus asks the priests to perform the inspection of the omens for the battle, according to Roman religious tradition. Chickens are brought up in cages, and set loose on deck. The senior priest steps forward, and from a bucket scatters grain for the chickens. The chickens are still frightened from the night before, and refused to eat.

"This is a terrible omen. The Gods are not pleased. The battle will not go well today. We should not attack today, and should make a sacrifice to the gods," says the head priest.

A murmur begins to flow through the crew and onto the other ships.

An angry Marcus shouts to his aides, "Throw those chickens overboard!" After the last of the chickens is thrown overboard, Marcus says,

"See that! The chickens won't eat but they do drink. It is a good sign. We will be victorious today."

No one seems convinced. The priest starts to protest but is cut short by a look from Lucius.

"Priest, can you swim?" Lucius asks.

"No, I cannot."

"Then consider your next words carefully, or you will drink with the chickens."

"It is as Marcus has said. It is a good omen."

At midmorning, Marcus orders the Cornicen to sound the call to attack. The signal is echoed by other Cornicens on other ships. Marcus then orders a single fire arrow fired high into the air. That is the signal to begin the attack, and notifies observers on land that the sea attack has begun. These observers ride off to inform Appius who has assembled his legions behind ridges out of sight of Syracuse but within an easy march.

The first naval legion leads the assault followed closely by the second. The third legion moves forward to find the range for its catapults. The ships with siege machines and Sambucas follow close behind the second legion in order to deliver their machines quickly to the land once a foothold has been gained near the walls.

The first legion commander plans to bypass the main walls of

Syracuse, and row pass the fort on the island of Otrigia. The second legion will attack the fort on Otrigia with missiles to keep the defenders from firing at the fist legion's ships as they sail through the narrow entrance into the Grand Harbor. Once inside the harbor, the first legion can beach on the undefended shore between the main city and Fort Olympia where there is room for the siege machines to operate, and knock down the walls. The commander is counting on speed to keep his ships safe from the huge stones that sank three ships yesterday.

The crews, tired of sitting onboard ships for days, are eager for battle. The ships reach maximum speed quickly, and head for the gap between the Fort Otrigia and a smaller fort on the opposite bank. Suddenly, the lead ship strikes something in the water. It gives a little initially but then stops dead in the water. The sudden stop throws all the oarsmen forward on top of the rowers in front of them. Crew members on deck are all knocked down or thrown overboard across the bow. The weight of their armor sends them to the bottom of the sea. A minute later the second ship strikes whatever it is under the water. The first ship commander rushes to the bow, and peers over to faintly see a chain just under the water surface. The Syracusans have stretched a chain between the two forts.

"Crack!"

A third ship strikes the chain and then a fourth. The trailing ships are alerted, and are able to slow down enough that when they hit the chain they were not going very fast. At least two thirds of the leading legion is now strung out in line along the chain. Ships that are hung up on the chain are shifting weight toward the stern, and rowing backward to get off the chain. Then the crews all hear the tell tale sound of catapults.

"Thump, thump, thump"

"Quickly, row backwards! Row for your lives!" yell the centurions.

Crews scramble but they know it is too late. Looking toward both forts they see the tiny specks that grow larger as they come closer. Stones! And on target! They strike the ships along the chain with deadly effect. Two ships take direct hits, break apart, and sink. Three others are only slightly damaged. The ships are just beginning to turn around when,

"Thump, thump, thump."

More stones are on the way. Oarsmen begin to panic, and scream with some marines throwing off their armor so they will not drown. Those that can swim drop their oars, and dive overboard. Most just watch helplessly to see if a stone is heading their way. This confusion results in a few collisions as ships row backwards into the ships behind them. The ship centurions grab whatever they can, and begin beating the oarsmen to row faster at the same time swearing to kill anyone who does not row.

"Crash!"

The second volley strikes two ships directly, and damages a third. Bodies begin floating in the water.

"Thump, thump, thump"

The crews watch as the tiny specks grow bigger to become huge stones. Though not as deadly as the first volley, this volley strikes one ship directly while tearing off the masts of two others. The damaged ships begin to take on water.

"Thump, thump, thump."

This is too much for the oarsman. Many more jump overboard. No one can remain calm enough to coordinate rowing on one oar let alone five banks of oars. Most ships come to a crawl or stop altogether. All eyes turn toward the shore to spot the huge stones in the air. One, two, three seconds pass. Nothing. Everyone stops to watch and to listen. Still nothing.

"They mock us by throwing nothing at us. They know that by now the mere sound will panic our men." say the legion commander. "Let's get out of here."

One by one each ship gets their oarsmen back into position, and begins to make headway, moving out of range. In half an hour, Marcus' flagship pulls up along the legion commander's ship, and Marcus climbs aboard. After a short conference, he decides that the first legion will attack again with the remaining ships. The point of attack is the southeast corner of the city wall where it turns from the west east run toward a south north run. Marcus reasons correctly that this should reduce the number of catapults that can be brought to bear against the ships.

Second legion will support the attack as before. Two hours later, the first legion begins its second assault of the day with crews that are on the verge of panic.

In the central tower of the sea wall, a nervous Hippo paces back and forth while Archi watches the new assault on the seawall taking shape.

"Apparently, Zoippos' spies failed to mention to the Romans that we had rebuilt the harbor chain," Hippo says to Archi.

"No, apparently not, which is odd since the chain has been used in past decades so it was not an original idea."

"That tells me that either Zoippos did not know of Marcus' plan of attack or he deliberately withheld the information."

"Probably both," replied Archi, "If he has lost the confidence of the Romans, then he can now say to Marcus that had he been told of the Roman plan of attack, he would have told them of the chain."

"I think you are right."

"Marcus planned his attack from the sea so that his fleet would have their backs to the sun, hoping to blind us, and cause us to miss our marks. Now that the first attack has failed, the sun is now in a position that is favorable to us. There is not a cloud in the sky. Hippo, I think it is time to show the Romans how we use the sun."

"Right! We are ready." Hippo puts on his helmet, and picks up his sword, "I will lead them myself."

Hippo goes to the base of the tower, and gives a messenger an order. Soon a cohort of infantry approaches at the double. Hippo directs them to a small door that leads under the seawall. The door opens into a trench, slightly deeper than the height of a man, and running parallel to the seawall. He leads the cohort into the trench until he is sure that the entire cohort is in the narrow trench. On his command, each soldier turns, and faces the wall toward the sea. On Hippo's next order, they step up on two steps and out into the open facing the sea, their shields in front of them. On another order, they raise their highly polished shields to catch the sun's rays, and reflect the light toward the attacking ships.

A hundred shiny shields reflect the sunlight onto the decks of the Roman ships where pilots, archers, and catapult crews are trying to work. The blinding light causes more than a few misses, and distracts the pilots. Archi had tried in vain to perfect a mirror that could set ships on fire but failed. Hippo keeps the cohort in position until a few arrows begin to find the range before he leads them back behind the seawall.

Archi watches as the Roman ships approach. In the water, indicating different ranges, float brightly colored gourds which are anchored to the bottom by a long line. Archi knows that it is difficult to hit a fast moving ship. His war machines are sited to strike at a set range for a given weight of stone. The gourds tell Archi the proper range, and the color indicates which machine can strike that position. When the lead ship reaches the first gourd, Archimedes notes how long it takes to reach the second gourd. Now he knows their speed. Before they reach the third gourd, Archi tells an aide near the rear window of the tower to raise a small flag that is the same color as the gourd being approached. On a large catapult on the ground below, the crew gets ready, all eyes on the aide in the tower. On Archi's signal, the aide rapidly brings the flag down, signaling the catapult crew to trip the trigger. Archi watches as the large stone flies over the wall toward the hapless ship. It strikes the water just in front of the ship, and sends a wave that nearly swamps the ship. Archi tells the aide who now raises a black flag that indicates a near hit. The crew cheers loudly. Archi tells the aide to raise two colors this time. Down below, two crews get ready. At Archi's command, the aide drops one color and a few second later, the other. Archi watches as the first stone rips the mast off a ship. The second stone crashes through the deck of another ship, and through the hull, immediately sinking the ship. The aide raises two red flags indicating direct hits. The two crews break into wild cheers, and jeer at the first crew with their near miss.

The attacking legion uses a staggered line formation consisting of two rows of ships with the second row filling the gaps behind the first row. As the legions come into range of Archi's machines, great stones begin to fall amongst the ships but with less accuracy this time. Some ships are struck, and the masts torn off. Other stones fall a little short but push up great waves that rock the ships, and cause some minor collisions. Two ships take direct hits and sink. With each "thump" crews panic, and jump overboard. Closer to the wall, smaller catapults with shorter range are employed by the Syracusans. While many ships are hit and damaged, none sink. As the second legion comes into range of the walls, they begin to launch arrows and missiles at the defenders. Marcus watches in awe and admiration as a large stone of maybe nine talents strikes one Sambuca midsection. The weight of the stone forces the structure backwards tearing its lashings from the first two boats. The two center boats are upended, and begin to take in water rapidly as men jump overboard. The last two boats are saved only by quick thinking soldiers who cut the lashings with their swords. The Sambuca falls into the sea pulling the center two boats with it. The second Sambuca is not hit directly but two of the boats supporting it are. The crews quickly cut the lashing to save the boats. The two that are struck break apart, but many of the crew makes it back to the surviving boats.

By this time the lead boats are less than a stadia from the shore. Suddenly, several boats have giant spikes driven up through their hulls, and they start to sink. They have tripped a trigger just under the surface which releases a great weight under water. This allows the weight to sink to the bottom, pulling ropes through a pulley system to drive huge spikes up through the bottom of the ships. The ships are dead in the water and easy targets for the catapults. As stones rain down upon the ships, water gushes in through the holes made by the spikes. The crews immediately abandon ship. Those who have not taken the time to remove their armor sink to the bottom. The ship centurions in the second line, all experienced seaman, drive their ships up to the rear of the damaged ships, and take on as many survivors as possible. Then by staying in the path of the damaged ships as much as possible, most of the second line of ships is able to slip by without striking other triggers. As rapidly as possible to avoid getting struck by catapults, the ships head for the shoreline. Near the beach, the ships sail head long into large spikes embedded along the shore just below the water line. Though impaled, their momentum carries them near the shore, and the soldiers begin to disembark. Slower ships that fell behind run their bows into the sterns of the impaled ship. Using the front ship as a bridge, they begin to unload their soldiers. A few of the soldiers stop to kiss "terra firma." The second legion, observing the landings, increases its volley of arrows and missiles in an effort to drive the defenders back from the top of the walls.

As the first echelon reaches the shoreline, Archi signals for the smaller machines to begin launching their missiles. The machines are sited to strike a primary spot where the terrain on shore will naturally cause the Romans to bunch up, creating a target. The crews continue to hurl stones at that spot until Archi signals them to shift their machine to strike a secondary killing zone. During the decades of peace, Archimedes has designed and built hundreds of war machines. The crews have practiced for hours to perfect their skills and efficiency. Syracuse has gathered thousands of stones, using many to build walls, roads, and theaters that can easily be dismantled when needed to defend the city. Elephants were used to drag the stones into place, and now are used to lift the huge stones onto the catapults and machines with a series of compound pulleys and levers.

Suddenly, a deadly rain of arrows comes from small slits in the wall striking nearly every Roman soldier who had made it to the shore. Hippo moves back and forth along the wall telling crews when to eject large timbers down upon the beached ships. Other timbers are released from the wall, and roll down onto the Roman formations, cutting huge gaps in their ranks. The soldiers begin to fall back toward their ships. As the marines start to climb back onboard the few ships that are not damaged, large beams swing out from behind the wall. Suspended from each beam is a large claw, like a giant hand. Once a claw is positioned over a ship it suddenly drops, and crashes down with great force. Upon contact with a ship the claw snaps shut, seizing the ship. Then the claw is drawn up, lifting the ship up on end. Soldiers and crews fall out of the ships into the water. After a few minutes the claw is released, and the ship lands in the water stern first. Very few survive the fall. Within thirty minutes every ship of the first legion is sunk or badly damaged. The legion commander orders a withdrawal, but the order is hardly necessary. Every ship still afloat, is trying to escape the deadly conflict. As the ships pull away from the shore they come under fire from the smaller catapults and then the bigger ones. Only the legion commander's flagship manages to get back out of range, and it is badly damaged. The commander lies on deck with a broken leg. Marcus calls off the attack, and orders a withdrawal out to sea and out of range of Archimedes' deadly machines.

Pro-Praeter Appius now begins his assault of Syracuse from the land side. The focus of his attack is the west wall of the part of the city called

Neapolis. He has timed his attack to start after the attack by Marcus is fully engaged. He hopes that Marcus' attack will draw defenders from the wall, and weaken the defense of the west wall. Appius forms his soldiers in a broad front using the standard checkered formation intended to extend the defenders along the entire wall, and conceal the point that he has picked to concentrate his siege machines for breaching the walls. It is a good plan except that it does not take into account how the defenders are deployed or the numerous machines of Archimedes.

As the Roman fleet withdraws, Archi and Hippo quickly move from the sea wall to the west wall of the city. They go inside a tall central tower where they can observe the entire wall. The Roman formations approach the wall but while their own catapults are still out of range of the wall, Archi begins to signal his catapult crews. On the land side, the various ranges are marked by painted rocks.

"Thump, thump, thump."

Huge stones begin to break up the Roman formations. The Syracusans are targeting the Sambucas. One by one the Sambucas are struck before they ever get near the walls. The smaller Roman catapults cannot be used while moving, and once in position, take several minutes to hurl their first stone. During that period the catapults behind the walls of Syracuse find their range, and began to shower rocks upon the Roman crews.

"Thump, thump, thump."

Some Roman catapults are hit and destroyed as they stop to set up. Others choose not to stop until they get closer to the wall, hoping to be too close to the city to be targeted by Archimedes' machines. They are wrong.

As Appius' legions advance toward Syracuse in an orderly fashion, the formations encountered thickets of thorn bushes and piles of rocks. These cause them to bunch up, and slow down as they make their way around these obstacles. Ditches and walls channel the formations into compact clusters. Whenever the soldiers bunch up, they are immediately hit by large stones fired from behind the walls of the city.

Appius has assigned each cohort a specific part of the wall to scale or breech. Archers and slingers are to attack the defenders on top of the wall, and keep them behind the walls so that the soldiers with ladders can scale the walls. When the formation gets close to the wall they realize that Syracuse is not a typical walled city. There is no top of the wall in the traditional sense. The top of the wall is covered so that the defenders fire their arrows from slits and windows. These slits are difficult targets for the Roman archers to hit. Other holes make it easy for the defenders to push away any scaling ladders. Large logs hang from ropes all along the wall that when they are released, roll down the wall and into the Roman formations with devastating effect. As soon as one log is released, another takes its place. The few soldiers who manage to escape the rocks and logs are cut down by arrows once they get within range of the archers. Nowhere along the entire wall is any cohort successful in erecting a scaling ladder.

"Thump, thump, thump."

A volley of a multiple stones is released at such a short range that the stones fall just in front of the walls killing many Roman soldiers. Suddenly, huge cranes with giant claws suspended from them swing out from the walls over the heads of the Romans. Just as suddenly, the giant Archimedes claws are released to fall upon the Romans, and seize whoever is not able to get out of the way. The cranes then lift the helpless victim into the air, and drop them from a fatal height. One by one the cohorts begin to panic as they watched their comrades being thrown about like rag dolls. Having to watch for falling rocks, rolling logs, arrows shot from the wall, and now giant claws that could lift a man high into the air, and drop him on his comrades is too much to endure.

"Thump, thump, thump."

The mere sound of the threatening catapults unnerves the army. The soldiers panic, and abandon all their siege equipment in a desperate attempt to get back out of range of the catapults and machines. The battlefield is littered with weapons, shields, and helmets as well as the injured and wounded. The Syracusan archers on the wall, one by one, kill the wounded and dying Romans that lie within range. The battle is over in less than an hour.

Marcus calls an immediate council of war aboard his galley. Lucius notices that there are some new faces; the killed and wounded commanders have been replaced. Several of the old commanders have wounds and new scars. Marcus asks Appius to explain his plan of attack and his opinion of what went wrong.

After reviewing Appius' plans, Marcus says, "Your plan was fundamentally sound. It would have worked against any other city in Sicily except Syracuse and Archimedes' machines. Does any one here have a plan that might have a chance of success?"

His question is met with silence.

Marcus begins shouting, "Very well then! I am surrounded with idiots! The entire might of Roma is stopped by the machines of one man, Archimedes. His machines toss our ships and soldiers about like toys. Can anyone here tell me if we actually inflicted any causalties on the Syracusans?"

Again, his question is met with silence.

"Very well! It is apparent that no Roman siege machines can get close enough to inflict any damage to the city walls. An all-out attack would result in many more losses, diminishing the ranks of valuable soldiers still needed to conquer the rest of Sicily. I see no other option but to stop the attacks for the time being, and start a blockade. The fleet can blockade the harbor, and that should prevent any aid from Carthage by sea. Appius, you set up a land blockade. That should not be too difficult either. We will defeat the other rebel cities one by one until Syracuse remains alone. By then the city may be compelled to capitulate."

Zoippos is the first to dare speak, "It is also possible that my agents inside the city might gain the upper hand, and open the city gates."

Marcus is so angry that he grabs a wine cup from the table and throws it at Zoippos, hitting him in the chest. "You did not tell us about the chain!"

Wiping wine off his face and chest, "Had you including me in your war plans, I would have. If you remember, I recommended a blockade in the first place."

Standing up, Marcus shouts back, "Your brains are in your ass! You know nothing of tactics." Marcus moves toward Zoippos but Lucius already has moved behind Lucius, and seized him from behind with his dagger at his throat.

Appius finally finds his voice, "Do not kill him yet, commander. We might need him."

Marcus thinks about Appius' warning. He places his face in Zoippius' face. "If you ever withhold information from me again, I will have you crucified. Do you understand me?"

With trembling lips, Zoippos manages a femble, "Yes, sir."

Lucius lets go of Zoippos. Marcus turns on his old friend, Appius, "However, something has to be done about the soldiers in your army who panicked, and ran in the face of Archimedes' machines."

Appius had anticipated this question would come up sooner or later. He is ready with his reply, "It is impossible to determine who had run and who had not. What is certain is that many who stayed and fought, died."

Marcus replies, "You are all so quick to remind me of our Roman customs. I want to decimate the ranks."

Seveal commanders protest, "You cannot be serious?"

Marcus stares around the group and again turns to Appius, "You will form up the entire army in a large open area. On my order, each of you will pass through your units, and identify every tenth soldier. Each soldier, as he is identified, will step forward three paces, and take off his armor. On another signal from me, the commander or Decurion of each selected soldier will step forward and kill that soldier. That is my order."

Appius breaks the silence, "Then the Syracusans will have caused the death of one tenth of our army without throwing another stone."

Marcus answers, "So be it. My order stands."

Lucius, who has never spoken in a council of war before now says, "Marcus, this is too much. Even the Lost Brethen were only banished when they ran from the field at Cannae."

Tuning toward Lucius, Marcus says, "I know that, you ass. And look what happened! There was no honor to be saved."

"But Marcus, there is no honor in being crushed by a stone, in drowning at sea, or being tossed about by a machine."

"Lucius, don't you see? The whole of the army ran but only a few must die for it. The honor of the rest is still in tact. Brutus, you know the senate's state of mind. What do you say?"

Brutus, who was hanging back to stay away form Marcus' anger steps forward and says, "If you do not do this, the senate will surely bandish the army to Sicily, never to return home."

Marcus asks Lucius, "Which is better? You tell me!"

Lucius hangs his head, "You are right, of course. It is better to sacrifice a few men to save the honor of the others."

The next day, Appius has his army form up in a large open field out of sight of the city walls. Each commander does as Marcus has ordered. The Decurion of each selected soldier thrusts his sword through the man's back and into his heart. Marcus had commanded that if any Decurion failed to kill his soldier, the entire centubernia of eight men would be killed. All the Decurions obey. They strike true and quickly, hoping for an instant kill so that their soldiers die without suffering. It is the least and most merciful thing the Decurions can do under the circumstances. The bodies are gathered into a large pile and burned.

After only one day of battle, Marcus concludes that Syracuse cannot be attacked directly, and turns his attention to blockading the city while conquering the rest of Sicily.

CHAPTER TWENTY THREE

(1499, Cesare's Campaign Headquarters)

"Leonardo, I never read anywhere that Syracuse defeated the Romans in Sicily. Are you sure about that? I thought that the city was eventually sacked by the Romans," says Cesare.

"Yes, sire. If you look for it, you will find it. History is written by the victors but the great historian, Livy, wrote about it, and so did Polybius. You are also correct that Marcus eventually did sack Syracuse. The story is an interesting one," replies Leonardo.

"How is it that Archimedes was able to design and build so many different machines, and employ them all around the city without the rest of the world knowing about it?"

"Remember, that Syracuse was at peace for nearly fifty years, and their walls had not been breached in centuries. Had they been attacked, the world would have heard about Archimedes' war machines. Just because they were at peace does not mean they were idle. They knew that some day they would be drawn into the wars between Rome and Carthage. They used that time to prepare their defenses. And while they had several cities that were loyal to them, they never engaged in conquest or aggressive wars. They paid the tribute to Rome, and supplied legions when required but never let their machines leave the city. Archimedes had learned much about making these machines while he was in Alexandria as Chief Engineer to King Ptolemy. He invented many types of gears, and made use of his knowledge of levers and pulleys. He tested many different types of weapons. When he returned to

Syracuse, he brought with him several elephants, which enabled him to move great stone blocks, and to accomplish much in a short period of time. King Hieron also made it a crime punishable by death to reveal any thing about the defenses of Syracuse to another kingdom, even allies. Archimedes also had help. Living in Syracuse were several families of engineers who had experience in making war machines. You recall your history concerning the exploits of King Phrrhos who invaded Italy some seventy years before these events?"

"Of course, he defeated the Romans twice and even marched into Latium. When he was finally defeated, Rome ruled the whole of Italy."

"Yes, and he was briefly king of Syracuse before he invaded Italy. He brought many Greek engineers to Syracuse to build his machines. He used war elephants so the people of Syracuse were use to them. Many of these engineers settled in Syracuse so Archimedes had many experienced engineers to employ on his inventions. Together, they designed and built the various machines I described to you."

"Amazing! Can we use any of these devices in my campaign?"

"Of course. I am working on many of Archimedes' ideas. The steam cannon is just one. But recall that Syracuse was for many years an ally of Roma. Syracuse was also a costal city. Carthage, at that time, was master of the sea, so Syracuse's defenses were built primarily to defend against an attack from the sea. When they were built, it was thought that Carthage would be the attacker, not Rome."

"So if Marcus could not break down the walls of Syracuse, how did he eventually sack the city?"

"You were right when you suggested it must be intrigue. Indeed it was, and if it had not happened, Syracuse may have never been conquered. Let me finish my story."

"Yes, yes! Please go on. I cannot sleep until I know how this ends."

Monte R. Anderson

(213 BCE, in Syracuse, Sicily)

On the advice of Hannibal, Hippo and Epi adopt a strategy of try-ing to cut the Roman supply lines, and to isolate Marcus in Sicily. They hope that Hannibal will eventually conquer Rome, and end the war. They also believe, convinced by Hannibal, that Carthage will send rein-forcements. Hannibal encourages them to tie down as many Roman legions in Sicily as they can to weaken the defense of Rome. Because of the blockade, Hippo and Epi cannot lead their own troops out of Syracuse, but using small boats that easily glide over the harbor chain, they are able to infiltrate through the naval blockade, and lead an army composed of allies of Syracuse. But each ally also has to defend their own cities, and can spare few soldiers. The Sicilian forces are hopeless-ly outnumbered, and one by one the independent cities loyal to Syracuse fall to the Roman army.

Near the city of Acilae, Marcus has the good fortune to come upon the camp of Hippo and Epi that is only partially fortified. Marcus immediately deploys his army and attacks. He captures the camp, killing nearly eight thousand men. With this victory, Marcus eliminates any threat from outside the fortified cities. Even the Carthaginian army retreats behind the walls of the few remaining cities. However, the two Syracusan brothers are able to escape with a small number of soldiers.

Later, Hippo and Epi make camp with a few followers after narrow-ly escaping Marcus' army. The small band of men lights no fires, and eat a cold meal.

"Hippo," asks Epi, "What shall we do?"

"I don't know. It seems certain that we will not be able to field another army, and fight in open battle. We need reinforcements from Carthage. We must send a message to Carthage. I think we should return to Syracuse, and command the defenses there. If Syracuse falls, all of the other cities will surrender to Roma, and Sicily will be ruled by Romans. Then Marcus can return to Roma, and fight against Hannibal. Hannibal will not be able to survive."

"I will deliver the message myself," says Epi. "I will go all the way to Carthage if I have to. You stay in Syracuse. You have a wife to pro-tect. When I get back, I will rally whatever soldiers I can find outside the city, and harass the Romans wherever we can. If we use hit and run tactics, we might still tie down many soldiers to protect their camps and supplies."

"We may be able to negotiate an honorable surrender," suggests Hippo. "The Romans know that they cannot capture Syracuse, but we cannot defeat them. Our allies are being defeated one by one. Unless Mars begins to favor the Carthaginians, they will be defeated. Tell the Carthaginians that if they do not break the blockade of Syracuse, and send us reinforcements, we will be free to make our own terms with the Romans."

"Then it is settled. We go tomorrow."

The next morning the two brothers say farewell, and go their separate ways.

Ω

(Two months later in Syracuse)

Archi and Hippo are supervising the repair of the walls and defenses of Syracuse. By means of compound pulleys and the power of elephants, large stones and stone blocks are again positioned on catapults. Other elephants help work crews replace the large logs that were used during the Roman attack. The spikes along the shore are repaired and reset. Triggers under the water surface in the harbor are reset as the great stone weighs are lifted by cranes mounted on large barges. All the hulls of the Roman ships are dismantled, and the wood hauled into the city for firewood. The training of catapult crews continues, even at night.

Archi and Hippo are standing on the city wall watching a crew of elephants maneuver a stone into place on one of Archi's machines.

"Hippo, have you considered sending Arsinoe to Alexandria?" asks Archi.

"Yes, we have discussed it. She does not want to go. It would be different, I think, if we had children."

"If you have a son, you should send him to the Museum at Alexandria to be educated. Nine is a good age to start. After ten years he will be ready to make his own contributions to science or the arts."

"You think he should be a scholar like you, and not a soldier like me?"

I think if we survive this war, you will be elected king of Syracuse. Your son would follow you as ruler of Syracuse. He would be a better ruler if he is educated," says Archi.

Hippo thinks about it for a minute. "I think you are right, but first, we have to have a son."

Archi says, "If you do have a son, and he does go to the museum, I want you to do something for me."

"And what is that, Master?" asks Hippo.

"You know my cedar chest in my work shop?"

"Yes, the one with the carvings on it? Often I have thought about all the great ideas you have in it."

"Hippo, when your son is eighteen, I want you to give him that chest. He will know what to do with it."

Even Hippo's bodyguards have laid aside their weapons and armor, and joined in the work. Most of the soldiers and workers have stripped down to just a loincloth in the heat of the day. However, Archi notices one soldier approaching wearing a cape, unusual in this heat. The soldier's face is partially blocked by his cape. Archi keeps an eye on him as he moves along the wall to a position behind Hippo.

Suddenly, the soldier throws off his cape, revealing his face, and rushes toward Hippo, sword drawn. Immediately, Archi recognizes Dinomenes, the former bodyguard turned traitor, who led the mob into the palace. Dinomenes charges Hippo at a dead run, hoping to catch him by surprise. Hippo has his back to Dinomenes, unaware of the attack. Archi shouts a warning to Hippo, and sticks out his staff, tripping Dinomenes. Two more assassins emerge from behind a corner of the wall and rush at Hippo. Hippo turns in time to draw his sword, and parry the thrust of the closest attacker. By circling sideways, he keeps the first attacker between himself and the second assassin. In this way, he can separate them, and fight them one at a time. Meanwhile, Archi disarms the prostate Dinomenes by striking his sword hand with the end of his staff, breaking all his fingers. As Dinomenes screams in pain,

Archi kicks his sword out of reach. He swings his staff again, striking Dinomenes in the knee cap, crushing it, and preventing him from standing. Dinomenes curls himself into a ball, trying to protect his head with his hands, and crying from the pain. Archi stands with his staff raised over his head, ready to strike again if Dinomenes should try to escape but Dinomenes is paralyzed with fear.

The would-be assassins do not wear any armor nor carry shields which leaves them largely unprotected. While Hippo also does not have armor, he is the better swordsman. The closest attacker lunges to stab Hippo. Hippo steps forward instead of backwards as he parries the thrust sword with his sword. At the same time, he uses his empty left hand to smash his fist into the man's face. Then, with a downward backhand swing, Hippo inflicts a severe wound to the forward leg of his attacker. Confident that the first attacker is disabled, Hippo turns to meet the second attacker who strikes at Hippo with an overhead swing aimed at Hippo's head. Hippo leans to his right slightly, and pivots on his front leg while he swings his rear leg to the right. This maneuver moves his body from under his opponent's sword and very close to his attacker - too close to stab with his sword. Using the hilt of his sword, Hippo strikes the attacker in the back of his head as the assassin lunges forward. The attacker's momentum and the strike to the head, sends him sprawling to the floor. Hippo follows close behind, and kills him with a sword thrust. He turns to face the first attacker on the ground when several arrows kill the first assassin. The bodyguards have arrived with their weapons to dispatch the would-be assassins. Hippo holds up his hand to stop them from killing Dinomenes too. He smiles when he sees the quivering Dinomenes on the ground trying to protect himself from Archi's staff.

"You have again proved that the lever is mightier than the sword, Master."

"This is the bastard that struck me when I tried to protect the women in the palace. He killed them all. I saw him leading the mob. I think he was the one who killed your father."

Upon hearing these words, Hippo kicks the beaten Dinomenes.

"You are a traitor!" yells Hippo. He raises his sword to kill him but then hesitates. He has another idea. He signals his bodyguards to pick up Dinomenes.

"Take him down by the elephants."

Hippo instructs the commander of his bodyguard how to execute Dinomenes. The commander has his men take Dinomenes over to a smaller stone, and forces him face down onto the stone. He then motions for one of the elephant handlers to bring his elephant over to Dinomenes. The handler immediately understands, and using his stick, guides the elephant into position at Dinomenes' head. Guards on either side of Dinomenes hold his arms, and place a foot on his back. Dinomenes finally realizes what is about to happen, and struggles harder, but his crushed kneecap keeps him from gaining any leverage to stand. The guard holding his broken fingers, twists them until Denomenes stops resisting, and lies still. The elephant's handler taps the elephant behind his knee, and the elephant raises his foot over Dinomenes' head. The handler, the guards, and Dinomenes all look up at Hippo and Archi standing on the wall above.

Dinomenes begins to beg for mercy, "In the name of Mars, no! Kill me with a sword! Cut off my head but not this! This is no way for a soldier to die."

"You killed people not in battle but by trickery," replies Hippo. "You are not a soldier. You were not even a good bodyguard. I heard that Damarata asked you for a sword, and you refused her. Now I refuse your request. I will avenge her death and the death of the other women you killed. I avenge the death of my father and mother, and the death of the king."

"Let me live, and I will tell you everything," pleads Dinomenes.

"It is too late for that. You should have come to me before you killed my father and the rest of the royal family"

"It was not my idea to kill the women," pleads Dinomenes. "Zoippos ordered me to do it, even his own wife."

"Zoippos?" asks Archi in disbelief. "You mean Zoippos ordered you to kill Heraclia, his wife, too?"

"Yes! Yes! He wanted me to kill all the royal family, and to assassinate your father and you. He is behind all the killing. He killed King Hieronymos. He wants no one left so that Roma can make him king of Syracuse. He was the one who ordered the beheading of the people in Leontini."

"That only confirms what I thought," says Hippo to Archi, "This man is not smart enough to have plotted all those attacks. Zoippos is behind all of this."

Archi shouts down to the helpless Dinomenes, "And what of King Gelo?"

"He was poisoned by his sister, Damarata, Hippo's own mother. She confessed it before we catapulted her into the harbor. Your family is not innocent, Hippo. Your father plotted against Roma. It is you and your whole family that are the traitors to the people of Syracuse."

An angry Hippo points to the elephant handler who then taps the foot of the great beast. With a thud, the huge foot falls on the head of Dinomenes which explodes with a crack, splashing blood and brains on the elephant, the guards and the bodyguards' commander. The guards drag Dinomenes' lifeless body, and the bodies of the other two assassins up onto the wall and throw them into the harbor.

Turning to Archi, Hippo says, "You saved my life. How can I repay you?"

"Save my daughter. Save your wife. Get her to safety. Send her to Alexandria."

Ω

(212 BCE in Central Sicily)

A centurion enters Marcus' tent, and announces his presence, "Sir?"

"Yes, what is it?"

"Sir, two days ago, we captured a small ship trying to leave the Syracuse harbor. There were two people onboard that we thought you might want to question."

"Why?"

"Well, sir, the skipper of the ship is a Lacedaemonian, by the name of Damippus. The other is a woman who says she is his daughter."

"They seem innocent enough. What are you not telling me?"

"Well, sir. I used to command a ship on patrol duty off these shores, and we stopped this person more than once. Each time he had a different story; he was a Phoenician, or a Carthaginian, or a Syracusan. Now he is Lacedaemonian? But he always carried letters from King Hieron or King Ptolemy of Alexandria and letters to and from Archimedes. The woman I don't know. But he never had a woman with him before. I think she is too young to be his daughter."

"Damippus you say? I know that name. Where are they now?"

"Outside, sir. I thought it best to bring them in case you wanted to see them."

"You did right. Bring them in."

The centurion leaves the tent, and returns in a few minutes with Arsinoe and Barnacle with a guard on either side, their hands bound behind their backs. Marcus studies them for a few minutes, and then looks into Barnacle's pockmarked face.

"Of course! Barnacle! We met in Alexandria many years ago along with Archimedes. You commanded that three-mast ship which was a gift for King Ptolemy. Am I right?"

"Yes, sir, and I was just trying to get back to my home in Alexandria."

Marcus slaps Barnacle across the face, "Don't play games with me. You are not in Alexandria now, and I will crucify you for the spy you are. Your home is not in Alexandria but in Syracuse."

"No! He is telling the truth. We were going to Alexandria," yells Arsinoe.

Marcus turns his attention toward Arsinoe, "I believe you were headed to Alexandria, but you were not returning home. You probably carry a message to the king." Marcus glances at the centurion who shakes his head no. "Or … you were trying to escape. Who are you?"

"I am Arsinoe, niece of King Ptolemy, and he will be angry to hear that you have stopped me."

"You are both lairs!" To the centurion, "Go get Zoippos."

"As you have commanded, sir," says the centurion as he leaves the tent.

Marcus directs the guards to tie the prisoners to separate supporting poles.

A few minutes later, Zoippos enters the tent. "You sent for me?"

"Yes. Can you identify these prisoners?"

Zoippos saunters over to Barnacle first, looks at him, then over to Arsinoe, and smiles at her.

"Yes, of course. You have Damippus, also called Barnacle, a shipping merchant and friend of Archimedes, and Arsinoe, daughter of Archimedes and the wife of Hippokrates, tyrant of Syracuse."

Pouring two glasses of wine, "Thank you. Have some wine, and stick around. You might be useful yet."

Marcus hands Zoippos a glass of wine. "Now then" turning toward Barnacle, "As I recall, you were instrumental in getting Archimedes and his wife, out of Alexandria when the king died."

Turning toward Zoippos, "What was her name?"

"Helena."

"Yes, of course, Helena. Now I remember. She was the one who was the niece of King Ptolemy. So now what do we have here? We have before us an old sailor who once built and commanded the fastest ship afloat, and is a personal friend of Archimedes and a young, beautiful woman who claims to be the niece of King Ptolemy but who is really the daughter of Archimedes and the wife of Hippokrates, tyrant of Syracuse and enemy of Roma. I am guessing that your husband has asked Barnacle to smuggle you out of Syracuse. Yes! That's it, isn't it?"

Marcus sips his wine, and smiles toward Zoippos who nods in agreement. Arsinoe and Barnacle do not answer.

"I met your mother, Helena, in Alexandria. She was one of the most beautiful women in Egypt. Not as beautiful as her sister, your aunt. I can see the family likeness now. You must be her daughter. You have her beauty. How is your mother?"

"She is dead, no thanks to you."

"I am sorry to hear that. Are you the only child?" No answer.

He turns toward Zoippos who answers for her, "She is the only child."

Marcus continues his interrogation, "How did your mother die?"

"She was murdered by an agent of the pro-Roman party who was trying to kill my father."

Marcus glaces sideways toward Zoippos, "Well, I'll be damned. Had that agent succeded, I would have conquered Syracuse a year ago."

Not wanting to admit that he had nothing to do with trying to kill Archimedes, and yet, not willing to take crdeit for trying to kill a man that Marcus admires, Zoippos remains silent.

"I see," says Marcus. "Archimedes wanted to spare his only daughter, so he asked his closest friend to smuggle her to Alexandria, or was it Hippo who arranged for your escape? No matter, you are my prisoners now. I imagine that your father and husband will pay a handsome ransom to get you back."

Turning to Barnacle, "And what shall I do with you? Well, I suppose you are just a bonus. If Archimedes doesn't want you back, I can use you to build faster ships for my navy."

Pouring another glass of wine, "Zoippos, I want you to get a message to Hippokrates. Tell him that I have his wife and the Lacedaemonian spy, Barnacle. If they would like to negotiate for their return, I am a reasonable man."

"Yes, sir."

"And tell them that if they will guarantee my safety I will conduct the negotiations myself. I will leave the meeting place up to them as an act of trust. Now hurry."

"As you have commanded, sir," draining his glass and departing.

Ω

Two days later Marcus enters into the city of Syracuse with a small party, wearing capes over their armor and weapons so as not to arouse attention. It is night and the city, under blockade, has very few lamps lit. They are met inside the gate by a cohort of soldiers who provide escort. Zoippos leads the way to the palace. The group of men must move slowly so that Lucius, with his flopping feet, can keep up.

"Why did you bring him? He only slows us up," Zoippos whispers to Marcus. "And why are you here? You could be captured or killed. I could conduct the negotiations."

"You forget that Arsinoe is my prisoner," says Marcus in a whisper. "Nothing will happen to me. Besides, I need to see the defenses for myself. That is why I brought Lucius. His slowness gives me time to observe the defenses without raising suspicions. I also do not trust you."

"Then it is foolhardy to bring Brutus, the second in command. What will happen if you both are captured?"

"Appius is quite capable of taking command if anything happens to us."

Zoippos does not say other word. Once inside the palace, Hippo greets them, dismisses the cohort, and guides the small group to a small inner room. Archimedes is already in the room when they arrive.

Hippo watches Lucius stagger across the room, "You were at Cannae?"

"Yes," replies Lucius with a surly attitude.

Ignoring his rudeness and disrespect, Hippo says, "It seems that the Romans are as hard on their own as they are with their allies."

"The Romans are, indeed, harder on their soldiers than they are on their allies, but Hannibal did this to me, not the Romans. I see that he treated you much better," replies Lucius with a touch of sarcasm.

"Yes, he treated my family well. My brother and I were his prisoners along with my father. Hannibal even had his personal physician treat my father's wound. He is much more civilized than you Romans."

"Then it is better to be a prince captured by Hannibal than to be a Roman centurion."

"Perhaps," turning back to the group, "This room will give us more privacy. I am Hippokrates, dictator of Syracuse, and this is Archimedes, my father-in-law and chief engineer. These others are my bodyguards."

Archi tells one of the bodyguards to bring a lamp closer to the group. As the light illuminates everyone's faces, Archi recognizes Zoippos. He takes his staff into both hands and raises it to strike Zoippos. As Hippo reaches to stop Archi, Lucius steps in front of Zoippos. Archi swings his staff as Hippo tries to grab it. The staff comes down hard but Lucius parries the blow with his forearm armor.

Hippo grabs Archi in a bear hug and whispers, "Not now, Master. We'll get Zoippos later. Right know we have to try to save Arsinoe."

Archi sighs, "You are right. I am sorry." He backs up, shaking with anger and glares at Zoippos.

Marcus salutes Hippo as the others follow his example except for Zoippos. Marcus glares at Zoippos who takes the hint and salutes.

As Hippo acknowledges the salute, Marcus turns toward Archi and using Brutus as translater, says, "Archi, it is good to see you again." He extends a hand out to Archi who refuses it.

"Archimedes!" says Archi.

"What?" asks Marcus.

"My name is Archimedes. Only my friends call me Archi."

"My pardon, sir. I meant no offense. Without you, Syracuse could not withstand my attacks for more than a month. But you have delayed my campaign for more than a year. As a soldier, I admire your skills and your machines. Congratulations."

Archi waves his hand, "They are nothing. They have no scientific value. They are merely toys, nothing else."

Turning to Hippo, Marcus says, "You are fortunate to have Achrimedes as your chief engineer."

Hippo replies, "He is my chief advisor too. He is also the only man in Sicily that is undefeated against me sword sparring."

All eyes stares at old Archimedes.

"It was a long time ago when Hippo was still my student, and we were developing the tactics which we now use successfully in battle," replies Archi.

Marcus is impressed. He would like to ask how this was possible, but decides now is not the time nor place. He starts the introduction of his staff, "I am Marcus Claudius Marcellus, commander of the Roman army in Sicily. On my left is Brutus, my second in command. This is Lucius, my personal bodyguard. Apparently, you already know Zoippos."

"If you mean the traitor who ordered his own wife killed along with the rest of my family, yes, we know him. Please, be seated and have some wine."

As the two leaders sit, Lucius takes up a position standing directly behind Zoippos. One of the bodyguards passes out bowls while a second bodyguard pours from a jug of wine. Everyone takes a wine bowl except Archi and Lucius, but no one drinks. Instead, they watch Hippo to see if he will drink the wine.

Noticing the stares, "Yes, of course." He takes a drink of wine and says, "See! No poison."

"One must be careful these days," says Marcus as he sips the wine.

"If I wanted to kill you now, I would not have to resort to poison," nodding toward Zoippos, "as some traitors do. I understand that you have taken my wife and good friend as prisoners."

"Not so much as prisoners but as my guests. I mean them no harm, and I will let them go."

"Just like that? No deals or trades?" asks Archi.

"Well, I didn't say that. The opportunity exists for Roma and Syracuse to end this war between us. Our mutual enemy is really Carthage, and the Carthaginians are losing. You should consider all the options."

"Return Arsinoe and Barnacle first," demands Hippo.

"No! If I do, you will not negotiate. That would leave me with nothing to bargain with."

"What is it you want?" asks Archi.

"I want you to stop this war, and sign a treaty with Roma. If you do, I will lift the blockade, and not occupy your city. If you refuse, I will conquer this city. You cannot win. In time, I will defeat you. You are isolated from the rest of Sicily. Carthage cannot help you."

"If you are going to win eventually, then why not ask for terms of surrender instead of a treaty?" asks Archi.

"Archimedes is right," says Hippo, "Thanks to him, you cannot defeat our defenses. It is you who has suffered the most casualties. We have enough food to last for ten years."

"Then we will conquer Syracuse in the eleventh year," says Brutus.

Marcus places a hand on Brutus' arm to silence him.

Marcus continues, "It is Roman custom that once our battering ram touches your gate, we will show no mercy. But it doesn't have to end this way. Syracuse was a good ally for many years. It could be again. However, thanks to Archimedes and his machines, you could hold out for another year or more and tie down many soldiers that I can use to fight Hannibal. But be certain of this, we will win in the end. Carthage cannot help you."

"And what of my daughter? Is she all right?" asks Archi.

"I won't let any harm come to her. If you desire a treaty, I will let her go immediately. If not, I will still release her anyway, and let Barnacle take her to Alexandria, out of harm's way. Roma has a long standing treaty with Alexandria. I would not harm a member of the Ptolemy family. I don't want her to be a factor in making your decision. I just wanted to use her to start the negotiations. Hippo, I am also prepared to offer you the kingship of Syracuse."

Brutus shifts his feet, and looks at Zoippos with a questioning glance.

Marcus continues, "You have only to sign a treaty with Roma and the Senate will forgive this unfortunate affair and crown you king of Syracuse."

Zoippos starts to speak, but he feels the point of Lucius' dagger pressed into his back. He stiffens as he feels Lucius' hot breath on his ear.

"One word and you are a dead man," whispers Lucius. "Let Marcus do all the talking."

Once he is sure that Zoippos heard and understood, Lucius takes one step back.

"I don't believe you." says Hippo. "How do I know she is all right?"

"I will send Barnacle at this time tomorrow under escort. You may talk to him about her. Afterwards, return him to me. Before he arrives, you can discuss your options with your war council. Send your answer back with Barnacle."

"Very well then, we will meet Barnacle at the same gate tomorrow night at the same time," says Hippo, standing up.

Zoippos glares at Lucius, and then leads the small party slowly back toward the city gate.

After walking several minutes in silence Zoippos says, "The kingship of Syracuse was offered to me by the Senate. You do not have the authority to crown Hippo king."

"I have the authority to do whatever I want to conquer this city. Beside, you forget that I was there when the Senate made a deal with you. The throne was offered to your wife, not you."

"But she was killed. Now the throne should pass to me."

"Yes, she was, wasn't she? How convenient! And if I understand what Hippo said tonight, you may have had a hand it that. I don't doubt it. But that is not the point. If you recall, I said that you must deliver Syracuse to us or you get nothing. The Senate went along with that. I will remind the Senate of that agreement, and hold you to it. Help me now, and you may still be king. Betray me, and I will kill you. Do we understand each other?"

Reluctantly, "As you have commanded."

After a few minutes of silence, Zoippos asks, "Do you really think they will sign a treaty?"

"No, of course not. They have not suffered enough. Besides, it is too late for that."

"Then why did you come into the city?"

"I wanted to see their defenses for myself. Do you see that tower over to the left there?"

"Yes, sir."

"Well the soldiers do not seem very alert, and the tower is not as formidable as the others. Here is how you can help. Do you think you can get some soldiers loyal to you assigned to that tower?"

"Yes, I think so. A few, perhaps."

"Also get men loyal to you at the nearest gate."

"Yes, sir. That should be no problem. The soldiers are always looking for someone to stand their post for them."

"When you do, let me know, and I will seize that tower. Once inside we can take the whole city."

"If you could stall for a few days," suggests Zoippos, "The city will celebrate the Feast to Artemis in three days. That would be a good time to attack."

"Describe the feast to me."

"I believe Artemis is similar to the Roman goddess Diana. In Syracuse, we worship her differently from the Greeks in the older Greek cities, who consider her a goddess of the hunt and mistress of wild animals. We Syracusans consider her to be the goddess of motherhood and childbirth. Many weddings are celebrated during the feast with much drinking. The guards on the walls will be reduced to the minimum. They could even be drunk."

"So be it. The timing is right for us to gain the element of surprise."

The group stops to wait for Lucius who has fallen behind. As they wait, Marcus looks around as the twilight begins to illuminate the surroundings.

Turning to Zoippos, "Syracuse is a beautiful city. You have many works of art. Is the entire city as beautiful as this section?"

"Yes, we have had many years of peace as an ally of Roma, and we have prospered by our commerce. Roma Pax, as it is called. The rich families of Syracuse have commissioned great artists to create all these works of art."

"We have nothing like this in Roma. We have been at war so long that all our money is spent on weapons and not art. When we conquer this city, I will take these art works back to Roma; not only the art but also the artists."

Lucius, who has been exaggerating his handicap, finally catches up with the group, and they proceed out the gate and back to the Roman lines.

Marcus calls for a council of war early the next morning. Present are Appius, Zoippos, Brutus, Lucius, and the other commanders.

Marcus, starts, "I found a tower which I think we can seize if we use stealth under the cover of darkness instead of a mass attack. Zoippos can lead a small raiding party to the nearest gate where loyal supporters will let us in. He will then lead the party to the tower. The tower guards are lax and may even be drunk. Once we have that tower, we should be able to let more small groups inside the walls to capture the other towers. We will seize one tower at a time until we are discovered. The key is surprise. If we can control most or all of the walls, then victory will be ours in a few hours. We will attack at night in three days. I can give you the details on how high to make the ladders and other things tomorrow."

"Sir," Appius speaks up. "I have a centurion who has trained a number of his men as assassins, mostly Lost Brethren. I had hoped to use them in battle to attack, and kill the enemy commander. This unit would be the best unit to lead this attack."

"Very well. I leave the details to you. Your mission is to capture and hold the northern walls. I want this done before sunrise. I want buglers placed all around the walls, and on my signal they will sound the call to attack. Secure all the gates in the northern wall to let the rest of the legions inside. At that signal, I want you to send two cohorts to seize the two gates in the inner wall that divides the city. We will need those gates to gain entrance into the southern part of the city. Zoippos, what is it called?"

"Achradian."

"Yes, Achradian. Once inside, send one legion immediately to capture Achradian. I want one cohort to capture the palace and the royal treasury. Guard the royal treasure. Use your other legions to fight the Syracusan soldiers. I will keep my headquarters on the tower until the palace is captured and then I will relocate there. Each legion will send two liaison officers to be with me at the towers."

"What of the loyal supporters?" asks Zoippos.

"You will provide guides to meet the legions at each gate. I will tell you which cohorts are to seize the gates. Work out a signal so that they do not kill the guides. Have one guide lead the cohort that is to capture the palace. Lead another cohort to capture the small fort where the end of the harbor chain is anchored. We need to lower the chain to let in the fleet. That will be a key to our success. Once the chain is down, the city is as good as captured regardless of what else happens. Brutus?"

"Yes, sir?"

"I want you to lead the attack to capture the chain and to let in the fleet."

"I was referring to the loyal citizens," says Zoippos.

"Of course. Tell all your loyal supporters to wear a white tunic with a red 'X' on the chest; men, women, and children. We will tell the soldiers not to harm anyone wearing such a tunic and not to enter their homes or to plunder them. Tell your men to disable as many catapults as you can. If everyone is drinking during the feast, that should not be too difficult. And Zoippos."

"Yes?"

"If Hippo finds out about this plan of attack, I will personally kill you. Understood?"

"As you have commanded, sir."

"Any questions?"

"Yes, sir." Appius asks, "What about the booty?"

Marcus pauses for a minute and then says, "We have fought hard for this victory and the Syracusans with their machines have inflicted many casualties upon us. They also betrayed us in violation of our treaty. For this they must be punished. However, within the walls of Syracuse we have many supporters. They must be protected as I have directed. I will allow plunder once the city is under our control, but it must end at sunset. Supporters of Roma must not be harmed in any way or their homes entered. Post guards. Zoippos will show which houses to guard. Do whatever you want with the Syracusans that did not support us. That includes their wives and daughters, their property, their slaves and treasures. But I do not want anything burned. Bring all the booty to the palace and we will split it there according to rank. I claim all the various works of art for myself. I want to take them back to Roma as trophies of war."

"Yes, sir. I will inform the soldiers."

"One more thing, Appius."

"Yes?"

"As soon as you enter the gates of Achradian, I want you to send an officer with some guards to Archimedes' house. I do not want him or his family harmed. Bring him to me along with all his scrolls and models. Do you understand?"

"Yes, sir, as you have commanded."

Ω

Hippo calls for a council of war with all the commanders and Archi.

Hippo begins, "I have met with Marcus, the Roman commander. He has offered to end this war between Syracuse and Roma. He holds my wife for ransom."

"What does he want in return?" asks one of the commanders.

"He has not asked for much. If we sign this treaty, he will be free to return to Roma, and to do battle with Hannibal. The Romans would crown me king of Syracuse. It would be as it was before the war."

I don't trust Marcus," says Archi. "I met him in Alexandria. He is a politician, and as such, he will say and do anything to achieve his goals. I think he is lying about the treaty. As soon as we open the gates, he will attack."

"I agree with you," says Hippo. "Inside the city we have lost few men while inflicting great losses on the Romans. I don't think they will forgive that. I have a feeling that the war with Hannibal is not going well. The Roman Senate may have even called Marcus back to protect Roma. Hannibal has not ever been defeated. Now King Phillip has entered the war on the side of Carthage. I think that soon, the Romans may be defeated. When that happens, I think Carthage will make Syracuse the ruler of all of Sicily. We just need to hold out for a little longer. Archi, what is the status of your machines?"

"We have had very little damage, mostly caused by their use, not by the Romans. All my machines have been repaired and we have plenty of stones for future attacks. The entire wall is still intact."

"What is the situation on food and water?"

"We are good," answers the minister for food and water. "We have enough food stored up for a year without killing and eating our horses and elephants. Most families have gardens. We have stored enough hay to feed the animals. Water is not a problem since we have cisterns that are full, and it rains often enough to refill them, thanks to the system of pipes that Archi designed. We can hold out for more than a year without difficulty."

"Good!" replies Hippo. "Then there is no reason to accept the terms Marcus gave us."

"But what of Arsinoe, your wife? My daughter? And what of Barnacle?" asks Archi.

"I think Marcus will let them sail for Alexandria."

"Can we take that chance?" asks Archi.

"Archi, I know how you feel. I love my wife. But this is war. There are many more lives at stake than these two. I cannot let them influence my decision. There is nothing else I can do."

Archi falls back in his chair, in despair.

"What of the Feast of Artemis?" someone asks.

"Ah, yes. I nearly forgot. I think we should celebrate. It will show the Romans that we are secure in our defense, and that we do not fear them. I think it will even demoralize them. Let's have a great feast. Make it loud enough for the Roman blockade to hear. It will also lift the spirit of the people, and make them feel safe. Let's celebrate."

"Hippo," says Archi. "This is foolishness. We have good defenses, but we cannot let our guard down. We must be vigilant. Don't do this, I beg of you. If there are any gods, they would not have let the Romans attack us in the first place."

"Calm yourself, Archi. This is for the people, and to convince the Romans that they cannot defeat us."

"It is foolishness. It will end in no good."

That night, Barnacle is escorted inside Syracuse to meet with Hippo and Archi. Hippo sends Barnacle back with a message informing Marcus that they will not negotiate, will not surrender, and will not sign a treaty. Marcus agrees to let Arsinoe and Barnacle sail on to Alexandria. The next day, Marcus releases them in their small boat to continue on to Alexandria. He has them supplied with enough food and water for the journey, and even gives them a scroll of safe passage to show any Roman ships that might stop them. Barnacle sails toward the open sea on a heading for Alexandria, but after sunset, Arsinoe convinces him to return to Syracuse under the cover of darkness. She decides to stay with Hippo until the end.

Monte R. Anderson

CHAPTER TWENTY FOUR

(1499, Cesar's Campaign Headquarters)

Cesare refills his wine glass as he summarizes Leonardo's last story with, "Leonardo, I do believe that intrigue is the down fall of many a king but, once again, it is the love of a woman that destroys kingdoms. It is almost a repeat of the tale of Helen of Troy but with a slight twist. When Arsinoe, Archimedes' daughter, fled Syracuse for the safety of Alexandria, and was captured by Marcus, that set the stage for the capture of Syracuse. It was Archimedes' love for his daughter that caused him to ask his good friend, Damippus the merchant, to smuggle her through the Roman blockade in the first place. Marcus used her to get inside the city, and discover the weaknesses in their defense. And it was Arsinoe's love for Hippo which drew her back to the besieged Syracuse. Love does not conquer all, it defeats all."

"You are correct that the capture of Arsinoe led to the sack of Syracuse. But, as you will see, it was even a worse tragedy than Helen of Troy."

"Really? Please go on then. I know it is late, but I must hear the end of this tale. I can delay my campaign one more day."

(212 BCE, the King's Palace in Syracuse)

Hippo is awaken by the sounds of foot steps in his royal chambers. He reaches slowly over to his sword hanging on the wall next to the bed. When he senses someone sitting on the edge of the bed, he leaps out of the bed on the opposite side, and draws his sword, ready to strike.

"Calm yourself, Hippo, it is me, Arsinoe!"

"Arsinoe? What are you doing here? You should be on your way to Alexandria."

"I know but I could not stay away. I made Damippus bring me back. My place is with you."

"Well, I do not approve, but I am glad to see you, nonetheless. What is done is done. I don't think the Romans will give me a second chance to smuggle you to Alexandria."

"I couldn't stay away. I love you so much. Beside, I couldn't let you celebrate the Feast of Artemis by yourself, now could I?" Pulling back the bed covers and smiling coyly, "The feast is for lovers. We could start to celebrate early."

Hippo leaps into the bed, and holds her in his arms. For one night he forgets that he is the dictator of a city under blockage by a Roman army, and is, once again, a husband and lover.

Ω

(212 BCE, Syracuse, Sicily)

The city of Syracuse celebrates the Feast of Artemis as it never has before. Hippo lets it be known that celebrating the Feast will convince the Romans that the people of Syracuse cannot be defeated, and have no fear of the Roman might. The citizens of Syracuse have been fighting the Romans for the last few years, and fighting a civil war within the city between those families loyal to Rome and those that want to ally with Carthage. They have not had much to celebrate. Weddings have been postponed. Now all the pent up tensions are released. The wine flows freely. Every family has at least one member who marries. Hippo allows the guard posts on the wall to be reduced to a minimum.

On the second night of the Feast of Artemis, a small band of Roman soldiers lead by Zoippos makes their way to the base of the city wall undetected. Each soldier wears only a loin cloth, and carries a dagger. Their skin is blackened with charcoal. At the gate nearest the tower, the small band meet men loyal to Zoippos, and are led into the tower where the guards are drunk and asleep. The Romans sneak in, and slit the guards' throats while they sleep. Once the Romans control the tower, they signal to soldiers below to scale the wall with ladders. Once inside the tower, the Romans put on the Syracusan armor and helmets, and wait until the next hour for the changing of the guards. The Syracusans change guards every four hours so the Romans time their raid near the end of one shift when the guards are tired and lax. Only three cohorts are on duty; one for the walls around Acradina, one around the walls of the northern part of the city, and the palace guards. As the relief shift enters the tower, the Romans, who greatly out numbered the relief guards, attack them from concealed places, and kill them all, quickly and quietly. Then a number of the Romans with Syracuse supporters form up on the wall and march to the next tower. The Syracusans in the next tower, thinking them to be their relief guards, are caught off guard and quickly killed. This ruse is repeated for the remaining towers that have not been relieved. One by one all the towers on the northern walls are captured during the night. The wall inside Syracuse, between the two halves of the city is not defended. Once the north wall is under Roman control, a runner is sent back to inform Marcus.

Two hours before sunrise, Appius orders his army to advance toward the city. They bring up no wagons or catapults so that their noise will not alert the city. The hooves of the few horses are muffled with cloth. Every soldier has wrapped his sword in cloth to prevent noise or reflection of moon light. Noise discipline is strictly enforced, no talking is allowed, but enforcing it is not a problem. The soldiers remember well what happened the last time they got too close to the walls of Syracuse; how Archimedes' machines threw their comrades about like rag dolls. They stop within arrow's distance from the walls, and await the signal to attack.

Marcus arrives on the walls just before sunrise. His officers congratulated him as if the city has already been taken. Marcus knows that even with the northern wall in Roman control, there will still be some tough fighting ahead, but victory is assured. Marcus is certain the Archimedes' machines cannot be directed inside the city. He looks over the sleeping city of Syracuse as the twilight light begins to light the panorama below.

"It is more beautiful than I thought. I have only seen it at night. It is obvious that this city has enjoyed many years of peace. Look at it."

"Yes, sir," says Brutus. "As in all Greek cities that I have seen, they value all the arts except the art of war."

"Still, it will be a shame to destroy all this. In a few hours we will plunder, steal treasure, rape women, and for what? Oh, well. Remind the men that the royal treasures belong to Roma. Once we break through the inner wall, you must lead a cohort to capture the fort that anchors the harbor chain. Give the signal to start the attack."

"Yes, sir. We are prepared."

Brutus points to a soldier nearby. Immediately, the soldier raises a signal flag on a long pole. Soon similar flags are seen on all the towers along the northern wall. Outside the wall, Appius' army can see the signal flags. Without orders every soldier silently stands, and prepares for battle. Once all the towers signal that they are ready, Brutus points to the soldier again. This time, the soldier quickly waves the flag back and forth. At this signal, buglers all along the wall sound the signal to attack. The sound of the bugles awakes the citizens of Syracuse from their stupor, and panic begins to spread.

Hippo is awakened by the noise, and rushes to the balcony. From the palace he cannot see the northern walls where most of the uproar seems to be centered.

"What is it?" asks Arsinoe.

"I don't know but it sounds as if we are under attack."

As Hippo and Arsinoe quickly get dressed, a messenger rushes into their bed room, "Sir, the Romans are attacking, and they have taken the northern walls. Their army is pouring through our gates."

Strapping on his sword, "What of the middle wall?"

"It is not captured yet but we have no soldiers on it."

"Tell all the commanders to go to the middle wall, and defend the gates. If we can stop them there, we can save most of the city."

"Sir, the Roman fleet appears to be forming up to enter the Grand Harbor."

"They won't dare to attempt to enter the harbor while the chain is still up." Turning to Arsinoe as the messenger leaves, "Go to your father's house and get him. Take him down to the harbor to Barnacle's' ship. He has a small ship that can get over the harbor chain. Tell him to make ready to sail. I have to go to the chain fort, and make sure that the Romans do not cut the chain. I'll get down to the ship as soon as I can. Now hurry!"

Hippo kisses Arsinoe, and runs out of the bedroom as she yells after him, "Be careful!"

As Hippo tries to make his way to the small fort that guards the northern end of the harbor chain, he begins to realize how bad the situation really is. People are in panic running into the streets. As in many old cities, the older part contains the various temples to the Greek gods. The fleeing mass of people seeks protection in the temples. Many are also heading for the small fort inside the city which seems to be the last line of defense. A passing soldier tells Hippo that the middle wall is breached, and the Romans are just minutes from reaching the palace. Hippo finally reaches the fort, and enters along with a throng of people. He sees an officer trying to organize a defense.

"Are you the commander of this fort?" Hippo shouts above the crowd.

"Yes, sir."

"You have got to close this gate. The Romans are coming."

"Yes, sir. We are trying to but the people keep rushing in. We can't close it. There are too many."

"We must close it. Now!"

Hippo throws his shoulder against the gate, and shouts encouragement to the other soldiers but the rushing mob is too great, and the gate stays open. Suddenly, the panic intensifies as Roman soldiers appear behind the crowd. The Romans, lead by Brutus, begin cutting through the swarm of people, killing anyone in their way. Hippo orders his men to pull back in order to reorganize, and prepare to fight the Romans. Before any organized formation can be formed, the Roman soldiers begin attacking the Syracusan defenders. In spite of the melee of one-on-one, hand-to-hand fighting, Hippo is able to get the defenders into a line across a small bridge just inside the gate of the fort. More soldiers fall in behind the first row, and finally a third row is formed. Slowing, the Syracusans begin to push the Romans back, step by bloody step. As one man falls wounded, another takes his place as the brutal fight continues. Suddenly, the Roman soldiers begin falling away, wounded or killed by a shower of arrows. Hippo turns to see that the fort commander has placed several archers on the fort wall, and they are now raining arrows down into the Romans ranks. The Syracusans begin to gain momentum as they push the Romans back through the open gate.

As the Romans start to fall back, Brutus stands his ground, urging his men to stay and fight. Whenever a Roman tries to run, he strikes the soldier with the flat of his sword. But the Roman line quickly dissolves into a mad rush to get out of the way of the Syracusans and the deadly rain of arrows. As the Syracusans push forward after the fleeing Romans, Brutus is left in an exposed position, standing alone in the middle of the bridge.

The Syracusan stop advancing when faced with this sight of a brave, but alone, Roman officer, standing his ground in the center of the bridge. They do not know whether to wait for his surrender or to cut him down where he stands.

Hippo moves to the front of his men, "So, Brutus, Marcus has sent you to die trying to capture our chain."

Realizing that he is hopelessly outnumbered, and abandoned by his own men, Brutus replies, "If I can't get the chain, I will settle for killing you."

He lunges at Hippo who easily parries the thrust with his own sword. For a second the two men stare at each other. At that moment, the morning sun shines into the fort. Hippo uses his shield to reflect the sun's rays into Brutus' eyes. As the light blinds him, Brutus panics and rushes at Hippo, but his sword finds only empty air. Hippo side steps Brutus' attack, and with one thrust through his heart, kills him. As Brutus falls, the last of the Roman soldiers rush out of the gate, and the Syracusans close the gate and secure it.

Turning to the fort commander, "They will be back with reinforcements. We must get ready. Are these all the men you have?"

"This is it, sir. Most of the men were with their families when the attack started. They did not have time to get back. A few might still make it, but most are probably trying to protect their families."

"We will have to make do. Get ready for another attack."

$$\Omega$$

A Roman officer arrives at Archimedes' house with two soldiers, and enters without knocking. The household, forewarned, is hiding inside. The soldiers enter with swords at the ready. One soldier admires a vase, and picks it up for booty. Clang, echoes the officer's sword as the broadside bounces off the soldier's helmet. With a crash, the vase shatters on the floor as the solder reacts to the ringing in his ears.

"Not now! We have work to do. Find Archimedes!"

With his sword, the officer motions for one soldier to go upstairs and the other toward the rear of the house, while he searches the courtyard. After a few minutes a soldier calls from the workshop.

"Up here, sir."

The officer races up the stairs three steps at a time, and finds the workshop with the soldier outside the door.

"In here."

The officer enters, and sees Archimedes sitting at his work bench drawing figures.

"Are you Archimedes?" No answer. "Are you the one called Archimedes."

Without looking up, "Yes."

"I have orders to take you to my commander, Marcus."

"Not now!"

"You are to come with me. On your feet!"

"Not now. Can't you see that I am working."

Turning to the soldier, "Keep an eye on him. I'll gather up these drawing and models."

The officer finds a large rug, and begins to place various drawings and models in the center. The second soldier comes in pulling Arsinoe by her hair.

"Look what I found hiding, sir."

The officer stops collecting items, and saunters over to Arsinoe and in Greek asks, "Who are you?" No answer.

The soldier grabs her by the throat, "Sir, this one is a pretty one. It would be a real pleasure to rape her."

Arsinoe tries to flee but the soldier grabs her hair, and pulls her to the floor. Ignoring Archimedes, the other soldier runs over, and pins a screaming Arsinoe's arms down while the first soldier starts to pull up her tunic. The officer removes his sword and helmet.

Now aware of what is happening, Archimedes yells, "Helena!"

Grabbing a short beam from his work bench, he starts to strike the officer. Before he can deliver a blow, one of the soldiers stabs him with his sword, and Archimedes falls to the floor. Realizing what they have done, the soldiers release Arsinoe.

"Abba! Abba!" yells Arsinoe as she rushes to her father. She tries to protect him from another blow with own body. The soldiers raise their swords to kill her.

"Stop!" the officer commands. "Put down your swords!" The soldiers comply.

Looking at her father's wound, "Abba! Abba!" Arsinoe attempts to stop the crimson flow, first with her hands, then with her tunic.

Opening his eyes, Archimedes says, "Helena?"

"No, father, it is me, Arsinoe."

Recognizing his daughter at last, "Arsinoe?"

"Yes, father. You were attacked by these soldiers."

"I sent you to Alexandria."

"Yes, Abba. But I couldn't go. My place is with Hippo."

"And the city?"

"Roman's have taken the walls, and are inside."

"Then all is lost. I cannot defend the city when the enemy is inside."

"Don't talk, Abba. We'll get a doctor."

"I tried to save you but I failed, just like I failed your mother. All is lost; Syracuse, your mother, and you!"

"It's okay, father. Be still! Do not try to talk."

"No! I have not been a good father. I should have saved you. I should have sent you with your mother months ago. Now all is lost."

With tears streaming down her face, "No, father. You did save me. I chose to come back. I must be with my husband, just like mother stayed by your side. You could not send us away. We are strong women who belong with our husbands. You are not to blame."

"Yes, you are a lot like your mother. But the city?"

"The Romans have seized the towers and walls. But the people are still fighting."

Coughing up blood, "Bury me with your mother."

"Yes, Abba."

"And Hippo?"

"Still alive I think."

"Save yourselves. I am killed. Syracuse is lost." Choking on blood, "I cannot see the stars."

"It is daylight, father. There are no stars to see."

Archimedes closes his eye, and dies in his daughter's arms. Arsinoe holds his head to her buxom, and strokes his hair, crying softly.

"Now you've done it," says the centurion. "Our orders were not to harm him, and to bring him in to Marcus. Marcus may kill us for this."

"Sir, it could not be helped. He was going to kill you. I saved your life."

"Well, we'll see if Marcus agrees with you. Bind her, and bring her along. Perhaps this will satisfy Marcus. One of you roll up that rug, and bring as much of these things as you can carry."

One soldier rolls up the rug while the other binds Arsinoe's hands behind her. Once everything is in order, the officer leads the soldiers with their prisoner to report to Marcus at the palace.

Much surprised to see Arsinoe, Marcus asks, "Well, what have we here? I thought I sent you to Alexandria. The moth is drawn to the flame." Seeing the blood on her tunic and hands, "Are you wounded?"

No answer. Realizing that the prisoners are Greek, Marcus asks, "Where is Brutus?"

"I do not know," replies the centurian.

"Oh, never mind. I sent him on a mission."

"I speak a little Greek, sir," says the centurian.

In poor Greek, the centurian repeats Marcus' question to Arsinoe.

Yelling at Marcus. "No, it is not my blood. It is my father's blood!"

Marcus turns to the officer, "You killed him? I told you not to harm him."

"Yes, sir, but this one showed up, and distracted us as we were seizing Archimedes. We did not know who she was, and Archimedes attacked me with a piece of wood."

"An old man and a young woman attack a Roman officer with two soldiers in full armor?"

Missing the sarcasm, "Yes, sir, and we had to restrain his daughter too. It could not be helped."

"You are a simpleton. I should cut off your ears for disobeying me. Where are his scrolls and models?"

"I have them outside but there are many more. I brought all that I could carry."

"Idiot! Couldn't you get a cart? The models will be destroyed."

"No, sir, but I left guards on the house."

"Where is his body?"

"We left it in his workshop."

"Show me! Bring her along too. She might be helpful."

The officer leads the group back to the house of Archimedes and up to his workshop. Marcus looks at Archimedes' body for a minute or two.

With a sigh, "You have killed the greatest military engineer in the world. Roma could have learned many things from this great man. His engines kept the might of Roma at bay until now. It is our loss. Show me his scrolls."

The centurion points to the work bench and around the room. Marcus began to pick up various pieces, and examines them.

Tuning to Arsinoe, "Do you understand your father's work? Can you explain it?"

"No. I never had any interest in it, and he never took the time to explain it to me."

"Pity!" Examining the water clock, "I want this machine put on my ship. Be careful with it, and don't break it. I will place it in the senate as a war trophy."

"Yes, sir."

Marcus ambles over to a model of the solar system, and finding a small crank, begins turning the handle. Immediately, the five planets, the moon and the earth began to rotate and circle about each other. Another model nearby indicates the location of various stars on a sphere. After examining one model after another, he spies the cedar chest. Walking over to the chest, he admires the carvings on the top and sides, and attempts to open it but cannot find any lock or key.

To Arsinoe, "Open it!"

A soldier unties her.

"I do not know how. My father never showed me but I know there is a secret lock."

Marcus pulls out his dagger, and carefully slides it along the edge of the lid until he finds the latch. Then with a quick jerk, the chest pops open. Marcus begins to examine the various tablets and scrolls in the chest.

"What are all these drawing and plans for?"

"Like I said, I don't know, but father called it his idea box. Whenever he had an idea but did not have time to work on it, he would write it down, and put it in there so he would not forget it. Later he would work on it."

"But there must be hundreds of ideas in here."

"He said that some of the ideas were his father's ideas. My father had a very fertile mind. He had more ideas than he time to work on them."

Closing the lid and standing, "Take this chest also. I must have it. I can probably get a high price for these ideas. Go get more men and carts. I want everything you can find taken to my ship."

Finally, after looking through the workshop, Marcus walks over to Archimedes' body, and kneels down next to it. Arsinoe starts to stop him but is restrained by her guard. Taking out his own handkerchief, Marcus tries to wipe blood from Archimedes' face but the blood is dried, and caked in his beard. Marcus settles for folding his arms across his chest.

Turning to Arsinoe, "Did your father have any special wishes about his burial?"

"Yes. He wanted to be buried next to my mother, Helena. He also wrote his epitaph."

"Would you mind telling me what it is?"

"It is a drawing really. It is over there," pointing to a tablet on a shelf. "He wanted a sketch of a cylinder containing a sphere, and under it he wanted written, 'The ratio of the volume of a sphere to the volume of the cylinder that contains it is two to three.'"

"A mathematical formula. Outstanding! Do you understand it?"

"No. But, he always felt that it was his greatest achievement."

"Really? His greatest achievement? It was his idea to put a hook into the boarding plank on our ships. That idea alone allowed us to defeat the Carthaginian navy. When I was in Alexandria, I saw the defenses he constructed around the city; the signal towers, the catapults, and other machines. His idea of using mirrors to signal commands was ingenious. I saw his invention of the water screw being used in silver mines in Spain. They even called it the Archimedes' Screw. I saw the ship he built, the Syracusia. It was magnificent. Had he been a general, he would have conquered the world by now. And yet, he thinks a mathematics formula is his crowning achievement. I will never understand these scholars."

"They live by a different code than you and I. That is the inscription he always said he wanted on his grave. I will honor his wish if I can."

"No, not an inscription! Much more! A statue, perhaps, or a relief, maybe. I will make arrangements for a proper burial. All my officers will attend. My engineers will build a tomb as you deem appropriate. We will have it inscribed as he wished."

"He was a simple man in everything except intellect. A simple tomb will do."

"As I recall, you were on your way to Alexandria."

"My place is with my husband."

"Yes, but you are not with him. Where is Hippokrates, your husband?"

"I do not know. I presume he died fighting somewhere inside the city."

"We did not find his body yet. Perhaps he is alive."

"I think not. He would have come for me by now."

"Show me the rest of this house. There may be other war trophies."

Arsinoe begins to show Marcus around, "This is his work shop, of course. He spent most of his time here, when he was home. Since mother died, he devoted much of his time in building up the defenses of the city."

After the upstairs, Arsinoe leads Marcus downstairs. At the foot of the stairs, a soldier whispers to Marcus.

"I am told that there are other people hiding in this house."

"The servants would not abandon Archimedes. They hid in the house."

"Get them out here, now!"

Arsinoe calls the servants who emerge from various hiding places. The soldiers have them line up in front of Marcus.

Turning to Arsinoe, "Are they all slaves?"

"No. None of them are slaves. My father did not believe in slavery. They are all servants, and all are paid."

"They are all slaves now. As the victor, I can claim them for myself."

"I know. You can do as you wish. But these are household servants, and not accustomed to hard labor."

"Tell you what I will do; if you cooperate with me and do not try to escape, I will let you stay here, and keep your servants. Or, you can come to Roma with me, with your servants. Would you rather stay here and take your chances with Zoippos as your new sovereign, or come back with me to Roma?"

"I am sure Zoippos has plans to kill me. I will cooperate and go to Roma with you, but let the servants go free."

"Very well! Stay here until arrangements can be made for your safety. I will have guards posted to ensure that no harm comes to you."

Marcus begins to inspect the servants who bow their heads as he walks by, "Greek?"

"Not all but many are Greek."

Marcus stops in front of a young, beautiful maiden with dark skin.

"This one is not Greek."

"No, she is Egyptian, born here of Egyptian parents, free parents."

Marcus fondles one of her breasts, and runs his hand down her buttocks. He walks around her, admiring her figure.

"Are you sure you wouldn't want to bring this young thing? I could marry her off to one of my officers."

"Marcus, these servants are my father's servants, not mine. Hippo, and I have other servants who, I am sure, have fled the palace by now."

"Of course. A pity. She is beautiful. Perhaps, in a few days you will change your mind. Have them stay here until I have finished seeing the rest of this house."

In the kitchen, Marcus examines a pipe over a basin. Arsinoe shows him how to open it so that water runs into the basin.

"Amazing! Water is piped into the kitchen! Are all the homes in the city like this one?"

"No, but many are. My father built a system of pipes and cisterns that are connected to the roof tops. The water is rainwater."

"No wonder the city was able to hold out for so long. Water was never in short supply."

As Marcus tours the house, he points to various models, machines, and works of art, and his soldiers take them outside to put on a cart. Finally, Arsinoe shows him the bath.

"Did your father design this bath?"

"No, my mother did. It is modeled after a bath in Alexandria. It always reminded her of her home there."

"Ah, yes. I recall hearing stories of her bath when I was in Alexandria."

"What stories?"

Marcus stops walking, and stares at Arsinoe for a minute. "Perhaps, there are some things that a daughter should not know about her mother. Your mother and father bathed together?"

"Yes. Before they were married, my father would use the public baths. He always said some of his best ideas came to him while bathing. When they returned from Alexandria, mother had this bath built, and they bathed often. But after my mother was killed, my father hardly ever bathed."

"When your mother married your father in Alexandria, I was there as ambassador from Roma. It was quite a scandal. Your mother was next in line to the throne of Cyrene and then in line for the throne of Alexandria. And she choose to marry a scholar. I never understood why King Ptolemy allowed it."

"I have heard the stories."

Pointing at a pipe, "I see that there was a system to supply water here too."

"Of course."

Asinoe then leads Marcus into the temple room containing the altar to Isis, the Egyptian god.

"Ah, yes. I recall now that your mother was a high priestess or something for the cult that worshiped Isis."

Arsinoe is taken back by his remark.

Noting her surprise, "I recognize the image of Isis. Was your father a believer too?

"My father has never believed in any gods. But mother did. The only time father ever came into this room was the day mother was killed."

"Killed? I was told by Zoippos that she died in an accident."

"An accident caused by one of Zoippos' men."

"You have my word that I had nothing do with the death of your mother. The first I heard about it was from your own lips. Your own kinsmen did it."

"I believe you. The things that happened the last couple of years have convinced me that we were defeated by ourselves and not by you. You arrived in time to seize the city before we destroyed it."

"Very well. Now, I must return to my duties. I will send for you tomorrow, after the city is secured, so you can return to the palace, and get ready to leave. It is not safe to be outside right now. Keep your servants here for a couple of days, and then you can let them leave. I have guards posted on your house. Until tomorrow."

Ω

Trapped in the small fort that anchors one end of the harbor chain, Hippo stands in the tower, and watches helplessly as one by one all the towers along the city wall are captured by the Romans.

Suddenly, the fort commander shouts and points, "Look!"

Hippo looks down into the streets below. Coming toward the fort is a huge battering ram and two cohorts of soldiers.

The commander says, "Sir, we cannot hold out very long against that ram. We were lucky so far but the end is near."

"I fear that you are right but we are trapped. We are surrounded."

"No, sir. There is a way out. The harbor chain is anchored inside the fort, and passes through an opening big enough for a person to pass through. We could climb down the chain, and escape into the harbor. The Romans have not captured the harbor yet."

"That is a good plan. Do it now. But let the women and children go first."

"Yes sir."

One by one, the women and children climb down the harbor chain to the beach, and run for the docks. The fort soldiers hold off the Romans as best they can before each, in turn, escapes. Hippo is the last to leave as he sees the Roman ram break down the fort's gates. He knows that soon the Romans will lower the harbor chain, and the Roman fleet will join in the attack on Syracuse. There is no hope to save the city now. He must find Arsinoe. He hopes that she made it to Barnacle's ship safely.

Ω

Arsinoe sits besides Archimedes' body softly crying. Suddenly, she is startled by a noise in the main hall. She finds a small axe from among her father's tools. If she is to be raped, she is determined to make some Roman pay dearly for the act. Axe in hand, she creeps over to the door, and peers around the corner.

A voice asks, "Would you kill your brother-in-law?"

Arsinoe is so frightened that she drops the axe to the floor. She turns to see Epi standing in the hall, grinning. She rushes to him.

When Epi sees the blood on her tunic he asks, "Are you bleeding?"

Arsinoe begins to cry, and shakes her head.

"Where is your father?"

In tears, Arsinoe can only point to the workshop. Epi rushes in, and discovers Archimedes' body.

"No!" he says, "I did not think they would kill him." After a minute, "We have to go. The city has fallen."

Finally, gaining control of herself, "How did you get here? Where did you come from?"

"It's a long story but I have been following the Roman army for days. When I saw them getting ready to attack, I snuck back into the city. Only, I am too late. Where is Hippo?"

"I do not know for sure but he said to meet him at the harbor at Barnacle's ship. That is where we must go. But there are guards on the house."

"I know. But there was only one on the back door. I killed him. We will go that way."

Arsinoe follows Epi through the kitchen, to the back door. Together, they rush out the back door before the guards in front realize what has happened. Holding hands, the two race toward the harbor. They arrive out of breath, and quickly find Hippo, Barnacle, and another young man getting the small boat ready to sail.

At the sight of Arsinoe, Hippo rushes to her, "Thank the gods you made it! And Epi too! You're alive! I gave you up for dead when there was no word from you."

"It is good to see you too brother. How did the Romans get inside the city?"

"I don't know. They captured the north wall before we knew it. But, I suspect, that Zoippos had a hand in it. We executed a traitor that confessed that Zoippos has been behind all the killings. He has been trying to make himself king. He even killed his wife."

Where is Archimedes?" asks Barnacle.

"Dead! Killed by the Romans," replies Arsinoe.

"Oh. No!" cries Barnacle as he falls against the rail of the ship.

Arsinoe turns to the young man, "Are you Barnacle's son?"

No. I am his grandson, Gelo."

"Gelo? Named after King Gelo?"

"Yes, I think so. Come on! Get in!"

At that moment, the Romans drop the harbor chain with a great crash.

"You have got to go now! Get in!" yells Barnacle.

They all scramble aboard except Epi and Barnacle who stay in the water to push the boat off the shore. As the boat is freed from the the beach, Epi and Barnacle wade back to shore.

Hippo asks Epi, "Aren't you coming? The Romans are nearly here."

"No brother, I will just be extra weight. I have something I need to do here."

"And you too, Barnacle, aren't you coming?" asks Hippo.

"No. I have a business to run."

Before, Hippo can reply, Epi and Barnacle turn, and disappear into the rushing swarm of people. Gelo hoists the sail, and steers the boat near the shoreline to avoid the Roman fleet that is starting to enter the harbor under oars. The Romans pay little attention to such a small craft as they head toward the city to participate in the looting. Soon the boat passes out of the harbor, and heads east toward the open sea.

Ω

That night, a tired Zoippos sleeps in the king's chambers of the royal palace. The sound of wine being poured into cups awakens him, and he senses, more than sees, that someone is in the room.

Sitting up, "Who goes there?"

No answer. He dimly sees the outline of a figure, and reaches for his sword only to discover it missing.

"Identify yourself or I will call the guards, and have you arrested."

"Your guards are dead," a familiar voice replies.

Zoippos recognizes the voice, "Epikyotes! How did you get in here?"

Epi uses a small lamp, the only light in the room, to light a larger oil lamp, and sets it on the table.

"Don't you recall how, as children, we use to sneak in and out of the palace?"

"Yes, I remember. Have you come to surrender? Surrender now, and I will spare your life."

"And drag me back to Roma in chains like you did to the king of Leontine?"

"If you have not come to surrender, what do you want?"

"I want to talk to you. Answer my questions, and I will surrender to you. But first, come, sit at the table. I have poured us some wine."

Zoippos gets up, pulling a bed sheet around his naked body, and sits at the table. He takes the wine cup Epi offers but just stares at it.

"Here, look!" says Epi, as he sips from his wine cup. See! No poison."

Zoippos takes Epi's cup from his hand, and gives him his cup. Then he takes a sip, and demands, "Give me back my sword."

"Not yet."

"What do you want?"

"I just want you to answer a few questions. I want to know if you killed King Gelo?"

Confident that Epi will surrender, Zoippos answers, "No. I am not sure who did. I suspect it someone in your family. I think Damarata may have done it."

"And King Hieron?"

"No. He died of old age. He would have died sooner if he had not been so stubborn that the gods did not want him."

"And King Hieronymos?"

"Yes. Him I killed or, at least, I had that idiot teenager killed by my agents."

"And my father?"

Zoippos pauses for a minute, and locks eyes with Epi, "Yes. Again, my agent."

"Why?"

Striking the table, "To be king! To take my birthright! When Gelo died my wife should have been queen. I would have been king."

"You are forgetting about Damarata. She would have been Queen."

"Sooner or later the people wold realize that your parents killed King Gelo. They would make my wife queen. But that does not matter now. Marcus promised me the kingship."

"You killed your brother-in-law and thousands of others to become king? You started this war, and destroyed Syracuse."

"No! Your father started this war. I only wanted what was rightfully mine."

"You caused all this suffering."

"I have suffered too! My wife! My daughters! But I will rebuild Syracuse, and restore her glory."

Epi starts to speak but his words are slurred.

Looking down at his wine cup, Zoippos yells, "This wine is poisoned!"

Epi nods his head. Zoippos tries to rush toward his bed to pull a dagger hidden under his pillow. But the bed sheet and the poison slow him down as he staggers toward the bed. He falls twice as Epi follows him, and unsheathes his own sword. Zoippos finds the dagger, and turns to attack Epi who is ready for him. Epi stabs Zoippos with his sword as Zoippos' dagger finds it mark in Epi's chest. Falling backward onto the bed, Zoippos pulls Epi on top of him and his dagger. The commander of the guard, hearing the scuffle, runs to the room to find his guards dead in the hall. As other guards arrive, they succeed in finally breaking down the door. They rush in, and kill the mortally wounded Epi as he lies tangled up in Zoippos's arms. In death, their blood runs together.

Ω

(212 BCE, at sea east of Syracuse)

As Gelo sails his ship toward Alexandria, Arsinoe and Hippo watch fires in Syracuse light up the evening sky.

"What will happen to us?" asks Arsinoe.

"We'll be safe in Alexandria. After all, you are a Ptolemy."

"Hippo, I want to have children, a boy and a girl."

"What will you name them?"

"The girl I will name Helena, after my mother. The boy I will name

Epi, after your brother."

"Not Archimedes?"

"No. There will never be another Archimedes."

(212 BCE, Syracuse, Sicily)

A few days later when the city is finally subdued, and the looting stopped, Archimedes is buried with full military honors. A cohort of Roman soldiers forms a cordon of honor along the trail leading to his newly built tomb. He is carried on a shield in the Roman custom but a Syracusan shield, not a Roman shield. Several slaves carry copies of his machines that are to be buried with him. All the Roman officers attend. His body is entombed in a small monument to his achievements near the Agrigentine gate outside of Syracuse. Helena's body is exhumed from her tomb, and placed along side his. All the surviving peasants of Syracuse are in attendance because he and his wife were loved by all. None of the surviving nobility of Syracuse attend. Once the bodies are entombed, buglers sound "Attention" and the Roman officers and the cordon of honor salute. After the ceremony, the Egyptian servants are allowed to prepare Archimedes' body, in the Egyptian custom, for the next world. When the servants are done, the tomb is sealed forever.

$$\Omega$$

CHAPTER TWENTY FIVE

(1499, Cesar's Campaign Headquarters)

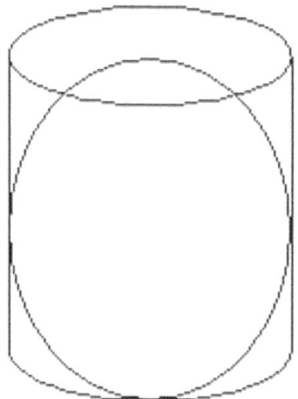

"You are correct when you say this was worse than a Greek tragedy," says Cesare as he stands and stretches.

"Yes, a great tragedy indeed," says Leonardo.

"So, all Archimedes' wisdom and inventions could not save Syracuse. Were all his inventions and models lost after all?"

"Not quite. Here, read this," Leonardo rummages through the cedar chest and hands Cesare a piece of paper. "It was written by Cicero."

Cesare reads aloud, "When I was questor in Sicily I managed to track down his grave. The Syracusans knew nothing about it, and indeed denied that any such thing existed. But there it was, completely surrounded, and hidden by bushes of brambles and thorns. I remembered having heard of some simple lines of verse which had been inscribed on his tomb, referring to a sphere and cylinder modeled in stone on top of the grave. And so I took a good look round all the numerous tombs that stand beside the Agrigentine Gate. Finally I noted a little column just visible above the scrub: it was surmounted by a sphere and a cylinder. I immediately say to the Syracusans, some of whose leading citizens were with me at the time, that I believed this was the very object I had been looking for. Men were sent in with sickles to clear the site, and when a path to the monument had been opened we walked right up to it. And the verses were still visible, though approximately the second half of each line had been worn away.

So one of the most famous cities in the Greek world, and in former days a great centre of learning as well, would have remained in total ignorance of the tomb of the most brilliant citizen it had ever produced, had a man from Arpinum not come and pointed it out!"

"Amazing!" says Cesare as he hands the paper back to Leonardo who places it back into the chest. "And what of Arsinoe and Hippo? Did they get to Alexandria? Did they survive? Did they have children? Did they ever return to Syracuse?"

"I have no knowledge of what happened to them after they left Syracuse. My information is incomplete."

"Leonardo, is this cedar chest of yours, the same chest that Archimedes called his idea box?"

"Who can say, sire? There is no documentation on its origins or history. I doubt it."

"I will tell you what I think. I think that Archimedes' idea box has, somehow, fallen into your hands, and you have been using it for years to invent machines."

With a slight grin, "As I have said, we stand on the shoulders of those who have gone before us."

"Yes, yes, but I want that box-as is. I will pay whatever you demand. Name your price!"

"Sire, I do not wish to offend you, but the chest is not for sale."

As Leonardo is speaking, Philippe enters the room followed by Salai.

"Duke," says Philippe, "Excuse my interruption, but morning mass is one hour away, and I know you would not wish to break fast before mass."

Behind Philippe's back, Salai mimics Philippe where only Leonardo and Cesare can see him. Leonardo chuckles and Cesare cannot help a slight grin. Realizing something is going on behind him, Philippe turns quickly only to see Salai straightening out his skirt. Philippe suspects that is has been made fun of but he lets it go...this time.

Cesare looks down at his half-full glass of wine, "Of course not." He finishes off the wine in one gulp. "I cannot believe that I have spent the entire night listening to this tale of Archimedes."

Salai steps from behind Philippe, "Master, you did not come home last night. Your bed was not slept in."

"Ah, Salai, I am glad you are here," says Leonardo as he locks up the cedar chest. "Please help me return this chest to my tent."

Cesare sees Philippe examining the empty bird cage, "Ah, yes! Philippe, remind me to buy another bird after mass. It seems that every time Leonardo comes to visit, my birds escape."

Leonardo grins sheepishly, "A coincident, I am sure, sire. I must take my leave now, and get ready for mass. I will see you there."

Leonardo helps Salai with the chest, and together they bow slightly, and leave the tent.

"Duke?" asks Philippe, "What tale would keep you up all night?"

"A tale of warfare, intrigue, love, and tragedy. I lost track of the time."

"And what is in that chest?"

"Ah, Philippe, if I only knew, if I only knew.

ACKNOWLEGMENTS

In writing this first novel, I decided to make use of a reading team. I owe a great debt of thanks to them. The story contains all the elements I love in life; history, engineering, military battles, intrigue, a love story, and politics. Therefore, I choose a team with a variety of talents. There was George Shoener, my West Point roommate, engineer, and retired army officer. I enlisted John Hart, another West Pointer with a MA in English and an author in his own right. Ed Darling, at one time my boss, an engineer, and a song writer was on the team. I also had the help of a librarian, Bayneeta Freeland. An old high school buddy, Steve Alber, was the sailor and a retired air force officer. I sent them the book one chapter at a time, and they provided me the much needed feedback. The truth is that I am a poor proofreader.

I also owe a debt of thanks to my wife, Kathryn. In the middle of writing this novel, I became unemployed, then found a position in New York and had to relocate. The burden of moving fell mostly on her shoulders. Without her help, the book may have taken much longer to complete.

I was inspired by an article in the March/April 2005 issue of Military History Magazine, a publication I thoroughly enjoy. The article was in the Weaponry column and titled, "Leonardo da Vinci's Steam Canon Foreshadowed the Steam Engines of the Industrial Revolution" by Nick D'alto. That got me started. I did most of my research online but I did read Nigel Rodgers' <u>The History and Conquests of Ancient Rome.</u> I did quote from the ancient historians Ploybius (200-118 BC),

Livy (59 BC - 17 AD), Cicero, and even Archimedes. I made some editorial changes when the ancient text was hard to understand. I used clip art from the public domain, although I did attempt some of the art work myself. The entire project was a labor of love.

www.ingramcontent.com/pod-product-compliance
Lightning Source LLC
Chambersburg PA
CBHW022205010726
47493CB00002B/422